By any other name . . .

Anthony Maitland, Viscount Ivers, took Georgy's chin in his hand. "I won't give you away, Georgy. Not until you give me leave."

"Thank you, my lord."

"Tony," he corrected.

"Tony?" Georgy smiled up at him. "It suits you."

He grinned back at her. "Better than Grace Vail suits you, I think. Whatever made you choose so prudish a name?"

"Perhaps a prudish name suits me better than you think." To prove her point she removed his hand from her chin, picked up the hideous dame-cap that lay in his lap and put it on firmly.

Maitland laughed. "If you think that cap has the power to deter me from my purpose, Georgy, my girl, you're out in your reckoning," he said, taking her in his arms . . .

A GRAND DECEPTION
A Regency Giant by
Elizabeth Mansfield

*Other books by
Elizabeth Mansfield*

Elizabeth Mansfield

A Grand Deception

CHARTER BOOKS, NEW YORK

A GRAND DECEPTION

A Charter Book / published by arrangement with
the author

PRINTING HISTORY
Charter edition / January 1988

ISBN: 0-441-30172-X

Charter Books are published by The Berkley Publishing Group,
200 Madison Avenue, New York, New York 10016.
The name "CHARTER" and the "C" logo
are trademarks belonging to Charter Communications, Inc.

PRINTED IN THE UNITED STATES OF AMERICA

10 9 8 7 6 5 4 3 2 1

Prologue

"To make an advantageous marriage is the goal, the purpose, the sum and substance of our existence," Lucy Traherne declared firmly, tying a satin, pearl-spangled sash on her henna-washed curls and observing herself fatuously in the dressing-table mirror. "Do you think this sash is too theatrical for a hairband?"

Her friend, Georgianna Verney, shook her head. "That," she declared with a firmness equal to her friend's, "is disgusting!"

Lucy stared at her reflection in surprise. "Good God, Georgy, does it look as bad as that?"

"Not the sash, you idiot. I'm not talking about your blasted hairband. It's your view of a woman's purpose that's disgusting."

"It is *not* disgusting. It is the way of life." She leaned toward the mirror and peered at her curls dubiously. "Are you certain this sash is not too . . . too *Babylonian?*"

"*You*, my dear girl, are too Babylonian! How can you sit there and speak as if women were nothing but chattel, to be bartered to the highest bidder?"

"What else were we raised for?" Lucy rejoined, turning her head to the right and left in an agony of indecision. "Are you going to give me an opinion on this hairband or not?"

The two friends, sitting in the upstairs dressing room of Lord and Lady Denham's townhouse (in which they'd deposited their wraps and were making final adjustments to their attire before descending the stairs to the ballroom where the final rout of the season was taking place), were a decided contrast to one another. Lucy Traherne, at twenty

1

years of age, was a little younger than Georgianna Verney, and would have been considered the prettier of the two if one looked quickly. With her dyed red curls and light eyes, she was more obviously pretty than her taller, more striking friend, and was a great deal more ostentatious. Lucy's blue eyes were underlined with blacking, her azure gown was tucked and flounced wherever possible, her décolletage emphasized by a double strand of pearls, and her hair (now bedecked with the jeweled hairband) was a curled, pomaded testament to her hairdresser's art.

Georgy, on the other hand, was the model of restraint. Only a keen observer could discover that her auburn hair, pulled back from her face with almost prudish severity into a tight bun, was thick and lustrous and that her features, completely unemphasized by any touch of rouge or eye-blacking, were almost Grecian in their sculptured perfection. She was taller than her friend, but seemed even more so by her proud carriage and the confident lift of her chin. That chin was square and perhaps a bit too pronounced for current tastes (which required that female features be softly rounded), but her nose and high cheekbones could not be faulted. Most noticeable, even to the unobservant, were her hazel eyes—wide and lustrous and sparkling with humor and intelligence. They did not require blacking to attract admiration.

But Georgy's beauty was more subtle than pronounced, and she refused to use cosmetic arts and feminine decoration to make that beauty obvious. Understatement was her style. In addition to the understatement of her coiffure and her lack of cosmetics, her neck, ears and arms were bare of jewelry. And most understated of all was the gown she was wearing. She'd chosen (over her mother's emphatic objections) to dress herself in a lilac jacquard so subdued in color that it was almost gray. Only those who looked closely tonight would decide that she was, in her way, as eye-catching as her gaudy friend.

At the moment, Georgy's eyes were flashing fire. "Is *that* what you believe, Lucy? That we were raised merely for the purpose of attaching ourselves to men of wealth?

That our minds and our characters were molded for no other purpose?"

Lucy gave her hairband a last pat and stood up. "What other purpose *can* there be?"

"What other purpose? I should think that being useful to society in some way is *one* possible purpose. Or becoming learned or wise. Or developing a talent. Or doing some *good* in the world."

"Do you know, Georgy," her friend said, shaking out the flounces of her skirt, "that sometimes you sound like an Evangelical?"

"If you're saying I sound like a wild-eyed preacher, you're right," Georgy admitted with a shame-faced grin. "I do sermonize a bit, don't I? I'm sorry, Lucy. But I hate the thought that making a good match is all we can accomplish in this world."

"There's nothing wrong with making a good match. If we can catch ourselves a pair of rich husbands—someone, say, like the famous Lord Maitland, who, by the way, Mama tells me, is expected to put in an appearance tonight —we can spend the rest of our lives doing exactly as we like."

"Is that why you've been adorning yourself like a crystal chandelier? To catch this Lord Maitland's eye?"

"Yes, why not? They say he's rich as a nabob, and attractive, too. There's nothing I'd like *better* than to catch his eye."

"But for the sake of argument, let's suppose he's not attractive. Let's suppose he's gross and vulgar—the sort who makes suggestive little winks and takes surreptitious little nips at your buttocks when no one is looking. Would you *still* wish to sell yourself to him?"

"Frankly, Georgy, my love, I don't much care *what* he's like, if he's as rich as they say. Once one is wed, you know, one can go one's own way—if one is discreet."

Georgy raised her eyebrows. "What do you mean, go one's own way? Do you mean . . . are you trying to make me believe that you'd be like Lady Whitbrough and that sort? Go about town with escorts not your husband? Invite gentlemen into your rooms to watch you dress? And . . . and have *affairs?*"

Lucy giggled. "I might. If one is rich enough, one can do anything, and people only think it stylish."

Georgy glared at her. "Now, that *is* disgusting!"

"There's nothing disgusting about it," Lucy declared defensively. "Letty Denham, our hostess, married advantageously, and everyone says she's the happiest creature in the world. But of course, why shouldn't she be? I certainly would be happy with a charmer like Lord Denham, who could give me clothes and jewels like that magnificent emerald her ladyship always wears. And Maitland is another such. Every unmarried female who's come tonight would barter her *soul* to engage Maitland's attention. And you'll never convince me that you don't have the same desire. You'll never make me believe, Georgianna Verney, that you don't want to catch Maitland's eye yourself, in spite of the fact that that dowdy jacquard you've chosen to wear isn't likely to turn *anyone's* head."

Georgy, caught off guard by her friend's abrupt attack, couldn't help laughing. "This gown *is* dreadful, isn't it? I only wore it to convince Mama that I won't be forced to 'exhibit my wares' on the Marriage Mart. She coerced me into attending this rout, but she'll never coerce me into playing this matchmaking game. I shall not agree to an advantageous match, even if one should ever be offered me."

"You're joking. You can't prefer an *un*advantageous one."

"If you want the truth, I don't want to marry at all. But you may take my word that, whatever I do, I shall *never* marry for money."

Lucy snorted. "You may think you're an idealist, Georgy, but I think you're a fool."

Georgy shrugged and rose from her chair. "Perhaps. But in the meantime, you may be missing the arrival of Lord Catch-of-the-Season Maitland. Are you ready to go down?"

Lucy bent down to the dressing table mirror for one last look. "Are you certain this sash is not *de trop?*"

"It may well be, my love, but surely you don't care, do you? So long as everyone notices you?"

"I don't care about everyone, only about Maitland. Do you think *he*'ll notice me?" Lucy asked hopefully as the two girls strolled to the door.

Georgy stopped, ran her eyes over her friend's beads, flounces, necklaces, bracelets, dangling earrings and jeweled headband and gave a ringing laugh. "How could he possibly help it?" she teased.

Lucy, satisfied, walked out the door. Georgy hesitated, took one last glance at herself in the mirror and sighed ruefully. "One thing sure," she muttered as she followed her friend and closed the door behind them, "is that he'll never notice *me*."

Chapter 1

There was not a female guest, no matter her age or marital status, who did not keep an eye on the entrance to the ballroom during the evening of Lady Denham's Annual Rout, for it was rumored that the season's most eligible bachelor, Anthony Maitland, Viscount Ivers (notorious as much for his exclusivity as for the fortune he'd made in the Indies), would actually be making an appearance. So rare were his public appearances that most of the women at the ball had never laid eyes on him. The gossips had variously reported that he was swarthy, pale, broad-shouldered, slight, nasty, pleasant, handsome, plain, noteworthy, undistinguished, talkative and silent. But the inconsistencies of the reports would surely be put straight this evening, when more than one hundred fascinated females would lay eyes on him at once. The suspense was all but unbearable.

Lady Horatia Verney, a tall, large-bosomed matron in her late fifties, was the only one of the dowagers (gathered like a flock of turbaned geese at the far end of the dance floor, where they could keep an eye on the dancers and the doorway, too) who was completely uninterested in Lord Maitland's arrival. Lady Horatia pretended to listen with her usual attention to the gossip and speculation circulating around her, but she felt no real anticipation. Although she was the mother of a marriageable daughter, she had no hope that his lordship's presence at the ball would have anything to do with her. She was not the sort to set her hopes upon impossibilities. Her daughter would never be considered eligible by the most eligible bachelor to come along in years. Why should she, therefore, be interested in all the speculation concerning Maitland's appearance and character? In truth, she could not concentrate on it. She had other, more pressing problems on her mind. All she could do was hope that her inner distress was not visible on her face.

Anyone could have told her that it was not. Her face showed nothing but its usual complacency. Of all the matrons of the polite world of London in the year of 1816, Lady Horatia Verney was believed to be the most self-satisfied. "And why should she *not* be satisfied with herself?" the Countess Lieven often remarked in her defense. "Verney was always the most loving and generous of husbands, even in his dying; he very obligingly passed away after giving her his best years and before burdening her with his worst. In addition, she has a son who passed through the wars with outstanding courage yet without sustaining so much as a scratch; and she has two enviable daughters—her eldest who is blessed with a strong and original mind, and her youngest who will undoubtedly grow up to be a beauty. With such a family, why *shouldn't* Horatia be complacent?"

Many of Countess Lieven's listeners were tempted to argue that the Verney offspring were not as special as all *that*, and that *they* had daughters equally (or more) brilliant and beautiful, or sons equally (or more) courageous and manly, yet *they* didn't find it necessary to gaze out at the world with such irritating smugness. But, since it was not expedient to argue with so influential a doyenne as the Countess Lieven, none of them said any of this aloud.

It would have been hard for Lady Horatia's critics to imagine how far from complacent she was feeling at this moment. She had spent the afternoon in fruitless argument with her daughter, and as a result had at last come to the realization that the prospects for her family were bleak indeed. If her daughter persisted in her decision to avoid matrimony, and if her son married a female who didn't want her and her daughters in her house, Lady Horatia might, one day soon, find herself having to move with her daughters to a little cottage somewhere in the country, living on a mere pittance, with only rags on their backs, a servant or two to do for them, and forgotten by the noble society among whom she'd always held a secure and re-spected place.

Horatia may have looked calm and self-satisfied on the outside, but inside she was in turmoil. She would have laughed bitterly if she'd been privvy to Countess Lieven's defense of her. In the first place the Countess was much mistaken in believing that it was obliging of Verney to pass away in his prime. Lady Horatia missed him sorely. She'd never had to trouble herself about business matters—or any other family problems—while he was alive. Dear Verney had handled everything. Every waking moment of every day that had passed since his demise left her more confused, more insecure and more bereft. How could that kind and loving man have planned so badly for her future?

In the second place, the son about whom the Countess assumed she was complacent had been so occupied with his military duties that she'd not laid eyes on him for three years. He, too, like his father, was kind and loving, and she did not for a moment believe that he would cast his mother out of the London house that had been her home for more than thirty years. But the house *was* his now (the son's inheritance of the property being mandatory by law), and since he was likely to marry before long (being practi-cally betrothed already to Rosalind Peascott, as cosseted and pampered a young woman as ever was), there was no guarantee that his bride would not prefer to live in the house without suffering the constant presence of her mother-in-law and two sisters-in-law. If the bride *did* prefer to keep the house for herself and her husband, who could really blame her?

And in the third place, Lady Horatia's eldest daughter, Georgianna (whom the Countess described as strong-minded and original) was turning out to be—hideous thought!—a bluestocking. A *bluestocking!* The signs were all there: the girl liked to read books meant for men, she despised all Tories, she refused to work at her embroidery, she never used eyelash-blacking or a curling iron, and she was more likely than not to declare publicly that dances and balls were ostentatious displays of wealth, wasteful of the resources of hosts and guests alike! If those were not symptoms of bluestockingness, Lady Horatia would like to know what were. And what good was it that Georgy had a pair of beautiful, hazel, "speaking" eyes, a slim waist, a head of thick auburn hair and the most enviable complexion in London if there wasn't a bachelor in the world who could honestly say he wished to wed a bluestocking?

Of course, Lady Horatia still had her other daughter, Alison, who would certainly be a beauty one day if she didn't grow too tall, but she was only fourteen. By the time she came of age the family would long since have come to ruin. What on earth, Horatia would have asked the Countess and anyone else who'd accused her of complacency, did she have to feel self-satisfied about?

Thus her ladyship sat at the edge of the dance floor in the Denhams' magnificent ballroom looking haughtily complacent on the outside and feeling desperate and miserable within. She had come to the ball (dragging her protesting daughter with her) only because her absence would have been noted. It would be quite the last straw if anyone guessed that she was in so difficult a financial predicament. It was essential to maintain the illusion of wealth if one were to have any chance at all of recapturing it. But she really had no wish to be here, sitting among all these chattering, turbaned dowagers, every one of whom was, at heart, more complacent and self-satisfied than she. *They* could all sit here contentedly observing their daughters whirl about the dance floor in the arms of actual or potential suitors (while at the same time keeping hopeful watch for Maitland's arrival), while *she* had to suffer the knowledge that her daughter would probably not be seen on the dance floor all evening.

Lady Horatia, not realizing that her face had remained impassive through all these distressing thoughts, and fearful that someone might notice her distress, forced herself not to think about her daughter. Instead, she concentrated her thoughts on trying to invent other solutions to her financial dilemma. But she could think of no way out. Her son had only the meager income from the property his father had bequeathed to him; it would be barely enough to support a family properly after he married. Even with the addition of his Captain's pay, his income would not keep his family in anything but modest comfort. If the responsibility for maintaining a mother and two sisters were added to his burden, he would lose what chance he had with Rosalind Peascott or any other female of substance. Horatia couldn't permit him to carry so heavy a burden. Thus the only chance the family had to improve their situation lay with Georgy.

Horatia almost sighed aloud. Why was it that every thought in her head came round to Georgy again? But the answer was obvious: her one hope lay with Georgy. If the girl could only be persuaded to marry well, the family might be saved. But would Georgy permit herself to marry well? Ha! That was as likely to happen as a puppy nibbling catnip. Horatia would consider herself lucky if she could persuade Georgy to marry at all!

Not that Georgianna Verney couldn't make a brilliant match if she set her mind to it. Why, there was almost nothing in the world the girl couldn't do if she wanted to! But the irritating creature had long ago decided that she didn't want to marry. Marriage, she would declare like a litany, was like selling oneself into slavery. And none of the arguments, pleas or threats that the mother had delivered *ad nauseum* during the four long years since the daughter had come of age had had the least effect on Georgy's stubborn mind.

Lady Horatia glanced across the large room at her daughter and winced. Why couldn't the girl even *dress* as the other girls did? she asked herself angrily. They'd quarreled about the gown for half an hour earlier that evening. Her ladyship had wanted Georgy to wear the emerald-colored lustring she'd had made for her daughter at extortionate expense, but the girl had insisted on donning that utterly inappropriate and dowdy grayed-lilac jacquard with the high collar trimmed with white lace and edged with black braid. It was, at best, a walking dress. Here in the Denhams' ballroom, matched against a roomful of revealing décolletages, frills, flounces, laces, gauzes and silks, the dull jacquard made Lady Horatia's daughter look like nothing so much as a cotton merchant's governess!

Her ladyship gave a hidden but hopeless sigh. She'd argued til she was hoarse to make Georgy change her mind, but she'd weakened in the end. As usual, Georgy had had her way. The girl was as immovable as a mule and had been so since she was a tot.

Georgy was standing on the sidelines, chatting comfortably with her friend, Lucy Traherne. She seemed utterly unaware of the discomfort her appearance was causing her mother. And her mother was certainly discomfitted. Lucy Traherne, with her reddish locks charmingly curled and her azure gown ruffled at the edge of its tantalizing décolletage with pearled lace, stood in painful contrast to her friend. With Georgy in the lilac jacquard and in a spinsterish bun, the pair looked, Horatia decided, like mistress and abigail.

Of course, her ladyship had to admit that, despite the gown, no fewer than three quite presentable gentlemen had already asked Georgy to dance. Three times the mother had watched with beating heart as each gentleman had approached, and three times her hopes had been dashed as her daughter had three times refused. Whatever was the *matter* with the girl? *But what else might a mother expect,* Lady Horatia asked herself, *from a deuced bluestocking?*

Not wishing to look at her irritating daughter for another moment, Lady Horatia got abruptly to her feet. "Do excuse me, ladies," she said to the group surrounding her.

"Where are you going?" asked Lady Aubert in surprise.

"I'm for a few hands of whist. Do you wish to come with me to the card room?"

"Heavens, no," Lady Aubert answered vehemently, her corkscrew side curls bobbing nervously. "What if we should miss Maitland's arrival?"

Lady Horatia shrugged. "It's already past eleven. I don't think the fellow's coming at all. You're all wasting your time." She was halfway across the room before she realized that she'd sounded exactly like her daughter.

But her friends had not wasted their time, for just before midnight Lord Maitland arrived. Lord and Lady Denham introduced him first to the circle of dowagers, then escorted him round the room to meet as many of the other two hundred and fifty guests as possible before supper was announced. Since they did not manage to get to the ladies' card room, however, Horatia was one of the few dowagers who missed being introduced to him. Not that it mattered, for at least three of her friends stopped by the card room to describe him to her. One said that he was somewhat taller than expected (adding in a whisper that perhaps he could use a little more meat on his bones), another reported that he was quite broad-shouldered and dark (though perhaps a little less swarthy than rumor had made him out to be), and the third, Lady Aubert, exclaimed effusively that he was soft-spoken and pleasant (though perhaps she would have preferred him to be a little more verbose). "And even if he's a bit too modest in his dress," she added with a matchmaking mother's gleam, "he has everything else to recommend him."

"Yes," Horatia muttered under her breath, "an income of more than twenty thousand a year."

But Lady Aubert, already pattering to the door to see if by some miracle the Viscount had asked her daughter to dance, did not like Horatia's jibe. "If you ask me," she said icily before departing, "he'd be considered the season's best catch with *half* that income."

Although Lady Horatia did not answer, she was secretly in complete agreement. No one could argue that the man wasn't a real catch even with half his income and even if he *was* (as Horatia now suspected) as thin as a stick, as dark as a Hottentot, and as taciturn as a stone. But since he was unlikely to take notice of Georgy when he was undoubtedly surrounded by every beribboned, bejeweled, bewitching young female in the ballroom, there was no point in admitting to Lady Aubert (or even to herself) that the fellow was the season's best catch. What difference could it make to her, under the circumstances? She put all thoughts of Maitland from her mind and returned her attention to her cards.

Considering the vagueness of the descriptions Lady Horatia received, it was not surprising that when she found herself standing at the buffet beside an unremarkable, tousled, lion-maned fellow with weathered skin, deep creases in his cheeks and attired in an evening coat whose cut was shockingly out of date, she did not guess that it was he.

The buffet had been set up in the blue saloon, a large, beautifully appointed room directly below the ballroom, and for the hour and a half since dinner was announced, a steady stream of guests had made their way down the stairs and up again. By the time Lady Horatia took herself down, it was quite late and most of the guests had already dined. Lady Horatia was hungry. She merely glanced at the fellow beside her and turned her attention to the food. "Oh, dear," she murmured aloud, "don't tell me the lobster cakes are all gone."

The fellow turned to her and smiled, the expression giving warmth to his entire visage. "I seem to have taken the last of them. But I haven't touched it. May I offer you my plate?"

Lady Horatia blushed. "Oh, no, thank you, sir! I couldn't *dream* of—"

"Please take it. I'm not particularly partial to lobster anyway."

Her ladyship shook her head. "Nonsense. I've never known anyone who didn't like lobster."

"Well, now you do." Meeting the look of disbelief in her eye, a grin lit his own. He took her empty dish from her hand and replaced it with his. "Even if I *did* like lobster, ma'am, which I don't for a moment admit I do, do you think I could possibly eat it now, knowing I was depriving you? Please, take it and think no more about it."

Lady Horatia was charmed. "Thank you, sir. You are most generous. Let me make it up to you by helping you to some of these poultry *filets à L'Orléans*. Letty Denham is famous for them. They're quite deli—"

To her chagrin, a familiar voice from the corridor just outside the doorway behind them distracted her and stayed her hand. The voice was completely audible and distinct; she knew at once it was her daughter's. "Why *should* I have danced with him, Lucy?" Georgy was saying as she and her friend strolled by the doorway. "He may be your brother, but he's a clod, a Tory and an absolute idiot."

Lucy, a blue-eyed vision (looking like a gaudy butterfly

beside Horatia's pale-gowned-moth-of-a-daughter), giggled loudly. "Georgy, really! You always say the most dreadful things! Just because Monte's a Tory doesn't mean he's an idiot, does it?"

"Yes, it does. Many men turn to Toryism in their dotage, of course—one expects that sort of change from minds turned stiff and clogged with age—but when a *young* man like Monte takes it up, it indicates not only a lack of mental acumen but a certain meanness of spirit. A young man should be a rebel, a radical, a fighter for the good of the weak and oppressed, not a supporter of the group that represents political hypocrisy."

"Political hypocrisy? You're not saying that my brother is a hypocrite, are you? Now, Georgy, *really*—!"

The gentleman standing beside Lady Horatia had turned round at the first sound of Georgy's voice. He stared at the girls in fascination as they passed by and then peered round the doorway after them until they disappeared from view. "What a magnificent creature!" he murmured almost to himself before turning back to Horatia.

"Yes, Lucy Traherne is much admired," Horatia said drily, returning her attention to the buffet.

"Oh, do you know her?" The gentleman followed her, eyeing her with renewed interest. "I thought the other chit called her Georgy."

"Other chit?" Horatia looked up at him in surprise. "Were you referring to *Georgy?* The creature in the hideous lilac-gray dress? Was it *that* one you spoke of as magnificent?"

"I didn't notice her dress. I did, however, notice her eyes. When she spoke of rebels and radicals and fighters for the weak and oppressed, they positively sparkled."

"Humph!" Horatia snorted. "I don't for a moment doubt they did." She handed the stranger a well-loaded plate. "Though much good her sparkling eyes will do her in that dress."

"That's where men and women differ, ma'am," the gentleman said with a smile. "Women put a great deal too much store in the efficacy of dress. Yet I'd wager that no man worth his salt would give a fig for what that young woman was wearing, not after he'd gotten a glimpse of those eyes."

"Do you really think so?" Lady Horatia looked up at the fellow in wonder. "I can't believe you speak for the majority, but I sincerely hope I'm wrong."

"And why is that, ma'am? Have you some connection with that fascinating young woman called Georgy?"

"Indeed I have. I'm her mother."

"Well, well!" the man said, his smile broadening. "I *am* in luck. Perhaps I can prevail upon you to introduce me to your charming daughter. I'd like to ask her to dance."

"I should be delighted to oblige, sir," her ladyship said with a sigh, "but I'm afraid you'd be wasting your time. She'd probably refuse you."

"Would she? Good God, am I as unprepossessing as all that? I know Lady Denham said that my evening coat was shocking, but—"

"No, no. I didn't mean to disparage your appearance," Horatia assured him hastily. "In fact I find you quite handsome, in a loose-limbed, careless sort of way."

The fellow laughed. "Thank you, ma'am," he said with a mocking little bow. "Then why are you convinced that your daughter would refuse me?"

"Because she's refused everyone who's approached her tonight," Lady Horatia explained with a hopeless shrug.

"Dear me. Everyone?"

"Everyone," Horatia intoned funereally.

"That does sound discouraging," the fellow said, taking her ladyship's arm and leading her to a table. "Nevertheless, I'd like to make an attempt. After you've eaten your lobster cake, of course."

"It's no use, my dear sir," Horatia warned, seating herself. "You don't know my daughter. She's immovable when she's made up her mind. And for some reason, she made up her mind not to dance tonight."

But the gentleman refused to be dissuaded. "Perhaps she'd weaken if you assured her I'm not a Tory," he suggested.

"She doesn't weaken. Not Georgy."

"Not ever? Not even for the Denhams' guest of honor?"

Lady Horatia, in the act of lifting a lobster-laden fork to her mouth, froze. "Guest of . . . *honor?*"

"Well, yes. So Lady Denham led me to believe."

"You?" Her ladyship gasped. "You're . . . *Maitland?*"

"Yes, ma'am, I am. Anthony Maitland, at your service."

Horatia gaped at him in disbelief. She could scarcely credit her ears . . . or her eyes. Why, the fellow was not at all what she'd been led to expect. A few moments ago, when she'd believed him to be just an ordinary, unexceptional guest, she'd found him handsome enough . . . even charming. But as Anthony Maitland, Viscount Ivers . . . well, it simply couldn't *be*. No wonder the gossip about him was so confused! He did not seem at all what one would have expected of a titled man of wealth. Why, the fellow had the tall, muscled slimness of a dockworker, the large hands of a stonemason and the broad shoulders of a farm laborer. He had unkempt, almost bushy hair, a strongly lined face and a modest, self-deprecating smile. In addition, his clothes were a disgrace. The cut of his coat was out of fashion, and his neckcloth was so carelessly knotted that it was clear that no valet had had a hand in tying it. That this shabbily dressed, weather-beaten, unpretentious man was Anthony Maitland was almost beyond belief.

But he *was* Maitland. The season's best catch, in the flesh, sitting beside her and asking to meet her daughter! As the implications sank into her consciousness, she felt her hand begin to tremble. She lowered her fork slowly, her mind in a whirl. What an incredible stroke of luck that she'd run into him like this at the buffet! Her ignorance of his identity had enabled her to engage in a much more natural conversation with him than would have been possible if she'd known him. And when she remembered the exact word he'd used when he'd spoken of her daughter, her heart began to pound in excitement. Anthony Maitland —*the* Anthony Maitland himself!—had described her Georgy as *magnificent! Good heavens*, she thought hysterically, *this meeting could change everything!*

Unaware of the turmoil the announcement of his identity

had caused in her breast, Maitland continued with his gentle prodding. "Well, ma'am," he asked, "don't you think my being the guest of honor might weigh with your daughter just a little? Just enough to convince her to stand up with me for a country dance?"

"We shall certainly try," Lady Horatia declared firmly, pressing a restraining hand against her heaving chest and rising from her chair. "Come along with me."

"But, ma'am, we needn't rush off now," he remonstrated, surprised by her sudden arousal into action. "You haven't yet eaten your lobster cake."

"Oh, who cares for that now?" she cried, grasping his hand and pulling him after her. "We must find Georgy before the next set begins to form."

The fellow stopped and grinned down at the flushed woman who was grasping his arm in a viselike hold. "Aha," he remarked with satisfaction, "then you think she *will* dance with me."

"She'll dance with you," the mother said between clenched teeth, adding to herself as she hurried her "catch" down the hallway, *she'll dance with you if I have to box her ears!*

Chapter 2

Georgy could tell by the fierce look in her mother's eyes that, unless she wished to take part in a dreadful scene right there on the edge of the dance floor, she had better not refuse Maitland's invitation to dance. She hesitated only a moment, glancing from the threatening glare of her mother's expression to Lucy's shocked one, and then she looked up at his lordship and nodded.

She'd been sitting with Lucy behind a bank of potted palms when her mother and Maitland had come up to them. Lucy had gasped in excitement, but Georgy had been unmoved. After Lady Horatia had made the introductions, Lucy had actually almost risen from her seat in eagerness, certain that it was she the Viscount was seeking. But it was Georgy he'd asked, and the shock had not yet left Lucy's face.

Throwing an I'm-surrendering-but-I'm-still-defiant glance at her mother, Georgy took the Viscount's arm and let him lead her onto the floor. She peeped at his face from under lowered lids as they took their places in the set. He was older than she'd thought at first, probably well past thirty. But there was a keen intelligence in his expression that she immediately admired and a lanky relaxation in his movements that she had to admit was attractive. Not that his attractiveness made her less angry that she'd been forced to stand up with him. If a young lady were permitted to speak her mind, she would have told him bluntly that neither his attractions nor his wealth interested her in the least. But no well-reared young lady could say such things aloud.

She became aware that they were standing together in

silence among the dozens of other couples who were all chattering away like magpies. Although the music had not yet begun, he was making no attempt to converse even though he must have known that it was his place to initiate a conversation. Was he too proud or too lazy to exert himself, she wondered, or was he just a bit peculiar?

Well, if he didn't say something, she would. "I suppose you realize that everyone is watching you, my lord," she said, hoping to shock him, "but you will not win much admiration for your choice of a partner."

He looked not at all shocked. "Why do you say that, ma'am?" he asked with mild curiosity.

The music began. "You can scarcely expect to be esteemed for choosing the most dowdy creature in the room to stand up with you," she informed him, taking his hand and stepping into place for the dance.

"Dowdy, ma'am?" He looked down at her with eyebrows raised in amusement and then went into the first turn. "Is that how you see yourself?"

"That's how everyone must see me."

"You are much mistaken, Miss Verney," Maitland retorted, "if you believe you can hide your beauty behind a drab gown and a severe coiffure."

Though surprised by this blunt response, Georgy didn't miss a step. "I seem to have hidden it very well so far this evening, my lord. This is my first dance."

"But it cannot be that I'm the first to ask you. If that is the case, the only explanation I can conceive is that the room is full of blind men."

That, my lord, was nicely played, she said to herself in unexpected approval. She looked up at him with the first glimpse of a smile. "No, you're not the first," she admitted. "I was not in the mood for dancing tonight."

"So your mother said. Why is that, ma'am? Are you not feeling quite the thing?"

"I'm feeling perfectly well," she responded as they parted to execute a figure.

"Then is it the *act* of dancing you dislike?" he asked when they came together. "That would be hard to believe, since you do it with perfect grace."

"Thank you. I like dancing well enough."

"Then is it that you hold our whole sex in dislike . . . or just the specimens of it who are present here tonight?"

A reluctant laugh escaped her. "It's just that dancing requires a bit of . . . of flirtation, and I don't care for flirting."

He cocked his head interestedly. "Don't you? Why not?"

Again the figure of the dance separated them, and when they came together she tried to change the subject. "Did you know that our hostess, Lady Denham, has acquired a Watteau oil for her gallery?" she remarked.

"No, I did not. What a fascinating bit of information. Is that your way of avoiding an answer to my question?"

"Question? What question?"

He looked down at her with narrow-eyed suspicion. "You know perfectly well what question."

"Do I indeed?" she challenged, meeting his eye. But a blush crept over her cheeks and gave her away.

He let the blush recede while they danced a few measures in silence. Then his smile lit his face again. "Don't you realize, my girl, that such evasion is in itself an act of flirtation?"

She studied his face speculatively and then dropped her eyes. "Yes, I suppose it is," she admitted, suddenly honest. "It's difficult to avoid being flirtatious in such a situation as this."

"Yes, it is. But I see nothing wrong in it."

"I do." They executed a perfect turn without ceasing to converse. "I find flirting to be superficial and insincere."

"So do I. But it has its uses. How are a man and a maid to become acquainted otherwise?"

They had to separate again, during which time she phrased her answer. "A man and a maid, if they wish to know each other better, can speak seriously about more important matters," she declared pompously when they met again.

His eyes twinkled. "Important matters? Like Letty Denham acquiring a Watteau, is that what you mean?"

She colored again. "Very well, my lord, your point. But

two people *could* discuss politics or philosophy or any number of edifying topics and become equally well acquainted, couldn't they?"

"Certainly they could," he said, trying not to smile. "And what edifying topic would you care to discuss right now?"

"You needn't laugh at me," she said, lifting her chin defiantly. "Any topic we choose would be a more sensible use of our time than flirting. We might discuss the Regent's reckless spending, for one thing."

"We could, of course, but I'd find such conversation not nearly so enjoyable as flirting with you."

"I, on the other hand, would be much more comfortable."

"I've never before encountered a female who was more comfortable discussing politics than flirting," he remarked, shaking his head in admiration.

"Perhaps in your encounters with females you didn't bother to try."

"Well done, ma'am, *your* point this time."

"Don't you find it reprehensible, my lord," she asked, firmly turning the topic to the Regent, "that Prinny seems to ignore the denunciations from Parliament and goes ahead with all sorts of wild extravagances in spite of them?"

"Oh, yes, quite reprehensible," Maitland agreed, and he proceeded to castigate the Prince's expenditures for the rest of the dance.

It was not until he was leading her back to her seat that he changed the subject. "I know your mother somehow coerced you into standing up with me, Miss Verney," he said earnestly, "but I hope the experience proved not too distasteful in the end. Speaking for myself, I found it quite the most enjoyable few minutes of the entire evening."

For the second time that evening she found herself admiring his manner of expressing himself, and her rare smile revealed itself again. "Are we reverting to flirtation again, my lord?" she chided.

He grinned. "I hope so. I'm certainly doing *my* share."

"Yes, you are, but don't expect any encouragement

from me. I do not change my views so easily." She put out her hand. "Thank you, my lord, for a not-distasteful experience. I wish you good night."

He took her hand and held it. "Good night, but not good-bye, Miss Verney. We shall meet again."

"It's quite unlikely. I rarely attend occasions like this."

"My dear girl," he said, pulling her close to him and laughing down into her eyes, "if you honestly believe that we won't meet again, you are greatly underestimating yourself." He lifted her hand to his lips, kissed it and let her go. "And grossly underestimating me," he added as he walked jauntily away.

Chapter 3

The shabby, ill-kept carriage that drew up to the marble steps of Verney House in Chesterfield Street was obviously a rented hack, but the uniformed young man who leaped out before the coachman had a chance to let down the steps was a vision of elegance. It was not only the brilliance of his brass buttons and gold braid that caught the eye of every passerby; it was the insouciance of the pompon atop his impressive hat, the pristine whiteness of his chest ribbands, the immaculate fit of the trousers round his well-shaped legs, the gleaming perfection of his high-topped boots, and most of all, the manly strength of his mouth and chin glimpsed beneath the visor of his shako that caused the passing ladies to sigh and the men to glance at him with surreptitious envy. "Fine-lookin' soldier, that," an elderly stroller remarked to the wife who was clinging to his arm. "Officer of the Scots Guard."

"Now how would ye know that?" his wife demanded suspiciously.

The old man chuckled. "From the medallion on his shako, that's how I know," he told her as they gave the soldier one last look before turning the corner.

The slovenly coachman had, by this time, clamored down from his perch and was removing his passenger's rucksack from the boot where it had been stowed. The officer, meanwhile, had been staring at the house with a strange intensity. It was an impressive dwelling, wide enough in front to accommodate a curved driveway. The front door was flanked with fluted columns that not only supported a narrow balcony running the width of the second story but continued up past the third story and but-

25

tressed a triangular pediment adorned with a sculptured crest at the apex. The officer's eyes seemed to dwell lovingly on the facade, but he shook himself from his reverie as the coachman came round with his baggage. "Here, I'll take that," he said and threw the rucksack over his shoulder.

"I kin carry it in fer ye," the coachman offered, wiping his nose with the back of his hand.

The soldier shook his head, tossed a coin to the coachman and made for the door. Before he reached it, however, it was thrown open by a portly butler who was smiling broadly. "Well, well, Master Jeremy, you've come home."

"Spiers!" The soldier took the butler's hand and shook it warmly. "You and the house haven't changed at all."

"Both a little grayer, p'rhaps, and a bit more—"

"Jemmy, Jemmy!" came a shriek from within, and the butler was almost overturned by a projectile whizzing past him—a blur of arms, legs and petticoats. "You're *home!*"

The soldier dropped his sack and held out his arms just in time to catch the creature who hurled herself at him. "Allie!" he gasped, embracing her tightly before lifting her high in the air and laughing up at her. "Good Lord, child, look at you!"

"Don't call me child," Alison Verney ordered magisterially, despite the awkwardness of her position in the air. "I've turned fourteen, you know."

"Have you indeed?" her brother sighed, setting her on her feet. "I quite believe it. Why, you've grown at least ten inches!"

"Well, what did you expect, you silly?" the girl giggled, patting her tousled skirt into place. She was a pretty creature, with unruly auburn curls topping a freckled face that still showed the rounded softness of childhood. "That's what usually happens, isn't it? After all, you've been gone three years."

"So I have." The soldier smiled at his sister affectionately. "And in that time you've almost become a woman."

"Almost," the girl agreed, looking down ruefully at the black-stockinged legs that protruded below the hem of her schoolgirl-length skirt. "If Mama would only permit me to wear longer frocks, I might almost pass for sixteen, don't you think?"

"You'll pass for sixteen when you *are* sixteen," said a hoarse voice from the doorway. It was Lady Horatia herself, come from the sofa, on which she'd been stretched all morning, to greet her son. "Jeremy, my love," she exclaimed, struggling to hide the depths of her emotion, "you've come at last!"

"Mama!" He stared at her for a moment, noting the unfamiliar streaks of gray in her hair and the deepened lines about her mouth. Then, shaken, he enveloped her in a bearlike embrace. "Forgive me, Mama," he whispered. "I should have come sooner."

Hiding her face in his shoulder, she smoothed his cheek with her fingers. "Nothing to forgive. You're not to be blamed if your father passed away just when Boney made his escape. The Duke needed you more than I."

"Well, Boney can't keep us apart any longer," Jeremy said, lifting her chin and kissing her cheek. "I'm home for good, now."

With an arm about his mother and sister, Jeremy crossed the threshold of the home he'd not seen for years. The entrance hall and the corridors seemed smaller to him than he remembered, and there was an air of decaying elegance over everything. The drapes in the drawing room looked faded, the carpet of the stairway slightly worn, and the sofas of the sitting room looked positively shabby. But the same portraits he'd seen from childhood still gazed down at him from the walls, the furniture still stood where it always had, and the fires in all the fireplaces still glowed with their old warmth. Nothing was out of place, and everything was endearingly familiar.

Overwhelmed with old memories, the returning soldier did not notice at first that someone was missing from the welcoming committee. It was only after his mother and the butler had urged him to the table in the morning room (where a light luncheon of barley soup, cold roast chicken, ham, pickled salmon, poached river trout, potatoes, greens, custard pudding and a variety of tarts had been set out) that he looked about him with a sudden, puzzled frown. "I say," he asked, "where's Georgy hiding herself? I've been home for ten minutes and have yet to get a glimpse of her."

Lady Horatia, her expression darkening, sank down on the chair opposite him. "Your sister Georgianna is not at home at the moment," she said, nervously rearranging her place setting.

"Not at home?" Jeremy looked from his mother to his sister and back again, his brows knit. "But . . . didn't she know I was coming?"

Alison opened her mouth to respond, but a glare from her mother silenced her. "We'll speak of Georgianna after we've eaten," her ladyship said firmly. "Meanwhile, Spiers, please serve some of this excellent soup to our re-turning hero."

Although conversation did not languish during the meal (for Jeremy was barraged with questions, and he obliged his mother, his sister and the butler by describing in great detail his part in the battle of Waterloo), the excitement of his arrival was considerably damped by Georgianna's ab-sence. Finally, after firmly refusing a second helping of custard pudding, Jeremy leaned back in his chair, faced his mother and said purposefully, "All right, Mama, we've eaten. The time has come for me to hear about Georgy. What's the mystery?"

Lady Horatia put down her teacup, lowered her hands to her lap and twisted her fingers together nervously. "It's because of Georgy that I sent for you," she said, taking a deep breath. She paused as Spiers leaned over to refill her cup, and then she turned to her daughter. "Alison, dearest, why don't you go to the music room and practice the piano for a while?"

"Practice?" the girl echoed in horror. *"Now?* When Jemmy's just *arrived?"*

"Yes, please. I wish to speak to your brother in private."

"But I want to *listen!"* Alison pouted. "I know all about Georgy anyway."

Lady Horatia frowned at the child. "Do as I say, girl, and without argumentation for once! Spiers, take the child away, and see that we're not disturbed."

Even after the butler and Alison were gone and mother

and son were alone, Horatia hesitated. "I'm sorry I had to ask you to come," she said after a long pause. "It must have been awkward for you."

"Not at all," Jeremy assured her. "The war is over. Napoleon will never again be a threat to us. It was only a matter of weeks before I would have returned in any case."

She reached across the tables and squeezed his hand. "I *am* glad. I do need you at home, Jemmy. Without your father to advise me, you see, I'm so often at a loss. And *now*—"

"Now, *what*, Mama? Has Georgy done something dreadful?"

"More dreadful than you can imagine. She's gone."

"Gone? What do you mean, gone?"

"She's left home. Run away. *Gone.*"

Jeremy gaped at her. "I don't understand. Gone where? With whom?"

"I don't know." The poor woman's facade crumbled, and the long-withheld tears dripped from her eyes. "I d-don't know *anything!*"

"Good God, Mama, don't cry! It won't do anyone any good to turn on the waterworks. I've never known you to do so before. Everyone's always admired you for being so . . . so *composed.*"

Her ladyship pulled a large handkerchief from the bosom of her gown and sniffed into it. "Composed? Ha! It's easy to be composed when one has nothing to be discomposed about. When your father was alive, I was rarely upset. Whenever anything went wrong, he took care of it. That's how I could be composed. But now everything's falling to *pieces!* The bills are piling up alarmingly—I'm afraid you'll fall into a taking when you total them—and then there's your sister . . . turning herself into a bluestocking and running off Heaven knows where . . . and just at this *crucial* time! How can I be *composed?*"

Jeremy, becoming quite alarmed himself to see his mother so agitated, tried to soothe her by patting her hand. "All right, Mama, cry if you must. But if I'm to understand, you'd better tell me clearly just what's gone amiss."

Horatia nodded, blew her nose resolutely into the handkerchief, took another deep breath and got hold of herself. "Yes, you're right. I must try to be calm and clear-headed. Very well, then, I suppose I must begin by admitting that Georgy and I have been quarreling badly. She just won't see that our future depends on her making an advantageous match."

The soldier frowned. "You shouldn't have been quarreling about that, Mama. Your future doesn't depend on Georgy. My income isn't large, but we can manage on it if we practice a little reasonable economy."

"No, you don't understand, Jemmy." She picked up a spoon and stirred her tea nervously. "You've been away so long . . . you *can't* understand. You won't be able to support us all indefinitely, especially after you marry. You must believe me, Jemmy, dearest. We have a real problem. I've thought and thought about what to do . . . and I've discussed all this quite openly with Mr. Hitchins, your father's man of business, but he had no helpful suggestions either. The only answer we could think of was to find Georgy a man of wealth. But you know your sister. She's not only unwilling to marry *well* . . . she's unwilling to marry at all."

"I remember her making childish remarks about never getting married," Jeremy said with a reminiscent sigh, "but I thought she'd have gotten over that nonsense by this time."

"I'm afraid she's worse than ever. Quite a bluestocking, your sister. She believes that *arranged* marriages in particular put women in bondage. I can't imagine where she comes by her strange ideas. It must be from those peculiar books she's always reading—she's forever quoting Bentham, for one, with his greatest-good-for-the-greatest-number theories . . . and that German fellow, Hegel, and Hannah More, the educationist, and Robert Owen—"

"Who's Robert Owen?"

Horatia made an impatient movement with her hand. "He's that fellow in Scotland who writes about the abuse of children in the manufactories. He's actually building schools for working-class children, Georgy told me. Not that I blame Georgy for admiring the man. Whenever one thinks of those poor little children working for pennies in those dreadful places, one must feel the utmost commiseration for them. But to get back to the subject at hand, my quarrels with your sister were not very serious at first, because there was no suitor pursuing her who was promising enough to offer me real hope. But then, you see, Maitland came along."

"Maitland?"

"Viscount Ivers. Surely you've heard of him? His story is quite romantic. He had a wild sort of youth and was sent abroad by his father some ten years ago. Seems he took himself to the Indies and made a fortune. The old Viscount passed on last year, and Maitland came back to claim his titles and estate. What with his inheritance and the fortune he brought back with him, they say he has more than twenty thousand a year!"

"That's impressive. But what has all this to do with Georgy?"

"I'm coming to that. Maitland is an old friend of Roger Denham, and he was the guest of honor at the Denhams' rout a month or so ago. Everyone was agog, because he rarely appears in public. I can tell you, Jemmy, that every unmarried female and every matchmaking mother was trying to attract his notice, but it was *your sister* the man was taken with! Though Heaven only knows why, for she was far from looking her best. She'd decided to wear a dreadful muslin gown that made her look like a churchmouse. But the man was so besotted, he told me she was magnificent. I swear to you, Jemmy, that was his very word for her, *magnificent!* And they danced together. It was the talk of the town for days, because Maitland hadn't asked anyone else to dance. But all I could get from Georgy afterwards was that she found him 'typical.'"

"Typical? Typical of what?"

"Typical of the men of his class. 'Makes use of the poor and downtrodden for his own advantage,' she said."

"How could she know that," Jeremy snorted, "after only one dance with him?"

"That's just what I asked her. She countered by asking

me how he could have made a fortune in the Indies without
taking advantage of the natives."

"Good God! She *has* become a bluestocking!"

"Isn't that what I've been saying?" Her eyes filled with
tears again. "I'm beginning to fear she'll become one of
those eccentric spinsters who dress themselves like Turks,
devote themselves to causes and surround themselves with
freaks."

"Don't be foolish, Mama. Georgy is too sensible for
that."

"Sensible? Do you think your sister is *sensible?* Would a
sensible young woman run away from the prospect of marriage to a rich nobleman?"

Jeremy shrugged. "Perhaps she took a dislike to him,
Mama. You can't blame her for that. After all, no girl of
spirit would wish to be shackled to a man she disliked,
even if he *were* rolling in soft."

"Don't use your free-and-easy barracks expressions to
me, young man," his mother chided. "Rolling in soft, indeed. And I don't think she disliked him. I think she was
hurt that he didn't call on her afterward."

"I can't blame her for that, Mama. If he didn't call on
her—"

"He left town. One can't call on someone if one is out
of town."

"If a man is taken with a woman, he doesn't *go* out of
town. At least not until he's established a stronghold."

"Will you *please* spare me your military metaphors?
This has nothing to do with establishing strongholds. The
fellow had to go to see to his estate. There *are* business
matters more pressing than the need to make calls, you
know."

"If the fellow cares more about business than he does
about matters of the heart, I'm not surprised Georgy disliked him."

"She didn't dislike him, I tell you. Maitland is a sur-
prisingly likable, unassuming fellow, Jemmy, really he is.
I'm not saying it merely because he's rich. You may take
my word for it, dearest, that I found him charming even
before I knew who he was."

"I *do* take your word, Mama, but Georgy evidently doesn't think as you do."

"Don't be too sure of that. It seemed to me that when they danced together, she positively glowed. It was only afterward, when he failed to call, that she became critical of him."

"It seems to me, Mama, that you're presuming a bit more here than is warranted. The fellow danced with her, but he evidently forgot about her once the dance was over. You say that they met more than a month ago. Has she had any word from him since then?"

"No, *she* hasn't, but—"

Jeremy threw up his hands. "You're building castles in air, Mama. It seems to me that you've refined too much on one dance." The young soldier fixed his eyes on her accusingly. "And then, I suppose, you began to nag at her to *like* the fellow."

"*Nag* at her? I, *nag?*" She drew herself up in offence for a moment and then lowered her eyes guiltily. "Yes, perhaps I did nag at her."

"Perhaps?"

"See here, Jeremy Verney, if you mean to imply that it's my nagging that drove her to run away, you're fair and far off! You'd better read her letter before you jump to conclusions!"

"There's a *letter?* Why didn't you say so at once? Let me see it!"

Lady Horatia withdrew from her bosom a much-refolded piece of notepaper and handed it to her son without a word. He unfolded it and scanned it hurriedly. *Dearest Mama,* he read, *I'm afraid you will think me Willful and Wicked for leaving you like this, but I have thought on this matter Long and Hard and am convinced that it is the Right Thing. You think that the Right Thing is for me to marry Wealth and thus save the family from Financial Ruin, but in Reality, no such offer has been made to me. And even if it were, I would not accept it. Such a marriage would only turn me into a Slave to the man who Bought me and you into a Poor Relation, dependent for your living on the Good Will of Another.*

*As you very well know—for you have heard me say it
Often Enough—I have long deplored the Subservient position of Women who must rely on the Generosity of the men
they marry for their very Livelihood. That sort of Enslave-
ment is repugnant to me, and I have therefore Determined
to make myself Independent. To that end, I have found for
myself a Post some distance from London which will provide for me Paid Employment, which in turn will permit me
to live Decently, with Dignity and Self-Respect. I have
always wished to live by my own Resources, and now I
shall.*

*If you choose to interpret this act of mine as Deserting
you in your Time of Need, so be it. But in my heart I am
not deserting you. Instead, I am relieving you of the necessity of Supporting me. I realize that this obliges you to give
up your Dreams that the Family Fortune will be saved by
my wedding a man of Wealth, and further obliges you to
begin to plan your life in a more Modest and Frugal style,
but I am convinced that this would be the best thing for
your Moral Character and for Allie's, too. It is almost
Decadent, I believe, for us to continue to live in the Plea-
sure-seeking, Wasteful style we have grown used to. It will
be better for all of us to learn to live like other Ladies of
Meager Means. We may no longer have a houseful of Servants and a new Bonnet for every gown, but at least we
shall be Independent.*

*Please do not be concerned for my Health and Safety.
The Post I have acquired is Secure and Respectable, so
you should have no cause to be in any way Alarmed. I pray
that some day you will find it in your heart to Forgive me
and that you come to believe that I am and Shall Always Be
your most loving daughter, Georgianna.*

"Good God!" Jeremy exclaimed after reading through it
twice, "the girl's become an Evangelical!"

"Oh, I wouldn't go as far as *that*," Lady Horatia said in
alarm. "Please don't repeat such a thing! If it were bruited
about that she's turned fanatical, that *would* be the end of
her chances."

Jeremy stared at the letter for a long moment and then
handed it back to his mother. "Perhaps it is only an odd

humor," he suggested with weak optimism, "a mere temporary conceit. Perhaps she'll find that this 'post' she's taken is a great deal more grueling and unpleasant than she supposed. Then she'll come back to us a changed woman."

"Yes, but by that time she'll have lost her chance with Maitland. I know you've convinced yourself that I'm only imagining he's taken with her, but I'm not. We've an invitation from him, you see."

"An invitation?"

"Yes. A very exciting invitation. Look at this!" She reached into a pocket in her overskirt and withdrew a card engraved with gold letters. She didn't cease her prattle as he scanned it. "He invites us—*all* of us, as you can see by the note he scrawled at the bottom—to visit his estate in East Riding."

"What's this he calls it? *Colinas Verde?* What sort of name is that?" Jeremy asked, staring at the gold letters.

"The Countess Lieven tells me that he's named it after his home in the Indies. He's refurbished the manor house completely, and he evidently plans to open it with a fortnight of festivities for some of his particular friends: the Countess, the Denhams, all that circle. What's particularly significant is that we scarcely know the man, and yet he's invited us! Surely that must prove to you that he's interested in Georgy. But the date is only a few weeks away." She gave a deep, hopeless sigh. "I tell you, Jemmy, when the invitation came, I was beside myself with joy! I had such hopes—!"

Jeremy handed back the card with a shake of his head. "Forget Maitland, Mama. If you want your daughter back, you must permit her to live her life as she sees fit. I can manage to keep us all going, I promise you."

"No, Jemmy, dearest, you haven't thought about this as I have. I know you would do all you can, of course, but you may not be able to stretch your limited resources as far as you think. After all, you'll be taking a wife one day . . . soon, I expect . . . and you'll have an uphill climb to keep yourself and your own family in comfort. And your wife may not wish to share this house with three female in-laws. And then, you see, you're very likely to have children before you know it, and even if your wife would have been willing to share her home before, she'd surely be quite *un*willing once children began to come. Under those circumstances, your sisters and I would have to find other quarters, and you would be severely hard-pressed to maintain *two* establishments. So you see—"

"Look here, Mama, if we were speaking in general terms about some unknown chit I've yet to meet, you might have some cause for concern. But it's Rosalind Peascott I intend to marry. You're speaking of *Rosalind.*"

"Am I?" his mother asked, lowering her eyes. "Are you still desirous of wedding her?"

"Of course I am. Did you think my years in service would make me forget her? I'm not so inconstant."

Her ladyship stirred her tea uneasily. She was not at all pleased that her son still harbored hopes of Rosalind Peascott. The girl had given no indication that she was equally constant; she'd been seen with a number of eligible escorts at a great many fashionable balls. And neither she nor Lady Peascott had paid a single call at Verney House during the last two seasons. Horatia could only hope that her son was not heading for heartbreak. "Rosalind Peascott has been accustomed to having every little wish granted," she said after a long pause. "If she weds you, you must not assume she would willingly share your home with us."

"Rubbish, Mama. She's as fond of you as she is of her own mother! And she adores Georgy and Allie, too. She would never wish to put you out."

Lady Horatia bit her lip. *If the girl is so adoring,* she asked herself, *where has she been for the past two years?* But aloud she only said, "She may be fond of us, Jemmy, but that doesn't mean she'd wish to live with us."

"Then I'll go round to the Peascotts' and ask her," Jeremy declared, getting to his feet.

"Right now?" his mother asked in some dismay.

"Yes, right now. I can't wait to see her. It's been three long years, after all."

Lady Horatia's face clouded. "You mustn't be upset, my dearest, if she doesn't agree to accept us as permanent visitors in your home. I don't want my situation to be an obstacle to your happiness."

"It won't be, Mama. I know Rosalind. She's as good and kind a girl as ever was." He went eagerly to the door. "And after waiting for me for three years," he added over his shoulder, "she'll be so delighted that we can wed at last that she'd probably agree to live in a stable with a family of cows."

Oh, very likely! Lady Horatia thought glumly as she watched her handsome son stride out of the room and down the hall. *Rosalind Peascott in a stable? Ha! I wish I may live to see the day!*

Chapter 4

Jeremy knew, from the stiffness of the Peascotts' butler's greeting, that something was amiss. The man, who'd known Jeremy since boyhood, barely permitted himself a welcoming smile. He ushered Jeremy into the library, said nervously that he would notify Sir Basil of his arrival and tried to bow himself out. But Jeremy stopped him. "I don't want to see Sir Basil," he told the butler bluntly. "I want to see Miss Peascott—as you know perfectly well."

The butler's expression remained passive, but his eyes fell. "Sir Basil gave me strict orders, Captain Verney, that whenever you chanced to call I was to notify him first."

Jeremy found those orders strange, but there was nothing he could do about them. "Will you please tell Miss Peascott I'm here *after* you've informed Sir Basil, then?"

The butler hesitated. "I . . . very well, Captain, if you wish me to." And with a last, uneasy glance at the visitor, he left the room.

When the door had closed behind the butler, Jeremy paced about the room, his brow puckered. He tried to tell himself that there was nothing ominous in the fact that Rosalind's father wanted to see him. What could be more natural than Sir Basil's wishing to welcome him home before any of the others? There was probably nothing more sinister in the matter than that.

But Jeremy's unease was not assuaged by such reasoning. There had been something in the butler's manner that was decidedly out of kilter, and Jeremy's instincts—not at all soothed by his brain's logic—warned him that the forthcoming interview with his prospective father-in-law would not be to his liking.

His instincts proved to be correct. Sir Basil's affability, as he entered the room, was an unmistakable attempt to mask an undercurrent of discomfort. Sir Basil was a heavy, ruddy-faced gentleman with a half-bald head and popping eyes. Jeremy had always liked his lack of ostentation and his tendency to blunt speech. But today it was plain that the man was hiding something. Although his greeting to Jeremy was warm and affectionate, and his expressions of gratification that the young soldier had come through the war so admirably and safely were undoubtedly sincere, Jeremy sensed that Rosalind's father had a more menacing purpose in arranging this interview. "Is there something else you wish to say to me, sir?" Jeremy asked, hoping to get to the crux of the matter without further roundaboutation.

Sir Basil lowered his large bulk into an easy chair and urged Jeremy to do the same. "Yes, my boy, there is," he admitted. "Shall I send for a bottle of spirits before we begin? I have some excellent Scotch whisky that might help bad news go down."

"If it *is* bad news, sir, I'd prefer taking it down without lubrication. Tell me at once, Sir Basil. Is something the matter with Rosalind? She's not ill, is she?"

"No, no, nothing like that." Sir Basil took a meerschaum and a tobacco pouch from the pocket of his coat and began to fill the pipe with what Jeremy found to be maddening deliberation. "I dislike to have to break this to you, my boy, on the very first day of your heroic return," he said, puffing at his unlit pipe between words, "but it don't seem right to put the thing off."

"Yes, sir," Jeremy said, getting up from his seat and going to the fire to light a wooden taper. "Put what off?"

"The bad news."

"Yes, sir," Jeremy said between clenched teeth. Trying valiantly to keep his impatience checked, he went to Sir Basil's chair and held the lit taper to the pipe. "But what bad news?"

Sir Basil ceased his puffing, looked up and met Jeremy's eyes. "You want it straight and clean, eh? Well, then, here it is. You're not to call on Rosalind any more."

For a moment Jeremy remained motionless, his eyes fixed on the flame of the taper he was still holding. *Of course!* he thought. *Why did I not see it coming?* Then he blew out the taper, threw the remains into the fire and calmly returned to his seat. "Has she formed an attachment to someone else?" he asked when he could trust his voice.

"In a manner of speaking," Sir Basil replied, his tone not without sympathy. "We intend to announce her betrothal to Monte Traherne within a fortnight. Rosalind didn't wish the announcement made until you'd been informed."

"That was kind of her," Jeremy muttered tightly.

"You mustn't believe that the girl switched her allegiance thoughtlessly," Sir Basil was quick to assure him. "Hang it, boy, I know for a certainty that she has sincere feelings for you. The girl's been loyal in her affection for you through all your long absence. Her mother and I had the devil's own difficulty in persuading her to forswear her promise to you, not that your youthful pledge to one another was in any way a binding agreement. As we told her, that pledge was premature and made in youthful innocence. A formal betrothal never came to pass, as you know."

"Yes, but we—"

"You were both very young, and neither your parents nor we ever came to an agreement."

"You needn't argue the case on technicalities," Jeremy said, a touch of anger flaring up in his voice. "We both—Rosalind and I—took it for granted that our families approved the alliance."

Sir Basil took a number of puffs before responding. "Three years ago, when you went away, we *did* approve. There ain't a fellow in all of London I'd rather have for a son-in-law, Jeremy. You know that."

"I *thought* I knew that. Yet you say that it was your desire, not Rosalind's, to end our attachment. Why, sir? What has caused you to change your mind about me?"

"I haven't changed my mind about you. You're a fine fellow... the finest. But I had a chat with your father before his passing. He gave me a complete account of your financial prospects." He puffed at his pipe glumly. "It gave me a severe shock, I can tell you."

Jeremy blinked. At last he was beginning to understand. "You learned that my inheritance was not to be as great as you hoped, is that it?" he asked with a sneer.

"You needn't sound so contemptuous, my boy," Sir Basil said. "I ain't a money-grubbing pinchfist. I only want the best for my girl. When you have a daughter of your own, you'll understand our feelings, her mother's and mine. We can't permit our little girl to throw herself away on a man who can only give her a life of genteel poverty. You may not have thought about your situation, my boy, but I have. You have a Captain's pay and a modest inheritance. With this you must keep a London house, an encumbered country seat, a penniless mother and two sisters. You are unable, in those circumstances, to offer my daughter the sort of life we wish for her. Fond of you as I am, I couldn't encourage my daughter to accept so much less from life than what she's accustomed to. If you were in my place, would *you* ask Rosalind to make such a sacrifice?"

Jeremy slowly lowered his head. "No, I . . . don't suppose I would."

"Ah, then, you *do* see." He puffed at his pipe in considerable relief that the worst of the interview was over. "Monte Traherne may not be your equal in appearance and charm, but he has two thousand a year. I'm sorry, Jeremy, but such is the way of the world."

"Yes, sir, I quite understand," Jeremy mumbled miserably.

Sir Basil looked at the young man's bent head and sighed. Then he rose and put a hand on Jeremy's slumped shoulder. "Don't take it too much to heart, my boy. These affairs always become a great deal less important as time passes. You'll get over it."

Jeremy, feeling dazed, struggled to his feet. "Yes, sir, I suppose so." He took his shako from the table where the butler had placed it and went to the door without conscious knowledge of what he was doing. But before leaving, he paused and said quietly, "Tell Rosalind that I . . . that is, offer her my felicitations on her forthcoming . . . betrothal."

Then, with unseeing eyes, he went out of the room and shut the door behind him.

Benumbed, he placed the shako on his head and went down the wide staircase. He felt oddly displaced. Rosalind, with whom he'd been in love for as long as he could remember, was now, with stunning abruptness, removed from his life. How was he to readjust his thinking, to rechart the map of his future? He had believed for so long that Rosalind was the most significant part of his future that now, suddenly, he seemed to have no future at all! What was he to do to fill this unexpected void? Where was he to look for the love and companionship he'd always assumed were his for the asking?

He stumbled on a stair and reached blindly for the banister. Like an old man, he used it for support as he made his slow way down. When he reached the bottom, he tried to pull himself together. He adjusted his tall hat, squared his shoulders and walked purposefully to the door. Just as he put his hand on the knob, however, he heard a soft, familiar voice whisper his name. He turned about quickly, his heart beginning to race.

She was standing in the shadow of the staircase, beckoning to him. He moved toward her in bewilderment. She looked just as she did in his dreams of her during the long nights of the military campaigns. Her hair was a dark cloud about her face, her tall slimness draped in a shimmering, rose-colored concoction that made her seem ethereal. And her eyes gazing at him were misty with love. "Oh, *Jemmy*," she breathed and threw herself into his arms.

He held her close, forgetting everything that had occurred in the past quarter-hour. He was aware only of her cheek against his, her arms clasped tightly round his neck, her bosom heaving against his chest. "Rosalind, my love," he murmured, kissing her eyes, her brow, her hair, "I've missed you so!"

After a while she drew away and looked at him. "You look so dashing, Jemmy!" she exclaimed, careful to keep her voice lowered. "Your uniform truly becomes you."

The whispered voice and her surreptitious manner reminded him of what had transpired upstairs. A wave of

bitterness washed over him. Even in this moment of greeting, after not seeing him for three years, she had not lost
control of her emotions. *He* had, at least for a moment,
forgotten her father's command that he was not to see her
again. But *she* had not forgotten. She'd carefully kept her
voice down so that no one would know she'd stolen downstairs to see him. "I suppose that Monte Traherne's mufti
must become him even more than my uniform becomes
me," he said angrily, turning his face away, "since you've
chosen *him* to wed."

"Jemmy!" the girl gasped. "How can you say so? *I*
didn't choose him. Mama did." Her voice took on the
tremor of tragedy. "How can you believe I ever could?"

"I can believe it because I've been informed that he is to
be your betrothed. That much is true, isn't it?"

"Yes, but only because Papa accepted his suit."

"But you agreed to it, did you not?"

Tears filled her eyes. "What was I to do, my love? Papa
said that if I married you it would be the ruin of us both. I
didn't want to ruin you. Oh, Jemmy, if only you knew . . .
just how much I've suffered!"

Jeremy's anger dissipated. Why should he blame her? It
was not her fault that his inheritance was inadequate. He
could not expect her to submit herself to a life of penury
for his sake. He drew her into his arms again and brushed
aside her tears. "Don't cry, Rosalind," he murmured, his
lips against her hair. "This pain will pass. Your father says
that affairs like ours are easily forgotten . . . after a time."

But her tears would not stop. "I shall never forget you,
Jemmy," she sobbed. "This pain will *never* pass! I shall be
utterly miserable for as . . . long as I live!"

His arms tightened about her. How could he bring himself to give her up? In the war he'd proved himself to be a
man of courage, but it seemed to him at this moment that
he had not enough courage for *that*. "Damnation, what a
muddle this is!" he muttered. "I don't know if I can bring
myself to say good-bye to you."

This provoked a fresh flood of tears. "Oh, I can't bear
it!" she cried. "I don't want you to say good-bye! Is there
nothing we can do?"

He was too choked to answer. But his mind lingered on the question she'd asked. Was there nothing to be done, no solution to this horrible dilemma? There had to be, if only a man were strong enough to find it. "I'll find a way," he said hoarsely. "I don't know yet how, but I'll find a way!"

"Will you, Jemmy?" She looked up at him with hope peeping through the eyes aswim with tears. "Do you think you can?"

"I'll have to, my love, for I don't see a future for me without you."

"Oh, Jemmy," the girl sighed, nestling her head in his shoulder, "nor do I without you."

He stroked her hair thoughtfully. "But it will take some time, I fear, and your father intends to announce your betrothal to Traherne quite soon."

"Don't worry about that," she murmured into his neck. "I'll see to it that the announcement is postponed for as long a time as you need."

"Postponed? For as long as I need?" He grasped her shoulders and held her away from him, peering earnestly down at her face. "Rosalind, my love, do you truly think you can manage it?"

She gave him a tremulous smile. "If you can find a way," she said, her eyes like stars, "then so can I!"

Chapter 5

Jeremy did not immediately return home. He walked the
streets of London in brooding abstraction until darkness
fell, and then, his cogitations being unfruitful, walked
some more. He noted somewhere in the back of his mind
that the air had turned chill (a marked change from the
afternoon, when the weather had been delightfully balmy
for September). It was a quiet night, so quiet that the sound
of his boots on the pavement reverberated loudly through
the streets. The black, starless sky hung heavy above him,
presaging rain. One could almost smell the wetness in the
air. It was not a night to be outdoors. He came upon other
strollers only occasionally, and as much as ten minutes
might pass between the rumbling of one passing carriage
and the next. There was little to distract him from his
thoughts.

He avoided the streets brightened by the gas lamps, pre-
ferring the darkness. The lights in the houses he passed
were flickering and dim, shedding but a few faint oblongs
of amber on the pavement. Only a glow in the sky from the
brilliantly lit streets near Pall Mall and the rumble of carriages from the still-busy thoroughfares near Picadilly reminded him that he was strolling through the largest, most
populous city in the world. Even when his meanderings
brought him to Westminster, and he came upon the
Thames, he did not sense the crowded vastness of the me-
tropolis. The river seemed an empty blackness before him,
the dancing lights of the ships looking like nothing more
than fireflies in the dark. Only the bridges, spanning the
river in arcs of light, gave indications of the breadth of the
great river flowing along below.

He walked to the end of the street and leaned on a low wall that separated the street from the water. Staring out at the river, his mind gnawed at his problem like a hungry dog at a bone. He'd thought of various schemes for improving his lot during the past hours, but none of them had stood up to careful scrutiny. If he sold the country property, for example, he'd have to pay off the encumbrances, which would severely limit his profit. If he got himself a post in the diplomatic corps (the only profession for which he was the least bit qualified), he could not expect a salary much above a pittance. If he sold the London house, invested the money astutely, and took Rosalind and his family to live in the country, they might manage; but he suspected that Rosalind, who'd lived all her life in London, would not wish to cut herself off from London society for long. And certainly her father would not consider such a solution at all satisfactory.

After a while the dampness and chill became oppressive, and Jeremy, still unable to devise a promising scheme to increase his wealth, decided it was time he returned home. By the time he got there it was well past midnight. The house was dark, except for a few lighted candles in the sconces on the stairway. It seemed that the entire household, even the butler, had gone to bed. But he didn't mind the absence of the family or staff; in fact, he was glad not to have to hide his feeling of depression and make polite conversation. He wanted only to fall into bed and enjoy the anodyne of sleep. He tossed his shako on the hall table and gloomily made for the stairs, hoping that some sort of inspiration would come to him in his dreams.

Before he'd climbed two steps, however, the door of the downstairs sitting room opened and Lady Horatia, with her hair hanging down in a plait, her head topped with a ruffled nightcap and her majestic form wrapped in a dressing gown, appeared silhouetted in the doorway. "Jeremy? Is that you?" she asked.

"Yes, Mama. Have you been waiting up for me?"

"Of course. I was worried. We expected you for dinner."

"Oh. Sorry, Mama, I didn't think."

"We waited dinner until almost nine. Are you all right?"

"Yes, Mama, quite all right. There was no need to worry. I've been taking care of myself for a long time. In any case, I'm home now. Do go to bed."

His mother ignored that suggestion. "Did you see Rosalind?" she asked, peering at him through the dim light in an attempt to read his mood.

"Yes, but I don't wish to talk about it now," he answered curtly, continuing up the stairs.

"Oh, dear," his mother sighed unhappily, "it's just as I feared. She won't have you now."

He stopped in his tracks and turned around. "It's her father who won't have me. You mustn't think Rosalind is a money-grubber, Mama. I found her to be as loving and generous as ever."

"Yes, of course you did," she agreed hastily, nodding so vigorously that the ribbons on her nightcap bobbed, "but if her father won't have you, it comes to the same thing." She walked to the foot of the stairs and looked up at her son with motherly concern. "I'm so sorry, my love. I know how much Rosalind meant to you. But—"

Jeremy groaned. "Please, Mama," he cut in, wincing, "if you're going to tell me that I shall get over it, you're much mistaken. I don't intend to get over it. I intend to find a way to nullify her father's objections."

Lady Horatia's eyebrows lifted. "Nullify his objections? What does that mean?"

"It means I'm going to find a way to make myself worthy of her."

"Make yourself worthy? Of all the—! You're worth *ten* Rosalind Peascotts, just as you are right now!" his mother declared passionately.

"Come, come, Mama, your maternal prejudices are showing. What I meant to say was that I'm going to find a way to make myself *financially* worthy," he explained.

"I don't see how you're going to do that." She sank slowly down on the bottom step and muttered in discouragement, "I really don't see how."

"I don't either," Jeremy admitted, turning and proceeding up the stairs, "but I'll think of something."

"I've thought of nothing else for months," his mother said to his retreating back, "but I haven't been able to hatch a practical plan."

"That doesn't mean *I* won't," he threw back over his shoulder.

"Is that so? Well, Mr. Hitchins can't think of anything either, and if he can't—"

Jeremy stopped in his tracks and clenched his fists. "Then, dash it all, I'll find where Georgy's gone and make *her* get us out of this fix!"

Lady Horatia's eyes widened. "What did you say?"

"I said I'd make *Georgy* get us out of this fix!" her son declared, stomping off toward his bedroom.

His mother squinted up at the shadows into which he'd disappeared, a look of triumph lighting her eyes. "But my love," she murmured as a smile slowly brightened up her face, "isn't that what I've been saying all along?"

Chapter 6

It was soon clear to Jeremy that finding Georgy would not be easy. No one in the household seemed to have any idea of where she'd gone. He and Horatia questioned all the servants, but even Georgy's own abigail, Betsy, had no knowledge of her movements. Jeremy questioned poor Betsy closely and at length, but the interview ended without Jeremy learning anything useful and with Betsy in tears, the distressed abigail blaming herself for not having watched over her mistress with greater zeal.

Were it not for Alison's desire to elevate herself to adult attire, the one clue to Georgy's direction would not have been found. Alison, on a naughty impulse, had stolen into her absent sister's bedroom and made free with the garments left behind in Georgy's wardrobe. She'd tried on one gown after another, relishing the feel of the long skirts brushing against her ankles, but the one she liked best was a cherry-colored, India muslin round gown with a white tucker gathered in a becoming ruffle at the neck. Swishing the skirt, she pranced across the room to admire herself in the pier glass. As she stood twisting and turning herself in delight, something fell from the cuff of the sleeve. It was a small slip of paper on which someone had scrawled the words *St. Martins-le-Grand* followed by the confusing notations, 8E and 530M. Suspecting at once that these mysterious jottings had something to do with Georgy's running away, she clenched the paper in one hand, lifted the cherry-colored skirt with the other and flew down the stairs to the sitting room where her mother and brother, she knew, were discussing this very matter. "Mama! Jemmy! I *found* something!" she clarioned.

Lady Horatia, who'd been sunk in the dismals because she and Jeremy had thus far been unable to determine where to begin to search for Georgy, looked up at her youngest child and gasped in horror. "Alison Verney!" she cried in a choked voice. "Whatever have you got on?"

"What?" Alison blinked distractedly and glanced down at herself. "Oh, this. It's Georgy's, but never mind it now. See what I've—"

"*Georgy's?* You've been wearing Georgy's *clothes?* How could you? March yourself up to your room and take that off at once! Immediately, Miss, do you hear me?"

"But, Mama, there's no need to fall into a taking. I was only trying it on. And if I hadn't, I wouldn't have found—"

"*Only* trying it on? Do you think that's an excuse?" The poor woman, already overwrought by her fruitless discussion with her son, found herself once again on the verge of tears. She drew out her handkerchief and sniffed into it. "Your sister has been gone less than a fortnight, and you're already robbing her grave!"

"Come now, Mama," Jeremy put in, "that's cutting it much too thick. No need to behave as if Georgy was dead."

"She'll be as good as dead to me if I'm never to see her again," Horatia moaned into her handkerchief.

"But Mama, if you'd just let me show you what I've found—" Alison begged.

"I told you to go to your room!" Horatia snapped, raising her head angrily.

"Very well, Mama, I'll go," the girl said, offended, "but if you decide you want to see the clue I've found, you'll have to beg me for it." And she turned on her heel to go.

"Clue?" her brother asked. "What clue, Allie?"

"Never mind," Alison retorted, nose in the air. "Mama wants me to go to my room, and I must obey." As she tried to stalk from the room, however, her air of offended dignity was made completely ineffective by the fact that she kept tripping on her skirt.

Meanwhile, Jeremy and his mother exchanged looks.

"Clue?" her ladyship muttered with hope dawning in her eyes. "Alison, come back here!"

"No, thank you. I'm going to change my clothes, just as you ordered," the girl said spitefully, lifting her skirt and whisking herself from the room.

But she did not get far. Her brother caught up with her and dragged her back. She permitted herself to be propelled to the sofa and, after sitting down and pouting for another moment or two, relented and showed them her slip of paper. Jeremy dropped down beside her and stared at it. "What is it?" he asked, bewildered.

"Don't you see?" the girl said excitedly. "It says St. Martins-le-Grand."

"But that's a street right here in London," her mother said, pressing her hands to her breast to keep herself calm. "You can't think she's *there*."

"No, of course not. But isn't that where the mail coaches start?" Allie asked.

"Yes, of course," Jeremy said, a light dawning in his eyes. He snatched the paper from his sister's hand. "And these numbers could very well be—"

"Times of departure," Alison finished triumphantly.

Jeremy nodded, but with less enthusiasm than his sister. "Possibly. Eight and five-thirty might be times of day, but how do you explain the *E* and the *M?*"

"I've thought about that," his sister said. "I'd wager the *E* stands for evening and the *M* for—"

"Morning! Of course!" Jeremy leaped to his feet. "That's just what this means! Allie, you're a treasure!" He leaned down, kissed the girl's cheek and ran for the door. "Mama," he called over his shoulder as he raced down the hallway, "I'd let the child wear that blasted dress if I were you. She deserves it!"

With Allie's slight clue in hand, Jeremy betook himself to the coach station at St. Martins-le-Grand and showed it to a high-hatted, large-bellied fellow who declared himself to be the dispatcher. The man, after pocketing the gold coin Jeremy offered him, studied the paper with a knit brow. "If the eight with the *E* yer showin' me does mean eight in the evenin', I cain't 'elp ye, Cap'n. All twennyseven of the mails depart prompt at eight, settin' out in every direction."

"Damnation!" muttered Jeremy, dashed. "Is that true about the other time as well?"

The dispatcher rubbed his chin. "This other time writ 'ere? Five-thirty is it? If it's A.M., then we're in a better case. There's a day coach t' Manchester, leaves 'ere five-thirty A.M. every day of th' week exceptin' Sundays."

Jeremy's delight at learning this news was quickly dissipated when the dispatcher added that the day coach to Manchester made stops at Northhampton, Leicester, Derby and Stockton, and that the drivers were not averse (for a small emolument) to dropping a passenger anywhere else along the route. This information was indeed discouraging; it meant that Georgy could have been dropped anywhere along the entire two hundred miles of countryside that the Manchester coach traversed. But he waited for the returning Manchester coach to come in and asked the driver (after baiting him with a gold sovereign and a drink of home brew at the tap room of Bull and Mouth Inn) if he remembered a young woman who'd traveled on his coach about a fortnight before. The driver was not at all certain. All he would say was that "per'aps" he'd taken up a young woman about a fortnight ago, who "per'aps" resembled the description Jeremy gave him, and who "per'aps" had asked to be set down at Whaley Bridge.

When Jeremy returned home, he could not tell his mother that he was hopeful. "It's a place to start," he told her as he threw a change of linen into a haversack, "but it may very well be a false lead."

"Yes, it may, but Whaley Bridge is not a very large town," his mother said, her spirit wavering between hope and despair as she sank down on the window-seat of his bedroom. "There will not be very many places in which to make inquiries."

"As to that, Mama, I must confess that I haven't the least notion of what to do when I get there," the soldier admitted.

His mother sighed in agreement. "Neither do I, but we must do something. I must confess that I grow more desperate every day. Today I met Lady Traherne at the milliner's, and she remarked that she'd missed seeing Georgy at the Althorpes'."

"Do you mean that you haven't told anyone she's run off?" Jeremy asked in surprise.

"Of course I haven't! Do you think I want your sister's reputation ruined?"

"But if people like the Trahernes and the Althorpes have missed her—"

"I told Lady Traherne that Georgy's ill. A putrid inflamation in the throat, I said. That should keep the gossips from guessing that something else is amiss . . . for a while, at any rate. But you must work quickly, Jeremy. We haven't much time."

Jeremy scowled. "I don't see how I'm to work quickly if I don't even know how to begin."

"Look about for a family that has recently taken on a governess," his mother suggested.

"Governess? Is that what you think she's run away to become? A governess?"

Lady Horatia shrugged. "She said in her letter that she's taken a post of respectability and dignity. What else could it be?"

"It can't be that," Allie said from the doorway where she'd been eavesdropping.

"Really, Allie, must you come creeping about listening to conversations that are not your concern?" her mother chided in disgust.

"Never mind that, Mama," Jeremy put in, looking at his sister with interest. "Why do you think Georgy can't have gone off to be a governess?"

"Because Georgy always said she felt sorry for governesses," his sister said with fourteen-year-old authority.

"Did she?" Jeremy asked. "Why?"

"Because they're not only demeaned by their employers, but even by the spoilt children they must instruct. That's Georgy's view in a nutshell."

Horatia frowned at the girl. "Then if she hasn't gone to become a governess, what do *you* think she's become?"

"I don't know. A milliner, perhaps."

"A milliner?" Horatia shuddered. "She wouldn't!"

"Why not?" Jeremy said. "Milliners are respectable enough."

"I can't believe my daughter would leave her home and family to work in a . . . a . . . shop!"

"There are worse places, you know, Mama," Alison said with a wicked gleam. "What if Georgy decided to become a scullery maid . . . or a tavern wench?"

Her mother glared at her. "Alison Verney, go to your room! A tavern wench, indeed!"

"'Go to your room, go to your room,'" Alison aped as she stalked off down the hall. "I'm sick and tired of being told to go to my room. And what's more, I think it not at all unlikely that Georgy's become a tavern wench."

Horatia strode to the door and angrily ordered her youngest offspring to hold her tongue. "Do not let me hear you utter such nonsense again! Sometimes, my girl, you go *too far!*"

But the spirited girl would not give her mother the last word. "Is that so?" she demanded, tossing her auburn curls saucily. "Well, it's my view, Mama, that your daughter is quite capable of it. I know my sister Georgy very well, and if you ask me, she is capable of *anything!*"

Jeremy, reviewing that conversation in his mind while being jostled about on the stage to Whaley Bridge, wondered whether his little sister was right about Georgy. If so, he would do well to visit all the shops and taverns in the town as well as the grand houses. His mother might have persuaded herself that Allie had gone too far in surmising that Georgy could conceivably allow herself to work in a shop or tavern, but he was not so sure. After all, not so long ago neither he nor his mother would have wagered a farthing on the chance that Georgianna Verney would run away from home. Perhaps it *was* Allie who knew Georgy best.

Jeremy leaned back against the hard cushion of the stagecoach and shut his eyes. Thinking of the possibility that his sister might at this moment be serving ale to drunkards in a tavern made him bilious, and the rocking of the coach only made him feel worse. Truth was sometimes a hard pill to swallow, and the truth he had to swallow right now was the fact that his beloved sister Georgy was quite capable of turning herself into a tavern wench. Or, as Allie had said, quite capable of *anything*.

Chapter 7

The coachman's memory had been remarkably accurate; Georgy *had* descended from the stagecoach at Whaley Bridge. What the coachman didn't know, however, was that a carriage had been waiting for her at the innyard where he'd set her down, and it had transported her to a small vicarage several miles east of Castleton, to the village of Ruckworth. The ride to Ruckworth took her through a part of the country she'd never seen, and she stared out of the coach window with great interest as they rocked along to their destination. Every time her eye glimpsed a child picking hops in a field or carrying a bucket of water down the road, her heart leapt up. *That might be one of my pupils,* she thought eagerly.

To help those children was her reason for being here. For the past few years she had felt discontent with her life. She was too thoughtful, too energetic and too sympathetic to the suffering of those less fortunate than herself to remain living in idle luxury in her mother's house. An avid reader, she had come upon the writings of Miss Hannah More, whose enthusiasm to educate the children of the industrial towns of the north became Georgy's inspiration. If Hannah More could devote her life to the education of poor children, so, too, could she. This post, schoolmistress of the charity school at Ruckworth, was the beginning of a new life . . . a life of usefulness and value.

When the carriage arrived at the vicarage—a low, rambling building made of stone with a thatched roof and narrow, mullioned windows—Georgy was handed down from the carriage by the elderly coachman who had said not a word to her during the drive east. After alighting and looking about her, she paused, waiting for him to take down her baggage from the boot. But the fellow did not move in that direction. Instead, he pointed to the doorway of the vicarage and said, "They're waitin' fer ye in there."

"But . . . my baggage . . ."

"I ain't goin' to unload yer blasted baggage, Miss," the fellow declared rudely.

Georgy's eyebrows rose. The man might be brusque, as many men became as they grew elderly, but age could not be used as an excuse for rudeness. She was not accustomed to being addressed in that manner. Was this what she must expect, she wondered, now that she'd given herself an ordinary name and had dressed herself in the clothes she thought a working woman would wear? She put a hand to her bonnet, which was the plainest she could find in her wardrobe at home. Was it the bonnet that had transformed her? It was made of twilled silk, but it was drab puce in color and trimmed with only a single row of ivory grogram ribbon. Had this plain bonnet and the simple blue poplin gown she'd chosen (covered with a short cape of the sort she'd seen her abigail wear) humbled her so completely that the coachman felt no compunction about treating her with disrespect? "I beg your pardon?" she said, drawing herself up proudly.

"I said I ain't unloadin'," the coachman reiterated. "Not 'til I'm told yer stayin'. There was another young miss come las' week, an' arfter I'd took down all 'er boxes, I was told that she wasn't even stayin' the night. I 'ad to load everything back agin. No use, all that loadin' and unloadin' fer nothin'. This time I'll wait 'til I'm told." And he shuffled off toward a group of out-buildings behind the vicarage without a backward look.

Georgy stared after him in considerable dismay. She had believed until this moment that the teaching post was definitely hers. She knew, of course, that this interview with the vicar and Lady Ruckworth was important, but she hadn't realized that there was a possibility they wouldn't like her and might send her packing. *Good God,* she wondered, *is it possible that they'll reject me? If they do, where can I go?*

She looked toward the vicarage doorway in sudden panic. She had been in correspondence with the vicar for this post for several weeks, and the tone of his letters had been very positive. She'd never considered the likelihood of rejection. She'd given herself a new identity in her letters to the vicar (she'd named herself Grace Vail, keeping her own initials so that her handkerchiefs would not have to be reembroidered) and, having written that outspoken and critical letter to her mother, had burned all her bridges behind her. She couldn't go back home now. The newly created Grace Vail *had* to have a chance to exist.

Georgy straightened her bonnet and walked slowly toward the door. Her stomach and her throat were both constricted in abject fright. She wondered if she'd be able to speak at all. The interview would certainly be disastrous if she were unable to answer their questions.

Now, Georgy, she scolded herself, trying to take herself in hand, *this is foolishness. You've been presented to dozens of important men and noble women since your come-out, including such awe-inspiring figures as the Duke of Bedford, Princess Caroline and the Prince Regent himself. Surely with all that behind you, you can speak calmly to a country parson and the local peer's lady.* Despite those brave thoughts, however, she knew she'd never felt such a nervous flurry in her chest in all her life. She approached the modest stone doorstep of the vicarage with real trepidation.

She was admitted by a stiffly starched housemaid and led through a low, arched passageway to the drawing room. Her quick glance about the room gave her an impression of a small but sunny space in which were crowded two sofas, a worn wing chair with books piled on the floor near it, a sideboard also covered with books, and a wide fireplace. But her gaze immediately fastened on a tea cart surrounded by three chairs which had been placed before the fire, for two of the chairs were at this moment occupied. A gentleman with a clerical collar sat on one, and a lady of more than middle age sat on another.

The cleric, a balding man of average height with a round, slack-cheeked face (made studious by a pair of nar-

row-rimmed spectacles) rose from the tea cart as the maid
announced Miss Grace Vail's arrival. "Ah, Miss Vail," he
said, crossing the room in quick, eager strides, "welcome
to Ruckworth Parish."

"Thank you," Georgy murmured as he bowed over her
hand. "Mr. Hunsford, is it not?"

"Yes, ma'am, indeed it is." His eyes swept over her
with what seemed to be decided approval, and then he
turned toward the seated lady. "And this," he said, leading
Georgy to the tea cart, "is Lady Ruckworth herself. Your
ladyship, may I present Miss Grace Vail?"

Lady Ruckworth looked up at Georgy with a mere formality of a smile. "Good day, Miss Vail," she said in a
voice that held no hint of warmth. "We have awaited your
arrival with considerable impatience. Do sit down and take
some tea."

"Let me pour," came a voice from the corner. Georgy
turned, startled to discover that another lady was in the
room. She had a pudgy face, with flat cheeks and pale blue
eyes, and what little of her hair that could be seen under a
stiffly starched cap was wispy and thin. She had been knitting in a chair on the far side of the fireplace, but she now
laid her work aside and came to the table. "I'm sure a cup
of tea will be welcome after your long journey," she said to
Georgy with a kind but uneasy smile.

"Yes, it will. Thank you, ma'am," Georgy answered,
wondering who it was she was addressing.

"Oh, I beg your pardon," the vicar said, pausing in the
act of pulling out a chair. "I seem to have forgotten you,
my dear." He laughed uproariously at his gaffe, not the
least bit discomposed. "This, Miss Vail, as you've no
doubt guessed by now, is my wife, Mary. Mary, Miss
Grace Vail."

"Enough of the formalities," Lady Ruckworth ordered.
"Let the woman sit."

Georgy smiled quickly at the vicar's wife, curtseyed
nervously to her ladyship and dropped into the chair the
vicar held for her.

While Mary Hunsford poured the tea and the vicar held
a scone over the fire to warm for her, Georgy studied Lady

Ruckworth's face covertly from beneath her lashes. Lady
Ruckworth was thin, with sharp cheekbones jutting out
forbiddingly over hollow cheeks. Her mouth was pursed,
deepening the wrinkles that ridged her lips. Her eyes were
coldly blue, and her iron-gray ringlets (tied into two
clumps, one over each ear) stuck out below her severe
black bonnet. A word popped into Georgy's mind to describe Lady Ruckworth: *formidable*.

Her ladyship did not indulge long in polite niceties.
Georgy had scarcely taken a sip of her tea when her ladyship waved Mary Hunsford back to her place in the corner
and opened the folded papers that had been lying beside
her plate. Georgy recognized them as the letters she'd
written to the vicar. "We'll get right down to business,
shall we? I have several questions to ask."

"Yes, of course, my lady," Georgy said, sounding to her
own ears disgustingly obsequious. Never in her life before
had she felt the need to play the toady. This feeling of
being at the mercy of a stranger's kindness was new to her,
and it made her decidedly uncomfortable.

"I would like to know something of your family background. You live in London, I take it?"

"I did, my lady." She lowered her eyes as she embarked
on the personal history she had fabricated in her mind before she came. She did not wish to begin her new life on a
foundation of lies, but she felt that she had no choice. If
she'd kept her old identity, she might be found and dragged
back to London. And if the vicar and Lady Ruckworth
knew that she was the daughter of a nobleman, they might
not believe in the seriousness of her intentions. So she
drew in her breath and launched upon her sea of lies. "The
Vails were originally from Yorkshire, but my father made a
home in London when he became secretary to Lord Verney,
now deceased. My parents, too, are now deceased. I have
been living with my brother, but since he is soon to be
married, he can no longer support me."

"I see. You are without resources then, Miss Vail?"

"Yes, ma'am."

"I am sorry for that, of course," her ladyship said, "but
we cannot award you the post simply out of charity. Our

school has always prided itself on the high quality of its teachers, and we fully intend to continue that tradition."

"Yes, of course, your ladyship," Georgy murmured, her hopes falling.

Lady Ruckworth looked again at her papers. "In your letters to Mr. Hunsford, you are rather vague about your education. Have you ever attended a girl's venture school or an academy of some kind?"

"I was educated at home, my lady, by my father and by my brother's tutors," Georgy explained. "As I wrote to Mr. Hunsford, I've studied history, have some proficiency in Latin, drawing and music, and I can speak French fluently."

"Heavens, girl," her ladyship snapped, "what good's all *that?* This is a *charity* school, not Harrow! We must train our children to be diligent and industrious, to praise the Good Lord for their bounty, to have humility and to know their station!"

Georgy felt her fingers clench. "Hannah More says that she labors to give children *principles,*" she stated bravely, putting up her chin.

"Yes, but *what* principles? It would not instill proper principles to teach them Latin or drawing. They mustn't be trained to aspire to a rank that will never be theirs. Music and French, indeed! It would have been a great deal better, my girl, if you'd been educated in Scriptures and needle-work."

The vicar cleared his throat. "I think, my lady, that Miss Vail can be relied upon to follow our curriculum. She is a sincere admirer of the work of Miss Hannah More, as we all are. She writes that, inspired by Miss More's writings, she wishes to dedicate her life to the education of the poor." He gave Lady Ruckworth a placating smile and drew her attention to a page of one of the letters wherein Georgy had listed a number of philosophical works with which she was familiar. "As you can see here, Miss Vail has read more widely than any of our other candidates. And she writes a fine hand. Very fine, I think. But even more important, her use of the language is certainly superior, don't you agree?"

"Hmmph," the lady snorted, bending her head over the letter only briefly. "That may be, but I fail to see where her reading of Bentham and Descartes is appropriate to our needs."

"I am not unfamiliar with Scriptures, your ladyship," Georgy put in, "and as for needlework—"

"I venture to guess that you haven't done a stitch of needlework in your life," her ladyship declared. "You may be the daughter of a nobleman's secretary, but you seem to have been raised like the daughter of the nobleman himself."

"I have done a great deal of needlework," Georgy responded, meeting her ladyship's scornful gaze with an angry glare of her own. But her eyes soon fell as an inner voice reminded her that she'd always hated needlework . . . every knot and cross-stitch of it. When she lifted her eyes again, Lady Ruckworth was no longer looking at her. Georgy, feeling herself rejected, rose from her chair, her throat stinging. "If you believed that I was unsuited to this post, ma'am, I can't help but wonder why you asked me to come all this way—"

"Sit down, girl!" Lady Ruckworth ordered impatiently. "I haven't finished with my questions yet. How much did you pay for your bonnet?"

Georgy gaped. Not only was the change of subject startling, but the rudeness of the question took her breath away. "My *b-bonnet?*" she managed.

"Yes, Miss, your bonnet. I venture to guess that it cost you ten pounds at least."

"I don't remember," Georgy responded, sinking down upon her chair dazedly, "but I suppose ten pounds is close enough to the sum."

"I thought so. Well, Miss, the salary here is twenty-two pounds per annum—we are not so well endowed as the schools in London where, I hear, they have the wherewithal to pay their teachers thirty-five or more—and at twenty-two pounds you will never afford silk bonnets again, that I can promise you!"

Georgy blinked. "No . . . I suppose not," she murmured in bewilderment.

"You have been used to getting yourself up much too fine for our purposes," her ladyship remarked. "Much too fine." She fixed an icy eye on her vicar. "It augers no good to choose a teacher who likes to dress above her station, don't you agree, Mr. Hunsford?"

The cleric, who had been very impressed with Miss Grace Vail's letters and was even more impressed by the girl in person, bit his lip and colored in chagrin. "I'm afraid I don't know much about matters of female dress, my lady," he said lamely, knowing that he could not oppose the views of the woman who was the primary support of his parish.

"No, of course you don't," her ladyship said in complacent agreement. "That's why I consider myself a better judge of females than you."

Georgy glanced over at the clergyman in hopes that he would once again come to her defense, but the vicar, catching her eye, dropped his own. With that single act of avoidance, the vicar caused Georgy's one last hope to shrivel and die.

Lady Ruckworth rose. "I must be off, Mr. Hunsford. I leave it to you to make the final arrangements." She wrapped a shawl magisterially about her shoulders and went to the door. "As for you, Miss Vail, I shall leave you with a bit of advice. A word to the wise, as they say. You must try harder to dress as befits your station. When in school, keep your head covered by a cap at all times. Mrs. Hunsford will, I believe, supply you with appropriate dame-caps, but you must provide dresses for yourself. The one you have on is too luxurious to wear in class—it will do for Sunday services, however, if you darken the blue by soaking it in black dye. One or two less elegant dresses in black or gray will serve you well enough for class if you keep them covered with aprons."

Georgy, bemused, stumbled to her feet. "But, ma'am, I don't quite understand—"

Her ladyship, ignoring the interruption, went on. "Mr. Hunsford seems to be convinced that your grounding in the principles of the Christian religion is sound enough. Since he is the vicar, I will accept his evaluation of that most important qualification. However, there are other qualifications to be considered. I am fearful, for instance, that your disposition is not sufficiently meek and humble for this post. Nevertheless, I am willing to reserve judgment for a while. As I said, Miss Vail, a word to the wise. I hope I make myself clear."

Georgy, glancing from her ladyship to the vicar and back again, felt that Lady Ruckworth had made herself anything but clear. "Does that mean you're offering me the post?" she asked, amazed.

Lady Ruckworth nodded. "I wish you success with your pupils," she said with no lessening of her forbidding manner. "Good day, Miss Vail. And may the Good Lord have mercy on us all."

Chapter 8

The town of Whaley Bridge was larger than Jeremy expected, and it took several days to explore all the possibilities. He introduced himself to the local vicar who gave him the direction of the one person in the town—a Lady Endicott—who had recently taken on a new governess, but when Jeremy called on her, he learned that the new governess was not his sister. Then he rented a curricle and drove into the countryside, where he made inquiries at every seemingly substantial homestead. And, finally, he visited every shop and inn within a five-mile radius. But after almost a week of fruitless searching, he was convinced that his sister was nowhere to be found in Whaley Bridge.

He walked about the town in utter discouragement, undecided about what next to do. He could go to Castleton, the nearest town to the east, and start again; he could try Bollington to the west; or he could give it all up and take the next stagecoach back to London. He had almost decided to return home when he rounded a streetcorner and came upon an open-air market in full swing. He stopped and surveyed the scene, feeling a surge of pleasure at the liveliness before him. It was the first lift of his spirits in several days.

The market extended down the length of the street as far as his eyes could see. It was a scene of boisterous excitement, full of the noise and color that are generated by the addition of a profusion of people and vendibles to a neighborhood that was ordinarily somnambulant and dull. But today the quiet, tree-shaded street was transformed, lined with carts and stalls whose awnings and pennants flapped in the light breeze. Dapples of sunshine glinted through the

trees, touching up the shabby hangings with a merry sparkle. Farmers and tradesmen were hawking their wares
loudly to the crowds who thronged the pavement. There
were people of all sorts milling about ogling the wares:
plump housemaids with baskets on their arms, elegant
ladies with bonnets and gloves, noisy children of all ages
(many of them eating pasties or fruits and dribbling the
juices down their chins), gentlemen in riding clothes,
workmen in leather aprons, and pretty girls with long hair
tied in ribbons. It was a cheerful scene, and Jeremy happily
became a part of it.

He strolled down the street, admiring the mounds of
autumn vegetables, the piles of fresh-baked breads, the
overflowing sacks of grain. He watched a fishmonger
skillfully fillet a trout with two swipes of his knife and a
farmer's wife cleverly parrying the bargaining attempts of a
housemaid trying to wheedle three onions for the price of
two. He turned about and found himself standing in the
midst of a circle of onlookers observing the talented hands
of a potter who sat at his wheel and shaped a bowl with
amazing concentration. Then he walked down the street
and discovered a stay-maker's stall. He couldn't help gog-
gling at the ladies who were trying on the stays over their
dresses right there in the open. It was only when one young
lady caught his eye and, instead of cringing, winked at him
flirtatiously, that he turned away in embarrassment.

Jeremy bought a sack of oranges at one stall, a box of
sugared plums at another, and a quaintly dressed rag doll
for Allie at a third. He was having so good a time that he
quite forgot what had brought him here. Thus it was with a
decided shock that he glimpsed his sister in the crowd.
He'd been merely looking about to see what he might buy
for his mother when his eye was attracted to the face of a
young woman who was at that moment passing through a
beam of sunlight. His heart constricted at the sight of the
familiar face. Although her hair was covered by a dreadful
faded-orange bonnet with a pathetic bunch of mock cher-
ries pinned to the poke, he knew immediately who she
was. "Georgy!" he gasped, dropping his parcels in excitement. "That was *Georgy!*"

He tried to push his way through the crowd. "Georgy!" he shouted, dodging and weaving his way round the dozens of shoppers who seemed determined to bar his path. "Georgy, wait! It's me, Jemmy!"

He lost sight of her for a few moments, and when he again caught a glimpse of the orange bonnet, her back was to him. She was standing near a watchmaker's booth, where a number of gold pocket-watches and small mantel clocks were on display. The watchmaker himself was haggling with a blue-coated gentleman, and, his attention thus diverted, did not see Georgy's hand slip out from the folds of her kerseymere skirt, snatch a gold watch and withdraw it stealthily to the protection of the skirt. Before Jeremy's astonished gaze, his sister moved in unobtrusive, backward steps away from the booth and then turned and walked quickly down the street. He couldn't believe his eyes! He had barely been able to envision his sister as a tavern wench, so how could he possibly imagine her as a *thief?*

Aghast, he raced after her, heedlessly elbowing aside all who stood in his way. Catching up with her, he grasped her by an arm and pulled her round to face him. "Georgy, what on earth are you doing?" he demanded in agonized alarm. "Have you lost your—?"

But the white-lipped girl who stared up at him was not Georgy. He could see that now. She was paler in complexion than Georgy and a bit smaller, her hair did not have Georgy's rusty glints, and her eyes were somehow different—browner and darker browed. Otherwise they were so much alike that it was only by this close scrutiny that he could realize his mistake.

"I b-beg your pardon, sir?" the girl asked in a frightened whisper.

"Oh! I . . . I thought . . . but . . . you're *not* Georgy," Jeremy stammered awkwardly. "I'm sorry." He peered down at her in amazement, aware that his heart was pounding in his chest with a strange combination of disappointment and relief—disappointment that he'd not found Georgy after all, and relief that it was not his sister who was engaged in petty thievery.

The girl licked her lips. "A mistake . . . yes. But it's all

right," she said, squirming from his hold. "I . . . forgive
you." She turned away and quickly continued down the
street.

"Just a minute," Jeremy ordered, gathering his wits together and dashing after her. He caught her by her wrist
and swung her round again. "I saw you palm a gold watch!
Let's have it, my girl."

"Wh-what? I don't know what you're t-talking about. If
you don't let me go, I shall . . . scream."

"Go ahead, if you wish to call attention to yourself."

"You're making another mistake, sir," she said, twisting
her wrist in a desperate attempt to free herself. "Please . . .
let me go!"

The blue-coated man who'd been haggling with the
watchmaker appeared suddenly at Jeremy's side. "Somethin' amiss, young lady?" he asked. "This 'ere 'andsome
young officer, 'e ain't botherin' you, is 'e?"

The girl flicked an enigmatic look at the newcomer.
"Yes, sir, he is. He won't let me go."

Jeremy tightened his hold on her wrist. "This *vixen* has
stolen a watch from the booth over there . . . the one where
you were just standing. I'm trying to convince her to give
it back."

"Oh, is that what ye've done, y' naughty puss?" the
man asked the girl as if scolding a child. "Come now, give
the bauble over."

To Jeremy's surprise, the girl put her free hand into a
hidden pocket sewn deep in the side of her skirt and pulled
out the watch. "Here," she said sullenly, handing it over to
the man in the blue coat.

"That's better," Jeremy said, glad to be able to end this
incident. "Now, if you promise not to engage in such mis-
behavior again, we can return this to the watchmaker and
let you go on your way."

The girl lowered her head and said nothing, but the
blue-coated man (who, Jeremy noted, was not much older
than himself, had a pair of ferretlike eyes and an evil-look-
ing scar that stretched from beneath his ear to his chin)
held up the watch by its chain and smiled at it with admiration. "An' a very nice little bauble it is," he said, nodding

with what Jeremy thought was considerable satisfaction.
"But we cain't just let this creature go on 'er way, can we,
Cap'n? 'Tis Cap'n, ain't it, sir? Yes, with that fine 'at on
yer 'ead, an' them gold epaulets, that's just what I tho't.
But as I was sayin', Cap'n, we cain't just let this little
canary bird go free on 'er own say-so. This 'ere watch is
worth more 'n ten quid, if I'm a judge, and that ain't no
petty theft. Besides, the puss 's prob'ly lyin' an' will return
to 'er life o' crime as soon as our backs is turned, don't ye
agree?"

"No, not necessarily," Jeremy replied. "I'm willing to
give the girl the benefit of the doubt."

"Y're a kind fellow, Cap'n, I'll grant ye that. I don'
know, though. 'Tain't right just to let 'er go." He swung
the watch by its chain and studied it thoughtfully. "I 'ave
it! I just seen my friend, Sir Thomas Cottle, goin' into the
Kings Arms Tavern round the corner there. 'E's the magistrate 'ere. Why don't we go along an' ask him? 'E's a fair
man. 'E'll know what to do with 'er. Prob'ly give 'er no
more 'n a good scold."

Jeremy hesitated. "What do you say, Miss?" he asked
the girl. "Are you willing to face the magistrate?"

The girl kept her eyes lowered and merely shrugged.

What a strange creature, Jeremy thought, eyeing her
curiously. *Hasn't she any fear of punishment?* He hesitated
for another moment and then threw up his hands. If the girl
herself was indifferent to her fate, why should *he* be concerned about it? "Very well," he said to the blue-coated
man, handing over the girl's now-limp wrist to his care,
"but let's return the watch first."

"Cain't do that," the man said promptly. "Need it fer
evidence, y' know."

"Very well," Jeremy agreed, wishing to escape the entire situation, "do as you think best." And he began to walk
away.

"Oh, no, you ain't goin', are ye, Cap'n?" the blue-
coated man asked, grasping Jeremy's sleeve. "We'll need
yer evidence, too. Y're the eye witness, arfter all, ain't
ye?"

Jeremy, sighing in acceptance of his civic responsibility,

fell into step beside the fellow as they turned in the direction he'd indicated. But when they rounded the corner, leaving the crowds of the marketplace behind them, Jeremy could see no sign of the King's Arms. They were in a narrow, winding street lined on either side with similar, slate-roofed houses. Not a soul could be seen, either on the cobbles or in the windows. Everyone had apparently gone to the market.

Jeremy began to feel uneasy. "Where *is* this tavern you spoke of?" he asked.

"Never mind the tavern," the man answered, his voice suddenly different. "Just 'and over the brass in yer pockets."

"My brass?" Jeremy stopped in his tracks. "What are you talking about?"

"Yer brass, yer blunt, every meg and copper-john on yer person, do ye understand me?" the fellow said with a leer. "I mean yer money, Cap'n." He pulled from an inner pocket of his blue coat a long-barreled pistol. "An' be sure I get *all* of it."

The young woman made a strangled sound in her throat. "Ned, no!" she whispered.

Jeremy winced, not because of the pistol but because of the unpleasant realization that he'd been six ways a fool. It was the man, not the girl, who was the real thief! He should have guessed at once that they were working together. The man had been distracting the watchmaker so that the girl could pocket the loot. He wanted to kick himself for his naiveté.

But though he'd been naive, Jeremy was no coward. The sight of a gun didn't frighten him; he'd faced a good many of them in the past. He looked the man up and down with icy scorn. "You damned maw-worm," he said calmly, "come and take it from me."

The man called Ned waved the pistol threateningly. "I ain't pokin' bogey," he said, his already beady eyes narrowing to mere slits. "I'd just as soon shoot ye down as not. So if ye don't want a 'ole through yer puddin', ye'll do what I say."

The girl pulled at Ned's arm, causing the hand holding

the gun to waver. "Let him go, Ned! He didn't do us any harm."

He shook her off. "Stay out o' this, Peggy!"

"No!" She grasped his arm again. "He wasn't going to turn me in. Let him be, Ned, *please!*"

The man she called Ned threw her a furious glare before turning his eyes back to Jeremy. "Let go o' my arm!" he hissed at her through clenched teeth.

"No, I won't! Let's leave him be and *go!*"

"I'm warnin' ye, Peggy, sister or no, I'll land ye a facer if ye don't let loose me arm!"

"I won't! If you don't release him this instant," she threatened, "I'll let out a scream so loud we'll have the whole mob on us."

Ned, keeping his eyes riveted on Jeremy, swung his arm up with such abrupt fury that the hand holding the pistol struck the girl on the face. She screamed in pain as she fell to the ground, blood trickling from her mouth. The man was unable to resist turning to see the effect of his blow, and in the instant of his turning, Jeremy leaped forward and knocked the gun from his grasp. It fell upon the cobbles with a clunk, and before Ned could stoop and recover it, Jeremy kicked it out of his reach.

With a cry, Ned leaped upon him. The two men fell to the ground, grappling each other and rolling from side to side. The girl whimpered and, lifting herself on an elbow, pushed herself out of the way of their flailing arms and legs.

"Damn yer 'ide," Ned muttered, pressing his hands on Jeremy's face in an attempt to reach his eyes, "I'll kill ye fer this!"

Jeremy made no attempt to reply but used his strength to break the fellow's hold on his face. He managed to do so, but in the process Ned rolled on top of him and began to pummel the side of his head. "I'll skewer ye proper and drop . . . yer carcass . . . down the nearest well!" Ned threatened with breathless satisfaction.

"You will . . . will you?" Jeremy managed to get his hands round the other man's throat and squeezed hard enough to weaken his hold. They rolled over again, this time with Jeremy on top, but the desperate Ned broke Jeremy's hold on his throat by kneeing him sharply in the groin. Jeremy groaned and fell over to the ground, pulling up his knees to his chest in pain. Ned, seizing his advantage, threw himself upon his adversary while at the same time feeling the ground with his fingers in a vain attempt to retrieve the pistol. But he couldn't reach it. Instead, he felt a loose cobblestone under his hand. This, he knew, would do nicely. He grasped it with frenzied fingers and pulled it free. Then, holding his struggling opponent down with his knees and his free arm, he raised his other hand to swing the stone at Jeremy's head.

"Stop right there, Ned Birkin," came his sister's trembling voice, "or that'll be the last thing you ever do!"

Both men turned their heads in her direction, Ned's arm poised in midair. She stood above them, holding the pistol in two shaking hands and aiming it down at her brother. Her bonnet hung down by its ribbons over one shoulder, her hair cascaded wildly over one eye, and her mouth was already beginning to swell while the blood dripped slowly from the split in her underlip. A passerby might well have taken her for a madwoman were it not for a certain cold steadiness in her eyes. Jeremy could see at once that the girl was in deadly earnest.

Her brother could see it, too. "C'mon, Peggy," he said, his voice a pleading whine, "give me the pistol. Ye know ye'd never shoot yer own brother."

"Don't wager your breath on it," she answered coldly. "Lay down that stone, nice and easy."

"All right, all right," Ned said impatiently, doing as she ordered. "There. Now kin I get up?"

She nodded, and Ned scrambled to his feet. Jeremy sat up, keeping his eyes fixed on the drama being enacted before him and drawing up his legs in order to be ready to leap to his feet the moment circumstances permitted.

Ned advanced toward his sister carefully, like a pup toward a hissing cat. "I'll let 'im go, like you wanted," he offered placatingly, "but cain't we take 'is moneybag first?"

"Don't come any closer, Ned, I warn you," she said tensely, her eyes wary. "You, sir, get up and on your way. Be quick!"

"Do you think I'll leave you to the mercies of this . . . this *blackguard?*" Jeremy asked, getting to his feet. "He's the sort who's bound to seek revenge, brother or no."

The girl threw him a surprised glance. "You needn't trouble your—"

The moment the girl took her eyes from him, Ned seized the opportunity to lunge for the gun. But he had to do it in two steps, and it took the girl only one to sense his movement, shut her eyes and shoot. The report shattered the quiet air, sending several cawing birds screeching into the sky.

Ned Birkin gasped and tottered backward, his right hand flying up to the place on his upper left arm where a bit of blue jacket had ripped away. "Damn you, Peg!" he cursed hoarsely as he removed his hand from the wound and gaped at the blood on his fingers. "I'll flog ye raw fer this!"

The girl was shaking from top to toe, but she continued to aim the gun in his direction. "Take yourself off, Ned. Right now!"

Ned, his face taut with pain, was attempting to staunch the flow of blood with a dirty handkerchief. Nevertheless, he looked up at her in scorn. "That pistol won't do ye any good now, ye noddy. Not 'til ye reload."

The girl's eyes faltered. "Reload?" she asked weakly.

Jeremy patted her shoulder reassuringly and turned toward the wounded man. "There's no need of further gunplay," he said, his voice quietly threatening. "In your present condition, I think I can take you quite easily without the assistance of a pistol. You heard the lady. Will you do as she says, or would you rather endure a short bout with my fists?"

Holding the handkerchief tightly against his wound, the blue-coated man looked from Jeremy to his sister and back again. "I'm goin'," he said, backing away down the street, "I'm goin'. But y' ain't seen the last o' me. An' as fer *you,* sister dear, ye'll get yours as soon as ye stick yer sneezer in the door!"

"I'll not cross your threshold again . . . not ever . . . as long as I live," his sister muttered to herself as the blue-coated man turned and walked away down the street. Jeremy and the girl watched unmoving until he'd turned the far corner and was gone from their sight. Then she shuddered and lowered her arms. The pistol fell from her numb fingers to the ground. With a choked sound that seemed to come from deep within her throat, she dropped her face in her hands.

Jeremy touched her lightly on her shoulder. "It was only a superficial wound," he assured her gently. "You did him no permanent harm."

She lifted her head slowly and stared up at him, her eyes—which, though a little darker, were so amazingly like Georgy's—aswim with tears. "It's not . . . that's n-not . . . it's only . . . I don't know what to do . . . n-now!"

She looked so pathetic, standing there miserably with the tears dripping from her eyes, that Jeremy felt compelled to slip an arm about her waist in what he hoped was a comforting embrace. But in truth he felt in need of a bit of comforting himself. Without having done anything wrong, he suddenly found himself saddled with a new responsibility. This girl was helpless and alone, and he could not, in good conscience, ignore her plight. After all, she'd come to his aid when he'd been in a tight fix; he was well aware of that. She might even have saved his life. It was clear, therefore, that he had to help her somehow. *But*, he asked himself in dismay, *how am I to do that?*

He handed the girl a handkerchief. As she sniffed into it she hunched her shoulders and seemed to snuggle more closely against him. She was like a homeless little animal that had found a warm hole in which to burrow. But, he reminded himself, she was not a little animal; she was a fully grown woman. It was too bad, really. If she were a little puppy, for instance, he could bring her home with him and install her in the kitchen in the care of the cook.

But he could just imagine what the cook would have to say if he came home with *this* little pet!

He exhaled a long, lingering breath. *What have I got myself into?* he wondered, panic-stricken. *And what on earth am I supposed to do now?*

Chapter 9

By the time Peggy Birkin stopped crying, the sun had set and the people at the market were dispersing. Jeremy took her back to the inn where he'd been lodging and bespoke a private dining room and a bedroom for the girl. While they supped, Jeremy asked her questions about herself. Why, he asked, had she permitted her brother to force her to steal? And how was it that her pattern of speech was more polished than his?

Peggy told him her story. She began slowly, trying to answer his questions briefly and without emotion. But soon the words came pouring out, and with them the tears. She'd been orphaned at the age of nine, she told him, and had been taken in by an aunt, her mother's sister, who had no children of her own. The aunt was delighted to have a little girl to cosset and to dress—to her mind it was not unlike playing with a doll—but she had no liking for boys. She would not take Peggy's brother, the already wild thirteen-year-old Ned.

The aunt's husband was a maker of fine boots. He made a good livelihood, and Peggy had been reared in genteel style. She'd even had a governess for a time. She'd lived contentedly with her aunt and uncle for almost ten years, when the aunt died suddenly of a liver ailment. It was then that Peggy's life took a tragic turn. The uncle, after a brief period of mourning, suddenly turned amorous toward his niece, forcing his attentions on her with increasing frequency. After a month of growing tension in the household, a night came when she'd been required to bolt her bedroom door. The next morning, she packed a few belongings and fled to the protection of her brother.

Ned had not been so fortunate in his rearing as she. He'd been taken in by his father's sister, a poor woman with four sons and two daughters of her own. There was little money in the home and less care. The boys were free to roam the streets of Manchester at will, earning pennies at odd jobs and stealing whatever they could. Ned, cleverer than his cousins, soon realized he could do better at thievery if he were on his own. By the time his sister came to him, he was well established in a life of crime. He offered her room, board and his protection on condition that she assist him in his "work." With no money and no prospects, she had no choice but to accept. "And that situation hasn't changed," she concluded worriedly, wiping her eyes with a handkerchief that was by this time soaked through. "If I don't think of something soon, I'll *have* to go back to him."

"Not on your life," Jeremy declared firmly as he escorted her to the door of the room he'd taken for her. "Let's sleep on it. By tomorrow morning, one of us will surely have thought of some way for you to go on without him."

The girl turned away from him, put her hand on the doorknob and paused. "Captain Verney," she said in a small voice, her head down, "I don't know how to . . . you've been so very kind . . ."

"If you're trying to thank me, Miss Birkin, you may save your breath. You prevented Ned from breaking my skull, and I won't soon forget it."

"Perhaps, but if it hadn't been for me, you and Ned would not have crossed paths at all." Her head lowered even more. "I've been a great deal of trouble to you, I fear. I wish I could . . . somehow . . . repay you."

Jeremy's brows knit as he studied the girl's bent head. Was she *offering* herself to him? *What sort of female have I befriended?* he asked himself. Not that the offer, if it was one, wasn't tempting. All at once he became aware of a fragrant smell that emanated from her warm skin. That, and the thought of what she seemed to have suggested, made him dizzy. Her hair, still wildly tumbled over her shoulders, was thick and silky, and he suddenly yearned to sift it through his fingers. Through the dark mass of hair he could glimpse a tantalizing bit of ear and the whiteness of her neck. Her shoulders and back were shapely, and the thin muslin of her gown only accentuated the slimness of her waist and the luscious curve of hip and thigh. Taking her to bed would make a delicious finish to what had been a troublesome day.

But *was* she offering herself? He'd caught her stealing, true, but he'd not caught her selling herself. And she'd run from the uncle who'd tried to misuse her. Perhaps he was doing the girl an injustice in his thoughts. He took a backward step away from her. "I've done nothing that requires repayment," he said brusquely. "Get a good night's sleep, Miss Birkin. I'll have the chambermaid wake you at seven. We'll make our plans at breakfast."

The night brought no inspiration to either of them, and the morning brought rain. They downed their breakfast in desultory silence, she wondering what was to come of her and he berating the fates for saddling him with this new responsibility. The heavy sky only underlined the darkness of their moods. Finally Jeremy jumped from his chair and threw the strap of his haversack over his shoulder. "Come along, Miss Birkin," he ordered, pulling Peggy to her feet. "We'll catch the morning stage."

"The stage?" She gaped at him in bewilderment as he pulled her to the door. "But why? Where are you taking me?"

"I've thought and thought about it, and it seems to me that there's nothing for it but to take you to my mother." He threw what he hoped was a reassuring smile over his shoulder. "Don't worry about it, my girl. My mother will know what to do with you."

It was dark when they arrived in London, and by the time he'd found a hack to take them from St. Martins-le-Grand to Verney House, everyone in the household had gone to bed. Jeremy, who'd spent the entire trip wondering how his mother would react to his bringing into her home a young female of shabby appearance whom he'd discovered stealing a watch, was glad that the necessary introductions could be postponed until the next day. Intending to install the girl in Georgy's bedroom and to forbid her to leave it until *after* he'd explained her presence to his mother the following morning, he unlatched the door with his key and tiptoed in, motioning Peggy to do the same.

Of course, he had to fumble about in the dark for a tinderbox and candles, and in so doing he knocked over a vase. It crashed to the floor and caused Peggy to scream. After he'd shushed her and lit two candles, he turned round to lead her to the stairs, forgetting that his haversack was still slung over his shoulder. The motion caused the haversack to swing out, knocking over a wooden hat rack. No sooner had that noise subsided than a light appeared at the top of the stairs. "Who's there?" came his mother's voice.

"Blast" he hissed under his breath. "We've wakened her."

A nightgowned figure, like an apparition, appeared at the top of the stairs holding a candle high in the air. "Jeremy? Is that—?" The candle wavered for a moment. "Georgy? Good God, I must be dreaming! Is that... *Georgy?*" Lady Horatia's voice was hushed with uncertainty. She stood there on the landing, frozen into immobility by the confusion in her breast of hope and disbelief.

"Now, Mama, don't fall into a taking," Jeremy warned. "It's not—"

Another nightgowned figure appeared behind Horatia. "What is it, Mama?" asked Allie sleepily. "I heard a noise."

Candlelight appeared at the back of the hall where servants were beginning to gather at the top of the back stairs. Meanwhile, poor Horatia, unable to make sense of her son's words, rubbed her eyes with the back of a hand as if to wipe away the the last vestiges of sleep. Then she held the candle out as far as she could reach. "It *is!*" she cried tremulously. "Oh, thank God! Georgy!" Overcome with joy, she dropped the candle and flew down the stairs. "Georgy, my love, you're home!"

"Mama, wait," Jeremy cautioned, trying to step between his guest and his eager mother, "it's not—"

But his mother had already stopped short. Having caught a clear look at the girl in the light of Jeremy's candles, she gasped in sharp pain. "But that's not . . . *no!*" she cried in agony. "You're not—!" She turned, trembling with disappointment, to her son. "Good heavens, Jemmy, that's not Georgy! What have you done?"

Chapter 10

Lady Horatia's disappointment was too great to be mitigated by Jeremy's labored, lengthy explanation. After she'd heard him out, she declined to discuss the matter further that night. She was, she said, too depressed to do more than return to her bed. Jeremy, realizing that his sojourn to Whaley Bridge had been a disaster, also went to bed in a state of abject depression. Not only had he failed to find Georgy but he'd saddled himself with a thieving female, and he'd let his mother down.

Therefore he was taken by surprise when he entered the breakfast room the next morning, carelessly attired in an old dressing gown (having slept until almost eleven and arisen too hungry to dress before breakfast), to find his mother restored to her normal complacency. "Ah, Mama, you look positively cheerful," he remarked in relief as he crossed to the sideboard and helped himself to some eggs and a muffin. "Are you no longer put out with me, then?"

"I was never put out with you, my dear," she said, smiling up at him over her coffee cup. "I've no reason to be put out with you."

"Haven't you? I didn't find Georgy."

"But you tried. One can't expect miracles, I suppose."

"That's true. It would have been a miracle if I'd found her. I didn't have enough clues to make a fruitful search." He sat down at the table and took a bite of his muffin. "But you have every reason to be angry that I've deposited a disreputable female in your home."

"I wouldn't call her disreputable, dearest. If the tale you told me is true, she is more unfortunate than disreputable."

"I don't know whether her tale is true or not," Jeremy

admitted, taking a spoonful of egg. "But I do know she saved my life. I owe her something for that."

Lady Horatia put down her coffee cup. "Perhaps your bringing the girl here will turn out to be fortunate," she remarked, smiling mysteriously.

Jeremy's eyebrows rose. "What's this, Mama? Are you hinting that you've thought of some way of dealing with the problem of Peggy Birkin?"

"Indeed I have," his mother gloated, rising from her chair. "Leave those eggs and come with me."

Puzzled, he followed his mother down the hall. She led him to the small sitting room and opened the door. He stepped over the threshold, stopped in his tracks and blinked. The light streaming in from the bow window somewhat blinded him, but his first impression was that Georgy was standing there in the center of the room, poised on a footstool, with Allie behind her tying her sash, and her abigail, Betsy, kneeling beside her busily hemming her gown. But of course it wasn't Georgy; he knew that. It was the girl he'd brought home with him.

When his eyes became accustomed to the glare, he saw that it was indeed Peggy Birkin standing on the stool. But she'd been remarkably transformed. Things had been done to her to make her look almost exactly like his sister, though he wasn't sure what they were. She was draped in one of Georgy's gowns, which Betsy was evidently shortening. Although Peggy wasn't as tall as his sister, no one would guess it today. He didn't know why, but in Georgy's gown Peggy appeared to be two inches taller. In addition, her hair had been washed, and it now glowed with the reddish glints that were so distinctive of Georgy's hair. Moreover, it had been pulled back from her face in a tight bun at the nape of her neck, just the way he remembered Georgy wearing it, making the resemblance between them even more startling. Even Peggy's eyes seemed to have been altered somehow. "Good God," he exclaimed, "she does look like Georgy."

Allie, who'd finished tying the sash, giggled. "Isn't it wonderful, Jemmy? She might pass for Georgy's twin."

"So she might," Jeremy agreed, gazing up at Peggy in

fascination. "Good morning, Miss Birkin. What have my mother and sister been doing to you while I slept?"

"I don't quite know," the girl replied nervously. "May I speak to you a moment in pri—?"

"What *have* you done to her, Mama?" Jeremy interrupted, his mind too preoccupied with the change in Peggy's appearance to take note of her agitation. "Even her eyes look different this morning."

"We thinned her brows," his mother said with satisfaction, "and arched them just like Georgy's. Isn't it remarkable what the shape of a brow will do? Then we trimmed her hair—"

"And rinsed it with henna," Allie added excitedly.

"And pulled it back in Georgy's Evangelical style. Then we picked out this gown from her wardrobe, and . . ." Here Horatia made a triumphant gesture toward the girl on the footstool. ". . . *voila!*"

"*Voila,* indeed," Jeremy said, nodding in reluctant admiration, "but I don't see why you've gone to all this trouble. We all agreed last night that the similarity is remarkable. I don't see what purpose you had in getting the girl up to pass for Georgy's twin."

Horatia shook her head. "I didn't 'get her up'—to use your repugnant phrase—to pass for Georgy's twin. I want her to pass for Georgy herself."

"Captain Verney?" Peggy whispered, trying again to get his attention. "May I take a moment of your t—"

Jeremy found his mother's statement so shocking that he didn't even hear Peggy's plea. "Pass her off—? As *Georgy?* What on earth do you mean?" he demanded.

"I mean exactly that. This girl will be Georgy . . . for a little while, at least."

"You can't mean . . . outside this house?"

"I certainly can't mean *inside* this house, you idiot," his mother laughed. "Everyone here knows she's not Georgy."

"Everyone outside will know it, too," Allie muttered.

"What makes you think so?" Horatia asked her daughter, her smile changing to a frown. "If she fooled your brother, and even me—and *before* we made these changes

—then what makes you think she couldn't fool everyone else?"

"She fooled you and Jemmy only until you looked closely," Allie retorted promptly. "Besides, she doesn't *sound* like Georgy, for one thing, and for another, her skin is paler. And furthermore, her eyes aren't the same color."

"I've thought of all that," her mother said complacently. "Luckily, I've been telling everyone who's asked for her that Georgy is ill with a putrid infection of the throat. Her illness will account for her pallor. And her illness will leave her with an impaired voice. She'll have to whisper when she speaks. As for her eyes, I'd wager nobody takes notice. One never notices the color of another's eyes unless they're unusually light."

"Captain, *please*—!" Peggy begged, wringing her hands.

But Jeremy was staring at his mother in disbelief. "Do you expect me to take you seriously, Mama? Are you truly intending to pass the girl off as Georgy herself?"

"Of course. What else did you think I had in mind?"

"Good God! Have you taken leave of your senses? Even if such an insane imposture could be carried out, what would be the purpose of it?"

"The purpose, you paperskull," his mother answered in the tone of a piquet player triumphantly revealing a winning quint, "is to pave the way for this girl to take Georgy's place at Maitland's house party."

Jeremy's brows rose in astonishment. "You can't *mean* it!"

"Of course I mean it. Why not?"

"Why *not?*" her son echoed, horrified. "Why *not?* Because, firstly, anyone who knows Georgy will see through it. Because, secondly, it's dishonest. And because, thirdly, the whole idea is ridiculous."

"Ha!" Allie couldn't resist smirking at her mother. "I *told* you Jemmy wouldn't agree to such a wild scheme."

"Be still, Miss Prattle-box! I shan't countenance another disrespectful word from you. Unless you are seen-but-not-heard during the rest of this conversation, you'll be banished from all adult companionship for a week!" She turned back to her son while her daughter flounced off to the window with a pout. "As for you, Jeremy, if you'll only give the matter a little thought, you'll soon see the advantages of this so-called 'insane imposture.' Georgy has disappeared, giving us no indication of when she intends to return. You and I have already agreed that our only opportunity for financial security lies in her making a good marriage. Maitland is the best candidate for our purposes. Not only is he wealthy, but he is *interested*. And, most convenient of all, he's met Georgy *only once,* and that was more than a month ago! He would be the very *last* person capable of realizing that this girl is not Georgy."

"Mama, you are not thinking clearly. There will be other guests at this house party, will there not? Londoners who are much better acquainted with Georgy than Maitland. They'll recognize Peggy as an imposter, won't they?"

"No, they won't, for I shall have tested the waters before we go. I intend to take Peggy to the Trahernes' ball next week. If she can carry that off, then we can attempt the Maitland's house party without a qualm."

A little moan from Peggy went unnoticed. Jeremy took a turn round the room and then spoke again. "I think, Mama, that you're out in your reckoning. Even if you could carry this off—and even if Maitland is fooled and offers for her—what then? Will you let him *marry* the girl?"

"No, of course not. I'm hoping that Georgy will return before Maitland actually comes to the point. We're bound to hear from Georgy sooner or later. When we do, we can get her back and have her step in and take over her rightful role. I'm only playing for time with this scheme."

"You can accomplish the very same thing, can you not, by just writing to Maitland and declining the invitation, explaining that Georgy is ill? That will give you just as much time, won't it?"

"No, that won't do at all! You can be sure that, if Maitland doesn't see Georgy for all that time, some other pretty creature with a matchmaking Mama will have coaxed him into a betrothal. My scheme will at least keep Georgy from

becoming a victim of the male tendency to forgetfulness—
the out-of-sight, out-of-mind phenomenon."

Jeremy ran his fingers through his hair. "And what if
Georgy never comes back?" he asked, knowing that his
mother was going much too far but feeling incapable of
controlling her.

"You cannot believe that your sister will never again
contact her family!" Horatia exclaimed.

"I don't know what I believe," Jeremy muttered unhappily. He took another turn about the room. "I don't know,
Mama," he said, shaking his head. "I cannot like it."

"You'll like it better when everything comes about
successfully . . . when *I* can dispense with financial concerns and *you* can settle down happily with your Rosalind,"
his mother assured him in her complacent way. "But I'm
not asking you to like it now. I'm only asking you to assist
me in this plan."

The girl on the footstool shut her eyes and clenched her
hands. "Captain Verney, I beg you—!"

Jeremy rubbed his chin ruefully. "Oh, very well,
Mama," he agreed, shrugging helplessly.

"No!" Peggy Birkin snatched the skirt away from the
abigail and jumped down from the stool. "Captain Verney,
please don't ask this of me! I couldn't possibly do it!" And
she threw herself against Jeremy's chest, shaking.

"Heavens, girl, don't make such a to-do," Lady Horatia
said calmly. "There's hardly anything you need to do, except to enjoy yourself hugely. You'll have lovely clothes,
good food, a warm bed, and, I warrant, more luxurious
accommodations than you've ever had before. So stop this
missish behavior, if you please."

Peggy grasped Jeremy's lapels and turned a pair of desperate eyes up to his face. "She doesn't understand," she
said urgently. "I can't pretend to be a . . . a lady of quality!"

Jeremy patted her shoulder comfortingly. "But you must
start to think of yourself as a lady of quality, Miss Birkin.
If you believe yourself to be one, then that is what you
are."

"That is *not* what I am, sir. The ward of a bootmaker is
a far cry from a lady of quality. Besides, even if I could

fool myself into believing I'm quality, I could never convince myself that I'm your sister. Please, sir, don't ask me to enact so great a lie!"

Jeremy looked up over Peggy's head at his mother. "The girl is right, Mama. The whole scheme is dishonest."

Lady Horatia drew herself up to her full height. *"Dishonest?"* The word resounded through the room. "Dishonest?" she repeated, her voice ringing in offended dignity. "How *dare* you use that word to me! It seems you need to be reminded, Jeremy Verney, that I am your *mother* and that my concerns are only for the good of my children. You, of all people, should know that this plan I've concocted will amount to nothing more than a harmless *espièglerie* . . . the merest prank that will hurt nobody! And I do it for the most *honorable* of motives: *to save the family!* Furthermore, I find it ironic indeed to be lectured on honesty by a woman who was caught *stealing a watch*. Let me point out to *you,* Miss Peggy Whatever-your-name-is, that after having spent a good part of your adult life in *thievery,* you only make yourself a laughingstock when you now take umbrage at the suggestion that you enact a little *lie.* So let us have no more of this rodomontade. Climb back on that stool like a woman of sense, and *let Betsy finish your hem!"* With a final, icy glare at the girl still standing in her son's embrace, she swept from the room.

Peggy Birkin, rendered speechless by Lady Horatia's diatribe, stared at the door for a long moment. Then she looked up into Jeremy's face with an expression of such pained surprise that he felt his stomach knot. "You *t-told* her!"

"Told her?" he echoed stupidly.

"About m-my th-thieving." Tears filled her eyes and began to roll down her cheeks. "You shouldn't have t-told her."

"But, Peggy, I . . . I *had* to, you know," he mumbled awkwardly, unable to account for the feeling of guilt that beset him. "I had to explain how I came to . . . how *you* came to . . ."

The girl wrenched herself from his hold. "You sh-shouldn't have!" She ran to the door, dashing the tears from her cheeks with the back of her hand. "You betrayed me!" And she fled from the room.

"Peggy, come back!" he begged, taking a step after her. But he could hear her footsteps already running up the stairs. Betsy, as upset by the quarreling as anyone in the room, darted past him and followed the girl out of the room. In utter bewilderment, Jeremy sank down on the footstool and dropped his head in his hands. What had he done, he wondered, that he should have done differently? Should he have forbidden his mother to make her plans? He was, since his father's death, the master of the house, but did he have the moral right to give orders to his mother? And had he been wrong to repeat Peggy's story? Or did his mother have the right to know the full particulars about any person he brought to stay under her roof? He sighed, remembering that he'd returned to civilian life less than ten days ago. He hadn't dreamed, in his army days, that home life could be so confusing.

He felt a hand on his shoulder and looked up to find Allie smiling down at him in sympathy. "We women give a man a great deal of trouble, don't we?"

He took her hand in his. "Not you, Allie, my sweet. Never you."

She giggled. "That's only because I'm not yet of age. I shall cause veritable pandemonium once I'm in long skirts."

He had to smile. "Is that what you want to do? Cause pandemonium among the gentlemen?"

"Of course. I should like nothing better. But, Jemmy, I don't think you should be sitting here listening to me talk fustian. Don't you think you'd better go upstairs and soothe Peggy?"

"Soothe her? But why? Do *you* think I was wrong to tell Mama about her?"

"I don't know. I suppose you had to tell Mama *something*. A gentleman doesn't bring a strange woman home, especially one as pretty as that, without some explanation. But you might have left out a few of the more ... er ... sordid details."

"I didn't find the details so sordid. She was forced into

thievery by her brother. It wasn't through any fault of hers."

"You needn't make excuses to *me*, brother mine," Allie said, taking his other hand in hers and trying to pull him to his feet. "Go up and make them to her."

But Jeremy held back. "I don't see why I should. I've been as kind and gentlemanly to that girl as I know how to be. What more can she want of me?"

Allie frowned at her brother in disgust. "You men are the stupidest creatures alive. You told her that she should think of herself as a lady of quality, didn't you? Well, then, how do you expect her to do so if she believes everyone takes her for a thief? If she *were* a lady of quality, would you stay down here, knowing she was crying her eyes out upstairs?"

Jeremy stared up at his sister in wonder. "Did you say you're fourteen? How did you become so wise in a mere fourteen years? Are you certain, Miss Alison Verney, that you're not forty?"

Allie giggled again. "I'm not old, only brilliant. Therefore, you should heed my advice and march upstairs."

Jeremy got to his feet. "You may be brilliant, my girl, but I'm not sure about your advice in this instance. Even if Peggy were a lady of quality, I'm not certain I would run up after her. Why is it my place to soothe her? I'm neither her father nor her suitor."

"No, but you *are* her protector, aren't you? How will you feel if she runs off?"

"Runs off?" Jeremy's brows knit in immediate concern. "What makes you think she might run off?"

Allie shrugged. "That's what I would do if I were in her place."

"You would?" He held up his hands in a gesture of surrender. "All right, all right, I'll go." He strode out the door muttering under his breath that he was doing this very much against his better judgment. "I'll be stubbled," he called back to her from the bottom of the stairs, "if the day ever comes when I understand women!"

Chapter 11

Allie's prediction that Peggy might be tempted to run off proved to be more accurate than she'd imagined, for Peggy didn't even take time to weep. As soon as she reached the bedroom that Lady Horatia had given her, she pulled off Georgy's gown, tossed it into the arms of the befuddled Betsy, threw on her own dress and was just dashing out the door when she came face to face with Jeremy. "Excuse me, please," she muttered, trying to pass.

"Where are you going?" he asked, grasping her arm.

She tried to wrench it free. "It's no concern of yours," she declared, her voice choked with unshed, angry tears. "You have no right to keep me."

For Peggy, this had been a very difficult morning. A bubble of romance, which had been bouncing about in her breast since she'd been caught by Captain Verney at the Whaley Bridge market, had abruptly burst and was causing her great pain. Ever since childhood Peggy had been a dreamer. She'd been raised in protected solitude by a soft-hearted but mawkish aunt who, from a misguided sense of generosity, had plied her niece's body and mind with a diet of spun-sugar confections. Pastries and fairy tales were Peggy's daily fare. Most children's characters were formed by their relationships with other children and by observing the adults around them, but Peggy, who grew up without either companions or siblings or even sensible parents to emulate, was forced to fabricate her own character—to create and shape and fashion it out of thin air, using the only sources she had available: her own imagination and the syrupy stories her aunt provided. Somewhere in the back of her mind she created a self to color the drabness of her reality; she saw herself as the quintessential secret princess, lofty, lovely and doomed to live under a cruel spell. And although she knew better than to believe it, she dreamed that a handsome prince would one day ride into her life and break the spell.

Those childish daydreams, which had so enlivened the loneliness of her early years, started to fade as she matured, for an innate part of her nature—a healthy portion of common sense—flowered as she reached adulthood. But the blow occasioned by the necessity of living with her brother so wounded her spirit that she retreated into childishness. The horror of her daily life with Ned brought back the necessity for daydreams. After each terrifying day in which her brother forced her into acts of petty theft, she would return to Ned's grim rooms, draw the curtains across the opening of the tiny alcove he called her bedroom, throw herself on the sagging, odorous cot that was her bed, and escape into her own world. In that world, the handsome prince whose face she'd recognized in a hundred tales would ride to her rescue. He became as real to her as the men whose pockets she picked.

It was not surprising, therefore, that when she gazed up into Jeremy's face at the Whaley Bridge market, her heart almost leaped out of her breast. There he stood, resplendent in gold braid and shako, the very embodiment of every stalwart hero of every fairy tale she'd ever cried over. In every detail of person and dress he was perfect. She'd dreamed him just this way, wearing the tall hat with its bushy plume, its visor tilted rakishly to one side. She'd seen the fair hair that could be glimpsed beneath, the contrasting darkness of his weathered complexion, the square chin with its single dimple, the broad shoulders made even more impressive by the gold epaulets, the immaculate coat with its brass buttons, the sash across the manly chest, the perfectly shaped trousers fitting tightly over muscled thighs . . . she'd seen it all before. He was her dream personified. And when the course of the day's events proved him to be truly her rescuer, it was almost more than she could bear.

When had a Cinderella ever enjoyed so romantic an encounter? She could hardly believe that the day's happenings had been real. That night at the inn she kept pinching herself to keep herself awake for fear that if she fell asleep she might wake up to find it had all been a dream.

But this morning had brought reality. Cold reality. She'd been awakened early by that overbearing harpy, his mother, who'd pulled her from bed, washed and dried her, dyed and curled her, tweaked and tweezed her, corseted and gowned her until she'd been remade into the image of her hero's sister, Georgy. *Georgy.* Peggy had soon come to hate that name. She didn't want to be Captain Verney's *sister!* That was the last thing in the world she wanted to be!

But the greatest disappointment had been the Captain himself. In the first place he'd slept so late that Peggy'd begun to fear he'd never show his face. Then, when he finally did make an appearance, he seemed completely different. He was not in uniform, and, since she'd never seen him that way before, she was surprised at his mundane appearance. He looked very—well, she could think of no other word for it—ordinary. Still handsome, of course, but certainly not heroic. He was tousled and unshaven and was wearing a worn dressing gown that he'd obviously outgrown years before. It was a severe blow; her prince was just a man.

What was worse, he took no notice of her at all, except to remark about how much she resembled his blasted sister! Even when she'd tried to appeal to him for help, he didn't heed her. It was as if she didn't exist! And then he'd let his mother override all his objections to her playing the role of his sister. She'd listened in growing despair as he'd made his step-by-step retreat. The truth was that her hero had behaved like a . . . a milktoast!

And there had been something else . . . something his mother had said. About someone named Rosalind, with whom, she'd said, he could settle down happily. Did that mean what she suspected—that Captain Verney was betrothed? The very thought of it made her feel ill.

But the cruelest blow to her dreams—the one that had finally burst the bubble that had persisted in dancing inside her breast—had been the discovery that he'd revealed the ugly secrets of her past to his mother. How could he have done it? How could he so heartlessly have shamed her and made her despicable in his mother's eyes? She'd told him her story—in confidence—protected by the romantic intimacy of the inn's dining room. It had been the loveliest evening of her life. She had opened herself to him as she had to no one else. How could he have betrayed that confidence? How could he have sullied her memory of that night? For that one lapse she could never forgive him. For that one lapse she would leave this house forever.

But now, here he was, holding her arm with cruel force and preventing her from departing. She tried again to free herself from his grasp. "I said, Captain Verney, that I want you to let me go."

"Go where?" he asked, tightening his grip. "I thought you told me that you've nowhere to go."

"That is none of your affair!"

"But it is, you know. You saved my life. I owe it to you to—"

"You owe me nothing. I absolve you of all your imagined debt to me."

He shook his head. "But I don't absolve myself. Don't be foolish, girl. You know I can't permit you to roam unprotected about the streets of London."

"I shall manage somehow. I did so before I ever laid eyes on you."

"Yes, I *saw* how well you 'managed,'" he retorted with cold irony.

Her cheeks whitened. "That was unkind," she said tightly. Wrenching her arm from his grasp, she turned her back on him. "I didn't know you could b-be so odious."

He heard the little quiver in her voice and felt suddenly contrite. "I'm sorry," he mumbled, abashed, "I didn't mean... I only wanted... Dash it all, Peggy, you don't want to go back to *that*, do you?"

"That?" She wheeled about to face him. "By 'that' you mean stealing for Ned, don't you? But I don't see that the choice you and your mother are offering me is so much the better."

"How can you say that, Peggy? We're not sending you out to steal."

"No, but you want to *use* me, and in much the same way as Ned did—for your own dishonest purposes. And when you finish with me, I'll still be in the same impossible situation that I'm in now."

Jeremy couldn't think of a quick answer. He was a soldier, untrained in dealing with women. Allie had advised him to "soothe" this angry female, but he didn't know how to do it. He brushed his hair back from his forehead in frustration. "Can't we sit down and talk for a moment or two?" he pleaded helplessly.

"There is nothing to talk about," she said, trying again to pass him.

"Come back inside. For five minutes only. I promise not to hold you if you still wish to go when we've finished." Seeing her hesitate, he drew her into the room where the abigail still stood watching them interestedly. He frowned at the woman. "Betsy, please leave us. Miss Birkin will call you if she needs anything."

Shaking her head in disapproval (though she was not quite sure at what), Betsy placed the gown carefully on the bed and trudged off down the hall. Peggy remained motionless until the abigail was gone. Then she sank down on the bed. "No one ever called me Miss Birkin before I met you," she said with a sigh. "When I hear you say it, I actually *feel* like a lady of quality."

"Then I shall call you Miss Birkin always," he said with a quick smile. He picked up a little upholstered bench from beneath the dressing table and carried it over to the bed. "Although I like the name Peggy," he added as he set the bench down in front of her. "It suits you."

"You may call me Peggy, if you wish. I like it better than Georgy."

"So do I. May I sit?"

She nodded. As he perched himself on the bench, she studied his face for a moment and then lowered her eyes. "I'd like to ask you something," she said hesitantly. "Something . . . difficult.

"Go ahead. You may ask me anything at all."

She lifted her chin. "Would a lady of quality permit you to converse with her in her bedroom?"

Jeremy grinned. "The door is open," he said reassuringly. "I am no expert on the rules governing the behavior of gentlewomen, but I would think the open door insures that the proprieties have been observed."

"Then please say what you have to say, Captain. I agreed to give you no more than five minutes of my time."

"I thank you for that, ma'am. Five minutes will suffice, I think. I want to tell you, first, that I don't intend to let you out of this house until we've found a place for you to go where you'll be safe. I had hoped my mother would think of something—that she might know of a friend who'd offer you a decent situation or a shopkeeper who might give you employment—but your amazing similarity to my sister seems to have driven the matter from her mind. That doesn't mean, however, that she won't still help us. I assure you that she will. Her behavior today notwithstanding, my mother is the most generous and warm-hearted of women. I regret that matters got out of hand this morning, but I give you my word that neither my mother nor I will ever use you ill. No one in this household will coerce you to do anything you've no wish to do. You will not be obliged to enact my mother's little charade against your will. But you must agree to remain here until we can find a proper place for you. You do see the necessity of that, don't you?"

Peggy frowned down at the hands folded in her lap. "I suppose so."

"Then you agree not to try to run away again?"

The fingers twisted in her lap. "I . . . don't know. I don't see how I can accept your mother's hospitality . . . and her assistance in finding a place for me . . . and at the same time refuse to do as she asks me."

"If it troubles you to refuse her, I shall keep her from asking you," he responded with a glib assurance he was far from feeling.

She glanced up at him dubiously. "Can you really do so?"

He shrugged. "I am, after all, the master of this house."

"But she's your mother. I should not like to be the cause of difficulty between you."

"If it can't be helped, it is something we must endure."

Peggy lowered her head. She could feel her resolve ebbing away. She would not give him back his position in her mind as the princely hero he seemed at first, but his words and manner suggested a gentle strength that she found hard to resist. Though he was perhaps less than heroic, he was at least manly. "What do *you* wish me to do?" she asked in a low voice.

"To stay, of course. Isn't that what I've been saying?"

"No, I didn't mean that. I meant . . . if I stayed . . . what would you wish me to do about your mother's intention to have me pretend to be Georgy?"

He gave the question a moment's thought. "As far as that charade is concerned, Peggy, I think there would not be much harm in it at worst, and probably some benefit at best."

"Some benefit to you, you mean," she murmured, peeping at him through lowered lashes. "You could settle down happily with your Rosalind."

He started in surprise. "How did you know about Rosalind?"

She shrugged. "Your mother said something about it this morning. Is this Rosalind your . . . your betrothed?"

Jeremy rose from his bench and turned away. "No, she is not. Her family does not find me good enough for her."

"How can that be?" Peggy asked in wonder. "I would think you good enough for a . . . a . . . duchess!"

Jeremy laughed mirthlessly. "That is kind of you to say. But you aren't familiar with the standards of the *ton*."

"No, I don't suppose I am. But I don't quite understand what the 'standards of the *ton*' have to do with your sister Georgy."

"Only that things would be different if Georgy married well," Jeremy admitted with some embarrassment.

Peggy stared at his bent head thoughtfully. "So if I play Georgy and catch the interest of this gentleman your mother spoke of . . . Lord Maitland, is it? . . . then your value will rise with Rosalind's family, is that it?"

"That is what Mama hopes."

"That is what you hope, too, is it not?"

He turned and met her eye. "Yes, that is what I hope, too."

It was true, then, Peggy realized. He was in love with another. Her shattered dream, like Humpty-Dumpty's shell, would never be put back together. He would never be hers. It was a foolish dream, and in the sensible part of her nature she'd known it from the first. He was a nobleman (for hadn't she heard the butler call him *your lordship?*); and she was a...a pickpocket. The distance between them was enormous. Love was sometimes a force strong enough to bridge even a gap as great as this one, but not in this case. Captain Verney loved Another. His Rosalind. After less than two days, the dream was over.

She gulped, swallowing the unshed tears that still stuck in her throat. She had to say something ... to make a decision. She had a choice of two alternatives: she could run off right now and find some sort of place for herself (for this was London, not Whaley Bridge, and there had to be many opportunities in this huge city for a strong, healthy woman to find honest work), or she could remain here and help the Captain to achieve *his* dream. She could sacrifice herself for him. In the stories of her youth, there had been two kinds of heroine: the Secret Princess who was rescued by her Prince, and the Selfless Lady who gave her life for love. If Peggy couldn't be the first, then she could certainly be the second.

She got up from the bed and went to him. "Very well, Captain, I shall stay. And, since you wish it, I'll enact your mother's little charade. I'll play the role of Georgy ... for you."

Chapter 12

Georgy stood before the notice board outside the door of the Ruckworth church and frowned at the placard she'd just tacked upon it. It was not a very large placard (she hadn't been able to find a larger card among the drawing supplies she'd brought with her), but she'd hand-printed it in block letters: *The Ruckworth Parish Charity School will reopen its doors on the second Monday of October. All children between the ages of six and fourteen are urged to enroll. G. Vail, Schoolmistress.*

She hoped her notice was large enough to attract the attention of the churchgoers away from all the announcements of banns and births. It was very important that the parishoners enroll their children. She needed at least a dozen pupils to enroll or Lady Ruckworth would not feel the enterprise useful enough to keep it going.

She stared at her handiwork, sighing worriedly. In six more days, she, Miss Grace Vail, would be starting her new career. She had less than a week in which to make preparations, and there was still a great deal to do. She hadn't even properly settled herself into her room as yet.

The vicar, Mr. Hunsford, had informed her early (in the letters they'd exchanged before she'd come) that while she was in the employ of the parish she would be expected to reside in a room in the vicarage. (She would only be charged eleven pounds per annum for her room and board, he'd written, which was very reasonable considering the substantial salary of twenty-two pounds per annum she would be receiving.) After the interview with Lady Ruckworth, Mary Hunsford had shown her to the little bedroom under the eaves that would be her living quarters. The room was very small—containing only a narrow bed, a dresser, a chair and a rickety bed table—but it was clean and cheerful and far down the hall from the rooms of the Hunsfords' three children. Georgy had assured Mrs. Hunsford that it would be quite satisfactory, and if in her heart she felt some dismay, she consoled herself with the thought that at least it was a place where she could be alone. The only other person residing near her was a timid housemaid who, she was sure, would not interfere with her privacy.

She was already fond of Mary Hunsford. The vicar's wife was much too self-effacing, but she was invariably helpful and kind. Her two daughters were much like her, modest and shy, but her eldest—a boy of twelve—was as talkative and confident as his father. She'd been with the family only a couple of days, but she'd already discovered that while the males in the household talked and talked, the women did the work.

Her first dinner with the Hunsfords had been an education for Georgy. (She'd been informed by the vicar that she was expected to take her meals with the family but could, if she wished, prepare luncheon and tea for herself at the school.) After grace was said, Mr. Hunsford and his son Edward had remained in their seats in kingly comfort while Mary and both little girls, aged six and eight respectively, rose from their places to assist the housemaid with the serving. Georgy had never before observed a household in which the women of the family were little better than servants.

Later, Georgy had asked the children if they would be attending her school, but the vicar intervened to explain that he himself was preparing young Edward for admission to a fine academy for boys in Manchester, and that his daughters would be trained in their letters and their catechism by their mother at home. "That, and the proper preparation for their future roles as wives and mothers, is education enough for little females," he said with a touch of smugness. "Besides, it would not be seemly for the children of the vicar to attend a charity school."

A sharp retort had sprung to Georgy's tongue. However, remembering that she was no longer Georgianna Verney of the London *ton* but Grace Vail, schoolmistress (and on temporary sufferance at that), she'd swallowed her resentment and kept her remarks to herself.

She didn't quite know what to make of Mr. Hunsford. She knew that he was eager for the school to succeed and for her to justify his judgment in appointing her by becoming a good enough teacher to win the approval of his patroness, Lady Ruckworth; but at the same time there was something disparaging in his attitude toward the school. It was plain that, to his mind, the school was not good enough for the education of his own children. Was the vicar a snob, or was there something about a charity school that made it a place to be avoided if one could afford some other kind of education?

There was something else about the vicar that made her uncomfortable. That discomfort had been caused by an incident that had occurred the day after she'd arrived. Mary Hunsford had just given her a tour of the house and had suggested that she take an hour or so to get some air. Georgy agreed, thinking that the hour could be well spent if she used the time to explore the village. The vicar, who was just entering the house as she came out the door, offered to accompany her. She accepted with gratitude, realizing that with his escort she would more quickly become familiar with her new environs.

The vicar took her arm in his and, pouring forth a steady stream of local lore, led her past the church (a small but lovely stone building with a tall pointed-arch spire), around the oval-shaped village green (in the center of which stood a stone market-cross that the vicar proudly informed her was built in the thirteenth century), past two rows of cottages in various stages of disrepair (about which the vicar said nothing to explain the existence of such poverty in the midst of an apparently prosperous village), and across a bridge over a muddy stream that led to a water mill so bucolic and picturesque that Georgy would have exclaimed over it in delight had she not been brooding over the condition of the cottages.

It was from those cottages that she would recruit her pupils. She'd known they would be poor, but she had not

realized the extent of their squalor. The prosperous-looking
farmhouses she'd seen from the road when she'd first arrived were not, she now understood, the homes of her prospective pupils. The few landowning farmers in the village
were prosperous enough to pay for their sons' tuition at
city grammar schools. *Her* pupils would all come from
those dank, dirty, run-down cottages where only farm laborers and ill-paid craftsmen lived. She knew very little
about their lives so far, but just seeing the outside of their
hovels disturbed her. And what disturbed her more was that
the vicar was evidently untroubled by those conditions.
Had his years in this village benumbed him?

By this time they'd climbed the hill to the gates of
Ruckworth Manor, an elegant brick edifice situated in
lordly superiority atop a hill overlooking the village. "We
are not going in, are we?" Georgy asked Mr. Hunsford in
alarm, not wishing to face Lady Ruckworth again so soon.

"Oh, no, indeed not," he assured her. "One doesn't call
on Lady Ruckworth without an invitation. Although I'm
sure you'll be invited for tea one day."

"One day?" Georgy asked, more amused than offended.

But the vicar did not see that there was cause either for
amusement or offense. "When her ladyship is convinced
that your work is satisfactory, she is certain to invite you,"
he said comfortingly. "She is very kind in that way."

"Yes, so she must be," Georgy murmured, suppressing
a smile. "But if we are not to call on her ladyship, Mr.
Hunsford, why did we climb up here?"

"For the view, of course," he answered, gesturing toward the village that could be seen in its entirety spread out
below them.

Georgy gazed down at what was to be her new home.
At that moment, a cold wind, harbinger of the harsh winter
that was not too far away, whipped up about them, causing
Georgy's skirts to flap and the vicar's tall hat to blow from
his head. She managed to catch it, but when she held it out
to him he did something that astonished her. He took it
from her hand and kept hold of her fingers. "You are a very
lovely young woman, Miss Vail," he murmured, staring
down into her face.

The remark could, of course, have been an entirely innocent one, the sort a fond uncle might make to a favorite
niece. But Georgy was discomfitted by it and withdrew her
fingers from his hold abruptly. "Thank you," she said and
turned quickly to look at the view. After a moment, she
glanced back at him. He was apparently unaware of having
committed a solecism, for he was gazing down at his parish with placid serenity. She looked away, scolding herself
for having had improper thoughts. The man had merely
indulged in an avuncular impulse. She should not make
more of it than that. She would brush the incident from her
memory. "That is indeed a lovely prospect, Mr. Hunsford,"
she remarked in a perfectly normal voice, turning from the
view to face her escort, "but you haven't shown me what I
most want to see."

"Oh? And what is that, Miss Vail?"

"The schoolhouse, of course. Can I see it from here?"

"Yes, you can. It's just behind the vicarage . . . there, to
the west. Look to the left of the little pond."

"Do you mean . . . ? Not that building with the tall
chimney?" Georgy felt a twinge of disappointment. "It's so
tiny."

Mr. Hunsford smiled indulgently and patted her
shoulder. "You'll find it large enough for the dozen or so
pupils you'll have."

Georgy didn't respond, for his hand on her shoulder
caused her to feel discomfitted again. But he removed it
almost immediately. Again she shook off her disquieting
thoughts and occupied her mind in studying the terrain.
She wanted to try, from this vantage point, to pick out the
shortest way from the vicarage to the schoolhouse. It
turned out to be simple: out the Hunsfords' back door,
through the small kitchen garden and across a large fallow
field. With that path fixed firmly in her mind, she'd told
the vicar she was ready to go back down.

That had been the extent of the incident. Not very significant, surely, but the vicar's behavior had made her wary
of him.

Now here she was a day later, still brooding over the
matter. She gave herself a shake to wipe the incident from

her mind. She had more important matters to think about. For one thing, days were going by and she'd still not visited the schoolhouse.

She took a last look at the placard she'd just placed on the board, the placard that announced her future. What did that future hold for her, she wondered? Would she be able to make the school a success? Would Lady Ruckworth find her work satisfactory? Would the pupils like her? Would Mr. Hunsford prove to be a problem to her? Would she be able to endure a prolonged absence from her family and friends? Would her mother ever forgive her? Would she ever be able to let her family know where she was, so that they could someday exchange letters and even visits? There were so many questions, but all of the answers eluded her. *Oh, well,* she thought, *the answers will come with time.*

Meanwhile, she reminded herself, she'd not yet visited the schoolhouse. That was what she determined to do next. With eager steps, she turned from the church door and ran off to take her first close look at the place where she expected to spend the most significant hours of her new life.

She crossed the green and the weed-choked field at a run, but her first look at the school building slowed her steps. She felt a sharp pang of disappointment. The building, though made of stone and thatched like the vicarage, was even smaller than it had seemed from the hillside. It had only one room inside, and a shed at the back for a privy. It wasn't at all what she'd imagined a schoolhouse to be.

She climbed the two stone steps that led to the unimpressive entrance and opened the door warily. As she paused in the doorway, her eyes were drawn first to the room's two windows, placed high on the wall opposite where she stood. They were grimy with neglect, the dirt as effective at keeping out the light as gray muslin shades would have been. Despite the faint light, however, she could make out the room's main features. No larger than her bedroom at home, it had four dusty rafters across its ceiling, a floor made of bricks set in the soil, cracked plaster walls of dingy gray, and a blackened fireplace in a corner. It was a most oppressive place, not unlike a prison cell . . . or, rather, what she imagined a prison cell must be like.

She stepped over the threshold into the dusty dimness and blinked the daylight out of her eyes, trying hard not to lose heart. The place could be improved, after all, she told herself. The floor could never really be swept clean, but the rest of the place could be brightened. There was no need for despair.

She looked carefully about her, taking note of the few furnishings and effects that gave evidence of the room's purpose: the round table and chair that were obviously for the teacher, the four low benches (but no desks) for the pupils, and the two wooden rails set low on the walls on both sides of the door into which brass hooks had been screwed at six-inch intervals. There were eighteen hooks. Would they all be taken? she wondered. Would there be eighteen little faces looking up at her next Monday morning . . . eighteen little minds eager to sop up the crumbs of knowledge she would impart? Her spirits rose as she imagined the room full of children. She touched a brass hook fondly. The room would be much cheerier, she told herself, when little coats and ribboned hats were hanging here.

But another look round caused her heart to sink again. The place was so *bare*. Except for a few shelves that had been hung between the windows over the teacher's table, the room's only decoration was a framed motto hanging crookedly on one of the two utterly blank walls. She crossed the room to see it. It was painted with ornate flourishes in red, black and gold, and it read:

WE ARE NEVER
TOO YOUNG
TO SIN.

That motto was quite the last straw. *Oh, my Lord,* Georgy thought miserably, *what sort of place have I come to?*

Chapter 13

Although the sight of the schoolroom with its oppressive message caused Georgy to suffer her first serious misgiving about the wisdom of her decision, she did not long indulge in regrets. Almost at once she shook off the doldrums and threw herself into the task of preparing for what lay ahead. Mary Hunsford, who had not failed to note the firmness with which Lady Ruckworth had ordered Miss Vail to darken the color of her gown, suggested that her first task should be the preparation of her school dresses. Together they dipped each one of the three gowns Georgy had chosen into a cauldron of boiling black dye. Mrs. Hunsford sighed in sympathy as one after the other of Georgy's lovely dresses—first the blue she'd worn when she'd arrived, next the silvery lilac she'd worn to the Denhams' ball, and the third a glowing green jacquard—were subdued to a uniform muddy-gray.

After the dresses were dyed, dried and pressed and the appropriate white collars, tuckers and cuffs affixed to them, Georgy set upon her next task: cleaning up the classroom. With the help of the sour old fellow who'd driven her to Ruckworth from Whaley Bridge, she patched and whitewashed the schoolroom walls. Then she swept the floor, cleaned as much of the fireplace as she could, waxed the benches and polished the coat-hooks until they shone. She scrubbed each of the thirty-six little panes of the windows to a sparkle and then prevailed upon the accommodating Mrs. Hunsford to help her sew two pairs of curtains for them. (The fabric they used was cut from the full skirt of a dimity gown that Georgy had brought with her but that she knew she would never be able to wear in this new life of hers because of its rich yellow color and sheer texture. But Mary, who'd never seen so beautiful a gown, was appalled at the thought of destroying it, and she actually wept as she watched Georgy cut into it. It was only when the curtains were hung, and Mary could see for herself how they filtered the light and illuminated the whitewashed walls with rows of glowing amber squares, that she was able to admit that Miss Vail had been right to sacrifice her dress.)

There was one last task Georgy was determined to perform, but for that she required no one's assistance. In fact, she hoped no one would catch her at it. One afternoon, when she was certain that nobody was loitering about in the field or on the road, she took down the motto from the schoolroom wall, hid it under her shawl, scurried down the road to the green, and then, with one last look about her to make sure that no one was about, dropped it, frame and all, down the well.

Once the deuced motto was disposed of beyond recovery, she returned to the schoolhouse with a bouyant step. When she arrived, however, she found Mr. Hunsford waiting for her. She froze in the doorway. Had he already discovered what she'd done? Would he accuse her of criminal behavior? Vandalism? Theft? Was she about to be summarily discharged from her post? But the vicar was smiling. "How very nicely you've transformed the place, Miss Vail," he said with sincere admiration. "I'm very proud of you."

He hadn't noticed! Although he surveyed the room many times before he took his leave, he never noticed that anything was missing. But Georgy didn't take a deep breath until he'd left.

Later, Mary Hunsford arrived with a pair of wrought-iron pokers and a brass grate she'd offered to donate for the fireplace. She also surveyed the room with pleasure, and she also failed to notice that a certain edifying motto was missing from the wall. She even gazed at the blank wall and wondered aloud if perhaps her ladyship might be prevailed upon to donate a picture or two. "A nice ocean scene, per'aps, or a meadow in spring . . . something pleas-

ant for the little tykes to stare at. But of course she won't,"
she added after second thought. "She'll only say that pic-
tures on the wall'd be a temptation to distract their thoughts
from God's message."

"Don't worry about it, Mary," Georgy said in delirious
relief. "I'll hang up some of the children's own drawings.
Those will surely brighten up the room."

"I s'pose so," Mary said, looking round somewhat
glumly. "That is, if you get any children to do the drawing." Sighing, she knelt down beside Georgy at the fireplace to help install the grate. "After all the trouble you've
taken, it'd be a shame to see you disappointed."

"Disappointed? What are you talking about?"

"If you don't get enough pupils, I mean. You'll have to
have at least nine or ten to keep the school going, but I
don't know if . . . I wouldn't count on more'n six."

Georgy was horrified. "Only *six?*"

"If you're lucky. They don't like coming, you know,"
Mrs. Hunsford confided, setting the pokers carefully in the
corner. "I shouldn't say it, being the vicar's wife and all,
but the children, they don't like it. All that praying and
hymn-singing and catechism. And having to wear the charity-school clothes. They don't like it. And their parents
don't, either. If the little tykes don't go to school, you see,
they can earn a few pennies gathering stones or scaring the
birds from the fields."

"Are you saying I shan't get enough pupils? That they
would *prefer* to gather stones?" Georgy sat back on her
heels and stared at Mrs. Hunsford in alarm. "But . . . but
Mr. Hunsford said there would be about a dozen."

"There were a dozen last year, when Mrs. Jayce was
here. But you're not like Mrs. Jayce, my dear. Not a bit.
And if you don't have enough pupils, I fear her ladyship
will decide the school's not worth keeping up."

Georgy peered at Mrs. Hunsford intently. "In what way
am I not like this Mrs. Jayce? What is there about me that
will keep the pupils from coming?"

"You're much . . . softer, you see. I don't mean any offense, my dear Grace, for I like you ever so much better
than Mrs. Jayce. But there's no getting round the fact that

she was . . . well, stronger than you. Mrs. Jayce was very
large and had a voice like . . . like a bellows. And her eyes
would peer into you as if she were St. Peter himself and
could keep you out of heaven if she found you undeserv-
ing. *Awesome*, Mrs. Jayce was. The children—and the
parents, too!—they were too afraid of her not to come. But
you are not so . . . so *scarifying* as Mrs. Jayce, my dear.
They won't be afraid to say no to you."

"Is that so?" Georgy got to her feet and brushed the dust
from her skirt. "We shall see about that." Her voice had a
firmness she was far from feeling. "Your Mrs. Jayce may
have looked awesome, but she wasn't St. Peter after all.
She was only a woman. And if *she* could entice a dozen
pupils to come to school, then so can *I!*"

But despite that ringing declaration, on Monday morning only four little children (three girls and a runny-nosed,
six-year-old boy) appeared at the schoolroom door. It was
Georgy's severest disappointment. Nevertheless, she
smiled bravely at each one of her pupils, helped them to
hang their hats and wraps on the hooks (which did nothing
to brighten the appearance of the room, for the girls' hats,
their three shawls and the boy's ragged coat were so grimy
that their colors had long since transmogrified to pauper
brown), learned their names, wiped their noses, started
them on learning their letters, gave them tea with jam and
then read aloud to them, to their very great delight, *The
True History of Sir Thomas Thumb*.

By evening (exhilarated by her first experience as a
teacher, enchanted by the children and touched by their
eagerness to shower affection on her), she was convinced
that she'd found her true vocation. More than ever, she was
determined to expand the size of her class to the twelve her
predecessor had claimed and thus to keep Lady Ruckworth
from closing the school. To that end, she set off right after
dinner to visit those cottagers whose young children had
failed to appear. She'd dressed herself in a proper gray
schooldress and one of the dame-caps that Mrs. Hunsford
had given her (its starched crown covering almost all her
hair and its two side panels flapping beside her cheeks like
the ears of a beagle) so that she would be immediately

recognized by the villagers as the new schoolteacher. Armed with a list of prospects from Mrs. Jayce's daybook, she marched down the road with high spirits, a resolute step, and not the slightest premonition of the possibility of failure. It didn't occur to her that the evening's encounters could result in disaster.

Her first call was on a family of six named Putman. When Mrs. Putman opened the door, Georgy was immediately assaulted by an overpowering stench of fish stew. On entering, she found herself in a smoky room that was obviously used for cooking, eating and every other purpose but sleeping. Mr. Putman, a ruddy, moustached man sitting in his shirtsleeves at a table from which the remains of the evening meal had not yet been removed, lifted himself halfway from his chair and nodded curiously at the visitor. Nearby, at the hearth, a little girl and boy sat on the floor taunting a cat and took no notice of her at all, while a slightly older girl, standing before a washtub scraping burnt grease from a pan, glanced over her shoulder at Georgy in shy fascination. Mrs. Putman, a pale, gaunt woman, nervously pulled out a chair from under the table. "Yer the new schoolma'am, ain't ye?" she asked as she gestured for Georgy to sit.

Mr. Putman lowered himself onto his seat. "Miz Vail, ain't it? What kin we do fer ye, ma'am?"

"How do you do?" Georgy said cheerfully. "I came to discover the reason why your children—you have four, I believe—did not come to school today."

"Tain't four no more. Sam'l, our eldest, is gone fer to work in the cotton mill over in Barstow."

Georgy consulted her list. "But it says here that Samuel Putman is not yet thirteen!" she exclaimed.

The man shrugged. "Big fer 'is age is Sam'l. He kin do a man's work."

Georgy stared at him for a moment and then glanced quickly at his wife. If the woman grieved for the loss of a son to the cotton mill, she gave no outward sign of it. Georgy, sighing inwardly, put a line through Samuel's name. "But what about the others? That must be Sarah standing back there, am I right? Twelve-year-old Sarah? And those two, Hester and William . . . what about them?"

"We need Sarah 'ere, to 'elp 'er mother," the man said coldly. "An' Willy goes out every day to pick 'ops."

"He picks hops?" Georgy winced. The boy was so small! With that cherubic face and short stature, he hardly looked his nine years. His little hands were filthy and covered with welts and punctures from picking the sharp, conical hops. School would be a much better place for him than the fields. If only she could persuade that stubborn man! "But the harvest is almost over, is it not?"

"There's still 'ops to be picked. And then, when they're gone, there'll be other chores the lad kin do."

Mrs. Putman leaned over and stroked her Willy's hair. "On'y nine 'e is, but 'e brought 'ome arf a shillin' last week," she told the teacher proudly.

"But surely he could be spared from work a few hours every day," Georgy protested. "And the girls, too. Shouldn't you be thinking of their futures?"

"There ain't nothin' you could teach 'em in yer school that'd make a difference in their futures," the man muttered, shifting in his chair as if he wanted to make an end to the conversation.

"Don't you think that they'd have a better future if they learned to read and write?"

"I got on wi'out it. An' the two years Sam'l spent in the Parish school didn't change nothin' fer 'im." He got up from his chair, crossed to the hearth and picked up the little six-year-old Hester. "'Twouldn' change nothin' fer this one neither. Thank 'ee fer stoppin' in, Miz Vail. Missus Putman'll get the door for ye."

Georgy had been rudely dismissed. Chagrined, she rose and turned to the gaunt woman who waited to show her out. "Do you agree with your husband, Mrs. Putman?" she asked. "Don't you want your children to have a little education?"

The woman hesitated. "I could spare Sarah for a few hours," she said to her husband quietly. "Most days, anyhow."

Mr. Putman glared at his wife and thrust the child into

her arms. "I said all that's to be said," he declared and stomped out to an adjoining room.

Mrs. Putman pressed her lips together. "Sorry, ma'am," she whispered, holding the door for Georgy, "but God bless ye fer tryin'."

Next door, at the Slopers', the outcome was about the same. Mr. Sloper answered all her questions with a grunt, his wife remained silent throughout the interview and the two children (Timothy, aged ten, and Molly, aged seven) watched impassively. "I'll think on it," their father said in conclusion.

But it was the third call that undid her. It was at the house of the Kissacks, the very poorest house in the row. It had only one room, a dark, crowded space with a loft hanging over it where all the family evidently slept. The large fireplace, used for cooking and heating, smoked badly and spread a coat of soot over everything. Georgy, glancing round the room as she stepped over the threshold, was appalled by the squalor of the place.

The only thing Georgy knew about the Kissacks was what she'd seen in the daybook. It listed six children in the Kissack family, but only two were eligible for school, for one was almost fifteen, one was a baby, and two were scratched from the list with the word "deceased" after them. Georgy didn't know what the poor children had died of, but she entered the house with a heart full of sympathy for the poor, bereaved family.

Even if Mr. Kissack could have sensed her feelings, he would not have been softened. Georgy could see at once that Mr. Kissack would be difficult. He sat at the table with a bottle of spirits at his elbow and a glass in his hand. He didn't bother to rise when she entered. In fact, no one— not the father, not the mother, not one of the three children sprawled near the hearth—even offered her a chair.

She'd barely introduced herself when Mr. Kissack let forth a stream of invectives that froze her blood. "Bloody hell and damnation!" he snarled, slamming a fist on the table so violently that he made both his bottle and Georgy's heart jump. "I don't take kin'ly to bein' plagued by the parish and their damn bloody school. Me 'n mine's 'ad

enough tubsters preachin' at us to last a lifetime. We don'
need no more. Any man what ain't a growtnoll knows it
don't do no bloody good, all that preachin' an' prayin'—

"Mister, 'old yer lushy tongue," his wife hissed as she
bent down to a rough-hewn cradle at her feet and lifted a
baby to her shoulder.

"Stay out o' this, Missus," he ordered, downing the
contents of his glass. "I ain't sittin' still to listen to no
bleedin' ol' maid with fine-lady airs tell me 'ow to raise
my brats."

Georgy tried to hide her inner trembling. "B-but Mr.
Kissack—"

"Quiet, woman! Don' try to tell me what goes on in that
school! I'll show *you* what goes on there. Benjy, Dorrie,
come 'ere an' do one of yer lessons fer us."

"Now, Mister," his wife objected as two children got up
eagerly, "there ain't no need to—"

The man glared the wife to silence. The two youngsters
took a pose in front of the fire. The eldest, Benjamin, a
strapping boy with intelligent eyes and a freckled nose
(who, Georgy realized, was the fourteen-year-old)
snatched up a dishcloth and draped it on his head like a
dame-cap. Making his sister face him, he crossed his arms
over his chest. "Now, child," he said in a high, mincing
voice that parodied every irritating schoolmarm he'd ever
known, "let us say that you're doin' an errand in the great
house, and you are tempted to pilfer somethin' like tea or
sugar or other things which you suppose will not be
missed. Even though they will not be missed, is this honest?"

The girl, Dorrie, a bony little creature with wild hair,
made a bobbing curtsey to her brother. "No, ma'am, it
ain't honest."

The boy frowned at her. *"Isn't* honest."

Dorrie grinned. "Isn't."

Benjy nodded. "Who does the tea and sugar and everything else in the house belong to?"

"The master," Dorrie responded promptly.

"Whose eyes would see you pilfer if the master is not
by?"

"God's."

"Who do victuals and drink belong to in that house?"

"The master and mistress."

"Is not robbin' them of these things the same as takin' their money?"

"Yes."

"Who sees people when they pilfer tea and sugar and such things?"

"God sees."

"Does God approve of such actions?"

"No."

"What will God do to thieves of all kinds?"

"God will punish them," Dorrie concluded, making another bobbing curtsey.

"There!" the father said scornfully, waving his arm at the performers. "That's what they learn in yer blasted school! 'S like the parish expects 'em all to be damn thieves!"

Georgy took a step toward him. "But, Mr. Kissack, *I* wouldn't—"

"Don' tell me what ye wouldn't!" he barked, rising from his chair. "Yer all alike, you an' all yer mealy-mouthed breed." He came toward her so threateningly that she backed away. "Takin' us fer liars and sinners, an' teachin' the children to be ashamed of their kin and theirsel's. You ain't no diff'rent from the rest of 'em, so don' try to say ye are. I know yer kind, with yer fine-lady talk an' yer hoity-toity airs, thinkin' y're so much better 'n us. Well, you kin keep yer fancy ways to yersel', hear? We don' want you or yer school, so don' come round lookin' fer us no more!"

By this time he'd backed poor Georgy to the door. Her knees were shaking so alarmingly that she feared they would give way. She had never in her life been spoken to with such venomous acrimony. She didn't know how to counter it, or even how to defend herself from it. How would Mrs. Jayce, her predecessor, have handled herself with this bullying creature? The thought of the 'awesome" Mrs. Jayce stiffened her a little. She couldn't let herself fail where Mrs. Jayce had succeeded. She braced herself against the doorjamb. "I didn't m-mean to imply that I'm your b-better, Mr. Kissack," she stammered. "I only wished to offer your children—"

"Don' offer my children *nuthin!*" he shouted, baring his teeth and thrusting his face close to hers. "Nuthin', I say! We don' need nuthin' from the likes of you!" And he raised his arm as if to strike her.

Her chest clenched in terror. He was going to hit her, she was sure of it! She could read the intention in the bloodshot, wild eyes and the black-toothed leer on his face . . . a monstrous face that loomed so close above hers that she could smell the spirits on his fetid breath. Her last ounce of determination, her last bit of courage, collapsed. She clapped a trembling hand to her mouth, threw Mr. Kissack one last, terrified look and ran.

He followed her out to the doorstep. "Don' come lookin' fer us again, Miss Hoity-toity Schoolma'am, do ye hear me?" he shouted after her as she stumbled, gasping in despair, down the road into the darkness. "Don' come 'ere again. We don' want yer damn school, an' we don' want *you!*"

Chapter 14

———⊸∞⊸———

Georgy fled past the row of cottages, across the green, round the church and into the vicarage. Brushing by the waiting Mary Hunsford with the barest of greetings, she ran up the stairs to her room, shut the door and leaned against it, gasping for breath. Never had she been so shaken. She could still see Mr. Kissack's face looming over her and his arm raised threateningly. But now she remembered that he'd not lowered his arm; it had remained poised in the air. He would not have struck her after all. She had been a coward . . . a foolish, namby-pamby, sniveling coward. Mrs. Jayce would not have let that man terrify her. She would have shouted right back at him.

A knock at the door interrupted her self-recriminations. "Grace? It's I, Mary. Has something happened to upset you?"

Georgy tried to pull herself together. "No, nothing, Mary, thank you."

There was a moment's pause. Then Mary asked in a troubled voice, "May I come in?"

Georgy wanted to tell her to go away, but she couldn't return Mary's kindness with such rudeness. There was nothing to be done but admit her. She wiped her eyes with the back of her hand and opened the door.

Mary took one look at her face and knew something had gone wrong. "Heavens, you're white as a sheet! What is it?"

Georgy sank down upon the bed. "You were right, Mary. I'm not fit to be a teacher."

Mary's flat cheeks puffed out in indignation. "I never said any such thing, Grace Vail! How can you—?"

"Perhaps not in so many words. But you did say that I'm not anything like Mrs. Jayce."

"Well, you're not. What has that got to say to the point?"

Georgy leaned her forehead against the bedpost. "The point is that I'm a failure. Whether you said it or not, I'm not fit to be a teacher. Not only haven't I been able to strike fear into the hearts of the parents I visited, as Mrs. Jayce used to do, but I . . . I let them strike fear into *mine.*" Her voice cracked as she went on. "Oh, Mary, I feel so . . . humiliated! I haven't been able to convince anyone to send me even one child!"

"Now, see here, Grace, stop talking such nonsense. It's not your fault if the cottagers don't want to send their children to school. In fact, it's more Mrs. Jayce's fault than yours. If she'd been such a good teacher, wouldn't the pupils be coming back for more?"

Georgy lifted her head. "Why . . . I never thought of that."

"Then think of it now. Mrs. Jayce was fearsome, but I wouldn't wish *my* little ones to be frightened into learning. I'd much rather send them to a teacher like you."

"Would you, Mary? Truly?"

Mary sat down beside her. "Of course I would. My girls adore you already."

"Oh, Mary!" Georgy threw her arms around the other woman in a tremulous embrace. "Thank you for saying that."

"No need to thank me, my dear. It's nothing but the truth."

The humiliating pain of the experience with Mr. Kissack was eased by the balm of Mary Hunsford's kind words, but Georgy's problem was not solved. Sighing, she folded her hands in her lap and looked down at them. "But even if I *am* a good teacher, it will do no good if I have only four pupils to teach."

Mary's smile faded. "I know," she admitted sadly. "Lady Ruckworth won't be pleased with only four."

"Tell me, Mary, do you think I should pack my things and steal away now tonight, and avoid further humiliation?

I could go back home to London, I suppose, and try to . . . to find a husband for myself."

Mary's eyes widened with sharpened interest. "A husband? Is there someone back in London that you care for, Grace?"

Georgy smiled at her eagerness. "No, I'm afraid not."

"But a girl as pretty as you . . . surely there must have been someone . . ."

"No, no one," she answered. But the words had no sooner left her tongue than a picture flashed into her mind of a dark-skinned, grizzle-haired fellow with keen eyes and a remarkable smile. *Good heavens,* she thought in surprise, *whatever made me think of Anthony Maitland at this moment?* But aloud she repeated, "No one."

Those words were nothing but the truth. There was no one in London whom she wanted to marry. But Maitland had been appealing. It was strange how that one meeting with him had remained so clearly in her memory. In fact, she'd even dreamed of him. His face had appeared to her in her sleep more times than she wanted to count. It annoyed her that she couldn't dismiss him from her consciousness, when obviously he'd dismissed her from his. He'd never kept the promise he'd made when he parted from her that evening. *My dear girl,* he'd said, *if you honestly believe we won't meet again, you are greatly underestimating yourself.* Ha! He'd never even *tried* to meet her again.

Mary was peering at her shrewdly. "You thought of someone just then, didn't you?"

Georgy felt herself blush. "Perhaps. Well . . . yes. But he's not for me."

"Oh? Why not?"

"Beyond my touch, I'm afraid. Besides, I hardly knew him. I only met him once."

"He must have been *something like* if you can blush at his memory after meeting him only once."

Georgy smiled. "Yes, I think he was 'something like'. But some designing minx is certain to have snared him by this time." *Lucy Traherne, I shouldn't be a bit surprised,* she thought.

"Handsome, I suppose he was," Mary speculated. "And clever, too. You'd not be captivated by anyone who wasn't clever."

"Yes, he was handsome and clever. Rich, too, they say." She grinned at her new friend. "Sounds too good to be true, doesn't he? No doubt if I'd gotten to know him better I would have learned that none of it was true."

Mary giggled. "You must be right. Handsome, clever and rich is too much to expect in any one man. So you may as well stay."

Georgy's face fell as the awareness of her present problem flooded over her again. "Stay? And wait for Lady Ruckworth to discharge me?"

Mary shrugged helplessly. "May as well, if you've nothing better to go to. Her ladyship's bound to wait a fortnight or two before deciding. In that time, perhaps something else'll turn up." She patted Georgy's hand comfortingly. "Let's hope for the best. Now, no more brooding. Get a good night's sleep. Everything'll look better in—"

"I know," Georgy said drily. "Everything always looks better in the morning."

Mary's platitude turned out to be true; everything *did* look better in the morning, for, as she approached the schoolhouse door, she noticed not four but six children waiting in front of the schoolhouse. Six! She stopped in her tracks and counted them to be sure, but she hadn't made a mistake. There were really six! Had a miracle occurred? Had one of the parents she'd spoken to last night relented? Perhaps Mr. Sloper had "thought on it" and sent Timothy and Molly. She hurried her step, but as she came closer she saw that the boy was much too big to be Timothy. Then, who—? She blinked in astonishment, not able to credit what she saw with her own eyes. The big boy was Benjy Kissack!

She forced herself to be calm and walked with unhurried step to the door. She gave greetings to each of the four pupils of the day before and sent them inside. Then she turned to the newcomers. They were indeed Benjy Kissack and his sister Dorrie, the two children who'd enacted the

little schoolroom dialogue the night before. "Good morning," she murmured, keeping her voice from revealing her
delight. "Does your father know you're here?"

Benjy shrugged. "Ye mustn't mind Pa, Miss," he said.
"He had a shove in the mouth too many last night. He
always rants on like that when he's cupshotten. He don'
mean anythin' he says."

"He certainly sounded as if he meant it . . . every word,"
Georgy muttered to herself before asking the boy, "Did he
send you to enroll?"

"Not me, Miss. Jus' Dorrie, 'ere. Ma says to tell ye
she's sorry 'bout Dorrie's schooldress bein' tore. She
didn't 'ave time to sew it this mornin'."

"That's all right," Georgy assured him, her spirits lifting
like the morning fog. "I'll do it for her. But why won't you
come in, too?"

"Oh, not me, Miss Vail," the boy said, backing off.
"I'm too big. I on'y come to bring Dorrie." And he ran off
down the path.

Oh, well, Georgy thought as she put an arm about Dorrie's shoulders and brought her inside, *at least it's one
more. Now I have five.*

She'd barely had time to enter Doreen Kissack's name
on the new class roll in the daybook when twelve-year-old
Sarah Putman appeared in the doorway with little Hester in
tow. "My ma tole us to come. She said that 'er girls would
learn readin' and writin' no matter what Pa thinks."

Georgy wanted to laugh out loud. She hadn't won Willy
Putman, who was more useful to his family picking hops
than going to school, but she had both the Putman girls.
The girls would show Mr. Putman what a little learning
could do! With a feeling of real elation, she entered their
names on her list. There were now seven.

Two days later, Molly Sloper joined the class. Her
friend Hester Putman had been coming home from school
and telling Molly about the wonderful stories Miss Vail had
told. Molly had begged her father to let her come. Her
father had "thought on it," she reported, and had decided
that if Sarah and Hester Putman were going to school, then
his girl would, too. "Wonderful!" Georgy exclaimed, feel-

ing a sudden surge of confidence in herself and in the future of her school. She added Molly Sloper's name to the list with a flourish. Now there were eight.

The following week Willy Putman came to school, his hair slicked down, his hands clean and his cherubic face shining. Georgy was surprised and delighted. "Don't you have any more hops to pick?" she asked him. The boy shook his head. "There's 'ops to pick 'til the first snow," he said, "but Pa says never min' the 'ops."

"Mr. Putman said *that?* But he told me he didn't think school was useful for boys," Georgy said, confused.

"That's so. But yestid'y Pa saw Molly write 'er name. 'E says if a little girl like Molly kin write 'er name, then a big boy like me should learn to write mine."

Georgy, overwhelmed, kissed his cheek. "And so you will, Willy, my boy. And so you will. You'll be writing your name by this evening, I promise. It won't take a fine nine-year-old lad like you more than one day. Here, come and watch me do it." And with the boy peering in fascination over her shoulder, she inscribed his name on the list. William Putman. That made nine.

When she announced the new total to the vicar at dinner that night, he raised a glass of port and toasted her. "Good for you, Miss Vail," he said heartily. "Lady Ruckworth will be pleased."

"*Everyone* is pleased," Mary whispered in her ear as she passed by with the serving tray. "Our new teacher is *something like.*"

Georgy was pleased, too, but not yet completely satisfied. Nine was not twelve, after all. And she'd not yet won the pupil she wanted more than any other to enroll: Benjy Kissack.

Every morning Benjy Kissack accompanied his sister Dorrie to the schoolhouse door. Every morning Georgy asked him to come in, and every morning he shook his head and ran off. There was no youngster. Georgy wanted more desperately in her class. She'd been very impressed by his clever mimicry of a teacher that night in the Kissack cottage, and she wanted to show him that not all teachers were so priggish. Besides, she was certain he'd make an able and eager student if he were convinced that the studies were more substantial than the little rote dialogues he'd been exposed to before. With his intelligence and a good education, he might make more of his life than his father had been able to do. He might learn to be a bookkeeper or a law clerk or a man of business. But she didn't know how to go about coaxing him in to class. Certainly she could not return to the Kissack cottage and speak to the father; she hadn't become *that* confident.

But one day Georgy devised a scheme. When he came to the schoolhouse to deliver Dorrie, she greeted him at the door with a cup of tea in her hand. "Won't you take some tea with us before you go?" she asked.

He shook his head and started off down the road, but then he thought better of it. "Don' mind if I do," he said, turning back. He came inside, and she handed him a cup. The tea was good and hot, and he had to sip slowly. While he drank, Georgy asked Sarah (who was closest in age to Benjy and was already a proficient reader) to read aloud a wonderful adventure tale about a boy without a name called "Nix Naught Nothing." Benjy could hardly tear himself away when his tea was drunk.

Benjy Kissack took tea every morning and lingered in the classroom until he saw the teacher's eyes on him. Then he snatched up his cap and ran out. Georgy began to despair of ever enticing the boy to enroll. However, she had better luck with Timothy Sloper. Molly had taken home a childish picture she'd drawn in class and brought it back the next day vastly improved. "Timmy fixed it," she told the teacher. Georgy was amazed at the sureness and confidence of Timothy's pencilings. She rolled the paper up thoughtfully. *That boy should be here at school instead of picking stones in the fields,* she told herself. *I ought to speak to his parents.* But she was reluctant to return to the cottages after the experience with the Kissacks. She hesitated for a while until she remembered that Timothy Sloper's father hadn't been nearly as frightening as Mr. Kissack. She convinced herself to try again.

That very evening she bravely presented herself at the Sloper cottage. "I think the child has real talent, Mr.

Sloper," she told the boy's father sincerely, showing him the drawing.

Mr. and Mrs. Sloper looked at the drawing dubiously. "It's on'y a little farmhouse," Mr. Sloper said, unimpressed, "an' the farmer ain't even got a face."

"But look at the horse," Georgy pointed out. "There aren't many children who have so keen a sense of proportion. And the barn not only has depth but character."

"The horse is real good," Mrs. Sloper agreed. "And the farmer . . . 'e looks sorta . . . strong."

Georgy beamed at her. "Exactly so, Mrs. Sloper. The boy's drawing has strength. You know, Mr. Sloper, I could give the boy some instruction in sketching. Don't you think Timothy could spend at least a little time in school?"

Timothy's mother and father exchanged looks. Georgy could see their pride. But Mr. Sloper only said, "I'll think on it."

The next morning, however, Timothy came to school and told Georgy to add his name to the list. There were now ten.

School had now been in session for over a fortnight. Mary assured her that there was no question of Lady Ruckworth's closing the school now. True, Georgy was short of the dozen that had been the goal, but ten was not an inconsiderable number. There was nothing to worry about. Nevertheless, ten was not twelve. She wished she'd managed to enroll twelve, as Mrs. Jayce had done, but ten seemed to be all she would have.

One morning during the third week of school, while the pupils were assembling, she heard the sounds of squabbling just outside the door. She went out to find Dorrie Kissack in tears and her big brother looking angry and embarrassed. "What is it, Dorrie?" she asked, kneeling down and wiping the girl's face with her handkerchief.

"It's all *his* f-fault!" the girl whined, giving her brother's leg a little kick. "I don' see why he has to w-walk wiv me every day. Molly comes by herse'f, an' she's no bigger'n me. Besides, she's my bestes' friend, an' we like to walk t-together. Wivout a b-big bruvver nuzzlin' in."

Georgy looked up at Benjy, whose ears immediately

turned red. "But if your mother wishes him to walk with you, Dorrie—" she began.

"Ma don' care. She knows I kin find the way by myse'f," the child insisted.

Benjy lowered his eyes and shuffled his feet. "Shut yer clappin' maw, Dorrie. Ye don' need to raise a dust. I won't take ye no more."

Georgy stood up and studied the boy speculatively. "If it's settled, then, Dorrie, you may go inside. I'll be right in. I want to speak to Benjy alone."

Dorrie ran off happily, but the boy looked more awkward than ever. "I'd best be goin', Miss," he mumbled. "Sorry to 'ave troubled ye."

"It was no trouble, Benjy. But there's something I'd like to know. Have you been accompanying Dorrie because you like coming in to the class?"

Benjy shrugged. "I s'pose. There was the tea and all . . ."

"Come now, boy, let's have the truth. You don't linger about for half an hour just to drink tea."

He threw up his hands in a gesture of surrender. "So I like comin'. What's it matter? I'm too big fer to go to yer school."

"No, you're not, Benjy. You're only fourteen."

"Closer to fifteen."

"But you do like coming to my class, don't you?"

"Yes, ma'am, I do. It's not like when I went to school before, just memorizin' prayers an' readin' scripture. Your class . . . it's more . . . you know . . . interestin'. Like the other day, the history lesson. How the Black Death come from fleas on the rats. I never know'd that."

"Then why won't you enroll?"

"'Cause I'm fifteen. The others'd all laugh at me."

"They don't laugh when they see you there in the morning, do they?"

"That's 'cause they know I'm on'y stoppin' by. Besides, I'm workin' steady. Apprentice to the smith I am. An' who ever heard of a blacksmith's apprentice goin' to school?"

"I don't care if it's unheard of, Benjy. If you'd truly like to come to school, we could find a way. What if you come

only for an hour or two? Would the smith you work for
permit that?"

Benjy rubbed his chin, his expression half eager and
half hesitant. "I dunno. He might. If I go in to the smithy
earlier, I s'pose . . ."

She smiled and took his hand. "Then it's agreed. Speak
to the smith and let me know your hours. I'll schedule the
history lessons for when you're here." She turned and
started for the door. "And if anyone should laugh, Benjy,"
she added, looking back over her shoulder, "why, then,
we'll—"

The boy grinned. "We'll let 'em."

She rejoined the class feeling truly pleased. *That,* she
told herself happily, *makes eleven.* It wasn't twelve, but at
least the eleven were there because they wanted to come,
not because they'd been frightened into it.

Two days later Mary Hunsford appeared at the schoolroom door, holding both her daughters by the hand. "Here
we are, Miss Vail," she clarioned from the doorway.

Georgy, who was sitting at her table with Hester on her
lap (instructing the youngest child in her reading by using
her own copy of *Mother Goose's Melody* while the rest of
the pupils were silently reading from the required *Book of
Common Prayer),* looked up at the figures in the door in
bewilderment. She set Hester on her feet, jumped up and
hurried to the door. "Mary? What on earth—?"

Mary gave her a conspiratorial smile. "Mr. Hunsford
finally agreed," she whispered. "Maggie and Betsy nagged
and niggled at him until he gave in."

For a moment, Georgy didn't grasp her meaning. "Gave
in to what?"

"To letting them go to *your* school!" Mary's eyes
glowed in triumph. "Grace, my love, I've brought two
more pupils for you."

Georgy could scarcely believe it. The vicar's daughters!
What a feather in her cap! And what was more, she'd out-
done her predecessor. The awesome Mrs. Jayce had had
twelve. But she, Grace Vail . . . she had *thirteen.*

Chapter 15

Once Peggy had made up her mind to take Georgy's place, she threw herself into the role with a will. She had less than a week to prepare herself for her first public appearance as Georgianna Verney, but she was determined to pull it off for Jeremy's sake. She listened for hours to Lady Horatia's recital of Georgy's history and dutifully memorized the names of all her friends, as well as their places of residence, their siblings and their family structures. She sat at the table every morning at ten while Spiers instructed her in such things as the proper use of the fruit knife and the dessert spoon, the difference between coffee and tea cups, and the way to hold a wineglass. Allie gave her daily lessons in curtseying and how to offer her hand for kissing. And every afternoon, she practiced the gavotte, the waltz and all sorts of country dances, with Jeremy as her partner and Allie playing the piano for them.

It was only the dancing that gave her pleasure. She took naturally to dancing, so the steps were not difficult to learn. And Jeremy was charming as he played the role of suitor, teaching her the art of ballroom badinage. She learned so quickly that she often set all three of them laughing uproariously. "You are looking especially lovely this evening, Miss Verney," Jeremy would begin, whispering the words in her ear with practiced gallantry.

"Thank you, sir," she'd riposte with a twinkle, "but I was told you are a dreadful flirt and that I should believe only half of what you say."

"Only half, ma'am?"

"Only half, sir. My problem is that I don't know what

half of 'especially lovely' amounts to. Does it mean that I look slightly better than my usual frumpish self?"

This would make Allie giggle, but Jeremy would remain in character and suppress his smile. "I assure you, ma'am," he would declaim in mock offense, "that whoever told you I lie has grossly maligned me. I have been wedded to truth since infancy."

"Oh? Am I to take it, then, that you are now a widower?"

Such a remark as that would send them all into whoops. Peggy loved playing these games. She loved flirting with Jeremy and making him laugh. She especially loved feeling his arm about her in a dance. Sometimes the touch of his fingers on her arm would make her skin tingle, and she would look up and catch his eye. He would color up at the ears, and she'd know that he, too, was affected by his closeness. It was hard, at such moments, to remind herself that this was all pretense.

But soon the time for laughter and game-playing was gone, for the night of the Traherne ball was fast approaching. Everyone became more serious. The "ballroom badinage" changed to repeated reminders that she must speak in a hoarse voice. Lady Horatia's quizzes became nerve-wracking, for mistakes could no longer be countenanced; Peggy would be bound to fail if, for instance, she called Monte Traherne Lucy's *cousin* instead of her *brother*. There was now an urgency in her ladyship's corrections. It was absolutely necessary that Peggy be completely familiar with all Georgy's friends. She had also to ape Georgy's posture and her gestures, and in these matters the whole family made corrections. Under this constant critical surveillance, Peggy became tense as a harp string, and only Jeremy's repeated assurances that he would be close at hand all evening to rescue her if she gave herself away had any soothing effect on her.

By the time the night of the ball arrived, Peggy felt benumbed. She put on the ruby gown Lady Horatia had chosen and sat wordless as Betsy dressed her hair. "Don't take on so," the abigail consoled her as she finished. "I've dressed Miss Georgy since she was no bigger than that stool, and I'd have to look real sharp not to be fooled myself. You'll do tonight, I promise you."

With that encouragement, Peggy threw a cloak over her shoulder and, holding her head at the angle she'd rehearsed and keeping her back straight, she descended the stairs. Lady Horatia, Jeremy and Allie were watching from the bottom. All three gave her encouraging smiles. Allie thrust a pair of white evening gloves into her hands and kissed her cheek. "It's almost as if Georgy's come back to us," she whispered.

Lady Horatia and Jeremy were cheerfully optimistic as they followed Peggy into the carriage, but Peggy herself was almost frozen with terror. Any error could ruin the plan and cause the Verneys to face a humiliating scandal. It all depended on her. Jeremy, noting her tense face, tried to relax her. "It won't be nearly as terrible as you think," he said. "Most people don't scrutinize others very closely. Their minds are too preoccupied with thoughts about themselves."

"Jeremy's quite right," Lady Horatia agreed. "Just remember not to behave like a frightened little mouse. You must speak up with confidence. A show of confidence will override anyone's doubts."

"Yes, ma'am," Peggy answered dutifully. But within herself she felt anything but confident.

Fortunately, the Traherne ball was a dreadful squeeze. Even though the season was long over and many of London's notables had already left town to winter in their country estates, there were enough remaining to choke the Traherne stairway and crowd the rooms. In such a crush, Peggy thought as she followed Lady Horatia and Jeremy up the stairs, she might not even be noticed. But no sooner had the thought crossed her mind than the sound of "Georgy! Georgy!" came floating down the stair. She looked up to see a young woman with beautiful auburn tresses waving wildly at her. "It's Lucy Traherne," Lady Horatia muttered without looking round. "Go up to her. Remember, *confidence*."

She threw a glance at Jeremy as she pushed past him.

He gave her a barely perceptible wink. "I'll be nearby if you need me," he whispered as she passed.

When she reached the top of the stairs, Lucy was waiting. "Georgy!" she exclaimed, flinging her arms about her guest. "It's been an *age!* I wanted so often to call on you during your illness, but Mama wouldn't permit—" She suddenly stopped speaking and gaped. "What is it, Georgy? You look so . . . so different."

Peggy was prepared for this. Shrugging carelessly, she answered in her rehearsed whisper, "So would you if you'd had a putrid fever for weeks. Do you think I look too fagged?"

"No, of course not," Lucy said, turning to wave at another friend who had just come up the stairs. "You look lovely in that color. I always said you shouldn't wear those mousy grays and puces you always choose."

Peggy felt lucky that there were so many guests squeezing by to distract Lucy's gaze. "I suppose you're right," she said, lowering her head so that her face would be shadowed. "But never mind about me. Tell me all the news I've missed."

"I've all sorts of things to tell you," Lucy said eagerly, slipping an arm about her friend's waist. "Come and make your greetings to Mama, and then we can find a quiet place to talk."

From the corner of her eye, Peggy could see Lady Horatia sigh in relief. Lucy had accepted her. The first and most difficult test had been passed.

Peggy suggested a loveseat in a dim corner of the ballroom as the setting in which to hold their tête-à-tête. "There, isn't this cozy? Now, what is the news?"

"I must be quick," Lucy informed her with a giggle, "for I've promised the first dance to Algy Colclough."

Peggy stiffened. Who was Algy Colclough? If Lady Horatia had ever mentioned such a ludicrous name, she would certainly have remembered it. She knew she'd never heard of the fellow before, yet Lucy's giggle indicated that he must have had *some* significance in their lives. "Not Algy!" she said with a noncommittal lift in her voice.

"Yes, do you *credit* it? Me, with Algy Colclough! I was certain it was you he secretly worshipped."

Here was the time to show confidence, Peggy realized. "Well, you can have him and welcome," she responded with daring. "I never had an interest in that direction."

"Oh, I know that, you goose. But you'd not admit to an interest in a man even if you had one. That's why I'm so delighted that Mama has agreed to accept Lord Maitland's invitation to Colinas Verdes. I'm going to keep close watch on you there."

"Are you going to Colinas Verdes too? How delightful!" Peggy tried to sound sincere, but in truth her heart failed her. It was plain that a real intimacy existed between Georgy and Lucy Traherne. If Lucy was to be a guest at Lord Maitland's place, it would be doubly hard for Peggy to succeed there. But this was not the time to worry about Colinas Verdes. She had tonight to deal with first. Fortunately, Lucy was too preoccupied with the doings on the dance floor to study her very closely tonight. Peggy looked Lucy bravely in the eye. "But why do you wish to watch me *there,* particularly?"

Lucy threw her a saucy grin. "I saw your face when you danced with Maitland all those weeks ago. Don't try to convince me, my girl, that you haven't an interest in that direc—Oh, blast, there's Algy bearing down on us. And Monte, too. Good God, what's Monte thinking of? I don't see why my idiotic brother wants to dance with you now."

The remark puzzled Peggy. "Why not now?" she asked.

"Because that's my other bit of news. It seems that Monte has got himself betrothed. *Almost* betrothed, to be accurate. Can you credit it?"

"Betrothed?" Peggy echoed, completely at a loss as to what to say. All she knew about Monte was that he'd been enamored of Georgy for years. But she'd not had the impression that Georgy returned his feelings. How was she supposed to react to the news of Monte's defection? If only she knew more about Georgy. *What sort of person is she?* Peggy wondered for the hundredth time. How would Georgy take the news that an old suitor had turned to another?

She didn't need the answer right at this moment, however, for Lucy had already turned to face her approaching
partner, Algy Colclough. "Make your bow to Georgy
quickly, Algy, for the set is beginning to form," she ordered, jumping up. "And as for you, Montague Traherne,
you may be my brother, but I must tell you that you're a
veritable bufflehead. You should be across the room giving
your arm to your—er, to a certain young lady—for the
first dance. If she sees you still hanging about after
Georgy, she'll be livid."

Peggy looked curiously at Monte Traherne. He was a
short, muscular fellow with an upturned nose and a wide,
slack-lipped mouth. He'd been keeping his eyes fixed on
Peggy's face during his approach, but he now turned and
glared at his sister. "I don't see where this is any of your
affair, Lucy, but if you must know, I've already informed
'a certain young lady' that I wished to pay my respects to
Georgy, not having seen her since her illness. Take my
odious sister away, Algy, so that I may visit with Georgy in
peace."

Lucy snorted and flounced off. Algy followed after
making Peggy a quick, awkward bow. Monte sat down
without further ado. "You look pale, my dear," he said,
taking her hand. "I can see you've had a bad siege."

"I thank you, Monte," she whispered in her carefully
rehearsed undervoice, "even though it's clear that by no
stretch of the imagination can that sentence be taken as a
compliment on my looks."

"I didn't mean to imply that there was anything wrong
with your looks, Georgy. It's just that you seem somehow—"

"I know. Different," she supplied drily.

"Yes. But lovely as ever, of course," he assured her.

"Am I indeed?" Peggy smiled, feeling more confident
now that she was engaging in the badinage in which she'd
been so carefully trained. "Are you sure you ought to say
that to me, Monte?"

"Why not?" he asked.

She gave him a sidelong glance. "I have it on good
authority that you're *almost* betrothed to another."

He reddened angrily. "Lucy told you! Damnation, she had no right! I wanted to tell you myself."

"You needn't fly into alt, you know. She didn't tell me the name of the fortunate young woman."

His choler and color subsided. "That's something, at least." He glanced over at her with a smirk. "It's Rosalind Peascott. The announcement's to be sent to the *Times* within a fortnight."

Her heart lurched. *"Rosalind—?"*

"Startled you, eh?" he chortled. "I thought it might. I wasn't good enough for *you*, but I stole Rosalind Peascott right from under your brother's nose."

Peggy stared at him in revulsion. No wonder Georgy had rejected this detestable creature. "That doesn't seem to me to be something to boast about," she said, withdrawing her hand from his hold.

"No? Well, I do. You always pretended to find me beneath your touch. I was not clever enough, not witty enough, not rebellious enough, not bookish enough, not musical enough... the list is endless. But Rosalind evidently doesn't find me so. She chose me over your so-admirable brother, whom you yourself would be the first to describe as handsome and clever and desirable. I think that gives me plenty of cause to boast."

Peggy turned her face away from him. "Then boast if you must, but not to me."

There was a moment of silence. Then she felt her hand being grasped again. "It is not too late, Georgy," he said in her ear. "The news of the betrothal has not yet been made public. I can still withdraw, if you give me the word. I offer myself to you one last time, even though you have no dowry and Rosalind's is considerable. It's you I've always wanted. Tell me you've changed your mind. Forget your childish objections and take me."

His hot breath on her neck revolted her. She wriggled her fingers from his grasp. "No, Monte," she whispered without turning her head, "I haven't changed my mind. I don't wish to marry you." She said the words without a moment's hesitation. She knew she'd said what Georgy would have wished her to say. In this one matter, at least, she felt she knew Georgy to the soul.

Monte got to his feet and glared down at her, his angry flush rising again to his forehead. "Very well, have your way. It will be better for me in the long run. Rosalind is the sort whose prettiness lasts, while you . . . you may be more beautiful now, but your illness has already subdued you. In a few years you'll be nothing but a withered, pathetic spinster. I feel sorry for you."

She watched with upraised brows as he strode away, feeling shaken but relieved. What a loathsome fellow he was, to be sure. If Rosalind had chosen him over Jeremy, the girl must be addled! She supposed that Jeremy would be hurt by this news (although he would not learn of it from *her*, Peggy promised herself), but she could not feel sympathy for him. If the silly Rosalind could tie herself to that repellent muckworm, she was not worthy of Jeremy's affections; and the sooner Jeremy was rid of her the better.

Before she could brush away her feeling of disgust at her last encounter, a young man presented himself to her and asked her to dance. He seemed to assume that she knew who he was, but she had no clue to his identity. She stood up with him for the next country dance but, lacking any information on what his past relationship with Georgy had been, said hardly a word to him. To make matters worse, she caught a glimpse of Jeremy dancing with a beautiful young woman who, she supposed (from the way Jeremy was gazing at her) must have been Rosalind. Her chest constricted with such a pang of jealousy that she didn't hear what her partner was saying to her. She answered with a mumble, wishing with all her heart she could be in another man's arms. Her partner looked decidedly chagrined and said not another word for the remainder of the set. After he'd returned her to her seat, she overheard him remark to a friend that Georgy Verney's illness had sapped her spirit.

She had to endure two more such dances in the next hour. When a fourth young gentleman presented himself to her, she felt she'd had enough. "I've decided not to stand up for this dance," she told him. "Pray excuse me, sir."

A GRAND DECEPTION 141

"Sir? *Sir?*" the fellow demanded furiously. "Do you think it amusing to speak with such ridiculous formality to someone you've known since we were both in swaddling clothes? Really, Georgy, it's the outside of enough that you haven't granted me a dance since your come-out. I know I trod on your toes at that time, but I assure you my dancing has improved a hundredfold since then!"

Peggy almost laughed aloud. If Georgy had no compunction about refusing to dance, even with fellows she'd known since childhood, then neither had she. "I'm certain it has," she said, her feeling of confidence blossoming like a rose, "but I'm too tired to put your claim to the test tonight."

The fellow glowered at her. "Hmmph!" he grunted before stalking off. "I heard Freddie say that your illness has sapped your spirit, but if you ask me, your spirit is as waspish as ever."

She returned to her place in the corner praying that no other dancing partners would present themselves. The strain was becoming too great. She lowered her head to keep any passing gentlemen from meeting her eye, but after a moment, to her dismay, she saw a pair of black-shod legs approaching her. Without lifting her eyes, she held up a hand. "Please don't bother asking," she said firmly. "I've had quite enough dancing for one evening."

But the black-shod feet did not turn away. "You can't refuse *me*, my dear," came a laughing voice. "I'm your *brother*."

"Jeremy!" She looked up at him in delighted relief. "Thank the Lord! You're the only gentleman who's approached me in the last hour whose name I know."

He grinned down at her. "I think you've done it, Peggy!" he whispered, taking a seat beside her. "Mama says that the only comment her friends have made regarding your appearance was that 'Georgy looks peaked'. Mama's overjoyed. And she's promised me that we can take our leave right after supper."

"Oh, good! Will they announce supper soon?"

"After the next dance, I believe."

Peggy's face fell. "Another dance? Must I—?"

"Yes, you must. You haven't yet stood up with *me*."

Her eyes widened. "With you? Are you cozzening me?" To dance with him just once this evening was all she'd been wishing for. If he could whirl her around the floor as she'd seen him whirl his Rosalind, Peggy might make him forget her, if only for a moment or two. And *she* could close her eyes and be a fairy-tale princess, if only for a moment or two. The prospect of dancing with him was so delightful she was almost afraid to believe it would actually happen. "Is it permissible for a gentleman to dance with his own sister?"

"Of course, you goosecap. Why not?" He stood up and offered her his arm. "But you must promise not to look up at me like that when we dance, for no sister looks at her brother so adoringly. A glance of *that* sort would give the whole game away."

Peggy lowered her eyes at once and let him lead her to the dance floor. She must indeed be careful not to look at him like that again, she warned herself. Another such adoring look might give away more than the game . . . it might give away her whole secret life!

Chapter 16

Peggy, having passed the preliminary skirmish, had now to be sent in to fight the major battle, to be held a few days hence at Maitland's estate in East Riding. Preparations for that encounter were hectic, for in addition to preparing Peggy, all the others had to prepare themselves. Even Alison had been invited to Colinas Verde, and she was as busily packing for the event as everyone else. A protracted stay in the country required dozens of costume changes; one needed morning clothes, out-of-doors raiment, afternoon dress, formal evening attire and bedclothes, to say nothing of riding clothes, sporting attire and traveling garments. In fact, for the four people in the Verney party, so many trunks, bandboxes and portmanteaux were required that an extra carriage was hired to transport them.

There was not time to alter every one of the garments that Georgy had left behind to Peggy's size, but Lady Horatia ordered Betsy to pack everything. "We shall be hard pressed to make do with what little Georgy left behind," she confided to the abigail worriedly.

"Miss Georgianna didn't take so much," the abigail argued, her loyalty to her missing charge as strong as ever. "On'y five gowns, as far as I kin count, and most of them too plain to use at Lord Maitland's."

"Perhaps you're right," her ladyship said, frowning at the pile of garments Betsy had heaped on Georgy's bed, "but most of these need still to be altered."

"Since y're takin' me with you to Colinas Verde, m' lady, I kin do the alterin' there," Betsy assured her. "Don't you fret about the clothes, ma'am. We'll manage."

But there was to be a great deal of fretting before the two carriages—one to transport the family and the other the baggage and the servants—set out for the north. There was so much last-minute scurrying and bustling (caused by her ladyship's nervous conviction that many essential items had been forgotten but which were shown, after protracted and harried searches, to have been packed after all) that they departed two hours late. Jeremy had hoped they could bed down for the night at an inn near Leicester, but they only made it as far north as Market Harborough, and even an early start the following morning did not prevent their arriving at Colinas Verde after dark. Thus they were unable to get a good view of the grounds. Their first sight of the mansion, however, caused them all to gasp. "Look Mama," Allie cried excitedly, "every window is alight!"

Allie was right. The windows gleamed, even the small, square ones on the third story. In their glow the visitors could see that the wide, three-storied edifice was awesome. Beautifully proportioned in its grandeur, its symmetrical facade was embellished by a slightly projecting entrance topped by a six-pillared portico two stories high. This, too, was alight; two enormous lanterns, hanging beneath the pediment, illuminated the portico with special brilliance. The entire building seemed to shed a jewelled radiance on the surrounding landscape.

Before the travelers had time to drink in the details, their host himself—followed by what seemed a regiment of footmen—came out to greet them. Maitland, already dressed for evening in a faultless coat that put his former evening wear to shame, looked every inch the wealthy peer he was. Lady Horatia, as he helped her down from the carriage, couldn't help gawking at him. Gone was the shabby, unkempt, weather-beaten fellow who'd given her his lobster-cake. His hair was cut and brushed into the fashionable "Brutus," his neckcloth folded in a "Waterfall" so impeccable that only a valet of the first rank could achieve it, and his coat so perfectly cut (surely by either Weston or Stultz) that even to *think* that his shoulders suggested a farm laborer's would be a gross calumny. If he'd looked like this when she'd first met him, Horatia would have known at once who he was. She was stricken almost speechless by the change in him. "Y-your l-lordship!" she stammered.

He looked at her quizzically. "You were calling me Tony when we parted at the Denham's," he reminded her with a warm smile that instantly transformed him to the fellow she remembered. "Is it my new haircut that's put you off? I assure you it will be shaggy again by the end of the week."

"Tony," she murmured in relief, giving him her hand. "How good to see you again! And I'm not in the least put off by your haircut. It is very *comme il faut.*"

"I hope so," he confided with a twinkle. "I did it to impress your daughter."

"You didn't have to cut your hair to impress *me,*" came a teasing voice behind him. It was Alison, who'd jumped down from the carriage as soon as her mother had alighted. "I need more than modish haircuts to be impressed."

"Alison!" her mother snapped, horrified.

But Maitland only laughed. "Ah, this is Miss Verney the Younger, I presume. What *would* impress you, Miss Verney?"

Allie giggled. "Oh, I don't know. Shirtpoints reaching to your ears, perhaps. Or satin lapels on your coat, even though they say Mr. Brummel dislikes them."

"Sounds too foppish for me, too, I'm afraid. Besides, Miss Alison Verney, pretty as you are, *you* are not the daughter I wish to impress."

She tossed her head. "I would be, if I were a bit older."

"I have no doubt of it," the Viscount agreed as he turned to greet Jeremy, who'd just descended. "Welcome to Colinas Verde, Captain," he said, extending his hand.

"How do you do, my lord?" Jeremy studied the older man's face as they shook hands. Despite the Viscount's modish garb, Jeremy could see that the fellow had a straightforward gaze, a strong face and a good handshake. He liked him at once. "I must thank you for inviting—" But at that moment Maitland's eyes lifted to the carriage door with a look of such eagerness that Jeremy stopped speaking.

Peggy stood in the carriage doorway, offering her hand

to a footman. But Maitland crossed to the steps in two strides and waved the footman off. "Miss Verney," he said with unmistakable excitement, "at last!" He took her hand and helped her down. "I *told* you we would meet again," he said triumphantly as he raised her hand to his lips.

"How do you do, Lord Maitland," Peggy answered with perfect propriety, gazing down at his bent head.

But perfect propriety and this modulated, whispery voice were not what Maitland was anticipating. His head came up at once, something of his delight washing out of his face. "It *is* Miss Georgianna Verney, is it not?"

"Yes, of course," Peggy answered nervously, trying but failing to radiate "confidence."

Jeremy held his breath as Maitland straightened and stared at Peggy from beneath a furrowed brow. "Are you feeling quite the thing, Miss Verney? You seem... different."

Jeremy was amazed at the man. Many people who'd known Georgy for years had noticed less than Maitland, who'd met her only once. Horatia, too, was amazed, but she didn't have time to ruminate on the matter. She had to move quickly to end this crucial encounter. "She's been ill, you know, Tony," she put in, taking Peggy's arm and pulling her away from him. "A dreadful siege of putrid fever."

"No, I *didn't* know," his lordship said in immediate concern. "Forgive me, Miss Verney, for keeping you standing out here in the chill. Come, let's get you all inside at once." And with the sincerest solicitude, he escorted them within.

The interior of the house was as impressive as the outside, but the Verney party had no time to look about. Dinner time was almost upon them, and they had to establish themselves in their rooms and change. By the time they came down again, the other house guests were already gathered in the library. Although the room was large, they made quite a crowd. Countess Lieven (whose husband, the Ambassador, was too busy with state affairs to leave London for a protracted country stay) had come with a handsome young nephew visiting from Austria; the four Trahernes—Lucy, Monte and their parents—were present, as were the three Peascotts: Sir Basil, his wife and his daughter Rosalind; Lord Denham (who was Maitland's closest friend) and his wife Letty (who had agreed to act as Maitland's hostess) completed the party. With their host and the four members of the Verney party, that made a lively group of sixteen. The warm, book-lined room rang with laughter and good fellowship, and everyone (except Peggy, who was convinced that a gaggle of hummingbirds had lodged in her stomach) seemed imbued with a delightful feeling of anticipation. The fortnight ahead promised to be filled with gaiety, games and good times, all set against a background of comfort and luxury. An aura of delicious expectancy hung in the air like the ladies' perfume; this glittering gathering was only the beginning of what everyone presumed would be a wonderful country holiday.

When the Maitland butler announced dinner, the guests —knowing they were about to partake of the very first dinner to be served in the banqueting room of the newly renovated mansion—paraded in carrying their aura of excited anticipation with them. Their excitement proved to be justified; the room was magnificent. It was large enough to accommodate a dinner party of twice the size. The walls were covered with pale blue damask, which also covered the chairs, a Persian carpet dressed the floor, and three glittering chandeliers hung on chains from a high, blue-and-gilt-painted ceiling. The table was set with gold plate, Sevres china and faceted crystal, all gleaming in the glow of four branched candelabra set at intervals along the table between large epergnes filled with exotic fruit. And, to insure that each guest was seated comfortably, a white-gloved footman stood behind each chair. To Peggy, the room was overwhelming. Even in her most romantic fancies of princes and castles, she'd never imagined anything quite like this.

Maitland took his place at the head of the table, and Letty Denham, elegantly attired in green satin, with her famous emerald hanging from a chain at her throat, sat opposite him at the foot as the hostess should. Peggy had feared that she would be seated next to him but discovered, to her relief, that she was placed several seats away. The place of honor at Maitland's right had been properly awarded to the Countess Lieven. Lady Horatia, seated in a place of quite satisfactory importance close to the head, found herself beside Roger Denham, who made a charming dinner companion. But she kept a close watch on her host and saw that he turned his eyes to Peggy very often. She could not read his expression with any certainty, but there was no doubt that he was studying her "daughter" much too closely for comfort.

Jeremy intended to keep an eye on Maitland also, but he found himself distracted by the presence of Rosalind just opposite him at the table. The girl looked very pink and nervous, and she assiduously avoided his eyes all through the long first course. The reason was soon made clear. During the second course, Sir Basil Peascott clinked on his glass for attention. When the talk quieted down, he rose to his feet. He first proposed a toast to the host, and then, when that had been made, he proposed a second. "You won't mind if I announce some news of a personal nature tonight, will you, Maitland?" he asked, his ruddy face beaming. "The news will be announced in the *Times* quite soon, but I couldn't resist passing it on now, among these good friends and in these magnificent surroundings, eh, what? So, although it's a bit beforehand, I'll speak my piece, eh? Glasses all full, are they? Then, here's to my daughter Rosalind, who has accepted an offer of marriage from none other than Mr. Montague Traherne, who is sitting there just two seats down from me! What do you think of that, eh?" He lifted his glass. "To Rosalind!"

An excited hubbub broke out as glasses were raised and congratulations and good wishes were expressed to the Trahernes and Lady Peascott. Peggy's eyes flew to Jeremy's face. The poor fellow's cheeks had whitened, and although he'd risen to his feet with the others and manfully raised his glass, she could see that he'd been dealt a blow.

Later that evening, when the men rejoined the ladies after their hour's masculine indulgence in port and politics, and card tables were set up, Peggy tried to speak to Jeremy in private, but he was snared by the Countess to make a fourth for whist. Peggy herself was asked by Maitland to join the circle at his table playing silver-loo, but she hoarsely informed him that she'd promised to join Lucy Traherne and Alison in a game of ombre.

The games seemed to Peggy to go on for hours. The strain of having to pretend to be familiar with a game she'd just learned unnerved her, despite Allie's quick-witted assistance every time she got into trouble. To make matters worse, she could not forgot the pain in Jeremy's face when Sir Basil had made his announcement. When at last the players began to drift away from the tables, and Lord Maitland announced that a late supper was being served in the East Drawing Room, it occurred to her that this might be her opportunity to seek out Jeremy and offer him some comfort. But before she found him, she saw Maitland approaching her, and, having no energy left to face the strain of a private conversation with *him*, she declined his escort to the buffet supper and asked to be excused. It had been a fatiguing day, she told him, and she wanted nothing more than to go upstairs to her bed.

Maitland kept up a cheerful-host facade for the rest of the evening, but he was painfully aware that somewhere beneath the surface of his consciousness he'd suffered a blow. Whether his depressed feelings were caused by Miss Verney's apparent desire to avoid him or his disappointment in this second encounter with her he didn't know. He needed a quiet moment to think, but he knew he would find no such moment until the last guest had bid him good night.

This did not come to pass until well after midnight. Then he had to confer with his butler about the plans for the next day. It was almost one A.M. when he finally made his way to the library, where he knew a comfortable chair, a banked fire, a bottle of brandy and some soothing solitude awaited him. But he found Lord Denham there ahead of him, clad in a dressing gown and lounging casually on a wing chair before the fire. "Roger, old boy, why aren't you abed?" he asked, pausing in the doorway.

Roger, who'd been Maitland's friend since their boyhood days at Eton, turned in his chair, propped an elbow on the arm and rested his chin on his hand, all the while eyeing his friend closely. "Letty and I both agreed that you seemed blue-deviled this evening," he said. "She ordered me to come down and inquire whether you have any need of my counsel, support or sympathy."

"I always have need of them," Maitland answered, entering the room and crossing to the table where the brandy bottle had been placed, "but there's nothing on my mind so urgent that it requires keeping you from your bed."

"Are you sure?" Roger asked earnestly. "I haven't seen quite such a look in your eyes since the day you told me your father had ordered you abroad."

"Do I seem as blue-deviled as that? Dash it all, Roger, I thought I was performing my host-role charmingly," Maitland muttered as he poured two brandies.

"So you were. No one but we could have noticed. What is it, Tony? The Verney girl?"

"Yes. Here, have a brandy. You can offer me counsel and sympathy as long as it takes to drink it. Then it's off to bed with you." He cast himself into a chair before the fire and put his feet up on the hearth. "Have I been an utter fool about her, Roger?"

"In what way a fool?"

"In every way. Believing that she was the woman I wanted from the very first moment I saw her, for one thing. Can a man have the measure of a girl at first glance?"

Roger shook his head. "Not very likely."

"But you and Letty . . . you knew at once, didn't you?"

"Not quite at once. Or rather, *she* did, but I met her many times before I even liked her. Women have better instincts for that sort of thing."

"Then you're saying I *was* a fool."

"I'm saying that your first impression could have been askew. Is that what's happened, Tony? Has your second impression of her undone the first?"

Maitland stared into his brandy glass. "I don't know. She scarcely seems like the same girl."

"I don't know Georgianna Verney very well, I admit, but she seems her usual lovely self to me. What is it about her that disturbs you?"

"It's hard to say. She seems a withdrawn, even frightened creature, not at all like the girl who so charmed me at your ball. That night she seemed like a . . . a . . . what is it you call those little firework things that whirl about and spin out sparks?"

"A girandole?"

"Yes, a girandole." Maitland shut his eyes, remembering. The girl *had* spun out sparks that night. She'd made the very air around her glitter . . . or so it had seemed to him. But there was nothing like a girandole about the girl he'd welcomed to his home this evening. "Can I have been so mistaken? So utterly besotted as all that?" he muttered in anguish.

"I don't know what to answer, Tony," Roger said, considering the question thoughtfully. "You've never said anything like this before. I've known you through many affairs of the heart . . . when we were young, and later during your travels . . . but they were always casual and brief. In fact, Letty and I were afraid that you were immune to the usual female wiles. So it's hard to imagine you as besotted."

"But this time was different. This girl touched a part of me I didn't know existed. I actually felt *smitten*." He looked across at his friend with knit brows. "Do you know why I rushed so with this renovation? Why I hired an army of workers, hounded them unmercifully, pressed Letty ceaselessly to help me choose the furniture and fabrics? Because I couldn't wait to ask the girl here! I wanted everything ready . . . everything perfect. I thought we could learn to know each other here in the very place I dreamed we would both one day inhabit."

Roger nodded. "Letty suspected it."

"But don't you see? I went off at half-cock." He stood up and leaned his forehead on the mantel, staring down into the fire. "It was all for nothing."

"I don't understand why you say that. She's been here only a few hours."

"Yes, but already I can see that her character is not as fascinating to me as I thought. And she seems equally uninterested in *me*."

Roger rose and joined his friend at the fire. "It seems to

me, Tony, that you're not being fair. Lady Horatia told me the girl has been quite ill. It would not be surprising if a long illness dampened her spirit, would it? And furthermore, she spent most of this day being jostled about in a cramped carriage on a long journey. How fascinating can a woman be expected to be after all that?"

Maitland stared at him speculatively. "You're right. I'm not being fair."

"Not to her, and not to yourself." He put an arm about his friend's shoulders and moved him toward the door. "It's much too soon to make judgments," he added as they made their way to the stairs. "You have time. There's a whole fortnight ahead."

Chapter 17

Jeremy did not easily fall asleep that night. Rosalind, of whom he'd dreamed for three years, had betrayed him, and the betrayal stuck in him like a knife. He tossed and turned in bed for what seemed like an eternity, but finally his thoughts became unfocused and his eyes closed. At that moment there was a scratching at his door. He came awake at once. Who could be at his door at this hour? he wondered. It had to be two in the morning, or later! He fumbled about awkwardly for his candle, the darkness and the unfamiliarity of the room making it difficult. When at last he'd lit it, he stumbled to the door. "Who is it?"

"It's me, Peggy," came the answer.

"Peggy!" He opened the door and gaped at the girl for a moment. She was clad in one of Georgy's dressing gowns, her feet were bare (entrancingly so, one part of his mind noted), and her hair was hanging loosely over her shoulders, the way it had been when he'd first seen her. "Good God, girl, what is it?" he whispered, pulling her in and shutting the door behind her. "If anyone's seen you, there'll be the devil to pay."

"Why?" she asked in bewilderment. "I'm supposed to be your sister, after all."

"That makes little difference. A lady doesn't come to a man's room in the dead of night, no matter who—"

"No one saw me, Jeremy. I waited until I was certain that everyone was asleep." She glanced up at him worriedly. "I just had to talk to you."

"Why? Is something wrong?"

"No, not with me. But I . . . I saw your face when Sir

Basil announced your Rosalind's betrothal. I couldn't sleep..."

He stared at her face in the candlelight, surprised and touched. "Because of me?"

"Yes, of course." She put a hand gently on his arm. "I hate to... to see you hurt."

"It's kind of you to concern yourself about me, Peggy, but I shall survive. You, however, will be in a worse case than I if anyone should see you. You must promise me never—and I mean *not ever,* no matter how pressing you think your problem is—*never* to go to a man's room at this hour! Do you prom—?"

A sound interrupted him—another scratching at the door! Their eyes met in horror. "Oh, my Lord," Peggy whispered, "who can it be?"

"I haven't the slightest idea," Jeremy muttered. "I feel as if I'm living some sort of nightmare!" He looked about him desperately. "You'll have to hide yourself."

The scratching at the door sounded louder now. Peggy's eyes were wide as saucers. "But where—?"

"There! In the wardrobe. Quickly, now, and don't make a sound!"

He set his candle down on his night stand, helped her climb in and shut the wardrobe doors. Then he crossed the room to the door. "Who is it?" he asked again. The only answer was another scratching sound. Gingerly, he opened the door a crack. It was Rosalind.

Stricken speechless, he stood aside as she stepped over the threshold in a rustle of filmy silk. Then, shaking himself, he closed the door behind her. "Rosalind!" he gasped.

"Oh, Jemmy, dearest!" she cried tearfully and threw herself into his arms.

He pulled down her arms and held her away from him. "Have you lost your wits? What are you doing here?"

"I had to see you, my love. To explain—"

"Explain?" he echoed absently, awkwardly aware that this scene was being overheard by his first visitor, now crouching in the wardrobe just behind him.

"About Papa. What he did tonight."

"Ah, yes, of course. Papa." Jeremy could feel himself

tighten. The anger that had kept him sleepless for hours flooded over him again. "He announced your betrothal, did he not? I was there, you know. I heard him. Did you come here in the dead of night, dressed in nothing but a . . . a chemise . . . just to repeat it to me?"

"This is not a chemise, you mooncalf," she corrected fondly. "It's a perfectly respectable morning robe. And of course I'm not going to repeat it. I only want to explain—"

He turned his back on her. "What is there to explain? You are betrothed. I find the facts quite clear. There is no need for explanations."

"You're angry, aren't you?" She came up behind him and slipped her arms about his waist. "Please, my dearest, don't be angry. It wasn't my fault."

"Wasn't it?" he demanded, forgetting the eavesdropper, the hour, the precariousness of Rosalind's situation in this room, and everything else but his own fury. "I suppose it wasn't you who told me—and with tears in your eyes, if memory serves—that you would give me all the time I needed."

"I know, dearest," she said, resting her head on his back, "but Papa insisted—"

"I'm sure he did. What did you expect? I would imagine *that* to be the very problem you'd prepared yourself to overcome when you promised me—it *was* a promise, wasn't it?—that you'd prevent him."

"I know I promised. But I didn't imagine it would be so difficult . . . and that it would take so . . . so *long* . . ."

He threw her arms from him and spun about. "Long? Three weeks, *long?*"

She lowered her head. Her underlip trembled, and she twisted her fingers together appealingly. "Three weeks *is* long when you're beset on all sides. And I *was* beset, my love. You d-don't know! When Papa learned that we'd been invited here with the Trahernes, he decided that this would be the perfect setting for the announcement. Nothing I said would dissuade him." Two big tears rolled down her cheeks. "I tried and tried—"

"Good God, Rosalind," Jeremy muttered, softening,

"don't start crying at this hour. You've got to get back to your—"

"I won't g-go until you've forgiven me! I couldn't eat or s-sleep if you don't!"

"What difference does it make if I forgive you or not? You're betrothed to another man now. I am no longer part of your life."

She threw herself upon his chest again. "Don't say that! *Don't!* Not ever! A betrothal is not a marriage vow, after all. I can always cry off, can't I?"

It was true, Jeremy thought; she was not lost to him yet. He shrugged in surrender, unable to resist her. He let his arms encircle her and put his lips against her temple. A nagging thought occurred to him that the girl in his arms was not behaving honorably to her affianced groom; she was using him, in fact, quite shabbily. But it was not her fault, he told himself. Her father had forced her into this unpleasant situation. And Jeremy would be a cad not to forgive her. "I love you, Rosalind," he murmured into her hair.

Her arms crept up and circled his neck. "Oh, so do I *you*, my dearest," she whispered and lifted her face to his. They kissed urgently, passionately, for a long moment. When he finally let her go, the clouds had all cleared from her face. "I knew everything would be all right if I could just see you alone," she crowed happily.

He brushed a curl back from her forehead. "That's only because I'm putty in your hands when you kiss me like that."

She giggled and drew him to the door. "I *do* know how to kiss, don't I? Good night, Jemmy. Remember that I love you no matter what befalls." She kissed him once more and slipped noiselessly out the door.

He stood at the door, motionless, bereft. His arms were strangely empty, and he shivered, feeling cold where a moment ago her body had warmed him. He sighed, thinking of the long fortnight ahead of him during which he would have to watch her performing the role of Monte's betrothed. If he ever came upon her kissing that worm, he might be driven to violence! Not that he was the hot-tempered sort, but it would give him enormous satisfaction to land a good right-handed facer on Monte's—

A sound behind him caused him to wheel about. "Good God, Peggy! I forgot you were—"

"Yes, so I gathered," she cut in, her voice icy.

He tried to see her expression, but she stood between him and the candle, her face shadowed. The only thing he could see was a halo of auburn hair. "I'm sorry, Peggy, I—"

"There's no need to apologize. I, too, would have forgotten everything if my beloved had fondled *me* so entrancingly."

There was a stinging acerbity in her tone that she'd never used before in speaking to him. He found it disconcerting. He wanted to make an equally stinging response. "See here, Peggy Birkin," he snapped, "I don't like your tone. Rosalind didn't 'fondle' me, as you put it."

"Oh, didn't she? I was here, you know. I have ears."

"It's not Rosalind's fault," he countered angrily, "if *you* had the poor judgment to come into a man's room in the wee hours of the morning!"

"And how about *her* poor judgment? I didn't hear you say anything about *that.*"

He glared at her shadowed face. "I don't wish to stand about here in the dead of night discussing Rosalind with you."

"Ooooh," she said in a sudden, exaggerated tone of self-abasement, "I'm sooooo sorry." The pitch of her voice was an unmistakable mockery of the voice of his beloved. "Please *forgive* me, *dearest* boy. I won't eat or sleep *ever again* if you don't," she mimicked.

Jeremy stiffened. "To make sport of a conversation you had no right to overhear is the height of vulgarity," he informed her coldly.

"Very well, then, I'm vulgar," she retorted, "but at least *my* behavior can't be called *stupid.*"

"Are you implying, ma'am, that I behaved stupidly? In what way, may I ask?"

"In every way! She led you by the nose, as easily as if you'd been her puppy!"

"I don't see—"

"No, of course you don't." She turned away from him in disgust. "You're too idiotic. Anyone but a fool could see that she is a conniving, designing baggage."

"Hold on there!" he ordered angrily, grasping the girl by the arms and forcing her to face him. "Don't say another word! I won't have you speaking that way about her!"

"I'll speak any way I wish! And I'm not speaking of her, I'm speaking of *you!* She let a couple of sham tears drip down her cheeks and you melted!"

He gave her a furious shake. "That's enough!"

"Ooooh!" she twittered in the high, mocking imitation of Rosalind's voice. "You're angwy, awen't you? Pweese, bewoved, don't be angwy. You'll make me cwy!"

Enraged, he pulled her to the door. "All right, Miss Birkin, you've played your little scene. It's time you took your leave."

"Yes, I'll go. I see you didn't need any comfort from me after all. A kiss from your little Rosalind chased all the doldrums away. I could have saved myself the trouble of coming."

"Yes, you could have. And I trust you'll not do it again."

She drew herself up proudly. "You can be sure of that. This is the last time I'll ever again come to your bedroom. But there is one thing . . . before I go . . ."

"What is that?" he asked suspiciously.

"This!" And to his utter astonishment, she reached up with both hands, grasped his neck, drew his head down and kissed him, hard.

His first reaction was anger, as if in response to an assault, and he tried to pull himself from her hold. But immediately he felt himself grow warm with desire. She was close against him, and he could feel every curve of her body through the soft dressing gown she wore. Her lips were full and moist against his, and the smell of her skin was intoxicating. He remembered the night at the inn, when he'd first met her; he'd wanted her so badly that night that he'd become dizzy. This present feeling was as dizzying as it had been then. He wanted to lift her up in the air, swing her about, feel her legs wrap round him and her bare feet clutch at his back. His arms, of their own accord, tightened about her waist. But the moment she felt his response, she broke away.

He peered into her face through the dim light. Was she laughing at him? "What was *that* for?" he demanded, trying not to reveal his breathlessness.

"Just to show you," she said, her hand on the doorknob.

"Show me what?"

"That your Rosalind is not the only one who knows how to kiss." And with that, she opened the door, ran out on her tantalizingly bare feet and left him alone.

Chapter 18

The gentlemen awakened early the next morning, for Lord Maitland had promised to take them shooting for grouse. The shooting party left the house before the first light, but the ladies, knowing that no gentlemen would be on hand until tea time, remained in their beds until midmorning—all except Peggy, who had not been able to sleep a wink all night. Humiliated by her unseemly behavior and heartbroken at the discovery of the depth of Jeremy's infatuation with Rosalind, she'd spent what remained of the night weeping. Early in the morning (it must have been before six) she heard the sounds of rain spattering her windowpanes, and, down below, the neighing of horses and the laughter of men. She went to her window and watched Maitland and his guests (Jeremy among them) troop off toward the woods as merrily as if the sun were shining. She watched until they disappeared and then returned to her bed, hoping to get at least a few hours of sleep. But it still eluded her.

Finally she gave up. She rose and dressed, and, knowing that there'd be no one downstairs with whom she'd have to make what she'd dubbed in her mind as "Georgy-talk," she went downstairs. As she hoped, the breakfast room was deserted except for a pair of footmen who were stationed there to help serve breakfast to anyone who should wander in. She let them load her plate with ham, eggs and muffins, and she sat down at the round table set in a bow window, stirred her coffee absently and let her food grow cold. It was there that, a few minutes later, she was discovered by the one she wanted least to face—Lord Maitland himself.

Lord Maitland had not slept well either. Only temporarily comforted by his talk with Roger, he'd been unable to find a place of emotional equilibrium between the heights of his anticipation of Georgianna Verney's arrival and the depths of his disillusionment when she'd finally arrived. As a result, he'd tossed and turned for hours. He'd eventually achieved an uneasy stability by promising himself to take the first opportunity to talk to the girl alone. This could be accomplished, he desperately hoped, the very next morning. With that goal in mind, he'd taken his guests to the home woods, set them up with their guns, assured them that rich numbers of their prey lay hiding in the underbrush, and left them on their own. He'd returned to the house determined to await Georgy's descent to breakfast, to detach her from whatever companion accompanied her, and to talk to her in private. Thus, when he discovered her alone in the breakfast room, he was overjoyed. "Miss Verney!" he greeted her heartily. "I *am* in luck! I expected to have to wait for you for hours."

She looked up with so distinct an expression of lugubrious dismay that it dashed out the flame of his eagerness with the effectiveness of cold water. "W-Wait for me?" she asked bewilderedly.

"Yes. I didn't expect you down so soon. Are you always an early riser, ma'am?"

"Yes, I suppose . . . I mean, no . . . that is, I sometimes . . ."

"Yes, no and sometimes?" He smiled down at her with beguiling charm, calculated to set her at ease. "Which is it, my dear?"

She tried to regain control of herself. Lowering her voice to the hoarse whisper she'd rehearsed, she answered, "I suppose it depends, my lord, on . . . on circumstances."

"Yes, it must, of course. But what circumstance brings you down so early today?"

She lowered her eyes. "I didn't sleep very well, I'm afraid."

"I'm sorry to hear that," he said, signaling to the footmen to leave them alone. He pulled up a chair beside her.

"I hope it wasn't the bed or something in the room that disturbed you."

"Oh, no, my lord, not at all! The bed . . . and all the furnishings, too . . . they are the most beautiful and comfortable and luxurious I ever . . . that is, I mean . . . they are lovely." Her eyes flew to his face in alarm. Had she become so mired in a tangle of awkwardness that she'd given herself away? But no. He was looking at her with nothing more than an expression of sincere concern. "I was just a little . . . overwrought. The journey, and all the excitement of our arrival, you see . . ."

He leaned back in his chair and stretched his booted legs out before him comfortably. "Yes, I do see, of course. It's strange, though. When I met you before, I had the distinct impression that it would take a great deal to make you overwrought."

"Had you, my lord? What was it that gave you that impression?"

"Just an air you had. You seemed so intrepid."

Peggy began to feel that she was being tested. There was something of a challenge in his comments, as if he were asking her why she seemed so different. She looked down at the table and stirred her coffee. "Did I?" she countered carefully.

"Yes, you did. Are you hinting that the impression was false?"

"Perhaps," she answered, using the bantering tone she'd rehearsed with Jeremy. "Although I suspect it was my reputation rather than my real nature that made you think so."

"Oh? Do you have a reputation for intrepidity?"

"Not that, exactly. La . . . Mama says I have a reputation for rebelliousness, which is close enough."

"Rebelliousness? How interesting! I wouldn't have thought of rebelliousness and intrepidity as synonymous, although they both suggest a bold-spirited nature. Nevertheless, it couldn't have been your reputation that gave me the impression that you are intrepid, my dear, for I'd never even heard of you before that night. No, it was something in *you*."

Peggy, not believing that her *own* nature could be called

bold-spirited, felt inadequate to her role. How could she make herself appear intrepid in his eyes? Georgianna Verney's shoes were becoming more and more difficult to fill. She did not know how to respond to Lord Maitland's challenge. The only thing she could think of to do, under the circumstances, was to resort to flirting. Not that she was in the mood for flirtation, for her heart was leaden inside her breast, but she didn't know how else to talk to Lord Maitland. "I hope, then, that intrepidity is something you *like* in females, my lord," she said, forcing herself to smile.

"Oh, very much," he assured her.

"Then please forget that I said I felt overwrought last night." She threw him a coquettish glance. "From now on I shall never be anything but intrepid in your presence."

His eyebrows lifted. "Good God, girl, I think you're trying to flirt with me!"

"Why the surprise, my lord? Surely many young ladies have done so before this."

"Yes, but not you. You said you detested flirting."

"Did I?" She put a hand to her forehead. *Damn you, Georgy Verney,* she thought, *why were you so blasted freakish? Why couldn't you have been like any other girl, so that I could have played this part with some confidence?*

The Viscount was studying her intently. "Don't you remember scolding me for trying to flirt with you?"

Peggy glanced at him from under her hand. She could say yes and try to bluff through the rest of the conversation, or she could say no and evade it. Lady Horatia had instructed her to claim poor memory if ever she found herself in trouble. "No, my lord, I'm afraid I don't," she said after a pause. "Everything about that evening is a little hazy in my mind."

His face fell. "Is it? I'm sorry to hear it." He got to his feet and stared at her for a moment, an unmistakable look of hurt in his eyes. Then he turned and stared absently out the window at the rain. "How ironic that you should have forgotten it all," he murmured, "and that I remember every word we said."

Peggy wanted to kick herself. Dash it all, she'd chosen the wrong reply. She'd probably ruined everything. Was there any way she could mend this rift? What could she possibly find to say? "I'd probably remember it all myself," she ventured, "if only I didn't have this blasted headache."

He turned round at once. "Oh, is *that* what's been troubling you? A headache? I'm so sorry. May I get you something for it? A James powder? A tisane?"

"No, thank you, sir. It will pass very soon, I'm sure of it. But now I must go upstairs and—"

"Please don't go yet, Miss Verney," he pleaded, sitting down again and reaching across the table for her hand. "Who knows when we shall have so good an opportunity to speak in private like this?"

But poor Peggy had had more than she could bear. The strain of pretense, added to the mortification of her experience the night before, made her feel unequal to the pressure this situation was placing on her. She couldn't face any more. Georgy Verney might be intrepid, but she, Peggy Birkin, had no more bold-spiritedness than a rabbit. "I'm sorry, my lord," she mumbled, snatching away her hand and getting up, "but I must go. I promised . . . Allie that I'd . . . I'd help her dress." And she turned and fled from the room.

Maitland watched her go, his brow deeply furrowed. After a moment he shook his head. "That's not the same girl," he muttered aloud. "I don't know how and I don't know why, but I'd be willing to wager a monkey that that's not *my Georgy!*"

Alison, meanwhile, was dressing herself. She'd gotten out of bed, taken a look at the weather and groaned aloud. It was bad enough that she was to be imprisoned in this place for a fortnight without the weather keeping her indoors! She'd looked forward to coming here, but now that she'd seen what sort of people had gathered, she knew she was in for it. There was not one person here of her age. Who was she expected to talk to for the next thirteen days?

The only possibility among the guests for interesting companionship for her was the Countess Lieven's nephew, Rudi. He was very good-looking in the blonde, Teutonic style, and, except for the heaviness of his Austrian accent, she found him very attractive. But he was much too old for her, being at least twenty. The only reason she could even consider him as a prospect for entertainment was that there were no other females with whom he could dally; of the three other unmarried ladies in the company, one, Rosalind, had just been removed from the lists by the announcement of her betrothal; the second, Peggy, would be occupied with Lord Maitland, and the third, Lucy, had already taken him in dislike. If she, Alison, could manage to attract his notice, she might, for the first time in her life, try her skill at the fine art of flirtation. But what man of twenty would even glance at a fourteen-year-old in short skirts?

To that end, Allie was dressing herself in the cherry-colored round gown she'd tried on a few weeks before. Some instinct had told her to pack it with her things. If she could wear this dress down to dinner this evening, she was certain that she would appear older and catch the handsome Rudi's eye. Her mother would be certain to object, of course, but if she could manage to keep out of her mother's sight until dinner was announced, it would be too late for her to do anything about it.

She pirouetted before the mirror, observing herself critically. The red color of the dress was perfect—just bright enough to attract attention but not so dashing as to be vulgar. Of course, the prim white tucker and cuffs made the gown inappropriate for evening; she would have to remove them. The dress would then be quite daringly décolleté. But was she developed enough to make the décolletage attractive? Might it not be cut too low and thus reveal too much of too little? If only she could take Betsy into her confidence, they could remove the white trim at once and see what the dress then revealed. But Betsy could not be trusted not to run to Mama and give her away. If the dress was to be worn tonight, Allie had to do the adjustments herself.

To that end, she asked a housemaid for a pair of scissors and began to cut the tucker from the bodice. After cutting through a few stitches at the back opening, she found she could easily rip the tucker away. But when she did so, a folded note, which had evidently been tucked in the little space between the tucker and the bodice, fell into her lap. Allie, realizing at once that this was something of Georgy's, opened it without a moment's hesitation. If Georgy had not disappeared so mysteriously, she would have at least *considered* the ethical question of her right to pry, but under the present circumstances, she had no such scruple. She read the letter at once. It was written in a curlicued, expansive script and it said,

> *My dear Miss Vail,*
> *I am Pleased to inform you that your letters have been Examined by Lady Ruckworth, the school's Patron, and she has found them to be Satisfactory. Therefore we may Proceed with the Plans as outlined in my Last Communication. Lady Ruckworth has Graciously consented to make herself available to Greet you on your Arrival. She will herself conduct an Interview at that time to settle any Matters which still may need Resolution. Until then, I remain Yours, etc. P. Hunsford, Vicar, Ruckworth Parish.*

Allie could make nothing of this. There was not a name in the missive that was at all familiar to her. None of it made sense. Why was Georgy carrying in her bosom a letter to a Miss Vail? The only thing that was clear was that a visit to the vicar of Ruckworth Parish might reveal some information. She was sure that Jemmy would agree. Her first reaction was to run to Jemmy's room and show this letter to him. But he was out shooting, she remembered, and would probably not be back until tea time. She supposed she should bring the letter to Mama, but that would mean explaining about the dress. Besides, if Mama and Jemmy became excited and hopeful of finding out about Georgy's whereabouts through this new clue, some hint of it would leak out—through servants' gossip, perhaps, or by means of chance remarks being overheard—to other guests here at Colinas Verde. One thing would lead to another, and soon everyone would know of Georgy's errant

behavior and Mama's trick of substituting Peggy for
Georgy. Then Mama would be humiliated and Maitland
disgusted. No, Allie decided, she would not show the note
to anyone . . . at least not yet. She would keep it hidden
away, at least for the time being. If matters came to a head,
if it became crucial that Georgy be sent for, that would be
time enough to reveal what she'd found. She, Alison Verney, was nobody's fool. If and when the time became right,
she would know.

Chapter 19

———————❧———————

Allie wore the dress to dinner, but it did her no good. Rudi the Teuton had already fallen desperately in love with Another and had no eyes for anyone else. He'd sat next to Peggy at teatime, tried to get her attention by plying her with iced cakes, clumsy jokes and heavy-handed flattery, but even when he unwittingly dropped his buttered scone into her lap, she'd barely looked at him. This utter indifference so charmed him that from that moment on he was irrevocably hers. Allie could have pranced in to the banqueting room in her underdrawers without attracting his notice.

But her mother noticed her *and* the long dress. Lady Horatia cast fulminating glares at her daughter all through the evening meal, and as soon as the ladies left the table, dragged Allie up to her room and locked her in, warning her in no uncertain terms that if she ever tried such a hoydenish trick again, she would be sent home to London where Spiers would keep her under constant surveillance, making sure she did nothing but work at her embroidery frame or practice the piano. Poor Allie could do nothing but remove the forbidden gown, pull on her nightclothes and, in utter disgust with herself and the world, throw herself into bed.

Peggy came up later to console her. Peggy was in a much better frame of mind than she'd been earlier. In the first place, she'd noticed that Rosalind was exhibiting bridelike affection toward her betrothed, Monte, thus causing Jeremy to grow increasingly irritated. This gave Peggy a perverse satisfaction; if *she* had to be irritated by his lovesick glances at Rosalind, it seemed only fair that *he* be irritated by Rosalind's love-sick glances at Monte. In the second place, the attentions that Rudi showered on her (which had at first annoyed her in the extreme) were turning out to be very convenient. Rudi was the one person among the guests who had never met the real Georgy. In *his* company she didn't have to worry about what she said. They had no shared past, no memories that could trip her up. When she realized that she could be herself in his company, she began to give the fellow some mild encouragement. That was all that was needed to keep him constantly at her side and effectively to keep Maitland at arm's length. Thus she had passed the evening with a minimum of tension.

Allie could see at once that Peggy's spirits were much improved. "You did well tonight, eh?" she asked, sitting up in bed.

Peggy shrugged. "At least I didn't say anything I shouldn't," she sighed, sitting down at the foot of the bed, "but that was only tonight. I don't know how I'll keep from coming a cropper for a whole fortnight."

"Confidence, my girl, confidence," Allie said in imitation of her mother. "Besides, two days are gone already. Only twelve to go."

Peggy shuddered. "Twelve! They loom ahead of me like years."

"I know," Allie said sympathetically. "They seem that way to me, too."

"Why you, Alison?" Peggy asked in surprise. "Aren't you enjoying yourself?"

"Enjoying myself? I should say not. How can I? There's no one here who'd miss me if I fell into the well and drowned! I *tried* to make that gawk Rudi notice me, thinking I might indulge in a little trial-flirtation, but the nodcock decided to fall in love with *you*. I actually went to the trouble of altering Georgy's cherry dress and doing up my hair *à la Sappho,* and all I earned for my pains was a whacking tongue-lashing from Mama."

"I'm sorry, Allie, I didn't think—"

"Heavens, Peggy, don't be a shatterbrain. It isn't your fault that gentlemen fall like dead leaves at your feet."

"Not all of them," Peggy muttered drily. She sat for a moment absorbed in her own confusion, wondering if, under other circumstances, Jeremy would have fallen at her feet. Of course it was out of the question now, her behavior of last night undoubtedly having given him a permanent disgust of her.

But Allie's voice interrupted her thoughts. "You don't really *like* Rudi, do you, Peggy? He's so stiff."

She shook her head. "No, of course I don't. He's only a boy, you know. Not yet twenty. But I like his company well enough. Nevertheless, I shall be happy to discourage him and give him a push in your direction."

"No, don't bother. Though why you want him hanging about is beyond my understanding."

"His company is soothing to me," Peggy explained. "He's the only one of the gentlemen here with whom I don't have to make 'Georgy-talk.'"

"Georgy-talk?" Allie giggled appreciatively. "I see what you mean. Most of the men here knew Georgy, so you *do* have to talk that way with all of them except Rudi. And Jemmy, of course."

Peggy dropped her eyes. "Yes, of course. Jemmy."

"Very well, then, keep your Rudi," Allie offered with blithe generosity, "since he's of more use to you than to me. I'll have plenty of time after I'm in long skirts—and when I have a bit more bosom—to practice flirtation. But, Peggy, you don't need to worry so about your 'Georgy talk'. You're doing it very well."

"No, I'm not," Peggy said glumly. "I'm terrified that someone will catch me up one of these days. Lucy Traherne or Maitland, most likely. I'll say something stupid, or Lucy'll take a good look at me in the daylight, or —"

Allie leaned forward eagerly. "I've been thinking about that, Peggy. Do you know what I think? I think Mama should order you to take a long rest in your room every afternoon. She can say it's on the orders of your doctor, to build up your strength after your long illness. That should take you out of difficulty for a good part of the day."

"Yes, it would, wouldn't it?" Peggy agreed, her eyes lighting. "That's a wonderful idea!"

"I'll talk to Mama about it tomorrow."

"Thank you, Alison." Peggy rose and planted a light kiss on the younger girl's forehead. "You've lifted my spirits considerably."

"And you've lifted mine." Alison looked after her thoughtfully as Peggy went to the door. "You know, Peggy," she added, "any time you tire of your Georgy-talk, you can always come to *me* and be yourself."

Peggy threw her a grateful smile. "I know that, Alison. You are the best of sisters. I hope Georgy knew how lucky she was."

They bid each other goodnight, and Peggy went down the hall to her bedroom, keeping a tight grip on the mood of optimism that Alison had instilled in her. But when she opened her door and found the room in almost complete darkness, the mood vanished. The room had never been left dark before. The servants always lit the bedside candles in the guests' bedrooms before they came upstairs. Was something amiss?

There was a small fire burning in the grate, of course, but it shed very little light. Peggy hesitated on the threshold. For some unknown reason, the dark room repelled her.

After a moment, she took herself in hand. "You are being childish," she said aloud, and she crossed the threshold purposefully. Once inside, she closed the door, crossed the room carefully and felt about on her bedside table for a candlestick and the tinderbox. Her hands shook as she fumbled with the tinder, for something—she knew not what—was making her feel distinctly uneasy.

As if to justify her fears, she heard the shuffle of a shod foot. The candle flared into brightness, and at that instant she saw a dark figure move toward her from the shadows. A scream rose to her throat, but before she could release it, a large hand was clapped over her mouth. "Don' yell, ye ninny," a familiar voice hissed in her ear. "It's on'y me."

As her eyes widened in recognition, the hand was removed from her mouth. *"Ned!"* she gasped, turning pale. "How —?"

"How'd I find ye? Easy. I been followin' ye ever since ye went off wi' that damned princock. Didn't dream 'e'd turn out to be a sprout off a noble line. *Lord* Verney 'e'll be, soon as 'e puts off 'is uniform, I 'ear."

Peggy backed away from her brother and stared at him in the dim light. Never had he seemed as sinister as at this moment, with the light from the candle accenting his sharp chin and deep cheek-hollows. He had some evil purpose for showing himself, she was sure of that. "Why did you follow me, Ned?" she asked bluntly, a pulse in her throat beating fearfully.

He propped himself comfortably on the arm of her bed-side chair. "I figured that wi' the proper lay, we could do some good fer oursel's, Cap'n Verney bein' a sprig o' the nobility."

"Captain Verney is not rich, if that's what you've been thinking," she said coldly, "so you needn't make any plan —or 'proper lay' as you put it—in that direction."

"I *was* thinkin' that Verney was flush, but that was before ye came 'ere. I been nosin' about wi' some o' the townsfolk down at the tavern, an' I whiddled the whole lay. Yer Cap'n Verney ain't nothin' compared to the Viscount what owns this mansion. There's *real* brass."

"I don't see what Lord Maitland's 'brass' has to do with you."

"It ain't me, my girl, it's *us*. Y're lookin' mighty fine wi' those silks an' borrowed jewels, but when the Verneys 'ave done with ye, what then? Where'll ye be then?"

"It's none of your affair where I'll be. I'll not come back to *you*, you can be sure."

Ned Birkin sneered. "No? Ye'll take to the streets, then?"

Peggy, who'd been worried about the answer to that very question, turned her back on him. "It would hardly be worse than living with you."

"But wouldn' it be better to 'ave a pile o' brass to start a new life fer yerself? Ye could buy a little shop, per'aps, an' set yerself up real fine."

Peggy sank down upon the bed. "Let's have it, Ned. How do you propose to get this pile of brass?"

"It'll be easy as pie," he said, leaning forward. "All ye need do is cozy up t' this Lord Maitland—"

"You're off the mark, Ned. Lord Maitland is in love with someone else entirely."

"But 'e thinks that someone is you, don't 'e? Isn't that the Verneys' lay in bringin' ye here?"

Her heart clenched in alarm. "How did you know that?"

"They call ye Georgy. I heard 'em. Yer brother ain't no fool. They're tryin' to pass you off as one of 'em."

She clenched her fingers nervously. "What if they are? It's Georgy that Lord Maitland wants, not me."

"But you resemble this Georgy, ain't that so? Resemble 'er so much that no one's any wiser. So you kin wheedle the fellow round to wantin' *you*, can't ye?"

"Even if I could, he's bound to find out sooner or later that I'm not who he thinks I am."

"Right. But by that time ye'll 'ave entangled 'im. Ye'll 'ave let 'em compromise yer reputation, if ye follow my meanin'."

"I follow your meaning," she said, shutting her eyes.

"An' that's when we'll have 'im!" Ned rubbed his hands together eagerly. "'E'll 'ave t' pay a plump bundle to rid 'isself of ye."

Peggy slowly rose to her feet, every muscle trembling. "Did you really think, *brother mine*, that I would agree to such a vile scheme as that? Then think again! I'm not a member of the muslin company yet. Get out of here, Ned Birkin! Go back to London, to your filthy friends and your filthy ways! There's nothing for you here."

He leered up at her, unangered and unmoved. "Y're sayin' no to a fortune, then?"

"I'm saying no to *anything* you might propose. So get out . . . and don't let me see your face again!"

He didn't even bother to rise. "I thought ye might say that," he chortled, reaching into his pocket. "That's why I copped *this*." His hand came out of his pocket, and he held it out toward the candle. Slowly he opened his fingers. Revealed in his palm was a glowing green stone.

"Why, that's . . . that's Lady Denham's emerald! Ned! You . . . you *wretch!* Give it to me!" And she made a lunge for it.

But he was too quick for her. He had it back in his

pocket before she reached him. They grappled together for a moment, but he soon had her wrists in his grasp. He pushed her against the bedpost with cruel force. "I could sell this bauble to a swagman an' come away with a pretty penny," he hissed in her face, "but we'd do even better wi' my first scheme. So I on'y copped this t' warn ye, Peg. If ye won't play the game my way, this little trinket is goin' t' find itself in yer Cap'n Verney's haversack." He leaned closer and tightened his grip on her wrists. "An' a little bird'll tell 'is lordship just where t' find it."

Peggy froze. "You wouldn't—!"

"Wouldn't I?" He smiled nastily, the yellow of his teeth looking grotesque in the candlelight. "Sweet on our Cap'n, ain't ye, *sister mine?* Y' wouldn't want 'im to be accused of stealin' from his friends."

Having made his point, he let her go. She backed away from him and rubbed her wrists. "All right, let me understand you," she muttered helplessly. "If I agree to try to attach Lord Maitland, you'll return the stone to Lady Denham's room?"

"I'll return the stone to Lady Denham's room *after* ye've attached 'im."

Peggy's mind raced about, trying to think of what to do. If she screamed and roused the household, Ned would be caught with the stone and punished. But he'd surely give away her identity and thus destroy the Verneys' plan and their reputation. If she refused to have anything to do with him, he'd plant the gem on Jeremy and destroy *him*. But if she agreed to Ned's ridiculous 'lay', she could buy herself some time to devise a plan of her own. "Very well, Ned," she said slowly, "I'll try."

He laughed. "I thought ye might. Then it's settled. But remember, y' ain't got long. I'll be watchin' ye. An' we'll talk again in a few days. Ye'd best 'ave made progress by then."

"I said I would try," she said icily.

"Here, old girl," he grinned, offering her his hand, "tip me a mauley t' seal the bargain."

She stepped back in revulsion. "I've given my word. That's enough."

"No, it ain't. A bargain needs a handshake."

She stared at his outstretched palm. *May God forgive me*, she said to herself miserably, and she put her hand in his.

Chapter 20

The weather was kind for the next two days, permitting the party to enjoy such country delights as a picnic on the lawn, an archery contest, a wheelbarrow race and an excursion to the ruins of Fountains Abbey. Lady Horatia agreed with Allie that these daytime excursions could be dangerous for Peggy, so for most of them Peggy was left behind, ostensibly resting in her room to recover the bloom of her health. But the most exciting activity was an indoor one, a formal ball held the third evening after their arrival, and for this Peggy certainly had to be available.

The gentry for miles about had been invited for this occasion; fifty additional guests toured the public rooms, gaped at the paintings and decor, swarmed about the buffets and thronged the dance floor of the breathtaking ballroom which was being used this evening for the first time. The new faces animated the houseguests and gave zest to the evening, and the glittering rooms rang with music and laughter.

Jeremy, however, did not find the ball at all zestful. He disliked the evening from the start, when he came into the ballroom and discovered Rosalind charmingly readjusting Monte's neckcloth behind a potted palm. Then she danced the opening dance with her betrothed and sat out the second in his company. When at last Jeremy managed to convince her to stand up with him for a country dance, his bristles were well set up. "You *love* playing the bride-to-be role, don't you?" he muttered through clenched teeth. "I wonder if you intend to call it off at all!"

"I've got to put a good face on it, don't I?" she countered with a charmingly girlish air of helplessness. "Papa warned me not to give Monte any reason to think I'm not sincere."

"Sincere, hah!" Jeremy snorted. "I don't know if you're capable of sincerity anymore."

"If you're going to speak to me in that way, Jeremy Verney," the girl pouted, "this is the last time I'll dance with you this evening. As it is, Papa will probably have my head washed for dancing with you this once!"

The dance ended in stony silence, and Jeremy stalked off in high dudgeon. He spent the better part of the next hour leaning on a pillar and watching her flirt with her Monte with all the exaggerated animation that comes with knowing one is being observed.

Jeremy would have spent the entire evening in that position had he not made an even more irritating observation. He discovered that Peggy was engaging in some animated flirtation of her own.

Peggy had entered the ballroom with more than her usual nervousness. Ned was very much on her mind. Somehow, she thought, he might be watching her. Since she'd thus far been unable to think of what to do about Ned, she felt herself impelled, at least for the time being, to try to implement his plan for Jeremy's sake. She began to flirt with Maitland as outlandishly as her reticent nature permitted, dancing with him three times, laughing at his quips and fluttering her lashes at him with nauseating coquettishness. Maitland's response to her efforts was peculiar: he didn't discourage them, but he didn't seem to have any particular liking for them either. It was as if he were merely watching her . . . watching and waiting to see what she would do next.

But Jeremy found her flirtations repulsive in the extreme. After having had his stomach turned over Rosalind's falsely fond attentions to Monte, he now found himself utterly sickened by Peggy's actions. Her behavior bothered him so much that he lost all interest in Rosalind's doings. Peggy's sudden animation, her affected coquetry, her obvious attempts to attract Maitland struck Jeremy as completely unwarranted. His mother had never asked her to flirt with Maitland, only to be there in the background, keeping Georgy's *place*, as it were. Now it seemed to him that Peggy had decided to catch Maitland for *herself!*

The more he watched her, the more agitated he became. What had gotten into the girl? he asked himself. Was she trying to play his mother and Georgy false? Was she doing this just to drive him, Jeremy Verney, to distraction? Or, worst and most painful possibility of all, had she suddenly fallen in love with Maitland? Whichever it was, his peace of mind was completely cut up. He wanted nothing more than to drag the girl into a dark corner and wring her neck!

He did not manage to get her alone until supper was announced. Finding her outside the banqueting room waiting for Maitland to escort her to the buffet, he gripped her arm and pulled her into a small room just off the corridor. It turned out to be a storage room for large silver serving pieces. A footman, standing just within the door busily polishing a huge tureen, looked up at the intruders in astonishment, but Jeremy merely glared the poor fellow out of the room and shut the door in his face. "Just what do you think you're doing, Peggy?" he demanded without preamble.

"What are you talking about?" Peggy asked, confused.

"This *ooh-la-la* with Maitland. Have you taken leave of your senses?"

"Ooh-la-la?" She gaped at him for a moment and then giggled. "Are you foxed, Jeremy?"

"You know damn well I'm not foxed. Answer me!"

"How can I answer *ooh-la-la?*" she laughed. "I have no idea what you mean."

"You know perfectly well what I mean!" he snarled, too angry to share her amusement. "Are you trying to snare him?"

"Snare whom? Maitland?"

"Yes, Maitland. Who else? Isn't *he* the target of your coquettishness tonight?"

Peggy finally understood. Full of misgivings herself about that very matter, she felt suddenly furious with Jeremy for confronting her with it. She thrust his hand from her arm. "Isn't that why we came?" she retorted.

"That is *not* why we came! We only came to gain time for Georgy."

"Well, that's just what I'm trying to do," she said dismissively, turning to the door.

"In order to do that, my girl," he sneered, pulling her round again, "it is not necessary to *throw* yourself at him."

Peggy drew herself up in offense. "I am not your girl, Captain Verney, so you may stop calling me such. And I was not 'throwing' myself at Lord Maitland, whatever you may think."

"It *is* what I think. 'Throwing yourself at him' is the perfect description of what you were doing."

She pulled herself free of his grasp again. "Even if I were, it is not your place to correct me. Your mother is perfectly capable of correcting any excesses in my behavior, and *she* hasn't seen fit to say a word of censure to me."

"That's probably because she wasn't watching you as I was. If she did, she would certainly have found it necessary to censure you."

"Would she, indeed? We have only your word for that, so it doesn't bear discussing." She flounced to the door and then whirled round again. "And furthermore, what business is it of yours to watch me so closely?"

"It's my business, ma'am, because it was my deuced doing that brought you to this family!"

"Oh? Are you implying that you're regretting it now?"

"Exactly so," he said cruelly. "If I'd known you'd be behaving like a wanton, I would never have—"

"Wanton?" Her whole body stiffened. "Do you d-dare call me wanton?"

"Yes, I dare!" He could feel his anger running wild, but he had no desire to bring it under control. "Also *strumpet, doxie* and *jade!* So there!"

Peggy felt the blood drain from her face. Everything she was doing was for his sake, yet *that* is what he thought of her! Trembling with hurt and rage, she lifted a hand and struck him hard across the face. Then, after the briefest hesitation (for she had never before in her life done such a thing), she turned and ran from the room.

Jeremy remained for a while just where he was, holding

his hand against his burning cheek and wondering why, since the girl was so flagrant a flirt and, in addition, had had the temerity to strike him, he was feeling so blastedly like a bounder.

Chapter 21

The morning after the glittering revelry of the ball everyone slept late. Thus it was not until midmorning that the houseguests became aware that the weather had taken a severe turn. The fourth day at Colinas Verde had dawned cold and rainy. A walking tour of the estate and a much-anticipated croquet match between the men and women had to be postponed. The atmosphere of good spirits that had so diverted the houseguests for three days was further dissipated by the news that Lady Denham's emerald pendant had disappeared. Maitland was chagrined by the occurrence, despite Roger's assurances that the bauble would turn up, and he ordered his butler to make discreet inquiries among the staff.

By the time luncheon was over, and the members of the party noted that the rain continued to pour doggedly down, a sudden lethargy seemed to overtake them. Jeremy and Roger Denham decided to fight the doldrums by challenging Monte and Rudi to a game of billiards, but the rest of the group surrendered. Most of the women retreated to their bedrooms to spend the afternoon with their hairdressers, while the older gentlemen retired to the library, covered their faces with their handkerchiefs and napped.

Allie, not having been invited to play billiards and wishing neither a nap nor a visit with a hairdresser, had nothing at all to do. She wandered through the rooms in utter boredom, finally casting herself down on a window seat in the south sitting room and staring out at the relentless rain. It was there that Maitland found her. "Poor Miss Verney the Younger," he greeted her. "I fear you are not enjoying this sojourn in the country."

"Not right now," she admitted, "although I did enjoy myself well enough yesterday."

"When you and I won the wheelbarrow race? I should hope you did. We made an unbeatable pair. But one can't live on the joys of yesterday, can one? What can I do to make you enjoy today?"

"You could have invited a boy or two that I could flirt with. That would have brought some excitement to my day."

"Is that all you like to do, flirt?" he asked in mock dismay.

"I don't know, for I've yet to try it," she admitted ruefully.

"What? Never?" He grinned down at her. "Are you trying to make me believe that you've reached the advanced age of . . . what is it? Thirteen?—"

"Almost fifteen, if you please."

"I beg your pardon, ma'am. Fifteen, then. You've reached fifteen without ever having flirted?"

"That, my lord," she sighed, "is the dismal truth."

He sat down beside her and took her hand. "I'm sorry I didn't think of inviting a handful of youths for you to cut your teeth on, Alison," he said. "I'm a dreadful host, I'm afraid. But that doesn't mean I have a moment's concern about your talent for flirting. In the long run, my dear, I'm convinced you'll excell at the flirting game beyond your wildest expectations. Take the word of an expert."

Allie glanced up at him incredulously. "Do you mean it, Lord Maitland, or are you merely trying to flummery me?"

"I have never been more sincere. But meanwhile, we need to do something to enliven the present. Let me think, girl!" He got up and began to pace about. "There must be *something* in this huge house that we can find to amuse you," he muttered.

She shrugged dolefully. "I don't know what it could be. Jemmy suggested that I find something to read in your library, but your books are not the sort to enliven a rainy day for a young girl. Nothing but history and political tomes. Don't you read novels?"

"Of course I do. Couldn't you find any? Come, I'll go back there with you and we'll see what we can find."

"No, not now, thank you, Lord Maitland. Sir Basil and Lord Traherne are napping there." She gave a mournful sigh. "I don't care to start a novel now, anyway."

"Then how about the music room? All well-reared young women seem to be proficient at the piano these days. Come and play for me."

Allie made a face. "Goodness, you sound like Mama. When I asked her what to do, she told me to go along and practice. I *hate* to practice."

Maitland sat down beside her again. "My, my, you *are* a sad case. Your brother advises you to read, but you can't find the right book. Your mother advises music, but you hate to practice. What does your sister advise?"

"Who, Peggy? She's a worse case than I. She's been sitting in her bedroom moping for hours!"

Maitland stared at her. *"Peggy?"*

Allie's eyes flew up to his for a startled moment. Then she dropped them and bit her lip. "Did I say Peggy? I meant *Georgy*, of course." Her legs unfolded and she sat up rigidly straight. "I suppose I must have been thinking of Peggy, my best friend at home," she said hastily, keeping her eyes lowered. "I've been missing her, you know. If she were here, I wouldn't be at a loss for what to do."

Maitland's breath caught in his chest, and it took him a second or two to expel it. Then he lifted Allie's chin and made her look up at him. "No, Alison, my dear, that little lie won't do," he said gently. "It smacks of too-hasty invention. You have no friend named Peggy, I'll warrant. That girl up there isn't Georgy, is she?"

"I d-don't know what you're t-talking about," she stammered, white-lipped.

"Yes, you do. You needn't look so terrified, you know. I shan't tell anyone else."

"Tell anyone else what?" Allie countered, her pulse pounding fearfully.

"That I know the Georgy upstairs is an imposter."

Allie pulled away from him and dropped her face in her

hands. "Oh, my God," she groaned, "I've destroyed *every-thing!* Mama will never forgive me!"

Maitland put an arm about her and nestled her head on his shoulder. "You didn't destroy anything, my dear. I'd guessed—well, *almost* guessed—already."

"That's not t-true! You c-couldn't have!"

"But I did. I swear it."

She looked up at his face suspiciously. "How could you have? Lucy hasn't guessed, and she's known Georgy for *ages*. And you only met Georgy once . . . a whole month ago."

He shrugged. "I don't know how to explain that, but the truth is that I felt uneasy about her from the first moment she greeted me the evening you all arrived. This Peggy is amazingly like your sister on the outside, isn't she? But perhaps the reason I felt a difference is that when I met Georgy I was drawn to something *inside*."

Allie nodded, frowning thoughtfully. "Yes, they're very different, really. Peggy's much more *in* herself, if you know what I mean. Georgy's ready to go out and embrace —or fight with—the entire world. Peggy would prefer to watch from a secluded corner. Not that she isn't a very sweet—" She suddenly stopped herself and winced. "What am I *doing?* How can I go on prattling when I've ruined Mama and Jemmy and everyone?"

"Please stop berating yourself, Alison. Nothing is ruined that I can see. I promise not to tell a soul that I have any suspicion that Peggy is not who she claims to be."

"Thank you, Lord Maitland. That is g-good of you. But everything is ruined anyway."

"I don't understand. What is it you think you've ruined? Who *is* this Peggy, a long-missing twin? And most important, where is the *real* Georgy? What I don't understand is *why* you've all decided to enact this charade."

"It's a sh-shameful story," Allie said, edging away from him on the seat and lowering her head. "If I tell you, will you promise not to be furious with Mama?"

"I don't know what to say to that, my dear. Am I *likely* to be?"

"Yes, but you must promise to forgive her, or I shan't tell you anything."

He couldn't help giving the child an admiring smile. "You, Miss Verney the Younger, are a clever little baggage, aren't you? You know that I won't be able to resist hearing your 'shameful' story, so you have me at gunpoint. Very well, I promise to forgive her for whatever it is."

Allie expelled a long breath. "Well, then, the truth is that Peggy is not a long-missing twin . . . or any relation to us at all. She's just a girl Jemmy found when he went searching for Georgy."

"Searching for Georgy?" Maitland interrupted in alarm. "Why—?"

"She'd run away, you see. That, of course, was bad enough, but it happened just when Mama decided that *you* would make her a perfect husband."

"Good God! Is that why she ran away? To escape from being matched with me?"

"No, I don't think so, for your invitation didn't come until after she'd gone. Although a match between you and Georgy was Mama's fondest dream—the only way she could see to get us out of the financial straits she's found herself in, you see—but until your invitation came, Mama did not have much hope of you."

Maitland knit his brows. "I thought I'd made it quite plain to your mother, and your sister, too, that *I* had hope of *her*," he muttered. "What a muddle I seem to have made of my intentions!"

"Are you going to be angry at yourself now, Lord Maitland? If you must be angry at anyone, it ought to be Georgy. If she hadn't decided to run away, none of this would have happened."

Maitland listened to the rest of the story without interrupting. His feelings as he listened were confused, but when he'd heard it all he realized that he wasn't angry at anyone . . . not at Georgy, who'd run away and caused all this, not at her mother, who'd been dishonest and manipulative, and not at Peggy, who had tried to deceive him. His strongest feeling was relief—relief that his first glowing impression of Georgy had not yet been proved to be a besotted idiot's illusion. The girl he'd dreamed of all this past month might still be real. He could still hope. The sense of relief that flooded over him came from the realization that hope had not died.

Alison was peering at him with anxious eyes. "What will you do now?"

He smiled at her reassuringly. "First, my dear, I think I should thank you for being so frank with me. You've no idea how invaluable this information has been for my peace of mind."

"You're welcome, my lord," she said glumly, not at all reassured. "And second?"

"Second, I shall request humbly that, in honor of our new-found intimacy, you stop calling me 'my lord'. My intimates call me Tony."

"And third, Tony?" she pressed, still worried.

"What do *you* think I should do?"

"Send us all packing, I suppose."

"Don't be a wet-goose. Why would I do that?"

"That's what *I* would do if I were you."

"No, you wouldn't. You would do exactly as I shall."

She cocked her head at him, birdlike. "Would I? And what would that be?"

He grinned. "Guess."

She wrinkled her brow in thought. "You'd make me tell Mama that I've told you."

"What would be the point of that? Do you think I want you punished for telling me the truth?"

"Then . . . you'll make Peggy confess to the entire company."

"What folderol is that? Didn't I promise not to reveal any of this? Do you think I would renege on a promise? What do you take me for?"

"Then, what—?"

"There's only one thing worth doing about all this, you know. I'm going to find your sister."

Allie's heart leaped in relief. "Really, Tony? You, yourself?"

"Yes, of course."

Her eyes widened in amazement. "Do you care for Georgy as much as that?"

"I think I do. But I won't know for certain until I find her." He got to his feet and started to the door. "So I think I should do so at once, don't you?"

"You mean *now* . . . today?"

"Just so."

"But your house party! All these people . . ."

He came to an abrupt halt. "Dash it all, you're right." Frowning, he rubbed his chin thoughtfully. "Perhaps Letty would agree to take over my duties in that regard," he murmured. "I'll tell her I must leave on urgent business."

"But where will you go? After all, even Jemmy didn't know where to look for Georgy."

"Yes, I know," he said, his brow knit in concentration. He came up to the window seat, knelt down before her and took her hand. "You must help me, Alison. You're the only link I have. Did she ever say anything to you . . . anything at all that might give us a clue to where she's gone?"

Allie studied him speculatively. "I've been all over this with Jemmy, as you might imagine, and there was nothing—" She paused, hesitated and then lifted her hand to her not-so-well-developed bosom and pulled from her bodice a folded note. "But I found something yesterday that might give you a place to start . . ."

Chapter 22

Georgy was, for the most part, quite pleased with herself.
School was going well. Two of the landowning farmers
had become subscribers to the school so that their daughters could attend. Even though they would not send their
sons (feeling, as did the vicar, that a proper academy
school would provide a better start for the boys), it was
flattering that they were willing to pay for their daughters
to have the same education that their laborers' children
were receiving free. Three new girls entered the class,
bringing its size to sixteen. Lady Ruckworth was so delighted that she actually invited Miss Vail to tea.

Except for that stiff, uncomfortable tea party, Georgy
had no social life at all. Despite the company of the Hunsford family at dinner time, she often felt lonely. Almost
every day she was tempted to write to her mother to ask
how things were at Verney House, but she restrained herself. If she revealed to the family where she was, they
might come and try to tear her away, and she wanted to
avoid such a confrontation at all costs. But when she lay
awake at night in her quiet room, she thought of them with
longing, imagining where they were and what they might
be doing, wondering if Jemmy had returned from the army
or if Allie was up to her usual mischief. Sometimes she
missed them so much she wept.

There was no one else of her London acquaintance
whom she missed or thought of very often, but strangely,
she found Lord Maitland rather frequently on her mind.
His name would pop without warning into her consciousness: Anthony Maitland, Viscount Ivers. Lord Maitland.
Tony, she'd call him in her mind. Georgy and Tony. The

pairing of the sounds pleased her ear. They'd had the briefest of connections, yet the occurrence seemed to glimmer
radiantly in her memory. She remembered with amazing
clarity his lanky, loose-limbed stride, the way his lean
cheeks creased when he laughed, and the taunting charm of
his voice when he said, *My dear girl, if you honestly believe we won't meet again, you are greatly underestimating
yourself.* Did he ever think of her? she wondered. It was
not likely that the encounter sparkled in his memory as it
did in hers, but did he at least occasionally entertain the
wish that he'd fulfilled that boast? Or did he not remember
her at all?

But when she was in the schoolroom, Georgy was far
from lonely. The children delighted her, and their progress
—not only in their studies but in their own self-esteem—
was a source of real pride. But pride, as the old saw so
rightly claims, is always followed by a fall, and for
Georgy, the fall was occasioned by a blow dealt by the
vicar.

Mr. Hunsford was very pleased that the teacher he'd
hired was admired by the locals, the children and his patroness, but when he paid a visit to the classroom, he felt
some decided misgivings. "The books you've chosen to
use, Miss Vail, are *not* the ones we had originally discussed," he chided after the class. "I think we should talk
this over. Please see me in my study this evening after
dinner."

That evening she reported to his workroom and, at his
invitation, took a seat beside his desk. "You are spending
too much of the school day in teaching reading and writing," he said to her in a critical tone, "and not always from
the books I suggested."

"Do you mean that I've been using *Aesop's Fables* and
Mother Goose for the little ones instead of the catechism
and the *Common Prayer?* But *Aesop's* and *Mother Goose*
are more entertaining for them while they're learning,
don't you think?" Georgy asked, eager to make him understand her methods.

"I suppose the children might think so, but our purpose,
Miss Vail, is not to entertain. Our aim is to keep the chil-

dren from vagrancy and idleness, to see that they are
always washed and combed, and to instruct them in their
duties by the catechism, so that they may become good
people and useful servants."

"Servants?" Georgy echoed, appalled. "Is that all to
which they can aspire?"

"That is the *best* to which they can aspire," the vicar
answered, peering sternly at her over his spectacles. "But
their aspirations are not my concern, nor should they be
yours. Yours should be to teach them to abhor vice, particularly the twin vices of cursing and swearing, to abstain
from taking God's name in vain, to avoid the profanation
of the Lord's day, and to despise idleness, which of all
vices is the most odious and contemptible. Those, second
only to the immediate service of God, are the principle
ends of education."

Georgy was left momentarily speechless. This exhorta-
tion had been delivered in a deep, Sunday-in-the-pulpit,
sermonizing tone that he rarely used at home. The effect on
her was as disturbing as a scolding from On High. She'd
based her teaching methods on the conviction that her
pupils should be taught more or less as she'd been taught
when she was a child, with the emphasis on reading, writing, history, arithmetic, music and drawing. A child, she
believed, should be taught to be virtuous, of course, but
that virtue should flow naturally from the civilizing force
of the education itself . . . a *side effect,* not the *end* of the
schooling. This criticism took her aback. She didn't know
how to defend herself. "Are you saying you're not pleased
with my work?" she asked, baffled.

"No, not at all," he hastened to assure her. Having made
his point, he was ready to revert to his usual, affectionate
attitude. He reached across his desk and took her hand.
"You must know that I am pleased at the response of the
parish to your presence. Our patroness, Lady Ruckworth,
is delighted by your ability to attract pupils, especially the
three paying ones. But she must not be permitted to receive
the impression that you spend time with the pupils frivo-
lously. Sunday evening, you know, will be the first of your
Quarterly Exercises. The children must perform for her la-

dyship and the other subscribers, and for whichever parents wish to attend, and naturally, you will want your pupils to be prepared in the serious matters that you were hired to teach."

The Quarterly Exercises. The very words made Georgy wince. She'd been hearing about them from the first. Periodically the schoolroom was opened on a Sunday evening for the patrons, subscribers and parents to examine the progress of the children. The children would be dressed in their Sunday best and would be expected to show how they recite Scripture, spell difficult words, read aloud with emphasis and clear enunciation and, in the case of the older pupils, make speeches or hold dialogues on some chosen Biblical passage. Georgy had been planning to surprise the audience with a different sort of performance—some singing of native ballads (for Sarah Putman had a sweet voice and had learned many lovely, homegrown songs at her mother's knee), an exhibit of drawings, and a humorous dramatization of the fable of "The Frogs Who Wanted A King." But now...

Mr. Hunsford could see that she was disturbed. He squeezed her hand comfortingly. "I did not mean to worry you, my dear. I can see that the children are progressing well. It is just that you must not permit frivolous pursuits to obscure the school's primary goals. Catechism and Moral Instruction, that is our purpose. Everything else must be secondary."

"Even reading and writing?" Georgy asked in a small voice.

"Reading is necessary for the understanding and performing of the catechism, but all the rest is secondary. It is a question of emphasis, my dear, only emphasis." He patted her hand. "Do you understand me?"

She wriggled her hand out of his grasp and rose. "Yes, Mr. Hunsford, I think I do," she murmured, deflated. She felt as if she'd been doused with cold water. She had been so proud of her accomplishments, of having inspired her pupils to take real pleasure in learning. Now she was told that it had all been *frivolous.*

He rose and escorted her to the door. "I hope you will not feel you've been chastised, Miss Vail. I only meant this interview as a reminder for you to keep the proper perspective."

"Yes, thank you, Mr. Hunsford," she said, giving him a feeble smile. "It's just the Quarterly Exercises —"

"Yes, I quite understand. They must seem frightening before the first occasion. But I'm certain the exercises will go well. You still have a few days in which to prepare. Here, take this. It's an opening prayer that will be more appropriate to the exercises than the simple Bless-Our-Lord you've been using." He handed her the sheet of paper on which he'd copied the prayer out for her.

She took it from him and bobbed. "Thank you, sir," she said. "Good night."

But he kept her from leaving by taking her chin in his hand. "Don't look so downhearted, my dear." He smiled down at her with unctuous solicitude. "I assure you that I . . . we . . . are all very pleased with you."

A wave of revulsion swept over her. She hated this tendency of his to find opportunities to touch her. He was always taking her hand or patting her shoulder or chucking her under the chin. But although his manner when he did so was invariably fatherly, it raised her hackles. This time she had an almost irresistible urge to slap his hand aside. But she resisted it. She turned her head so that her chin came free, backed away, thanked him again and whisked herself out of the room.

When she got to her room, she closed the door and looked down at the paper still clutched in her hand. The prayer he'd given her read:

> Make me dutiful and obedient to my benefactors,
> And charitable to my enemies.
> Make me temperate and chaste,
> Meek and patient,
> True in all my dealings,
> And content and industrious in my station.

She groaned aloud. The vicar was trying to make her into another Mrs. Jayce. This was just the sort of prayer her fear-inspiring predecessor would have chosen. Mr. Kissack, if he decided to attend the exercises, would find it just what he disliked most. But Georgy knew she had no choice; the pupils would have to learn this for Sunday evening. "Make me temperate and chaste, indeed," she muttered, throwing herself upon her bed. "It's *you* who ought to say this prayer, Mr. Any-Excuse-To-Fondle-A-Girl Hunsford!

As the week went on, the tension over the coming Quarterly Exercises increased. Georgy spent each day drilling the children in their new parts and trying to prepare them for what was supposed to be a treat but was becoming a trial. What most disturbed Georgy was the closing hymn. Mr. Hunsford had given her a copy of the selection that had been the traditional close of every one of the past Quarterly Exercises. It began:

> Obscured by mean and humble birth
> In ignorance we lay.
> Till Christian bounty called us forth
> And led us unto day.

She felt that, in combination with the opening prayer, this closing would place entirely too much emphasis on the feeling of gratitude the children were expected to bestow on their benefactors. She could not accept it as a proper closing sentiment for the school program. Without discussing it with Mr. Hunsford, she selected instead a favorite hymn of her own. It was called "Light Shining Out of Darkness." The words were written by the poet William Cowper, the music was simple but charming, and the sentiments were beautifully optimistic. Two of her favorite verses from the hymn expressed just what she would have wished the children to grasp of Christian theology:

Ye fearful saints fresh courage take,
    The clouds ye so much dread
Are big with mercy, and shall break
    In blessings on your head.

Judge not the Lord by feeble sense,
    But trust him for his grace;
Behind a frowning providence,
    He hides a smiling face.

Certainly there was nothing in the hymn to which anyone could object, she told herself. And nothing she could
think of would make a more appropriate message for the
children to learn and for the evening program to express.

As each day passed before the Sunday festivities, Mr.
Hunsford, and Mary, too, grew more nervous—the vicar
because her ladyship would be casting her critical eye on
his protegée, and Mary because her daughters would be
among the performers and because her friend Grace's future might be at stake. Georgy, however, became less and
less concerned. She did not let herself dwell on the conse-
quences; she merely concentrated on what had to be done.

By Sunday evening everything was in readiness. The
front of the room had been cleared of furniture and was
brightly lit with candles. The wall between the windows
was covered with children's drawings. And the children
themselves, lined up and nervously facing the visitors,
were resplendently shiny-faced and clean. The girls wore
new aprons that Mary had made, and the boys sported new
pocket handkerchiefs and neckcloths. Their hair was
combed, their shoes polished and their smiles angelic.

The back of the room was packed with visitors: all the
parents (even Mr. Kissack, Georgy noted uneasily), Mary
and Mr. Hunsford, a visiting curate from Whaley Bridge, the
church deacon and his wife, other church officials and even a
few parishoners who did not have children in the class but who
came out of curiosity to see the much-talked-of teacher in
action. There was only one empty seat; an arm chair, placed
squarely in the middle of the crowd, was conspicuously
empty. Lady Ruckworth had not yet arrived.

When fifteen minutes had passed beyond the hour appointed for starting, Mr. Hunsford came up to Georgy and whispered, "I understand that her ladyship has an unexpected but important houseguest. I suppose that's caused this delay. Perhaps we'd better begin without her."

Georgy nodded and signaled the children to begin. They launched into the carefully memorized prayer Mr. Hunsford had given her, and then each in turn read a selection from the scriptures. Georgy, seated on the first bench right in front of the children, did not look round to see the parents' faces, but she could hear murmurs of approval after each child read. After the fourth reading, Georgy heard a commotion behind her. Lady Ruckworth and her party had evidently arrived and were taking their places. From the corner of her eye Georgy could see Mr. Hunsford run over to greet her, but her ladyship must have waved him away. "Hush, hush," the patroness whispered, "I don't wish to make a disturbance. Just let the program proceed."

When Georgy heard those words, she felt free to keep her attention on her pupils and to omit performing the ceremony of welcome that would have been expected of her had her ladyship been prompt. The readings proceeded, each one greeted with the enthusiastic approval of the audience.

When the readings were completed, Mr. Hunsford invited the visiting curate to conduct a spelling bee using place names from the Bible. This was carried out with much seriousness, and when the winner proved to be little Molly Sloper, the whole crowd broke into cheers. Then Benjy retold the story of Noah in his own words, while the children performed the action in dumb-show (Georgy's compromise after discarding the more "frivolous" dramatization of the fable). Benjy's version of the story was in rhyme and full of imaginative detail (like the inclusion of rats and fleas in the parade of animals into the ark). The pantomine was attended with rapt silence, and when it was over Georgy heard her ladyship murmur, "Charming, charming."

It was all going well. Only one thing remained to complete the program — the closing hymn. Georgy rose, the children grouped themselves in front of her according to their size, and she lifted her arms to conduct them in the opening stanza of the song she'd chosen:

> God moves in a mysterious way,
> His wonders to perform;
> He plants his footsteps in the sea,
> And rides upon the storm.

Georgy beamed at them as they sang. She was overwhelmed by the blending of the tender simplicity of the song and the sweetness of their faces. The children, realizing that their efforts this evening had been wildly successful, sang the praise of God with innocent fervor. And when Sarah's pure voice rose to sing alone the "blessings on your head" verse, Georgy felt a lump rise in her throat. She'd never believed that a ceremonial exercise of this sort could be so beautiful! A man in the back coughed, and Georgy knew it was Mr. Putman, Sarah's father, trying not to cry.

When the children completed the "God is his own interpreter" stanza and brought the hymn to its conclusion, Georgy stood motionless as the echo of their voices reverberated among the rafters. Only after the sound had completely dissipated did she dismiss them. As they ran in eager triumph to the arms of their parents, Georgy looked over her shoulder and saw Mr. Kissack, of all people, standing in the far corner brushing a tear from his cheek before scooping little Dorrie up in his arms.

Then it was over. Parents and children rushed together and hugged, made their bows and their "thank-ye's" to her ladyship and set out for home. Mary, with her girls in hand, threw Georgy a triumphant grin before departing. Georgy had nothing left to do but sigh in relief and wait for words of congratulations from Mr. Hunsford and the school's benefactress.

Lady Ruckworth was surrounded by the church officials, all of whom seemed to be offering her their evaluation of the evening's exercises. Mr. Hunsford, at Lady Ruckworth's elbow, had his back to Georgy, evidently fawning over an elegantly dressed fellow who, Georgy supposed, was her ladyship's important guest. Before

Georgy could get a look at the stranger, however, Lady Ruckworth broke away from the circle of hangers-on and came up to her. "I must inform you, Miss Vail," she said coldly and loudly, "that your closing hymn was completely inappropriate."

Georgy froze. The effervescence of spirit that she'd enjoyed during the past few moments changed to a heavy lump and sank like a stone in her chest. "Inappropriate, my l-lady?"

"Yes. Completely. And, what was worse, to have a *solo* sung in this school is beyond anything. Didn't you realize that 'singing singly' is not allowed?"

"No, my lady, I didn't," Georgy answered, cut to the bone and miserably aware that there was not one person among the silently staring group remaining in the room who would say a word in her defense . . . not Mr. Hunsford, not the curate from Whaley Bridge, not the deacon nor his wife, not anyone. She turned her head away so that no one would see the tears gathering under her eyelids. "Why is it not allowed?"

"Because it gives the soloist a pride in herself," Lady Ruckworth declared in disgust. "You, who are teaching these children, should know that we cannot encourage self-pride. Humility is the virtue we must encourage."

"Oh, I don't know about that, Lady Ruckworth," came a new voice, the voice of the elegantly dressed stranger. "A bit of solo singing can't possibly lead to harm. And I, for one, found that little hymn enchanting."

Georgy, her entire being suffused with gratitude, whirled round to face the speaker. "Thank you!" she breathed, her eyes lifting from a black-coated chest, past a pair of impressively broad shoulders, to a dark, lined face. Then she gasped, her expression changing from beatific gratitude to utter stupefaction. She was looking up into the laughing eyes of Tony Maitland.

Chapter 23

"Lord Maitland, it is kind of you to pay so effusive a compliment to our teacher," Lady Ruckworth said in a manner that clearly expressed her disapproval of his interference, "but she must nevertheless be made aware that our children are not to be misled into believing that blessings will rain down on them from the sky, as her hymn says. Blessings will *not* rain down on them. They must not dream of easy gifts from a generous heaven, for that is not to be their lot in life. The appropriate message with which the school program should close is that of gratitude for the bounty which has been given them by Christian charity. I hope you will remember that, Miss Vail. Miss Vail, are you attending me?"

Georgy, who'd been staring at Lady Ruckworth's guest in disbelief, shook herself and turned her eyes to the school's benefactress. "Yes, of course, your ladyship. I will remember next time."

"I realize, your ladyship, that as an outsider it is inappropriate for me to interject my opinions in these matters," Maitland said, smiling down at his hostess with disarming charm, "but I would like you and your Miss Vail to know that I, a jaded fellow who has seen the best of theatrical presentations in my time, found myself completely captivated by the children tonight."

Lady Ruckworth's antagonism melted away. She'd been much taken with Lord Maitland from the moment of his arrival, and she was delighted by his surprise visit. Widowed and childless, Lady Ruckworth was aware that, despite her wealth and importance in this little world of hers, her life was for the most part drab. When Maitland had presented himself on her doorstep this afternoon, explaining that he'd come on his deceased father's instructions to pay his respects, she'd been overjoyed. A visitor of the fame and elegance of Lord Maitland was an unexpected source of stimulation and excitement in an otherwise too-placid existence. She wanted to keep him as a guest as long as possible. She'd worried, earlier this evening, that he would find the Quarterly Exercises a great bore. She'd explained to him that it was absolutely necessary for her to attend but that she was quite willing to excuse him from any obligation to accompany her. She'd offered him the run of her house and a bottle of her husband's best port to keep him company, but he'd insisted on joining her. The fact that he'd not found the program dull was a decided relief to her. "I'm so glad you enjoyed it, my boy," she said. Then, turning to Georgy, she added in a much more kindly tone, "And if you will take to heart what I've told you, Miss Vail, then I believe enough will have been said on that score."

Mr. Hunsford, however, glanced over at Lord Maitland in some resentment. He sensed that the famous, high-born visitor had played the role of Knight Protector to Miss Vail in the subtle battle that had been waged between the teacher and her ladyship, and he saw in Miss Vail's eyes a gleam of gratitude. He was stricken with jealousy. He, too, wanted to earn such a gleam from the young woman's eyes. "We wish you to know, Miss Vail," he said in a sudden rush of courage, "that Lady Ruckworth and the church officers and I found the *rest* of the program to be quite satisfactory, did we not, your ladyship?"

"Yes, quite," her ladyship agreed magnanimously, "although the pantomime might have troubled one or two of us. How did *you* feel about the pantomime, Lord Maitland? Did it strike you as being, perhaps, a shade too frolicsome for its subject?"

"No, indeed it did not," Maitland responded promptly. "In fact, I found it delightfully imaginative and innocent. But your ladyship," he added, turning from his hostess and smiling down into Georgy's still-startled eyes, "you have not yet made your talented young teacher known to me."

"Oh, I do beg your pardon, my lord. May I present Miss Grace Vail to your lordship? Miss Vail, this is Anthony Maitland, the Viscount Ivers, whose father was a good friend of my late husband's."

"Ah, Grace Vail, is it?" Maitland asked with an enigmatic smile as he bent over her hand. Georgy responded with a deep but nervous curtsey, her head in a whirl. Did he not recognize her at all, she wondered, or was he merely pretending? She peeped up at him as she straightened from her curtsey, but she was not sure she could read his expression. All at once, however, she was struck with embarrassment. Whether he recognized her or not, she must look a fright! Her hand flew to the dame-cap that covered her hair. For the first time, she hated it. Those dreadful flaps that hung over the ears made a woman look hideous.

"It was such a pleasant surprise," Lady Ruckworth was explaining to Mr. Hunsford, "to find Lord Maitland at my door this afternoon. It seems that his father ordered him— on his deathbed, mind you!—to call on Frederick Ruckworth's widow at his earliest opportunity and pay his respects. It was such a surprise. I'd heard my husband speak of the late Viscount Ivers, of course, but I had no idea that they were so well acquainted."

This explanation of Maitland's presence among them sounded incredible to Georgy. She glanced over at the Viscount in sudden, puzzled suspicion. Maitland met her eye with one raised eyebrow and a look of saintly innocence. "Her ladyship has been most hospitable," he said, turning with smooth aplomb to the vicar. "She welcomed me very cordially, even though we were perfect strangers."

"How can you think of me as a stranger, my lord," Lady Ruckworth asked, taking his arm with motherly affection, "when our families have been so close? I hope you are giving serious consideration to my invitation to extend your stay. I don't want to hear of your departing for at least a week."

"We shall see, my lady. I should like to accept, of course, but—" Maitland threw Georgy a quick glance. "—but the length of my stay depends on a . . . a message I am waiting to receive."

Lady Ruckworth beamed at him. "Then you are at least giving me hope. But come, everyone, to the carriages. My cold collation awaits."

"Cold collation?" Maitland asked as she urged him to the door.

"I always arrange to hold a late supper for all the officials of the church and their wives after the Quarterlies," her ladyship explained. "It will be a most special occasion, tonight, with your presence among us."

Maitland held back. "Does Miss Vail have a carriage to transport her?"

Lady Ruckworth blinked. "Miss Vail? I hadn't thought ... but of course, Miss Vail, you are most welcome. I'm certain Mr. Hunsford can take you up."

Georgy flushed. If Maitland did not already sense the low esteem in which she was held by the school's benefactress, he must certainly do so now, for the invitation was so obviously an afterthought that her pride would not possibly permit her to accept. "I thank you, my lady, but I beg you to excuse me. I am very tired after all this exertion."

"Yes, I quite understand," her ladyship said indifferently. "Then we bid you good night, Miss Vail."

Maitland, being inexorably drawn to the door, looked over his shoulder with unmistakable chagrin. "Er . . . yes . . . good night, Miss Vail." And he was gone.

Georgy lay awake for hours that night, trying to make some sense of this startling occurrence. Could it possibly be coincidence that brought Lord Maitland to the very town in which she'd chosen to hide herself? And if he'd truly come to offer the respects of his deceased father to Lady Ruckworth, had he really failed to recognize her? Neither the first nor the second possibility seemed likely. Assuming that both those possibilities were false, then he must have had another reason for coming here. Could he possibly have come here seeking *her?* If so, what right had he to do such a thing when they barely knew each other? Had Mama sent him? And how on earth could he have discovered her whereabouts?

It was a great puzzle. When she looked back on the events of the evening, it seemed to her that he *had* recog-

nized her. He'd given her a number of looks that seemed to
speak volumes: looks that told her he was glad to see her;
that he admired her work; that he was disappointed she
would not go to partake of her ladyship's "cold collation."
Or was she, on the other hand, reading more into his expressions than was truly there?

She found no answers that night nor all the next school
day. It was a bewildering, endless day in which she could
not concentrate for a moment on her work. Her mind
seemed befogged, and she wondered when and how she
would ever clear away the confusion. But when she
emerged from the schoolhouse at dusk, Lord Maitland's
carriage was standing in the schoolyard, and his lordship
himself was waiting beside it. "I've come to escort you to
tea," he said, removing his hat and coming to meet her.
"Her ladyship insists."

"Now?" Georgy gulped, her breath deserting her.

"Yes, right now. May I help you up?"

"But . . ." Absurdly, her hand flew to her cap again. Of
all the questions, suppositions, accusations, theories and
sensations that had clogged her mind all day, the only feeling that now emerged was dismay that he was seeing her
again wearing that dreadful cap. "But I'm not . . .
dressed . . ."

"Don't be absurd," he said, grasping her waist with his
two hands and lifting her bodily into the coach. He followed right behind her, pulled the door closed and dropped
down beside her. The carriage moved forward, but neither
one of them noticed, for their eyes were locked together in
an intent scrutiny. After a moment he put his hands to her
cheeks and tilted her face to his, studying it as if to imprint
every feature in his memory. "Oh, Georgy," he murmured,
expelling a long breath, "it *is* really you."

Those few words, if she'd analyzed them, would have
answered a number of her questions, but her mind was
unequal to analytical thought at that moment. His face was
just as she'd seen it in dreams, and it seemed to her fogged
mind that she was dreaming now. That she was dreaming
was the only explanation that made sense. Where else but
in a dream would his face be so endearingly familiar?

Where else but in a dream would she feel so comfortable and warm in spite of the fact that his face was so close and his lips only a breath away? And when he closed the gap and kissed her with the hunger that the long postponement had engendered, where else but in a dream would she let herself respond? If she were awake, the kiss would have been uncalled-for, insulting, alarming. But this kiss was none of those things. It had all the irrational inevitability of an occurrence in a dream.

She felt herself press closer against him, and his arms, in response, tightened about her until she could hardly breathe. But she didn't care, nor had she any will to struggle. Instead she let herself surrender to a series of sensations that were, if one had to find a word for them, nothing less than blissful. She shivered, and one arm, as if it had a will of its own, moved slowly upward to clasp him about the neck. As it rose, her hand brushed her cap . . . the dreadful dame-cap with its unflattering earflaps. The feel of the starched fabric brought her suddenly awake. It was a detail of reality that had nothing of a dream about it. Her mind snapped into action and sent out a loud alarm. It told her that she'd lost her wits and was permitting herself to be intimately embraced by a man who was practically a stranger! "Lord Maitland," she exclaimed, pushing him away, "what are you *doing?*"

He grinned down at her sheepishly. "I do beg your pardon, Georgy, my dear. I was a bit carried away."

"Carried away?" she echoed, appalled at what she'd let him do and at his unrepentant reaction.

"Yes, carried away at having you—the real you at last! —all to myself."

"I don't understand." She stared at him in bewilderment. "You *did* recognize me, then. Last night, I mean."

"Of course I did. I'd recognize you anywhere. Even under that deplorable cap you seem to require in your new life."

A laugh bubbled up from the mire of her confusion, and she felt herself blush. "It *is* deplorable, isn't it?" She reached up and pulled it off. "But please, my lord, don't distract me from the matter at hand. I want to understand.

You didn't . . . you couldn't have . . . come here to find *me*, could you?"

"Why else do you think I'd have come to this out-of-the-way backwater?" he asked, taking the cap from her hand and fingering it fondly.

"But Lady Ruckworth said . . . your father . . ."

"I don't believe my father ever heard of Frederick Ruckworth in his life. I know *I* certainly didn't. I made up that tale out of whole cloth."

"Are you saying that, without having any knowledge of Lady Ruckworth at all, you marched up to her door, invented a family connection and brazenly imposed on her hospitality?"

"Yes. Brazenly. I learned from a servant that she was a widow, and the rest was easy."

"But, my lord, I still don't understand *why.*"

"How can you ask? I had to find you, did I not?"

"No, you did not." She fixed a frank gaze on his face. "There was nothing between us to require you to seek me out."

"Wasn't there, my dear?" He took her two hands in his and looked down at them. "If there wasn't, I've seriously misjudged what happened between us at our first meeting." His head came up, and he turned to her with an expression of disarming sincerity. "Did I misjudge it, my dear? Can I have been a conceited coxcomb?"

She caught her breath, and her fingers trembled in his hold. There *had* been something between them at their first meeting, she knew that. If there had not, she would not have thought of him so often and so fondly all these months. But to admit it to him now would muddle the plans she'd made for her life. In any case, the events of the past day had unbalanced her. She needed time to think. To gain that time, she deliberately turned her face away from the question in his eyes. "I can't answer that now," she said quietly. "I'm too confused about all this."

"What confuses you, Georgy? I'll explain anything you wish to know."

"How you found me, for one thing. That confuses me."

"It was Alison. She found a letter among your things,

written from Ruckworth Parish, from a Mr. Hunsford to a
Miss Grace Vail. I came here to question the mysterious
Miss Vail, hoping that she might have some knowledge of
your whereabouts. But folks in small towns are cautious
with strangers, so I decided to proceed slowly. Making the
acquaintance of the local gentry seemed the best course, so
I introduced myself to Lady Ruckworth in the manner I've
already described. I was delighted when she invited me to
attend Miss Vail's Quarterly Exercises, but that was nothing to the delight I felt when I saw who Miss Vail really
was."

She shook her head in admiration. "You certainly handled everything remarkably well. You discovered my identity without giving me away."

"I didn't wish to do that without your permission. But
now I'm looking forward to this tea, to which I've shamed
her ladyship into inviting you."

"Yes, I wondered about that. How did you manage it?
She's invited me to tea only once before in all the time I've
been here."

"I merely pointed out that you hadn't been properly re-
warded for your efforts at the Quarterlies and that it was a
shame you weren't persuaded to attend the 'cold collation'.
Lady Ruckworth was quick to take the hint." He chuckled
mischievously. "I can't wait to see Lady Ruckworth's face
when I tell her at tea today that the girl she snubbed last
evening is Lord Verney's daughter."

Georgy's smile died. "Oh, no, you *mustn't!*" she exclaimed in alarm, withdrawing her hands from his.
"Please, my lord, I'm not. . you can't . . . don't give me
away now."

He stared at her for a moment in disappointed bafflement. He had thought, when her response to his impetuous
embrace had been so warm, that she would be as eager to
go home with him as he was to take her. But now it seemed
that it was not so. She had reservations. Something he did
not understand was keeping her from going back. He wondered what had driven her from home in the first place.
Had her mother been too demanding? How would she feel
if she knew that her mother had substituted a look-

alike to entrap him? In that moment, he decided to tell her nothing of the occurrences at Colinas Verde. The girl had enough on her mind.

He sighed in what he thought of as temporary defeat and took her chin in his hand. "I won't give you away, Georgy. Not until you give me leave. I realize that all this has happened very quickly and that you need time to take it all in."

"Yes. Thank you, my lord."

"Tony," he corrected.

"Is that what you're called? Tony?" She smiled up at him. "It suits you."

He grinned back at her. "Better than Grace Vail suits you, I think. Whatever made you choose so prudish a name?"

"Perhaps a prudish name suits me better than you think." To prove her point she removed his hand from her chin, picked up the cap that lay forgotten in his lap and put it on firmly.

He laughed. "If you think that cap has the power to deter me from my purpose, Georgy, my girl, you're out in your reckoning," he said, taking her in his arms.

She put her hands against his chest to hold him off. "Don't, my lor—Tony! We've no time for waggery. We've been riding for quite a while, have we not? We'll be arriving at the manor at any moment."

"Don't worry about that, ma'am." He gave her a wide grin and pulled her close. "We've more time for 'waggery' than you think. I told the coachman to take the long way round."

Chapter 24

For Georgy, taking tea at Ruckworth Manor this time was vastly more entertaining than it was before. From the moment she and Maitland arrived, the afternoon proved interesting. They were greeted with a scold from Lady Ruckworth for being late, which Maitland countered by explaining (with a twinkling glance at Georgy) that Henry, his coachman, had an alarming propensity for frequently taking the long way round on any route. "I always berate him soundly for it," he said with a helpless shake of his head, "but nothing I say has any weight with the fellow." Lady Ruckworth, having a sense that she was being in some way teased, didn't long dwell on that subject. She gave Miss Vail a cursory greeting and then took Maitland forcibly by the arm. "My lord, I wish you to make the acquaintance of Lady Symonds and Miss Carolyn Symonds," she said eagerly, and she drew him across the room to the window where two women—mother and daughter—were sitting. "May I present my very best friend, Lady Elizabeth Symonds, whose estate is no more than five miles distant, and her charming daughter Carolyn."

It was obvious at once that Lady Ruckworth was matchmaking and that Miss Symonds had been occupied all day with preparing for this meeting. Her hair had been frizzed and curled with such pains that there was not a lock that did not bounce when she moved her head, and her dress, ornately edged with seed pearls and glass beads, was more suited to a court ball than a tea party. In addition, the girl was flushed with excitement. The moment the introductions were made, she attacked his lordship with so vigorous a barrage of quips, questions and comments that he was not able to put in a word of his own. And on the few occasions when she paused for breath, her mother entered the conversation with her own barrage.

Georgy was given her tea and relegated to a seat in the far corner of the room. She didn't mind the virtual banishment from the rest of the company, for she quietly enjoyed watching the scene being played out across the room. It pleased her to watch Maitland react with quiet politeness to the fawning of the three women. Everything about him was generous and manly, and Georgy could not help but feel overwhelmed by the knowledge that she'd made so deep an impression on him that he had come all this way (and subjected himself to foolish social entanglements such as this one) for her sake.

As soon as he could, he excused himself from the company of the Symonds women and, picking up a tray of cucumber sandwiches, walked deliberately across the huge room to offer them to Georgy. "Are you enjoying the tea, Miss Vail?" he asked blandly.

"Yes, very much. But not quite as much as you must be, my lord," she murmured in a voice too low to be heard by anyone but him as she accepted a sandwich with a smile. "Miss Symonds seems to bubble over with charm."

Maitland rolled his eyes. "Babble over, you mean," he muttered under his breath.

"Oh? A very fluent young lady, is she?"

"She has the entire world at the tip of her tongue."

Georgy's lips twitched. "But, my lord, you must admit she is very animated and bright-eyed."

"I think a better description would be 'bride-eyed,'" his lordship whispered. "Don't you think her mama should tell her that pursuit is more effective if the object doesn't know he's being chased?"

Georgy couldn't help letting a little gurgle of laughter escape her. This caught the ear of their hostess. Lady Ruckworth frowned at them in disapproval. "You two mustn't make jokes between yourselves, you know. Come and sit here near Miss Symonds and me, my boy, and tell *us* a joke or two. And oh, yes, Miss Vail, I just remembered. I have something for you. Ask the butler to show you to the library where you will find several copies of *The Poor Girls' Primer*. It is the book that Mrs. Jayce used to teach reading to the younger girls. You'll find it more suitable than *Aesop's Fables,* which Mr. Hunsford tells me you've been using."

If Georgy felt chagrined at this abrupt dismissal, one look at Maitland's face showed her that he felt even angrier. She rose from her chair, pressed a restraining hand surreptitiously on his arm to calm his temper, and went swiftly to the door. The butler led her to the library where she lingered over the books for as long as made sense, and then, tucking them under one arm, she returned to the sitting room hoping to be able to take her leave. The sound of Lady Ruckworth's voice, however, made her pause in the doorway. She peeped round the doorjamb and saw that the three ladies had surrounded Maitland on the sofa. "You *must* stay for the Assembly this Saturday, my boy," Lady Ruckworth was urging. "I don't normally approve of fetes and dancing, for those sinful diversions encourage ungodliness and depravity, but our Assemblies here in this district are not the sinful sort."

"No, they are not," Lady Symonds agreed. "They are most decorous. It will be a delightful affair, I assure you."

"Not only will I and the Symondses be there," Lady Ruckworth continued, "but we believe that the Wangells are planning to attend this year, and Lady Wangell, you know, is closely related to Lord and Lady Holland."

"Oh, yes, Lord Maitland," Miss Symonds urged eagerly, "you *must* come. We would all be *flying in alt* to have you there!"

"Is there anyone else I've met here in Ruckworth Parish who is to attend?" Maitland asked incorrigibly. "The Hunsfords, for instance . . . or Miss Vail?"

"Miss *Vail?*" Lady Ruckworth exclaimed in astonishment. "We are hardly likely to include *servants* on the Assembly list, my lord."

"Servants?" Maitland asked, reddening. "Do you consider Miss Vail a servant?"

"My dear boy, I don't know what sort of society you

maintain in East Riding, but here we consider a charity-school teacher to be nothing else." Her brows knit, and she peered at him curiously. "You seem to take an inordinate interest in Miss Vail, my lord. Why are you so concerned with her?"

"Because, ma'am, I'm considering setting up a charity school of my own in East Riding," he retorted promptly, "and I am seriously considering stealing Miss Vail from under your nose."

At this point, Georgy deemed it advisable to reenter the room. Whether Lady Ruckworth was about to take offense at Maitland's retort or take it as a joke would never be determined, for Georgy's presence effectively put a damper on the conversation. After a few desultory remarks, Georgy curtseyed to her employer and begged to be excused, thus bringing the tea party to an abrupt end.

Georgy returned to the vicarage in as much of a muddle as when she'd left it that morning. In place of the questions that had been answered, a new, larger question now loomed up: what should she do about Tony Maitland? In one day he'd changed from an inaccessible dream-figure to a real man, a man more appealing to her than any man she'd ever met. In one day he'd acted as her defender, her companion and her beau, and in each one of those roles he'd been charming, witty, strong and endearing. He'd made it quite clear that he cared for her and wanted to take her back home and wed her. He'd not said it in so many words, but his intention was plain. He'd not pressed his suit, but he surely would before very long, and she would have to have an answer for him.

Until today, her goal had been firm and unshakable. She'd charted her course in life, and she'd had no intention of wavering from it. But Tony Maitland had offered her a detour more tempting than any in her life before, and she didn't know if she had the strength to refuse.

Sometimes, however, ordinary everyday events provide us with answers to questions of extraordinary importance, and ordinary events did just that for Georgy the next day. As she came round the schoolhouse from the hayfield that morning before school was to begin, she found Mrs. Putman waiting for her. "Miz Vail," the gaunt woman said, holding her shawl tightly about her thin shoulders, "I brung ye somethin'. A small . . . gift, ye might say." And she held out a package wrapped in brown paper.

Georgy stepped back in surprise. "There's no need for you to do that, Mrs. Putman. It isn't my birthday or anything like that, you know. And even if it were, I couldn't—"

"Please take it, Miz Vail. It ain't much. I jest wanted ye to 'ave a token of my . . . gratitude, ye see."

"Gratitude?"

"Fer what y're doin' fer my Sarah. Fer the others, too, acourse—Billy writin' 'is name so pretty, an' Hester makin' out the words in 'er Mother Goose. Right lovely it is. But it's Sarah, ye see. She ain't been a 'appy child." The woman's lips trembled, and she pressed them together for a moment to steady her emotions. Then, after taking a shaky breath, she went on. "Ye see, she was the sort wut's always keepin' to 'erself an' lookin' at everyone wi' those fearful, sad eyes . . . used to break me 'eart to see 'er. But now she goes about singin' to 'erself all day. *Singin'!* Ye don' know, Miz Vail, wut a joy it is to 'ear 'er." She tried unsuccessfully to sniff back her tears. "An' the way she sounded in school on Sunday, singin' that hymn part all by 'erself in front of everyone, not a bit scared. She sounded like a bird, didn't she? A *bird!* Miz Vail, I cain't tell ye . . ." She shook her head, unable to continue. Then she gulped, wiped her cheeks with work-worn, bony fingers and thrust the package into Georgy's hands. "Thank ye, Miz Vail. Thank ye."

Georgy watched the woman hurry away and then walked slowly into the schoolhouse. She placed the package on the table and stared at it. It was like an omen . . . a Greek augury in which one could read a message from the gods. And the message was very plain. She didn't even have to open the package to read it. It told her that *this* was her place, her work, the reason for her being on this earth.

This was the answer to her question. It didn't matter what was inside the package. What mattered was what Mrs. Putman had told her: that this was where she was truly needed . . . that here was where she had to be. Nevertheless, she had to know what Mrs. Putman had given her. With a mixture of elation for what she'd so far achieved with the children and misery for what she was about to give up for them, she opened the wrapping. It was a jar of blackcurrant jam.

She found Maitland waiting for her after school just as he'd been the day before. "Am I to take tea *again*, my lord?" she asked in surprise.

"No, I would not subject you to that again so soon. But you didn't think I could endure a full day at Ruckworth Manor without at least a glimpse of you, did you? Will you take a drive with me, ma'am?"

She hesitated. "They will miss me at the vicarage . . ."

"Tell them you were summoned again to the manor. Please, Georgy. The only way I was able to endure a second visit from the Symonds ladies was the expectation that I would soon be visiting with you."

"A second visit? Today?"

He nodded. "At luncheon. The conversation was as heavily sprinkled with sugar as the dessert. And both were equally lacking in subtlety."

She laughed. "Poor Tony. I shan't refuse you, then. Besides, I have something I must say to you."

He helped her up and jumped in beside her. "May I kiss you first? I've been longing to do so all day."

"No, you may not," she said firmly, moving as far away from him as the seat allowed. "You've pushed us into intimacy much too quickly, my lord, and I'm afraid you've made assumptions about my responses that may not be true."

"Have I?" he asked, his expression turning watchful.

"I think you have. You may have forgotten what I told you when we first met—that I am not given to flirtation."

One of his eyebrows rose. "Flirtation? Is *that* what you call what has been passing between us?"

"Yes, I must, because this sort of thing *is* flirtation if it is not meant to have a . . . a serious result."

"I'm afraid, my dear, that I don't know what you mean. What serious result?"

Her cheeks grew hot. How was she to explain that she was rejecting him when he'd not yet even asked? "I mean when two people have ... er ... ah ... serious intentions toward each other."

"And you think we have not?"

She clenched her hands tightly. "No, we have not," she said pointedly.

His brows knit in anger and bewilderment. "Can you have forgotten what happened here yesterday? Then let me remind you!"

He seized her by the shoulders and forced her into an angry embrace, as if to compel her to feel with her body what she was denying in her mind. But neither his feelings nor hers were at all the same as those of the day before. This time, instead of warmth and delight, there was confusion and hostility surging below the surface. The violence of the pressure of his lips on hers infuriated her, but she could not push him away. His insistence enraged her even more. But enraged as she was, she nevertheless found her pulse racing and her heart hammering in her chest in a response that had nothing to do with flirtation.

Abruptly he let her go. "Was that serious enough for you?" he asked, breathless but cold as ice.

"That was not serious," she retorted, as breathless as he. "That was *belligerent*."

He winced, suddenly aware and ashamed of having bullied her. "Yes, I suppose it was. I'm sorry."

"There's no need to apologize," she said, her anger fading. "I was also at fault. I made you angry. I did not mean to belittle ..." She made a helpless gesture, not knowing what name to give to what had been between them.

"I'm not sure I understand you, Georgy. You cannot believe that I'm not serious ... that I've been toying with you!"

"No, I know better than that. What I mean ..." She lowered her eyes. "What I mean is that I ... I won't be going back with you."

There was a long silence, broken only by the creaking

of the carriage. When it became clear that he was not going to speak, she glanced timidly up at him. He was sitting back against the squabs, still watching her, but the tightness about his mouth showed that her words had had a powerful effect on him. "I suppose you'll have a dreadful scene with my mother when you tell her," she said, feeling capable of nothing more than nervous bibble-babble.

"No, there'll be no scene. I have no reason to tell her anything about this."

"But . . . wasn't it Mama who sent you here?"

"No. Your mother knows nothing about it. It was all my own idea. I had Alison's help, of course, but no one else knows anything about it."

Georgy gaped at him. "I don't understand. You told me they'd found a letter—"

"Not 'they'. Alison."

"Are you saying that Allie didn't show Mama the letter? That Mama doesn't know any of this?"

"No one knows but Allie and me."

"But why did Allie keep the letter from her? And why didn't you tell her you were coming to find me?"

"I think Allie's motive to keep the letter secret and mine to keep silent about where and why I was going were the same. We didn't wish to reveal anything about you without first asking your permission." He spoke abstractedly, as if his mind were elsewhere. "We felt that you must have had a good reason for what you did, and we wished to respect your privacy."

"That was good of you . . . both." She fixed her eyes on his face. "Do you intend to *continue* to respect it, now that you've found me?"

"Good God, Georgy," he burst out impatiently, "what is it you're asking of me? To keep your whereabouts secret from everyone? To go back home and refrain from telling any of them where you are? Is that what you want?"

"Yes, that is what I want. I left home for what I think are good and sufficient reasons. They have not changed just because you found me."

His mouth tensed. "Haven't they? I think they *should* have changed. Do you think my coming after you has no significance? Do you think your response to my embrace means nothing? Can you ignore what you obviously feel for me and I for you? Dash it all, girl, I *love* you! It is, perhaps, too soon to ask you to marry me, but that was my intention from the first. Are you going to refuse me because you're reluctant to go home and face your *mother?*"

Her eyes widened. "Can you really believe *that* to be my motive? How little you know me, my lord. I'm refusing you because I want to remain here to teach. That is why I came, and that is why I shall stay."

"To teach? I can't credit that for a moment!" he said angrily. "Are you expecting me to believe that you'd rather remain here as a servant to Lady Ruckworth—yes, that is how she thinks of you . . . as a servant!—than to be my wife, the Countess Ivers, and mistress of Colinas Verde?"

"You may believe it or not," she snapped, flaring up angrily herself, "but it is true. I realize that it may be difficult for you, puffed up as you are with your own wealth and importance, to accept the fact that I would prefer to stay here with my pupils than to be wedded to your titles and estate, but—"

"You would *not* be wedded to titles and estates. How can you even think such a thing?"

"*Everyone* would think it. And Georgianna Verney has sworn she would never marry for money!"

"Oh, has she indeed?" he sneered with nostrils flaring. "How very noble of her!"

"I don't pretend to be noble . . . only to be a woman of principle."

"And what *is* that principle, ma'am?

"To do some *good* in this world, instead of dedicating my life to marrying advantageously, as most girls of my class are raised to do. I think it reprehensible to marry wealth."

"But you would not be marrying wealth," he said between clenched teeth. "You would be marrying *me!*"

"It is much the same thing, is it not?"

"I have always thought," he answered icily, "that I am a *man*, distinct from and more than my titles and possessions."

"But you are *not* distinct from them. They are part of you."

He stared at her, appalled. "Part of me? How can they be? They are only things, no more part of me than my clothes! Would you find me acceptable if I dispensed with them all—my clothes included—and came to you penniless and draped in sackcloth and ashes?"

"I cannot even imagine you doing something so foolish," she answered.

"No, neither can I."

They eyed each other warily from their opposite corners, Georgy pale from the strain of breaking from him and Maitland tight-lipped and furious. To her, this act was a commendable deed, abounding with self-sacrifice and nobility of purpose. To him, her behavior was both mystifying and heinous, a painful rejection of his character and his love, and at this moment altogether unforgivable. "I suppose there's nothing more to be said," he muttered at last.

She bit her lip. "I suppose . . . not."

He tapped on the carriage roof for the coachman. "Back to the vicarage, Henry, if you please," he ordered.

They rode back in silence. When the coach stopped at the vicarage door, Maitland jumped out and handed her down. "I shall tell no one that I've seen you," he assured her, "since that is what you desire. Good-bye, ma'am. My very best wishes to you for a successful and happy future with your . . . er . . . principles."

"Thank you, my lord," she murmured unhappily, her eyes on the ground. Then she flicked a quick glance up at his face. "Wh-What will you do now?"

"Do, ma'am? What will I *do?*" He gave her an unexpected, sardonic, lopsided smile. "I would have thought you'd guess. I shall go at once to someone who *is* enamored of my titles and estates. I'm off to ask for the hand of Miss Carolyn Symonds."

Having delivered himself of that riposte, he climbed back in the carriage and shut the door. She stood watching as the coach disappeared up the road, her breast heaving with a flood of regrets and misgivings that she could no longer keep at bay.

That night at supper, Mr. Hunsford brought the news that Lady Ruckworth's famous visitor had departed. He'd informed his hostess that urgent business required him to leave at once. In spite of the fact that the information that Lord Maitland was no longer in the vicinity came as no surprise to Georgy, it left her feeling utterly bereft. As soon as supper was over, she excused herself and went up to bed with the only comfort left to her . . . her principles.

Chapter 25

～

The mood at Colinas Verde was as gloomy as the weather during Maitland's absence. Letty Denham racked her brain devising pastimes for the ladies, but cards and gossip were all that seemed to stir their interest. Lucy convinced some of the younger set to engage in rehearsing an amateur theatrical, which occupied them contentedly for a few hours during the rainy afternoons, but otherwise there was little to entertain them. The men played billiards and hunted quail on those mornings when the weather was bearable, but none of these activities seemed to have the spontaneity and excitement of the earlier days. Everyone looked forward to Maitland's return, somehow convinced that only his presence would restore the house party's previous glow.

Peggy spent a good part of each day in her room, taking advantage of the excuse that she was following doctor's orders. She spent the time reading novels from Maitland's library and helping Betsy alter Georgy's gowns. These methods of passing the hours were not fascinating, but they were preferable to the hours spent downstairs among the rest of the guests. There she had always to be on her toes; with almost everyone in the group she had to guard her tongue; with Lucy she had to try her best to avoid intimate exchanges (during which there was a greater likelihood than at any other time to slip into error); with Rudi she had to endure an overabundance of effusive compliments; and, worst of all, when she came face to face with Jeremy, she had to try to ignore his lingering, glowering disapproval. Even though she could not possibly flirt with Maitland while he was away, Jeremy remained unreasonably, furiously angry with her.

Ned was unreasonably angry with her, too. He appeared in her bedroom two nights after Maitland had gone. "Have ye bedded 'is lordship yet?" he demanded.

"Bedded him?" Peggy echoed, shuddering. "I have no intention of—"

"No intention? No intention, Miss 'Igh-in-the-Instep? Then will ye please tell me 'ow else y're goin' to compromise 'im? How else, eh?"

"I don't know," she said in disgust, dropping down on her bed and leaning her forehead on the bedpost. "This is your idea, not mine."

"I know it's my idea. My idea, noddypate, is to *bed* 'im. There ain't no other way 'e'll pay off."

She looked up at him levelly. "I won't do it, Ned. There's no use pressing me. Besides, he wouldn't do it even if I agreed. He isn't the sort."

"Every man's the sort. Take my word on it."

She gave a sneering laugh. "I wouldn't take your word for the time of day."

He walked toward her threateningly. Grasping a handful of her hair, he pulled it up, using it to lift her painfully to her feet. "I'll brook none o' yer lip, Peg Birkin, so mind yer manners," he snarled into her face. "Ye know what I 'ave in my pocket, don't ye? 'Ave ye fergot a certain green stone? Do ye want me to drop it off in yer Cap'n's room tonight?"

"Let me go!" she cried, wincing in pain.

He pulled harder. "Well, shall I? Yes 'r no?"

"No!" she gasped.

He released his grip and let her fall back on the bed. "That's a good lass," he chortled in triumph. "That's usin' yer noddle. So when will it be, eh? T'morrow?"

She rubbed her head with shaking fingers. "How can it be tomorrow? His lordship is not here."

"Then, when—?"

"How can I say? I don't know when he'll be back. Lord Maitland doesn't take me into his confidence."

"Ain't 'e said nothin' to anyone concernin' 'is plans?"

"Not that I know—"

The sound of a light knock at the door caused them both to freeze. "Who's that?" Ned hissed.

"I don't know. Get under the bed, quickly."

"No. I'll step be'ind the drap'ries there. Watch what ye say, girl. I'll be listenin'."

The knock sounded louder. "Who is it?" Peggy asked, slipping on a robe.

"It's I, Jeremy," came a whispered voice.

Peggy groaned inwardly. She didn't want Jeremy, of all people, to be overheard by her brother. What on earth did he want with her? She opened the door only slightly and peered out. "What is it, Jeremy?"

"Let me in, Peggy. I must speak to you," he pleaded softly.

"No, I . . . I'd rather not. You told me yourself that these nightly visits are not proper."

"I know. But it will take only a moment." He gave her a boyish, hesitant smile. "We'll leave the door open."

She opened it wider and let him in. He held up his candle and looked at her curiously. She seemed disheveled and somewhat distressed. "Is anything wrong, Peggy?"

"No, nothing. If you have something to say, Jeremy, say it quickly. I wish to retire."

"Very well, then. Peggy, about the other evening, I . . . I want to beg your pardon. If I said anything offensive, I didn't—"

"*If* you said anything offensive!" She drew herself up proudly. "There is no *if* about it. You called me names that could not be considered anything *but* offensive."

"Yes, I know. I'm very sorry. I haven't been able to sleep since then, thinking about it."

"Is that so? Then why have you been looking down your nose at me in that churlish way these past two days? You've been behaving as if you'd like to bite my head off."

"Have I been? If I've seemed angry, it was only at myself."

She made a dismissive gesture with her hand. "That's very touching, Jeremy Verney, but I don't think your self-reproach or your loss of sleep makes up for anything, do you?"

"No, I suppose not. But I *am* apologizing now. Can't you forgive me? You must realize that I didn't mean any of it."

"Why must I realize it? You sounded sincere enough at the time."

"No, I was completely beside myself that evening. I said things I never intended to say. I don't know where they came from. I don't know what maggot lodged in my brain, but when I saw you dancing and laughing with Maitland, I quite lost my head."

Peggy's heart began to pound. She peered at him in fascination through the dimness, yearning to hear the full details of this revealing explanation, but she knew she ought not to encourage the outpouring. What she ought to do, she told herself, was to make short shrift of this conversation and urge Jeremy out of the room. But she could not. What he was saying was of vital interest to her. She had to hear him out. "Lost your head?" she prodded. "Why?"

"I don't know," he answered helplessly. "All I know is that when I saw you with him I went mad. Utterly mad. I don't know why."

Peggy wanted to stamp her foot in irritation. Was *this* the outpouring she hoped for? With an impatience that was usually foreign to her nature, she took him by the shoulders and turned him to the door. "Then go back to your bed and think about it," she said curtly, pushing him out. "When you think you know the answer, let me know."

"But ... are you saying you won't forgive me?" he asked, balking in the doorway.

"That's exactly what I'm saying. When you discover your motives, only then will I consider forgiving you." She gave him a final push. "Good*night,* Jeremy."

As soon as she'd shut the door on him, Ned emerged from his hiding place. He was grinning broadly. "That was a bit of *all right!*" he exclaimed. "Ye 'ad 'im eatin' out of yer 'ands. Just ye 'andle Lord Maitland that same way an' we'll soon be livin' on a bed o' roses!"

Chapter 26

Jeremy returned to his room, shut his door, ripped off his neckcloth and threw himself upon his bed. He'd humbled himself before that damnable female and had gained nothing for his pains but an increased feeling of discomfiture. It was a feeling he hadn't had before and which he couldn't easily describe. It was as if he'd been unhoused, dispossessed. He was uncomfortable with himself, with others, with his surroundings. He wished he were back in military service. The dangers of army life had never frightened him. And *there* he'd never felt this unpleasant sense of not belonging.

It was all Peggy's fault, of course. Peggy's and his mother's. If he hadn't taken her under his wing . . . if his mother hadn't pushed them into this elaborate charade . . . but there was no point in dwelling on that. The deed was done, and it was too late now to undo it.

But perhaps it was unfair to lay the blame for this unhappy feeling at their door. It had come upon him only in the last few days, and though it was somehow bound up with Peggy, it was very much his own mind that had created it. He had explained his rudeness to Peggy by saying he'd gone mad, and the chaos in his mind was not unlike a kind of madness. Peggy had somehow become to him a wild obsession. He thought about her all the time. Her image seemed to hover over him like a low-hanging cloud on a hilltop. All day long he breathed her in. He had only to shut his eyes, and her face would appear before him, sometimes looking furious as she had the other evening when he'd so cruelly berated her, sometimes looking yearningly adoring, with her lips parted and her eyes beckoning. If he didn't know better, he would believe he was in love.

But he knew he was not in love with Peggy. It was Rosalind he loved, he knew that. He'd loved Rosalind since boyhood. He'd carried her in his heart through his school days, through his early manhood, through the battles and boredom of years of war. He'd never thought of loving anyone else; his image of his future had always included Rosalind as his wife. There had been other women who'd come his way, but he'd always known that they were interim indulgences, temporary and insignificant, and he'd made sure that they had known it too. Peggy, however, was different. She'd taken on a significance and importance he hadn't believed a woman could have in his mind. She'd somehow gotten under his skin.

He'd been so preoccupied with Peggy of late that he hadn't even paid heed to Rosalind's behavior. In the last couple of days he hadn't concerned himself with Rosalind at all. It was almost as if he felt *relieved* that she had to occupy herself with Monte.

But if what he was feeling for Peggy was not love, what was it? Was this obsession, this hunger to take her in his arms, nothing but lust? He sometimes thought that if he could have her once—just once!—he could rid himself of this turmoil. But it was not to be thought of. Peggy was not a lightskirt, in spite of the names he'd called her that night. She was a sweet, lovely young woman who deserved more than life had thus far offered her. If he was any sort of man, he would find her a good husband and see her comfortably established when this masquerade was over. But the thought of seeing her happily wedded to another made him wild. Had he truly become a madman?

There was only one thing he could think of to do. He had to get away from Peggy. He could not spend the entire week that still remained of the house party in such close proximity to her. He would wait until Maitland returned, and then he would tell his mother that he had to get back to London. Once he was safely back home, far from the distraction of her closeness, he would forget Peggy. He would leave it to his mother to arrange for her future. He would concentrate on the state of his finances. By the time the country sojourn ended and his mother and the Peascotts and all the others returned to London, he would be ready to make his case to Rosalind's father. He would have all the facts and figures ready to make Sir Basil see that he and Rosalind could manage well enough. Then Sir Basil could nullify the ridiculous betrothal to Monte before it became an embarrassing *on dit*, and he, Jeremy, could marry Rosalind and get on with his life.

Jeremy propped himself up on his pillows, folded his hands behind his head and stared up at the ceiling. He knew he wouldn't sleep, but he did feel somewhat better. He'd at least plotted a course of action. In a few days, alone in the London house and far from the attractions that were now so maddening to him, he would be able to sleep at last. All he had to do was wait for Maitland to come home.

Maitland returned the next evening. Letty Denham had managed, in the three days he'd been gone, to keep the party going, but it had not been easy. Combatting both the weather and the resultant lethargy of the company had taken all her resources as a hostess, and when Maitland walked back in the door after his three-day absence, no one was more delighted than she. The rest of the group brightened also, each one of them expecting a resumption of the gaiety and good spirits of the first few days. Even the weather seemed to welcome Maitland home; the sky cleared and the stars came out.

If Maitland's trip had dampened his spirits, no one was aware of it. Dinner that evening was noisily festive. Everyone was dressed in his finest clothes and highest spirits. The ladies chirped excitedly over the first course, and the men roared over the smallest witticisms. Even Peggy, who'd been quiet and restrained during Maitland's absence, seemed to come out of her shell and flirt with her host outrageously. Dozens of bottles of champagne were poured, Sir Basil made a number of toasts, Lord Traherne kept everyone laughing with his imitation of the notorious Sidmouth making a speech in the Lords', and Lucy announced that she, Monte, Rosalind, Alison and Rudi had prepared an amateur theatrical for presentation that evening in honor of their host's return.

When the men rejoined the ladies after their port, the entire group assembled in the music room, where seats had been arranged around an area against the far wall which had been cleared of furniture and designated as the stage. For two hours they were entertained with a much-abbreviated version of *The School for Scandal*, with Lucy performing famously as Lady Teazle, Rudi bringing down waves of laughter as a German-accented Snake, and Alison winning the most applause for transforming herself into a swaggering, handsome Charles Surface.

Maitland tried to concentrate on the performance but could not. The fury that Georgy had stirred up in him for dealing so painful a blow to his self-esteem had been a buffer that shielded him thus far from his deeper feelings. The anger had lasted through the long ride home, through the reunion with his guests and through the long dinner. Now, however, with the theatrical performance distracting his guests' attention away from him, his mind was free for the first time in many hours to roam where it willed, and it roamed, naturally, to Georgy. It permitted him to relive the two days he'd spent in her company. He let himself remember it all, every detail: her instinctive, almost passionate reaction to his first embrace, the noticeable pleasure she took in his company, and then her brave, painfully uttered declaration of her principles. Reliving it all, he felt his anger receding. It was hard to keep himself angry at the girl; she had so obviously struggled with herself to bring herself to reject him. Her reasoning may have been foolish and girlishly idealistic, but he couldn't help admiring a young woman whose ideals were more substantial than the trivial, self-indulgent ones that preoccupied most of the ladies of the *ton*. He'd fallen in love with her because she was uniquely free-thinking and independent. He could not now be furious at her for the same qualities.

But as his anger died, his pain increased. He loved her. How could he now face the emptiness that life would bring without her? He was no callow youth who believed that hearts break and lovers die of thwarted love, but although he knew the illness was not fatal, the pain was damnably real. How could he make it endurable? Some men were able to ease it by quickly indulging in a new romance, but he knew that such a solution would never work for him. Another Georgy would be impossible to find, and someone less would not cure him. He had somehow to learn to live with the emptiness. And to do that, he needed to be alone.

But he was not alone. His house was full of guests. While they remained with him, he had no hope of finding peace. He was sorry now that he'd invited them. He could perhaps have found some comfort in confiding in Roger, but he'd promised Georgy not to reveal her secret, so there was not even the prospect of that mild anodyne. He would have to grit his teeth and endure it. There was still another week before the fortnight was over, a week that loomed ahead of him like a prison sentence. He had, before anything else, to get through that.

The prospect of the next week had no bright edges to its clouds. Not only would he have to deal with his personal pain, but he'd have to wear a cheerful face. He'd have to invent more amusements and pastimes for his guests. He'd have to continue to pretend that Peggy was Georgianna Verney and to counter her more-and-more obvious overtures without giving offense. And he'd have to discover who in his household had stolen Letty's emerald. No, it would not in any way be a pleasant week.

When the play ended, he resumed his smiling-host aspect and led the players and the audience downstairs for a late supper. It was there that Alison, looking utterly charming in the breeches and neckcloth she'd worn as Charles Surface, took him aside. "I've been waiting on tenterhooks for your return," she whispered eagerly. "Well, Tony? What did you find out?"

He lifted her chin gently. "I'm sorry I raised your hopes, my dear. I learned nothing."

Her face clouded in disappointment. "Nothing? How can this be? Did you find that woman . . . what was her name? Miss Vail?"

He sighed. "Don't press me, Allie. I've nothing to tell you."

"But you must have learned *something!*" the girl insisted. "How did such a letter fall in among Georgy's possessions if there wasn't some connection?"

He dropped his hand and turned away from the intensity of her gaze. "I learned one thing only . . . that your sister doesn't want to be found. Perhaps we have no choice but to honor her wish."

"But how did you learn that?" she persisted.

He made a helpless gesture. "I can't say. But it would be a disservice to your sister to speak further about the letter, about Miss Vail, or about any of this. I hope you'll say nothing more on this subject—to anyone."

Allie went round and peered up at his face. *"You're* more disappointed than I am, aren't you? I'm sorry, Tony. I didn't mean to pry."

"You had every right to pry, my dear. It is I who should be sorry. I wish I'd been able to restore your sister to you."

She nodded knowingly. "Don't take it so badly, Tony. She'll come back when she's ready." With a small, sympathetic smile, she turned and walked away.

"Your performance tonight was delicious, Allie," he called after her. "You make a most charming young man."

She turned back. "Did you really think so?"

"Yes. Really."

She walked slowly back to him. "I'll make an even more charming young *woman,* my lord," she taunted, "If you're willing to wait a few years."

He laughed. "I know you will."

"Perhaps even more charming than Georgy." She kissed him quickly on the cheek and ran off.

Even for someone as adorable as you, my girl, he said sadly to himself as he watched her go, *that would take some doing.*

Chapter 27

Jeremy had watched Peggy flirt shamelessly with Maitland all through dinner, and the fury that had driven him a few days before to berate the girl returned in full force. She *was* a wanton! He wanted, more than he'd wanted anything in his life before, to strangle her with his bare hands.

This was all becoming too much for him. He'd been a soldier, but he'd never considered himself to be a brute. Yet Peggy was turning him into one. If his character was not to degenerate into bestiality, he had to get away. And the sooner the better. All he had to do was inform his mother and go.

When the evening's activities were over, and the guests trooped up to their beds, Jeremy went down the hall to his mother's room and tapped on her door. At her prompt "Come in," he entered. He found her sitting at her dressing table, already clad in her nightdress. Betsy stood behind her plaiting her hair. "Jeremy, my love," Horatia greeted him, "how serious you are looking. Is anything amiss?"

"No, ma'am, but I'd like to speak to you."

Horatia stayed Betsy's hand. "Of course, my boy. Do sit down. Betsy, you may go to bed. I shall finish without you."

He perched on the edge of her bed and waited silently for Betsy to close the door behind her. When they were alone, his mother turned on her chair and faced him. "Something *is* amiss," she declared. "I can see it in your face. Is it Rosalind?"

"No, Mama, it is not Rosalind. It is only that I've had enough of ruralizing. If you don't object, I'd like to go back to town. It won't inconvenience you, I promise. I've planned it all out. I'll only pack a saddlebag so that I can go on horseback, leaving you the carriages. You can take the rest of my things with you when you leave."

Horatia eyed her son suspiciously. "Yes, yes, the details are perfectly satisfactory. I don't care about them. What I wish to know is the reason behind this sudden decision."

"No special reason. I'm just bored."

"No, that's not it. I've observed you when you go out with the other men on a hunt or when you play billiards. You are not the least bored. But in the evenings I've seen you prowl about like an angry lion looking for its mate. It *is* Rosalind, isn't it? You cannot accept her betrothal to Monte."

Jeremy glared at his mother in irritation. "If you know the answers for yourself, Mama, why do you bother to ask me the questions?"

Horatia's natural complacency kept her from taking offense. She turned back to the mirror and took up plaiting her hair where her abigail had left off. "If you were to ask my opinion, Jeremy, I would be pleased to tell you that you're lucky to have Rosalind off your hands. She is a spoilt, selfish creature who would not have brought you a day's happiness."

"But I didn't ask for your opinion, ma'am. And she is not 'off my hands', as you put it. We still have every intention of marrying. This betrothal to Monte is her father's doing, not hers. As soon as I can convince Sir Basil that I am sufficiently solvent, Rosalind will cry off."

"And how do you intend to convince Sir Basil, may I ask?"

"That is what I am returning to London to take care of. When I set my accounts in proper order, I'm sure we'll find that I'm capable of supporting a wife."

"You may be able to support a wife who has a sense of economy, my boy, but you will *not* be able to support a wife like Rosalind Peascott," his mother said bluntly.

"We shall see about that, Mama."

She sighed. "I suppose we will. If only Georgy were here, I might have been able to offer you some hope. But as things are, I don't blame you for feeling that those hopes are dashed."

"I have no dashed hopes, I assure you. I never expected anything of Georgy, nor of this scheme of yours. I was convinced from the first that you were overly optimistic about Georgy's snaring Maitland. And surely nothing will come of substituting Peggy in her place."

"Yes, I'm beginning to see that you're right about that. Maitland shows no real interest in her, in spite of the lures she's been putting out to him." She shook her head in reluctant admiration. "I didn't think Peggy had it in her, but the girl has become as bold as brass."

Jeremy clenched his fists. "You needn't sound as if you *approve* of that behavior," he said savagely. "If I were you, I'd order her to stop."

"Why should I do that? When a marriageable girl finds herself in close proximity to a catch as splendid as Maitland, it is almost her *duty* to throw out lures. Lucy's wiles are even more brazen than Peggy's, yet I haven't heard anyone express disapproval."

Jeremy was astonished. "Lucy flirts with Maitland, too? I hadn't noticed that."

"Then I don't know where your eyes are. On Rosalind, I suppose." She reached for a jar and absently began to rub cucumber cream on her face. "The girls' efforts are all wasted, I'm afraid. Maitland seems utterly immune. It would have been interesting to see if Georgy herself could have snared him."

"I'd wager that Georgy would never have 'put out lures,'" her son muttered.

"No, I suppose not. Certainly not in the way that Peggy does. It's strange about Peggy. The more I see her, the less she resembles Georgy in my eyes. I almost don't see the resemblance anymore."

Jeremy rubbed his fingers against his temples as if he were trying to erase the pain of a headache. "No, neither do I."

"I suppose she's become, to us, a person in her own right. Yet everyone else has accepted her as Georgy without question. Isn't it amazing? I think the reason is that most people are so absorbed in themselves and their own concerns that they don't pay close attention to what's under their noses."

"Yes, you're probably right." He lifted his head, trying to shake off the weary depression that had engulfed him. "Speaking of Peggy, Mama, what do you intend to do with her?"

"*Do* with her? Play out the masquerade for the rest of the week, of course."

"Yes, I quite see why you must do that. But when it's over—?"

"I don't know. I haven't thought much about it. I won't put the girl out on the street, if that's what's worrying you. Perhaps we can engage her as a housemaid or something of the sort."

"In *our* house?" he asked, horrified.

"No, I don't suppose that *is* a good idea. When Georgy comes back, it won't do at all to have Peggy anywhere about." She looked thoughtful for a moment and then gave a dismissive shrug. "I ought to find her employment somewhere far away. I shall have to think about it."

"Yes, I wish you would. We must play fair with the girl, you know." He got abruptly to his feet. "Well, Mama, with your permission, I'll say good-bye."

"Very well, if you insist. But rushing back to town to set your accounts in order won't do you any good with Rosalind, I promise you. But go, if you're determined on it." She held up her cheek for him to kiss. "Good-bye, my love. Have a safe journey."

He stepped out into the hallway, determined to go down to the stables and ride off at once. His saddlebag was already packed. All he had to do was pick it up in his room. He started down the hall, but after only a step he stopped in his tracks. Some distance down the hallway something had moved in the shadows. It was a man dressed in black. He was sure of it. He blinked his eyes to sharpen his vision, but the candles in the hall sconces threw only small, dim circles of light. Between those circles were deep shadows. It was impossible to see clearly. Yet he could have sworn

that the dark figure had emerged from the fourth door
down. *Good God!* The realization hit him with a blow.
Peggy's door!

He wanted to shout for the fellow to stop, but the cry
stuck in his throat. He couldn't shout—he'd wake everyone on the floor. He dashed off at once after the man, but
the shadowy figure was already disappearing into the darkness all the way down at the end of the hallway. Jeremy ran
as noiselessly as he could down the hall after him. When
he came to the end, however, there was nobody there.
Puzzled, he was about to turn away when he noticed a door
swinging shut. He pushed through it and found himself on
a narrow stairway. He raced down the stairs but couldn't
catch a glimpse of the shadowy figure who, he was certain,
was always one flight ahead of him.

At the bottom, the stairs led into a long, narrow shed
evidently used by a gardener for storage. It was completely
dark. He should have pulled a candle from one of the hall
sconces before coming down, he realized. He paused and
peered into the darkness, listening for sounds. He was re-
warded by the click of a door closing at the far end of the
shed. He ran toward the sound, tripping once over some
obstacle he couldn't identify. Cursing under his breath, he
burst out of the door. There he stopped. He could see nothing, for there was no moon. He knew that he was at the
back of the building's west wing and, from the smell of
fragrant herbs, that he stood in the kitchen garden. But
trees and shrubs made deep shadows everywhere. If the
fellow he'd been chasing had hid himself in one of those
shadows, he'd be impossible to find.

Jeremy kicked viciously at the nearest shrub, but the
action did nothing to calm him. Abruptly he wheeled about
and ran back the way he'd come. As he raced through the
shed he collided with the same obstacle that had tripped
him before, and he cursed again. But he did not stop. With
a fury building up in him stronger than any emotion he'd
ever experienced, he took the stairs two at a time til he
reached the top floor. He burst through the little door and
ran down the hall to Peggy's door. Heedless of the distur-

bance he might cause, he pounded on it. When his knock was not immediately answered he pounded again. This time it opened a crack. Peggy, holding a candle, peeped out cautiously. "Jeremy?" she whispered in surprise. "What—?"

Furious, his breath coming in painful gasps, he shoved the door open, causing her to totter backward. He stomped over the threshold and slammed the door behind him. "Who was he?" he demanded through tightly clenched teeth.

"The door," she murmured in confusion, frightened by his wild eyes and heaving chest. "You closed the door."

He grasped her shoulders savagely. "Who *was* he?"

She blinked in bafflement. "Jeremy? What is it? You shouldn't have closed the door. You told me—"

He could feel her skin through the thin cotton nightdress. Its smooth warmth drove him further into insanity; his only thought—and it maddened him—was that the black-coated fellow had *touched this skin!* He shook her ferociously. "Who was here with you tonight?"

Her eyes widened with sudden fear. "No one. No one was here."

He caught that flicker of fear. *"Slut!* Don't lie to me! I *saw* him."

She tried to push him away. "Jemmy, *please*—"

"Who was it?" he repeated, holding her tighter. "That fawning boy Rudi? Maitland himself? One of the footmen?"

"You're hurting me, Jemmy!" she gasped, struggling to free herself. The candle she was still clutching in one hand wavered widely, throwing their huge shadows into an exaggerated struggle on the ceiling. "Let me go!"

"We've been here a week," he snarled, his eyes murderous. "How many visitors have you had here in that time? One? Seven? Tell me!"

"Please, Jemmy!"

"Or was your caller an old lover . . . someone who followed you from Whaley Bridge?" He slid his hands from her shoulders up to her neck, gripping her cruelly and tilting her face up to his with his thumbs. "Has he been here every night? Was he hiding under the bed when I came in here last night to apologize for calling you a wanton? That must have been a splendid comic moment for you both."

She closed her eyes to shut out the terrifying ferocity of his face. "Jemmy, don't . . . ! You don't understand—"

"Understand? What is there to understand? That a man was here? That he saw you like this, in this negligible nightdress, with your hair undone like this and your body trembling? Were you trembling like this for him?"

"*Jemmy!*" Appalled, she wrenched her head abruptly from his grasp and backed away. "Please, my dear, you don't know what you're saying. Go away now. Please. We'll talk about it tomorrow, when you're calmer." She held out her hands to him, one still holding her candle and the other open, palm up, with fingers outspread in a pathetic plea.

He was distraught but not fallen so far into madness that he failed to hear the pathos in her voice or see the frightened innocence of her eyes. He blinked for a moment in confusion, but his jealous rage made him brush that confusion away. His imagination had conjured up too powerful an image of a dark-coated stranger kissing those full, trembling lips and running brutish hands over the curves of her body under that thin shift. "No, not tomorrow," he said, stalking her until she backed into the bedpost and could move no farther. "We'll talk right now."

He thrust her arms aside and moved in as if for an attack. He was terrifyingly close to her. "Jemmy, I *swear!*" she cried desperately. "No one has—"

"Damnation, must you lie to me *still?* I tell you I *saw* him." With a savage cruelty, he pulled her to him. "Did you let him hold you like this? Did you let him smell your skin and tangle your hair in his fingers?"

"Jemmy, d-don't—"

His mouth was on her cheek, and all at once he could taste her tears. The tears confounded him. In the light of her candle he could see, with a start, the widened whites of her eyes. He was *terrifying* her! He realized with sudden

self-loathing that he was turning into the beast he'd feared
he would become. His obsession with her had been gnaw-
ing at him for days, and this spark of jealous madness had
ignited something inside that had almost undone him. But
the taste of her tears on his tongue seemed to have a magical, medicinal effect on the fever in his chest. What was he
doing here? he asked himself, shaking off the violent rage.
What right had he to make accusations or to seek ven-
geance? Abruptly he released her and turned away. "I'm
sorry," he muttered, struggling to restore himself to sanity.
"Your doings are none of my affair."

"No, they are n-not," Peggy answered, choked with
tears. "I am n-not your s-sister, after all."

"No, you're . . . not my sister."

"N-nor anything else t-to you."

"No, nothing!" he snapped, wheeling about. "You're
nothing at all to me! But I was fool enough to think that I
might be—*ass* that I was!—that I *might* be *in love* with
you."

She stared up at him for a moment, lips parted and
breath arrested. Then, with a shudder, she turned her back
to him. The candle slipped from her hand, and she grasped
the bedpost with both hands and leaned her head against it.
"You *w-were* an ass if you th-thought so," she said in a
hopeless whisper. "You can't love s-someone you think of
as a . . . slut."

Absently, without taking his eyes from her bent head, he
picked up her still-flickering candle, let the flame restore
itself and placed it on her bedside table. The fact that he'd
said that word to her filled him with an inexplicable shame.
But why should he feel this way? He'd *seen* the fellow
leave her room!

The evidence of his eyes notwithstanding, Jermey
wanted nothing more than to take her in his arms and beg
forgiveness. She looked so fragile, standing there huddled
against the bedpost, her fingers clenched around it, her
forehead leaning upon it, her shoulders hunched and shaking. Every nerve and sinew in his body yearned for her,
every muscle ached to hold her to him. But he would not

let himself touch her. He would not play the beast, but he would not play the fool either. "Love!" he exclaimed with a bitter laugh. "I don't know what it is anymore. I think that I despise you now." He stumbled through the shadows to her door. "Almost as much as I despise myself."

Chapter 28

When Peggy failed to appear for breakfast the next morning, no particular notice was taken. Many of the women liked to sleep through breakfast, and although Peggy was not usually one of them, it did not trouble anyone that she'd decided to do it this time. And her failure to appear at luncheon was commonplace; she always spent afternoons resting in her room. But when she made no appearance by dinner time, several of the guests took note. Horatia, waiting in the drawing room for dinner to be announced, sent Alison up to see what was the matter. Allie returned with a puzzled look on her face and drew her mother aside. "She's not there," she whispered.

"What do you mean, not there?" her mother asked sharply.

"Just not there. Her room was empty."

"Empty? How can that be? Where can she be hiding herself?"

"I have no idea, Mama. Do you think she's run away, too?"

"Run away? Like Georgy? Don't be ridiculous. Where could she run to?"

"I don't know," Allie answered with a shrug. "Where could Georgy have run to, for that matter?"

Lady Horatia threw her daughter a repressive frown. "I wish you will not be flippant with me, Alison. This may be serious."

"Not necessarily, Mama. Perhaps we're being unduly worried. Perhaps she's just gone out for a walk or has closeted herself in the library with a book, or engaged herself in something equally innocuous."

"At dinner time? It hardly seems likely. However, we shall say nothing to draw attention to the matter right now. Let's wait and see what transpires. We needn't say anything until we're sure she's gone. That will give me a chance to think."

"But what if someone asks where she is?"

"Then simply say you have no idea. That is nothing but the truth, after all."

The men, who'd been out all day shooting, were gathered in one corner of the drawing room sipping their preprandial drinks and laughing over the day's adventures. Jeremy (who, his mother noted, had not left for London after all) was among them. He'd spent the day with the shooting party, but now he seemed to wish he were somewhere else. He kept looking over his shoulder for someone he couldn't seem to find. After a while, he excused himself from the masculine conclave and crossed the room to where his mother was sitting. "Have you seen Peggy?" he asked.

She frowned at him. "No, I haven't seen *Georgy*," she corrected pointedly, glancing about her to make sure no one was close enough to hear. "But I didn't expect to see *you* here today. I thought you intended to leave."

"I changed my mind," he murmured absently, scanning the room nervously. "Isn't Peg—Georgy coming to dinner?"

"Why wouldn't she?" She smiled up at her son and smoothly changed the subject. "Have you merely postponed your departure, Jeremy, or do you intend to stay the week as originally planned?"

"I don't know. We'll see," he said and wandered aimlessly away.

Jeremy had had a terrible day. Ever since last night he'd been feeling like a cad. He'd accused Peggy of wanton behavior and had even seen a man leave her room, but all night, after he'd left her there weeping, he'd hated himself. He could not explain why he was assailed with doubts, but it was difficult to recall her innocent eyes and still believe the girl was a lightskirt. Although she had not identified the man who had come to her room, he found it hard to

believe the fellow had been a lover. Had he blundered
badly?

He could not accept the evidence of his eyes. Something
nagged at him, some inner voice repeating in his ear that
he'd utterly misjudged her. If he had, he'd said things to
her that she would find unforgivable. He had to talk to her
again, to ask her for the truth. He wanted to hear her deny
his accusations. Whatever she said he would believe, so
greatly did he long to trust her again. If he'd been wrong,
he would no longer be able to live with himself unless she
forgave him. He didn't understand himself, but all day
long he felt an irresistible urge to see her, to hear her de-
nials, to fall at her feet and beg her pardon.

But she did not appear at the dinner table, nor was she
sitting with the women in the music room when the men
rejoined the ladies after their port. Several of the guests
inquired of his mother where she was, but Lady Horatia
merely shrugged. "You know Georgy," she said. "A mind
and a will of her own has my daughter. I can't keep track
of her."

Jeremy, miserable and troubled, wandered about the
rooms in search of her. He tried her room first, but there
was no answer to his persistent knocking. Then he returned
downstairs, but he didn't find her in either of the sitting
rooms, the morning room, the blue saloon or the portrait
gallery. He entered the library as a last resort, but it was
unoccupied. The light of the fire showed only the glowing
backs of leather books and a number of empty seats. He
turned back to the doorway in despair, wondering where
next to search, and came face to face with Rosalind. "Oh,
here you are," the girl clarioned happily. "I've been seeking you all over."

"Oh, Rosalind," he said glumly. "It's you."

"My dear boy," she exclaimed in mock offense, "I've
had warmer greetings at a burial! You *are* blue deviled."

"I'm sorry, Rosalind. I've been looking in vain for . . .
er . . . Georgy. Have you seen her?"

"No, I haven't. Your sister hasn't shown her face all
day. But it can't be your *sister* who's put you in a pucker,

can it? No, of course not. *I* know what has you in the dismals."

"No, you don't, Rosalind. But I haven't time to banter with you right now, my dear. If you don't mind, I'll take myself off."

"But I *do* mind," she said, softening her words by flashing a brilliant smile at him and taking his arm cozily in hers. "And I *do* know what's been troubling you. But, my love, I have wonderful news for you . . . just the news you need to drive off those dismals. Come, let's sit right there, on the sofa near the fire."

He let her draw him down beside her. "What news is it?" he asked curiously.

She turned toward him, curls bouncing and eyes dancing. "What news would you most like to hear of anything in the world?"

"That you've seen Pe—Georgy waiting for me just outside the door."

"Jemmy!" she pouted. "Can't you forget your blasted sister? Come now, what is the news you've been urging me to give you for so long?"

"I don't know," he said impatiently, feeling a rising irritation with her coyness. "May we skip over the guessing games?"

"Oh, very well, I'll tell you, since you insist on being a spoilsport." She threw her arms about his neck. "I've told Papa."

"Told Papa what?"

"What do you mean, what? You know what."

"See here, Rosalind," he said, untwining her arms from his neck and placing them firmly at her sides, "I told you I have urgent business. Tell me what it is you have to say and let me go."

"Well, *really*, Jemmy," she said, her brows arching angrily, "I don't know if I should tell you, now that you're behaving like a dog in the manger."

"Suit yourself, my dear," he said, starting to rise.

She pulled him back at once. "I suppose I deserve this," she said, smiling again and clinging to his arm. "I've been leading you a chase, my sweet, I know. Papa always says

I'm a naughty little puss. But I've told him at last, so you needn't get on your high ropes any longer."

"Told him *what*, confound it!"

"That it's not Monte but *you* I wish to wed, of course!" She beamed at him. "Isn't that what you wanted me to do?"

He stared at her as if she'd just made a speech to him in Greek. "What?" he asked stupidly.

Her smile faded. "That *is* what you wanted, isn't it, my love?"

"Yes, I . . . of course," he said, stunned. He stumbled to his feet and went to the fireplace, his head swimming. He leaned his forehead against the mantel and stared down into the flames. Rosalind was his at last, and instead of feeling elated, he felt sick.

"*Isn't* it what you wanted?" she asked again, her light voice quivering with shaken confidence.

But he couldn't answer her. The habitual response, which had come so readily to his tongue for so many years, was not there. The truth burst on him like an explosion: *No*, it was *not* what he wanted! Why had he ever thought that this silly, spoiled coquette was the woman he wanted to marry? All at once it was impossible to believe that he'd ever really loved her. Love, he realized with a shock, was not spun of sugary phrases and teasing glances. His feeling for Rosalind had been built on a boyish fantasy that, because of their lengthy separation, had hung on past its time until it had eventually become a habit of thinking. He wondered how far that habit of thought would have carried him if he'd not been overcome with the onrush of a deeper emotion. Would he have gone on pure habit to the wedding itself?

But now such a wedding was impossible for him to contemplate. He now knew why he hadn't been able to think of anyone but Peggy since the day they met. Real love *was* a deeper emotion than the adolescent feeling he'd had for Rosalind. Love was such a tangle of feelings—pain and jealousy and this awful agony of yearning. Love was a feeling so overwhelming that it overcame the worst suspicions a man could have.

So there it was. He did not love Rosalind, but Peggy. It was so clear to him now that he could hardly believe he hadn't recognized it days ago. The pattern of thought that had become a habit with him had kept him from seeing what was to Peggy as obvious as sunlight. She'd suggested, the other night, that he ask himself why he'd been so madly jealous, but he'd refused to face the truth of his feelings. Now all he wanted to do in life was to take her in his arms and tell her how he felt. He didn't care at all what she'd been before or what she'd done. He loved her! He wanted nothing more than the opportunity to tell her so.

Meanwhile, however, there was Rosalind. She was sitting just behind him, bewilderedly waiting for an answer, and he had no idea what to say to her. He lifted his head. "What made you decide, Rosalind, to tell your father about us *today?*" he asked, looking over his shoulder at her. "Did you quarrel with Monte?"

"Quarrel with Monte? Is *that* what you think?"

"Is it so strange a thought? You didn't see fit to tell your father before, no matter how I begged. But suddenly, today—"

"Are you suggesting that I've come to you because Monte and I have broken it off?" the girl asked in outrage. "How *dare* you, Jemmy!"

Jeremy studied her as if scales had fallen from his eyes. It was suddenly quite clear that she'd been playing with him . . . and probably with Monte, too. She had a sentimental, romantic attachment to him which she was reluctant to end, but she knew that Monte was the better catch, so she'd been holding on to both of them for as long as she could. But she'd intended to wed Monte from the first, or else she would not have ignored *him*, Jeremy, so blatantly throughout this past week. His mother had seen it, but he'd kept himself blind. "I dare, my dear," he said softly, "because I saw during this past week how very content you've been in his company. If suddenly you took this action, it seems to me a very logical consequence of such a quarrel. And your violent denial is strong evidence that I'm right. 'The lady doth protest too much,' as Shakespeare says.

How nice for you that I'm so conveniently close and so ready to step into his place at the snap of your fingers."

"But I love you, Jemmy, you know that. I always have."

"Perhaps we loved at first. But it's long been just a habit, I think."

"Jemmy!" she cried, her eyes filling. "You can't believe that! The way you're speaking, one would think I find you second best! That's not *true!* You must believe me. I never found Monte *nearly* as handsome or manly as you."

He came back to the sofa and sat down beside her. "But I *am* second best, my dear," he said, taking her hand gently. "Our parents know it, and at heart I think we know it, too. I've discovered that my mother was right when she said that I cannot afford you. There isn't much I can do to change my financial situation, I fear, so if you married me you would find yourself without the resources you've always taken for granted. Can you see yourself scrimping and saving and going without new gowns and pretty bonnets? Whereas, with Monte, you will have all that and more . . . jewels and fripperies and all sorts of luxuries."

"I d-don't care for j-jewels and f-fripperies," she said, sniffing her tears back bravely.

"Of course you do. And I would be a beast to deprive you of them. As your father once pointed out to me, it would not be right to force you to live below the style you've always been accustomed to."

She gaped at him in disbelief. "Do you mean, Jemmy, that you are g-going to *give me up?*"

"I suppose it had to be done sooner or later," he said, ashamed to be playing out this sentimental scene but soothing his conscience by reminding himself that it was the kindest way to extricate himself from this entanglement. "We may as well face it now. Go back to Monte and make it up with him."

She pulled her hands from his and dropped her head in them. "But I c-can't. When we quarreled and he called me a j-jingle-brain, I told him that he was a c-clunch and that it was you I really l-loved."

He patted her shoulder and got up. "No matter, Rosalind. He will forget it if you play your cards well." He went hastily to the door. "Just tell him that you didn't mean a word of it, and that you could never love a gudgeon like Jeremy Verney when you had an out-and-outer like Monte Traherne to compare with him. He will fall at your feet, I promise you."

Chapter 29

He loved her—that was what he had to tell Peggy! That was the foundation upon which his hope for his future was built. If she cared for him—and he'd seen signs that perhaps she did—he and Peggy could ignore the past and start afresh. It was just possible that there might be a future for them both. Jeremy had not understood himself before, and that ignorance had driven him to behave like a lunatic. But now that he knew what had driven him, he could handle the situation with some sense. If she had been misguided in the past, he could learn to forget. If, on the other hand, he had misjudged her, perhaps he could convince her to forgive.

With that in mind, Jeremy ran up to Peggy's room as soon as he'd extricated himself from his entanglement with Rosalind. He knocked once and then again, but there was no answer. His need to see her was so urgent it felt like a physical pain. He tried to turn the knob, but the door was locked. He knocked again, pounding with both fists. But there was still no answer.

It suddenly occurred to him that something might be very wrong, and his blood turned to ice in his veins. In a rush of absolute terror, he threw himself against the door with all his might. It gave way with a loud crunch of broken wood, and he tumbled in. He lifted his head at once and saw the empty bed and the cleared dressing table. Peggy was gone.

Before he had time to identify the feeling of crushing disappointment that washed over him, a movement at a window to his right caught his eye. He turned his head in time to see a black-coated man climbing over the sill. The feeling of jealous madness returned in a blinding rush, and in one swift movement he leaped to his feet and threw himself upon the fellow, pulling him down to the floor. They scuffled desperately for a moment, until the intruder managed to free one foot and used his boot to kick Jeremy powerfully on the chin. Jeremy grunted with pain and fell back, thus permitting the man to squirm out of his hold and make for the window again. Jeremy, wincing in pain, could hardly see, but he grabbed for the fellow anyway. He managed to clutch the man's coat, ripping the pocket, and he heard something fall to the floor. But the man was out of the window and gone from view.

Jeremy rubbed his eyes and shook his head to clear it. When he could see, he noticed something gleaming on the floor. He stooped, picked it up and stood staring at it in stupefaction. It was Letty Denham's emerald.

"Good God!" came a voice from the doorway. "What's happened here?"

"Oh, it's you, Maitland," Jeremy muttered breathlessly. "Look at what I've found."

"The emerald!" He stepped over the shattered door and came in. "Wherever did you find it?"

"There was a fellow here . . . wearing a black coat—"

"What fellow? The thief? Did you see who it was?"

"No, confound it! He got away from me." Jeremy leaned out of the window and tried to see where the man could have gone. Again it was too dark to distinguish anything or anyone who might be lurking down below in the shadows. But, Jeremy reasoned, the man could not be down there in the garden; they were too high above the ground for him to have jumped. The only possible means of escape was a narrow ledge below the window which ran the length of the building.

Maitland leaned out beside him. "He can't have used this ledge, can he?"

"I don't see what else—Wait! What was that?"

Maitland looked in the direction in which Jeremy was pointing. He too could see a shadow, just a shade darker than the wall itself, moving slowly away from them. "Dash it all, he'll break his neck!"

"I don't think so," Jeremy said, pulling back inside and quickly throwing off his coat. "He's done this before, I believe."

Maitland looked over his shoulder at the younger man, his brows lifted quizzically. "How do you know th—?" Then, noting the preparations Jeremy was making, he whisked himself back into the room. "Damnation, Jeremy, what are you doing? You're not thinking of going after him! Not on that *ledge*. I forbid it! It's not worth it. We have the stone back, and that's enough."

"I have a personal reason for going after him. Stand aside, Tony, please."

Maitland took one close look at Jeremy's tight-lipped expression and did as he was asked. Then he helped Jeremy up to the sill, but before he assisted him onto the ledge he peered out into the darkness to locate the moving shadow. "Wait a moment!" he exclaimed suddenly. "I know what that fellow's making for. There's no easy way down from that ledge, but the frieze just above us projects out at the corners of the building, and he can undoubtedly grab onto it and pull himself up to the roof. There are several stairways, not frequently used, down which he can make his escape. See here, Jeremy, why use the ledge when you can get up there faster and safer by the stairs?"

"I might lose him." He turned about carefully on the sill and set one foot gingerly on the ledge. "I lost him once before, and I don't want to do it again. If you've a mind to help me, Tony, *you* take the stairs. Then, between the two of us, we can corner him on the roof."

Maitland nodded in quick agreement, and Jeremy lowered his other foot onto the ledge. "Take a gun, Tony," he muttered before disappearing from view.

Maitland quickly ran down the hall to his bedroom, where he rummaged through a chest for his box of dueling pistols. He'd carried them all through his travels but had never used them before. He lifted one of the pair from its velvet bed and ran out of the room. The nearest stairway was in the servants' passage, and he made for it at once. It was only one flight up to the roof. The door opened at the slightest pressure (he made a mental note to speak to his butler about seeing to it that these doors were locked in future), and he stepped out onto the roof. It was too dark to make out anything but unidentifiable shapes outlined against the starless sky. He stood still for a moment, trying to get his bearings. If the thief had followed the plan he'd outlined to Jeremy, he would be somewhere ahead and to his left. He moved stealthily in that direction, trying to balance himself on the roof's slight pitch and holding the pistol out before him. All at once, he saw a shape—much further to the left than he'd anticipated—move along the edge of the roof. "Stop where you are!" he shouted.

The man froze for a moment, and then slowly began to back away in the direction in which he'd come. "Stop, I said!" Maitland ordered. "Stop or I'll shoot!"

"No, don't shoot him, Tony," came Jeremy's voice. "Not until I can question him."

Maitland could now make out Jeremy's silhouette, a shadow rising slowly above the edge of the roof. The thief, finding himself between Maitland on his right and Jeremy on his left, turned around and ran straight back, Maitland and Jeremy dashing after him. When he reached the edge, the thief paused, looking about him in desperation. Maitland, though he couldn't see the man's face, could almost tell what he was thinking. He was cornered, trapped on the sloping roof of the main building, more than three stories above the ground. The only possible escape was a leap onto the roof of the west wing, one story below. But that roof, at right angles to this one, left a wide gap between its edge and the place where the thief was poised. "Don't do it, fellow!" Maitland warned. "You won't make it."

The fellow's silhouetted head turned to where Jeremy was slowly approaching him. He hesitated for only a heartbeat and then turned and bent his knees as if to make the leap. "Oh, no, you don't!" Jeremy shouted and sprang at the fellow like a tiger.

The thief leaped. Jeremy's hands grasped nothing but air, and he fell on his face at the very edge of the roof. But the thief! Whether it was Jeremy's lunge or the impossibility of spanning the distance between the two roofs that caused the fall, they would never know; but the thief flew,

arms outstretched, into the air and then plummeted down-
ward out of their view. Maitland stood motionless as the
dull thud of the fall reached his ears. Then he went forward
and helped the prostrate Jeremy to his feet. They peered
over the edge of the roof but could see nothing. "We'd
better get down," Maitland murmured.

They found the body face down in a rose bed. Jeremy,
completely shaken, could do nothing but stare at it. It was
Maitland who knelt beside it and turned it over. Calmly, he
closed the staring eyes and brushed the mud and dead
leaves from the bruised cheeks. "Oh, my God!" Jeremy
gasped in horror. "It's Ned!"

Maitland looked up at him. "You *knew* this fellow?"

Jeremy fell to his knees. "It's her brother," he groaned,
dropping his face in his hands.

"Peggy's?" Maitland asked shrewdly.

Jeremy nodded, sunk in despair. All he could think of
was that this monstrous occurrence was his fault. He'd
killed Peggy's brother! Only after a long moment did Maitland's one-word question trigger a reaction in his consciousness. He lifted his head slowly. "Did you
say . . . Peggy?"

"Yes. That *is* her name, isn't it?"

Jeremy was stunned. "How long have you known?"

"Almost from the first."

"From the *first?*" A wave of shame washed over him,
shame for his mother, for himself and for Peggy who'd
been coerced into becoming part of this ugly subterfuge.
But the shame soon changed to anger as he realized that
Maitland had been toying with them in some sort of cat-
and-mouse game. "Then why didn't you *say* something?"
he asked, glaring at the other man angrily. "Did you enjoy
playing us for fools?"

Maitland got to his feet and brushed the knees of his
breeches. "I didn't enjoy any of it, Jeremy. But surely you
didn't want me to speak up and embarrass you all before
my guests. Besides," he added, helping Jeremy up, "I had
my own reasons for wishing to play out the charade."

"Oh?" Jeremy studied him curiously. "What reasons
were those?"

"Perhaps I'll tell you one day. But for now, since the game is not over, I'll hold my tongue."

"But it *is* over," Jeremy said, looking down at Ned's body. "It will all come out when we explain *this*."

"It needn't. This matter can all be explained without involving you or your family. I shall cover the body temporarily and call in the local magistrate. We need tell him only that the thief who'd stolen Letty's emerald—and who was still prowling about, undoubtedly for the purpose of making off with other baubles belonging to my guests—had the misfortune to fall off my roof. That is all. We shall say we know nothing of his identity."

"That is good of you, Maitland. You have been kinder to the Verneys than we deserve. But there is still Peggy."

"What about Peggy?"

Jeremy drew in a deep breath. "She should be told about Ned."

"Yes," Maitland agreed, "she should be."

"If I can only *find* her." Jeremy shivered, aware for the first time that the night air was too cold for shirtsleeves. He took a few impatient steps, swinging his arms about to warm them. "Damnation, where can the girl be hiding herself?"

"She's gone back to London."

Jeremy wheeled about, startled. "What? How do you know?"

"I provided her with a carriage," Maitland explained impassively.

But Jeremy did not feel impassive. "Provided her with a *carriage?*" he exploded. "Why the devil did you do that?"

"Because the girl was in great distress, that's why."

"Oh, you know that, too, do you?" Jeremy clenched his fists. "What else do you know of all this?"

"Nothing else, so you needn't get on your high ropes. I was taking my horse for an early gallop this morning and spotted your Peggy walking along the road. She had obviously been weeping, but she put a good face on it. She said she had an urgent need to go to London and was heading for town to take the stage. When I saw that I could not dissuade her, I did the only other thing I could think of to

assist her: I offered her a means of transport. She accepted
with gratitude, suggesting with what she believed to be
great subtlety that I need not say anything about her destination until asked. Since I saw no reason to do otherwise, I
kept silent about the whole incident until now."

"I'm sorry, Tony," Jeremy said, abashed. "I tend to be
slightly lunatic in matters concerning that girl."

"Oh?" Maitland grinned at him. "Is that the way the
wind blows?"

"Yes, but I'm making the worst mull of it. Do you know
where she was going?"

"London was all she said. Why?"

"Why do you think? I've got to *find* her! To tell her . . .
well, to tell her about her brother, for one thing. Where in
London do you think she's gone, Tony?"

"I don't really know. She is always so carefully playing
her role as Georgy in my presence that she is never sincere
with me. I have the impression that she was going to your
house to get her own things, but I don't think she intended
to stay there for long."

"My house, eh?" Jeremy muttered, his mind racing.
"And she left this morning? Then she's had at least a
twelve-hour start. But she'll surely have stopped somewhere for the night. If I ride horseback and make no long
stops, I can gain six hours or more."

"Then go at once, by all means," Maitland urged.

"Yes, I shall, as soon as we've taken care of the problem of poor Ned Birkin."

"Ah, yes, our *homo ad patres.*" They gazed down at the
body ruefully. "I hope, now that he's 'gone to his fathers,'
that he'll do better than he did here on earth. But you
needn't wait around on his account, Jeremy. I'll take care
of him. You'd better get started, old fellow, or you'll miss
Peggy entirely. Tell my stableman to saddle Negrino for
you. He is as untiring as any mount I own and as swift as a
racehorse."

Jeremy threw him a look of heartfelt gratitude. "Thanks,
Tony. I'll be going, then." He set off at a run. "Someday,"
he threw back over his shoulder, "I'll find a way to thank
you properly."

Maitland watched him go, a feeling of envy in his chest, the envy of the spurned lover for the successful one rushing off to be reunited with his beloved. "If you truly want to thank me, Jeremy Verney," he muttered to himself as he pulled off his coat and bent down to cover the body, "bring your sister back to me. Your *real* sister."

Chapter 30

Jeremy's real sister was discovering that the only thing certain in life was uncertainty. Georgy had been certain she'd made the right decision in dedicating her life to Good Works instead of Selfish Pleasure, but the moment after that decision had become irrevocable, she became *un*certain. No sooner had she sent Maitland packing than everything began to come unglued. She'd been certain, when she'd sent him away, that her appointment as teacher of the Ruckworth Parish Charity School was now permanent, that the quality of her teaching was considered by her employers to be more than satisfactory, and that she could face the future with some sense of purpose and security. But less than two days after Maitland had gone, she began to discover that none of those things were sure.

In the first place she found that, as happy as she was with her children in the classroom, as soon as she left the school her vision of her future became bleak indeed. Tony Maitland had twice waited for her in the schoolyard—only twice!—yet ever since then she'd come out of the door hoping he would be there. There was no reason for that hope, no logical reason at all, she told herself. She tried to banish it from her mind. But her sense of disappointment when she found the schoolyard deserted was overwhelming.

Sometimes she wished he had never come. If he had not, she would not have known how sparkling the days could be when a girl sensed that a lover was nearby. She would not have experienced the excitement of the development of an "attachment," or the thrill of an unexpected, passionate embrace. And she would not now have to en-

dure the feeling of emptiness, a feeling that was heightened
and sharpened by comparison with the two days that had
been so full. If he had never come, such a comparison
could not have been made.

In the second place, it was becoming clear that lady
Ruckworth did *not* find her teaching satisfactory. It was
difficult enough learning to endure that powerful, aching
loneliness that Maitland had left in his wake, but having to
deal with Lady Ruckworth's opposition to her methods
only added more weight to her heavy heart. She had tried
to follow her ladyship's instructions: she'd taken *The Poor
Girls' Primer* into class and tried to teach reading from it,
but neither she nor the little girls for whom the book was
intended could bear it. It was sermonizing and tedious, and
no one could expect little girls like Hester Putman and
Dorrie Kissack to prefer:

> Swear not at all, nor make a Bawl,
> Use no bad words at all, at all,

from the *Primer* to the delightful, wicked fun of the selection from *Mother Goose's Melody* that was the girls' favorite:

> There was a man in our town,
> And he was wondrous wise;
> He jumped into a bramble bush
> And scratched out both his eyes.
> And when he saw his eyes were out,
> With all his might and main,
> He jumped into another bush
> And scratched them in again.

So Georgy took the *Primers*, stowed them away on a
shelf and returned to her preferred curriculum, hoping that
Lady Ruckworth would forget that she'd ever suggested
the change. Lady Ruckworth, however, did not forget. She
paid a surprise visit the very next day and scolded the
teacher loudly and nastily right in front of all the pupils.
Georgy, humiliated almost to tears, was forced to return to

the use of the *Primer*, making the reading time far less enjoyable for everyone, including the teacher.

Lady Ruckworth, when her vituperative scolding had been delivered, must have marched herself straight from the schoolhouse to the vicarage and instructed Mr. Hunsford to keep a firm eye on Miss Vail's activities, for he appeared in the schoolroom that very afternoon. The children had just left, and Georgy was stacking away the now-forbidden *Aesops* and *Mother Gooses* on an upper shelf. "May I help you, Miss Vail?" the vicar offered, coming up behind her.

"Oh, no, it's not necessary," Georgy said quickly, uncomfortably aware that he was standing much too closely behind her.

But he did not pay attention to her refusal. He put his arms up, took the books from her hands and shoved them on the shelf. When this was done, he did not move away. Georgy turned and found herself nose-to-nose with him, with less than two inches separating them. She tried to duck under one of his still-raised arms, but he suddenly lowered them and threw them around her. "Oh, Miss Vail," he breathed, gazing at her mistily through his spectacles, "you are such a *very* lovely creature!" And before she could recover from her astonishment, he pulled her close and was splattering kisses all over her face.

"Mr. Hunsford!" she cried, pushing against him with all her might. "Have you taken leave of your senses?"

"I can't help it!" he declared, panting heavily and holding on gamely despite her resistance. "You have inspired in me . . . the most overwhelming . . . passion."

"Overwhelming *passion?*" she echoed, appalled. She pushed at him so furiously that he fell over backward onto the floor, causing a bench to topple over with a noisy crash and his spectacles to slide from his nose. "But you're a man of God!" she exclaimed furiously to his supine form. "How *could* you?"

He lifted his head and peered at her myopically. "But one can't help one's . . . feelings . . . can one?" he asked, feeling about with no success for his spectacles.

"Can't help one's feelings? Can't help them? If *you*

can't help them, who can? You, who preach adherence to the Commandments and the moral benefits of self-restraint! You, the spiritual leader of your flock!" She looked down on him with an expression of utter disdain. "How *can* you have sunk to such depravity?"

He gazed up at her with frightened eyes. "But surely you must have sensed . . . before this . . . that I . . . I . . . ached with desire for you."

"If I did, I would not permit myself to believe it of you." She bent down, picked up his glasses, placed them on his nose and, not pausing for a moment in the delivery of her stern reprimand, helped him to his feet. "Instead of asking *me* so foolish a question, you should be asking *yourself* how so good and respectable and God-fearing a man could have so misled himself. In short, Mr. Hunsford," she declared ringingly, "you should be *ashamed* of yourself!"

"Does this mean," he asked dolefully, "that you have not any spark of feeling for me?"

She blinked at him for a moment in disbelief. *"Feeling* for you?" she exclaimed, poking a reproving finger in his chest and backing him to the door, "If you mean passion, sir, I do not see how you can even ask! You are a married man! Go home to your wife, sir, your dear, sweet, loving Mary who has given you three children and the best years of her life! But first, Mr. Hunsford, go to your church, and kneel down. Yes, kneel down, sir, and thank God that He has given such a wife to such a worm as you!"

With that, she pushed him over the threshold and shut the door in his face. *Good heavens, Georgy,* she said to herself, leaning in exhaustion against the door and expelling a long breath, *you are a virago!* Her eyes fell on the overturned bench, and suddenly, the recollection of the vicar lying there and declaring his passion from his ludicrous position on the ground was too much for her. She burst into uproarious laughter, a spasm so overpowering that she had to sit down until it passed. But when she regained control of herself, she realized that it was truly not a laughing matter. Mary was her friend, and it was disturbing that Mary's husband, the vicar himself, could harbor adulterous thoughts. Was it wise for her to go on living at the vicarage? Were there other arrangements she could make? What excuse could she give to Mary for wishing to move to other quarters? She had to find a solution for each one of these problems. She realized, with a sigh, that her laughter had been an inappropriate reaction. Tears would have been more to the point, for the fact was that she'd received a disconcerting blow.

Another blow followed quickly. The next morning, Georgy, depressed and heavy-eyed, found Benjy waiting for her outside the school. When he saw her, he pulled off his peaked cap. The sight of him made her gasp. His right eye was red and swollen and the cheek below was completely covered with a purplish bruise. "Benjy!" she cried. "What happened to you?"

"It ain't nothin', Miss Vail," the boy said hastily, returning the cap to his head and tilting the peak down to cover as much of the bruise as he could. "I came to tell ye I won't be comin' to school no more . . . er . . . *any* more."

Her heart sank. Benjy was very dear to her, and the most promising of all the pupils. "But my dear boy," she said urgently, "you *must* come. I have such plans for you . . ."

"Please, Miss Vail, I cain't. It'll be better this way. I'm too big fer schoolin' anyhow."

"Who decided this, Benjy?" she asked tightly. "Your father? I'd be happy to go to speak to him on your behalf." She would not be happy, of course, for her fear of Mr. Kissack had never quite died. But she would endure entering a lion's cage for Benjy's sake.

"No, it ain't my father. It's the smith. I was readin' in the smithy yesterday an' I let a shoe sit in the flames too long, see. It melted down and made a terrible botch. The smith was right sore, an' I don't blame 'im."

"Did *he* give you that bruise?" Georgy asked, clenching her fists.

"I deserved it, ma'am. I'm lucky 'e didn't sack me then and there. I 'ad to promise there'd be no more readin' an' no more schoolin'. I'm sorry, ma'am. It'd be nice to be able to stay, but I cain't afford to come no—any more. Smithin' is good work, y' see, an' I'm glad to 'ave it."

"Oh, Benjy," she moaned, heartbroken, "isn't there any way we can—?"

"No, ma'am." He pulled off his cap again. "I'd best be off. Thank ye fer everything ye tried to do fer me. Goodbye, Miss Vail."

She walked sadly into the schoolroom and took out her daybook. When she drew the line through Benjamin Kissack's name, it cut through her like the slice of a surgeon's knife through flesh. One down. She'd lost one. And he had been the best.

Chapter 31

———❦———

"Set not much by this —" Hester read laboriously from her place on Georgy's knee, "who is a . . . ag . . ."

"Against," Dorrie Kissack assisted, leaning over Georgy's shoulder, her eyes fixed on the book.

"Against thee or with thee, but so do and . . . care that God be with thee." Having completed the paragraph, Hester looked up at the teacher in triumph.

"That was very good, Hester," Georgy said, smoothing the child's hair. "Very good indeed."

She was reading with the smallest girls. On the first two benches Sarah and the older girls were bent over an atlas studying the geography of Europe. The older boys, grouped in the rear, were working on subtraction problems, and Timmy was sitting at the teacher's table exploring for the first time the mysteries of water-coloring. Into this peaceful scene sailed the school's benefactress, Lady Ruckworth. "Good morning, children," she said from the doorway.

The children got to their feet. "Good morning, your ladyship," they said in unison.

Georgy lifted Hester from her lap and set the child down on the chair. "Good morning, Lady Ruckworth. How nice to see you in our classroom," she said with as much sincerity as she could muster.

Her ladyship gave Georgy a curt nod. "And what are we doing here?" she asked Billy Putman.

"Subtracshin, my lady," he said, showing her his paper.

"Very nice," she muttered, not looking. "And here?"

"Geography, ma'am," Sarah volunteered with a little curtsey. "It's Europe, y'see."

"Yes, I recognized it," Lady Ruckworth said drily, looking round with a frown. "But I see no signs of needlework."

Georgy's heart sank. "Needlework?"

"You did receive the muslin work-pieces I sent round, did you not, Miss Vail?"

"Oh, yes, I did indeed, Ma'am. They are right... er..." She glanced over her shoulder quickly. "...right over there."

Lady Ruckworth looked up at the shelf Georgy indicated. "So they are. But I see that they have not yet even been unwrapped."

"Well, no, ma'am. Not yet."

"And when did you intend to unwrap them, Miss Vail? Next month? After Christmas? At Lent?"

Her tone was so icy that little Hester, fearful for her teacher, began to cry.

Georgy lifted the child in her arms and patted her comfortingly. "I mean to do so very soon, your ladyship. Tomorrow, if you wish."

"Hmmmph," Lady Ruckworth muttered in disgust. "I've heard that before. You told me some time ago that you would have the girls knitting 'tomorrow'. Have the girls done any knitting, Miss Vail?"

Georgy dropped her eyes. "No, ma'am." The truth was that Georgy did not know how to knit. She had intended to ask Mary to teach her, but she'd been too busy so far.

"I see." Lady Ruckworth shook her head as if at a hopeless child. "I think, Miss Vail, it is time for us to have a talk. I shall come down to the vicarage at thirty minutes past four this afternoon. Thirty minutes past four precisely. See that you are there, Miss Vail."

At thirty minutes past four precisely, Miss Vail entered the Hunsford drawing room. The tea cart had been drawn up before the fire, exactly as it had been the day she first arrived, and seated at it, just as they'd been then, were Lady Ruckworth and Mr. Hunsford. And in a corner on the other side of the fireplace, Mary sat huddled in her rocking chair. Georgy immediately sensed that this would not be a pleasant meeting, for Mary's eyes were red-rimmed and she could not summon a smile to acknowledge Georgy's surreptitious wink. Mr. Hunsford rose from his chair. "Do sit down, Miss Vail," he said, not meeting her eyes.

"Will you have a cup of tea, Grace?" Mary asked, leaning forward.

"No, thank you, Mary," Georgy answered, seating herself at the tea cart.

"Then we may as well begin," Mr. Hunsford said, sitting down again. "Our benefactress, as you know by this time, Miss Vail, has very high standards for the school." He hesitated, glancing uneasily at Lady Ruckworth, who gave him a queenly nod indicating that he should proceed. He sighed, took off his glasses, fiddled with them a bit, replaced them and reluctantly went on. "They are standards set, not by her own whims, but by such outstanding educationists as Mrs. Sarah Trimmer and Hannah More herself."

"Yes. Quite right," Lady Ruckworth declared.

The vicar folded his hands on the cart and looked down at them unhappily. "Her ladyship feels, Miss Vail, that you have consistently refused to adapt your curriculum to those standards."

"That, Mr. Hunsford, is nonsense," Georgy said impatiently. "I have tried in every way I know to conform to those standards. I'm even using her blasted *Poor Girls' Primer.*"

Her ladyship gasped. Mr. Hunsford threw her a disapproving look. "Really, Miss Vail, there's no need for vulgar language."

"At least vulgar language is better than vulgar *behavior.*" Georgy snapped back. When the words were out, she wanted to bite her tongue. She should never have said that with Mary in the room. But a glance at Mary showed that she didn't seem to attach any significance to the words.

"You haven't conformed in any way at all," Lady Ruckworth said coldly. "If you had studied Mrs. Trimmer's *Teacher's Assistant* as you should have, you would be aware of your failings."

"She hasn't any failings, if you ask me," Mary put in, unable to contain herself. "The children *love* her!"

"Mary!" her husband barked.

Lady Ruckworth lifted her chin haughtily. "I think, Mr. Hunsford, that your wife may be excused."

"Mrs. Hunsford," the vicar said, rising imperiously, "perhaps you'd better go and see to supper."

Poor Mary reddened to her ears. "Yes, Mr. Hunsford," she said, getting up slowly from her rocker. "Good evening, your ladyship." She crossed the room, giving Georgy a look of heartbroken helplessness, and went out, closing the door behind her.

"Now," Lady Ruckworth continued calmly, "we may proceed. I was saying, Miss Vail, that you have not followed the precepts set forth by Mrs. Trimmer."

"That's not so, your ladyship. I've studied the *Teacher's Assistant* very carefully. I follow Mrs. Trimmer's advice in almost everything I do," Georgy declared.

"Mrs. Trimmer recommends that girls learn to spin wool and linen," Lady Ruckworth pointed out. "Have you taught the girls to spin?"

"Well, no . . . but—"

"She recommends that they learn how to sew shifts and shirts. Have your pupils sewn a single shift? A single shirt?"

"No, ma'am. But many of the girls already know how to sew."

"Perhaps they do and perhaps they don't. If you don't see their work, how can you tell?" She opened up a copy of *The Teacher's Assistant* that lay on the cart at her elbow and read aloud. " 'Lesson Five, Learn to knit Hose, Learn to Bake and Brew and Wash, Learn to clean Rooms and Pots and Pans'. Have you instructed your pupils in *any* of those subjects, Miss Vail?"

Georgy leaned forward. "Lady Ruckworth, the girls will learn those things anyway," she explained earnestly, "if they have not already done so. Don't you think the school curriculum should emphasize more intellectual . . . more *uplifting* subjects?"

"No, I do not. Nor do I think it is your place to criticize Mrs. Trimmer's precepts in these matters, nor to alter them to suit your own purposes." She rose majestically from her chair, motioned the others to remain seated, and turned to the vicar. "You see, Mr. Hunsford, that the woman is quite incorrigible. I warned you from the first that her disposition was insufficiently meek and humble for this post. I believe that further argumentation is pointless. Miss Vail, the day you arrived I informed you that I was reserving judgment on your suitability. Well, I have now made that judgment. You are *not* suitable."

Georgy should have been expecting this, she now realized, but it struck her with a shock. "Do you mean you're sacking me?" she asked, so startled that her only emotion at the moment seemed to be wild amusement.

"Just so. Though I would not have phrased it quite so vulgarly." She turned once more to Mr. Hunsford, who had remained seated and was unhappily staring at his still-folded hands. "I leave the rest to you, Mr. Hunsford. You may pay her for three months, although her service to us did not come quite to that."

The vicar stumbled to his feet. "If she remains at her post until the end of the month, however —" he suggested, a gleam of hope dawning in his bespectacled eyes.

"Good heavens, Mr. Hunsford, are you mad?" her ladyship asked in horror. "Can you imagine what we should have to endure if she returns to the classroom even one more day? I shudder to think of it. All those tearful good-byes, the children sullen, the parents petitioning for me to change my mind! No, no, Mr. Hunsford, it must be a clean break. Pay her for the time I've specified and send her off at once. Mrs. Hunsford may take over her duties until a suitable replacement is found. Good-bye, Miss Vail. May God go with you."

Chapter 32

Georgy sat squeezed into a corner of the crowded night mail to London, staring out into the blackness. The other passengers all seemed to be sleeping (the huge man next to her, in fact, was snoring loudly), but she could not. All she could think of was that Grace Vail was no more. This night journey seemed to be making a symbolic passage, traversing a black tunnel between two worlds. She'd entered it on one end as Grace Vail, woman of purpose and ideals, and she would emerge on the other as Georgianna Verney, impoverished spinster, muddleheaded runaway and failure. The far end of the tunnel—her return home to a reproachful mother and a wasteful life—was something she was not yet ready to think about. And the near end of the tunnel—her life as Grace Vail—was something she was not yet ready to put behind her.

It was more difficult than she'd ever imagined to leave Grace Vail behind. She had not even been permitted to say good-bye to her beloved children. She and Mary were able to embrace tearfully and make promises of eternal remembrance, but she'd been denied that bittersweet comfort in the case of the children. It would have meant so much to be able to embrace them, to tell them not to feel deserted, to urge them to persevere toward a more hopeful future. She had left them a letter, of course, which Mary had promised to read to them, but it was not the same as being able to see their faces once more.

The only satisfying leave-taking had been her parting with Mr. Hunsford. He'd carried her baggage down and then asked shyly if she would permit him a word in private in his study. Since it seemed hardly likely that his intentions were dishonorable (she being already cloaked and bonneted for the journey, and the carriage already waiting at the door to take her to Whaley Bridge), she agreed. She even permitted him to close the door.

"I hope you don't think, Miss Vail, that I . . . I *encouraged* her ladyship to discharge you," he began.

"No, of course I don't," she assured him. "Why would I think such a thing?"

He reddened. "Because of . . . of my foolish behavior yesterday afternoon. I thought that you might believe I supported her ladyship's action out of . . . of a desire for revenge."

"I assure you, Mr. Hunsford, that I had no such notion."

"I'm glad. Thank you for that, Miss Vail. To be honest, I think I would have enjoyed taking a bit of revenge if this had happened yesterday. I felt such a fool yesterday, you see. But your words rang in my head all night, and by this morning I was grateful for them."

"Were you, Mr. Hunsford? I'm pleased to hear it."

"And more than that, I realized that you had no intention of revealing my . . . er . . . my indiscretion to Mary or anyone else."

"Goodness, how can you have imagined I would?"

"There are many women who, had they been in your place, would have babbled to the world. You spoke the truth to me, and then kept silent. That showed character, Miss Vail. Truly worthy character. I only wish I could have told that to Lady Ruckworth." He removed his spectacles and rubbed the bridge of his nose with shaking fingers. "It is I who lack character, I'm afraid."

Georgy felt a rush of sympathy for him. "But you mustn't think for a moment that I suspected you of being party to the decision to discharge me, Mr. Hunsford. I understand fully that the matter was out of your hands."

"Yes, it was. Her ladyship has always been completely beyond my power to control." He replaced his spectacles and drew himself up bravely. "But she will *not* prevent me from writing you a letter of commendation, Miss Vail. I promise to do so, whenever you request it of me."

Now, in the coach, remembering his brave words,

Georgy had to smile. Mr. Hunsford's brave promise was so typical of him; there was no bravery in it, for it was not a promise that endangered him in the least. Lady Ruckworth was hardly likely to censor his mail!

As the hours passed and London loomed nearer, Georgy forced herself to think about the other end of the tunnel. She wondered if things would be much changed at home. Mama would undoubtedly be furious with her. She would probably have to endure hours of recriminations. She hoped Allie would be forgiving. It would be difficult enough to endure Mama's harangues, but to endure them without having Allie as an ally would be insupportable. Perhaps Jeremy was home at last. He might possibly take her side if Mama began again to plague her about making a good match.

All the old problems were returning to haunt her, the problem of matchmaking in particular. It loomed up before her more fearfully than ever. If she'd opposed marriage before, she was even more strenuously against it now. Before, she'd opposed it on merely theoretical grounds, but now she had a quite specific reason. She was in love. No one else but Maitland would do for her now, and Maitland himself was out of the question. She'd refused him when she was independent and self-supporting. Now that she was penniless (well, almost penniless—her wages, five whole pounds, were safely tucked in her reticule at the moment), it would be humiliating to accept him, even in the unlikely event that he asked her again. She could not accept him out of *need* when she'd rejected him out of *love*.

But what if Mama still hoped that a match with Lord Maitland was a possibility? Would Mama engage in machinations to promote such a scheme? If she did, Georgy would find herself more deeply in the suds than ever. She would not be able to bear being thrown at Tony now.

There was one way out, she realized with a start. She could try to find another school. There were other charity schools that needed teachers. It could be done. After all, she'd done it before. Why, this time she'd even have a recommendation. Hadn't Mr. Hunsford promised to write a letter for her? *Grace Vail could live again!*

With this encouraging plan before her, Georgy was able to face the far end of the tunnel—and the dawn now brightening over the roofs of London—with an almost cheerful spirit. She was going *home*. She would see Mama and Allie and perhaps even Jemmy, for at least a while. That, she had to admit, was a heartening prospect.

By the time the coach pulled in at the Swan it was bright daylight, and by the time she found a hack to take her to Verney House the morning was well advanced. She had not slept for almost two days, and she was rumpled and weary, but a sense of anticipation was growing within her and keeping her spirits high. The day was windy and brightly crisp, perfect for late fall, and the closer she came to home the faster her heart beat. When the carriage turned the final corner, Georgy felt her pulse racing like the wind in eagerness.

When they at last drew up before the house, she leaped out and ran up the front steps, leaving the coachman to take care of the baggage. Stiers opened the door. "Good morning, Stiers," she grinned.

The butler peered at her for a moment in a kind of stupor. "Miss Georgianna? Is it—?" Then he gasped. "It *is* you!"

Georgy saw nothing unusual in his reaction. She merely laughed. "Is Mama in? Don't say a word, Stiers. I want to surprise her."

Stiers kept staring at her as if her face wasn't quite as he remembered it. "Her ladyship is not at home, Miss. They're all gone."

Georgy's face fell. "All?"

"Miss Alison and Lord Verney, too."

"Lord Verney? Do you mean Jemmy? He's back, then!"

"Yes, Miss, but they've all gone to East Rid—"

She held up a hand. "Don't say anything more, Stiers. I'm too excited to take it all in. Since no one is at home at the moment, I shall go upstairs to my room and catch my breath. Then, when I've pulled myself together, I shall come down, and you'll tell me everything that's passed in the three months I've been gone." And she started for the stairs.

"Yes, Miss," Stiers said, following her across the hallway, "but there's something you should —"

"In a moment, Stiers. Just a few moments."

"But you don't understand, Miss Georgianna," the butler called up from the foot of the stairs. "I don't believe you've been told about Miss Birkin. She's in your —"

"Later, Stiers," Georgy said, disappearing round the landing. "You can fill me in on everything later."

She strode down the upstairs hall feeling heady with pleasure. The house had never looked better to her, nor the prospect of her lovely, large, luxurious bedroom more inviting. Three months of nights spent on a narrow, lumpy bed in her tiny vicarage room had been endurable, but when she added to that the eighteen hours of bruising discomfort in the coach, the anticipation of throwing herself upon her own huge, soft featherbed was delicious. She could hardly wait.

She threw open her bedroom door, took one step over the threshold and stopped short. She was not alone. A young woman was kneeling before the chest at the foot of her bed, folding some garments into it. This unfamiliar female was also sniffling rather loudly, which explained why she hadn't heard the door. Georgy was conscious of a wave of annoyance. Who was this person? She was too slim to be Betsy. If she were a new housemaid, there might be some excuse for her presence here, but even a maid had no right to open her chest and make free with her things. "Just what do you think you're doing?" she demanded.

The person on her knees turned her head sharply, her eyes widening in astonishment. Georgy's mouth fell open. She was staring into her own face.

Chapter 33

They stared at each other in shocked silence, each one taking in the other from top to toe. Finally Peggy lifted herself slowly from the floor. "You're *Georgy*," she breathed, brushing away the tears from her cheeks while keeping her eyes fixed on the other girl's face.

"I *think* I am," Georgy said, stupefied.

Peggy came a step closer. "You're beautiful! I don't know how I ever convinced anyone that I was you."

"I can't imagine why you would want to, but I'm sure you could," Georgy said dazedly. "I must be dreaming. Looking at you is like . . . it's like looking into a mirror." She shut her eyes and opened them again. "Am I having some sort of hallucination?"

Peggy gave her a strained smile. "It's no hallucination. Do sit down, Georgy. You look as if you're ready to sink."

"Thank you for the invitation, Miss Whoever-you-are, although you, may I remind you, are in *my* room."

"Yes, of course I am. But this has been my room for so long that I almost forgot. I'm sorry."

"*Your* room? What are you talking about?" She shook her head in utter bafflement. "Perhaps this isn't an hallucination. Perhaps it's only a nightmare." Then she peered at the other girl with a kind of hopeful desperation. "That's it, isn't it? A nightmare. I shall wake up in a little while and find myself still being jounced about on that blasted mail coach."

"I'm sorry, Georgy, truly I am. This must be very strange to you." Peggy sighed, and a shadow seemed to cross her face. "It is quite like a nightmare to me, too, but I know I shall not wake up from it." She forced a smile. "My name is Peggy. Peggy Birkin."

"How do you do? I don't suppose I have to give you *my* name. You seem to know it."

"Oh, I know it, all right," Peggy declared, her smile brightening. "I've been using it for almost a month."

"Using it?" Georgy asked, baffled.

"Yes. I suppose you could say I borrowed it."

"Borrowed my *name?* Why?"

"Because I've been taking your place. Do you realize, Georgy—I hope you don't mind my calling you that. I feel as if I know you too well to call you Miss Verney—do you realize that seeing you is the only good thing that's happened to me since this whole thing began? You have no idea how I've longed to meet you!"

"Have you indeed?" Georgy murmured, sinking down upon the bed but keeping a fascinated eye on the other girl. "Why is that?"

Peggy took a deep breath, as if to clear away whatever had depressed her and make room for something cheerful. "It's so exciting even to hear your voice," she exclaimed, pulling up a footstool and perching at Georgy's feet. "We don't sound at all alike, do we? That's why I had to pretend to everyone that my throat was still infected and went about whispering all the time."

"This is the most confusing conversation! Miss . . . Miss Birkin, is it? . . . please, dear girl, I'm completely at sea. Tell me who you are and why you are in my room. And, most confusing of all—though in this ocean of bewilderment, it is ridiculous for me to rate the confusion in degrees!—*why,* Miss Birkin, do you keep talking about pretending to be me?"

"Well, you see, pretending to be you is the reason I'm here. When your mother saw how great the resemblance was, she set about training me to take your place."

"Take my place? Good God! Whatever for?"

"For the house party at Colinas Verde."

Georgy stiffened. "Colinas Verde? That's . . . that's Lord Maitland's estate is it not? Has *he* anything to do with this?"

"Well, of course!" Peggy exclaimed in surprise. "Didn't you realize that? Lord Maitland is ... well, he's the whole point. Lady Horatia wanted to keep him from forgetting you and falling in the clutches of one of those designing females like your friend Lucy Traherne, you see."

Georgy shut her eyes, shook her head and put a trembling hand to her forehead. "No, Miss Birkin, I do *not* see."

"I wish you would call me Peggy. It's a very simple story, really. You and the family were invited to Lord Maitland's house party at Colinas Verde. Since you were gone, your mother asked me to stand in for you at the house party, that's all."

Georgy gaped at her, aghast. "To stand in for me? At Maitland's house party? And you say that's *all*? Good heavens, it's the outside of *enough!* It's the most ridiculous, the most embarrassing, the most *humiliating* idea I've ever heard of! I'd like to give my mother a good, sound tongue-lashing! How did she ever think of such a deplorable trick in the first place?"

"I think your mother has a talent for ... for arranging things."

"What a kind way to put it," Georgy said, glancing at the other girl appreciatively. "And how did my 'arranging' mother manage the miracle of finding someone who looks so much like me as you do?"

Peggy smiled ruefully. "You have it backward, Georgy. The 'miracle' came first. *Then* the idea."

"Oh, I see. I *think* I see. No, I don't see. Do you think you could explain it to me step by step?"

"I think so. It was Jeremy who found me at a—"

"Jeremy?" Georgy exclaimed in surprise. "You know my brother?"

Peggy lowered her head. "Oh, yes, I know your brother. As I was saying, he found me at a street market in Whaley Bridge. He was there looking for you and spotted me in the crowd. For a moment he thought I was you. Then, because I had no place to go—which is a long story I won't bore you with relating—he took me home with him."

"Did he really? I'm glad my brother can be so gallant."

Peggy's fingers twisted in her lap. "Yes, he can . . . sometimes. In any case, when your mother saw me, she conceived the idea of substituting me for you. The idea was very frightening to me, as you can imagine, but he . . . they persuaded me."

"Ah, now I *do* see. My leaving home seems to have upset my mother more than I thought, if it drove her to devise so desperate and foolish a scheme." She gazed down thoughtfully at Peggy who was looking quite baleful, sitting with her eyes lowered and hands folded in her lap. Georgy reached out and squeezed the other girl's hands. "You mustn't think I blame *you* for any of this, Peggy. You must be a very brave young woman to have agreed to perform such a dangerous masquerade."

"More foolish than brave, I think," Peggy answered, looking up. "You are very kind, Georgy. I'm beginning to see why Allie and so many others think so well of you."

They smiled at each other in mutual liking. Then Georgy, sighing tiredly, leaned back against the pillows and closed her eyes. "Thank God," she murmured, "that I'm home in time to prevent Mama from perpetrating such a despicable scheme."

Peggy drew in a sharp breath. "What do you mean, in time?"

Georgy opened her eyes in surprise at Peggy's tone. "I mean, now that I'm back, I will see to it that neither one of us attends his lordship's house party."

"But, Georgy," Peggy said, rising slowly from the footstool, "you don't understand. It's . . . it's too late. It's over."

"What's over?" Georgy said, sitting up abruptly.

"The house party. At least . . . it's almost over."

Georgy paled. "What are you trying to tell me? That you actually have *been* there?"

"Well, yes. Of course. For more than a week."

"For more than a week? At Colinas Verde?"

"Yes. I thought you understood. We were all there, Alison, your mother and . . . and Jeremy, too."

Georgy lifted two trembling hands to her forehead. "Let me be sure I understand you. Are you telling me that you and my whole family have been visiting with Lord Maitland for over a week, during which time you have been pretending to be *me?*"

"Yes," Peggy said, beginning to feel unnerved by Georgy's strange reaction. "That's exactly so."

Georgy swung her legs over the bed and stood up abruptly. "What sort of lies have you been telling me?" she asked furiously. "Lord Maitland was visiting with *me* only three days ago!"

Peggy gasped. "With *you?* How can that be?"

"You may well ask. How can you claim you were with him in his country home when he was visiting with *me* in another place entirely?"

Peggy shook her head. "I'm not lying to you, Georgy. Your family is still there."

"What?"

"Truly. Lady Horatia, Alison and . . . and your brother, too. They're all there. With Lord Maitland and the rest of the guests. Your friend Lucy, her brother, Rosalind Peascott, the Countess Lieven, Lord and Lady Denham . . . all of them. They're still there!"

The two young women stared at each other speechlessly. Georgy could see the sincerity in the other girl's eyes. She sank down upon the bed in real turmoil. "But . . . he came to see me in Ruckworth. Three days ago. How can you explain that?"

Peggy wrinkled her brows. "He *did* leave the party for a few days last week, Georgy. On urgent business, he said. He put Letty Denham in charge in his place. But if he went to *you* . . ." She shut her eyes in horror. "If he went to you, then he must have *known* . . ."

"Known?"

"That I was an impostor."

Georgy let herself fall back upon the pillows. "This is all too much for me," she said. "I don't know whether to believe you or not."

"I don't know whether to believe you either!" Peggy snapped defensively. "How did Lord Maitland know where to find you when no one else did?"

"He said that Allie found a letter that led him to me."

"A likely story! If Allie found a letter, why didn't she tell your mother or your brother? Why did she tell Lord Maitland?"

"I don't know. But I know that *I'm* telling the *truth.*"

"And so am I!" Peggy declared angrily. "You can ask Spiers where your family is if you don't believe me."

Georgy sat up again with a gasp. "Yes, you're right! Spiers did try to tell me something about East Riding. Forgive me for not believing you, Peggy. It's just that this whole business is a bit hard to swallow. All those people whom you named—Countess Lieven and Lucy Traherne and the rest, people who've known me all my life—how could they be so easily fooled by a . . . a pretender?"

Peggy shrugged. "It's hard for me to believe it myself. But it seems that people don't pay much attention to anything but their immediate concerns, you know. Nobody gave me close scrutiny. Your mother told them that you— that is, I—had been sick, and I spent many hours in my room, supposedly resting. I was in their company mostly in the evenings. In the candlelight even Lucy didn't seem to notice how different I was."

"And you truly are amazingly like me. It's quite incredible. But what else is incredible is that Tony, who hardly knew me, was apparently not taken in."

"Tony?" Peggy asked, cocking her head interestedly.

Greorgy bit her lip. "He asked me to call him that."

"I see," Peggy smiled. "He came to see you in Ruckworth—urgent business—and he asked you to call him Tony. Yes, I see."

"You needn't make more of it than that, Miss. Something flared up and then died. It is now over."

"Oh? I'm sorry. Maitland deserves . . . but never mind. I don't mean to pry. But at least I can see now why he wasn't taken in. Now that I think of it, I remember that the first morning I spent there, he came in from a hunt just to join me for breakfast. He seemed to be quizzing me. I think it was then that I must have failed."

"You have no reason to feel a failure, Peggy. My mother never should have suggested such a scheme. It is she who should be ashamed. And Jemmy, too, for going along with it."

Peggy was silent for a moment. "I can't help wondering about something, Georgy. If Lord Maitland guessed I was an impostor, why didn't he expose me?"

"I don't know. And why didn't he so much as hint to me, when he saw me at Ruckworth, that all this was going on?"

"A deep sort is our Lord Maitland," Peggy observed. "It's not easy to fathom what goes on in his head."

"Certainly too deep for Mama to have imagined she could get away with playing such a ridiculous trick on him."

Peggy nodded gravely. "I never did believe that I would get away with it for an entire fortnight. And now, of course, I've botched it all."

"Botched it? What do you mean? You said that Tony didn't give you away, so how have you botched it?"

"Running off as I did," Peggy muttered, lowering her eyes.

"Yes, I've been wondering about how it is that the rest of the family is still in East Riding and you are here."

Peggy turned away and walked to the window. "I would rather not speak of it, if you don't mind," she said quietly.

Georgy peered at her. "Something else went on at Colinas Verde, didn't it? I wish you would tell me about it, Peggy. Perhaps I could do something to set it right."

"You can't set it right. No one can."

"But shouldn't I know, if you were playing me?"

"But I wasn't playing you. N-Not then."

Georgy swung off the bed and came up behind her. "Yes, I remember now. You were crying when I first came in. Please tell me this, at least, Peggy—was it something concerning Tony?" she asked softly.

"No, not him," Peggy said, feeling the tears welling up inside her again.

Thank goodness, Georgy thought, *that it wasn't Tony that hurt her.* But some man had. Georgy recognized the signs. She put an arm about the other girl's shoulders and let her mind roam over the strange conversation they'd just had: two young women who'd never met but who had evidently shared more than just looks. They'd shared a name. Then Georgy remembered that at one point a shadow had crossed Peggy's expressive face. What had they been speaking of at that moment? *It's been a nightmare to me, too,* the girl had said, *but I know I'll never wake up.* What had happened to her at Colinas Verde? The only other man she'd mentioned besides Tony was Jeremy. But Jeremy was not the sort who . . . or was he? Now that she thought about it, the girl had dropped her eyes every time Jeremy was mentioned. "Peggy, look at me," she ordered. When Peggy looked up, Georgy faced her squarely. "Forgive me for asking, Peggy. I don't like to pry. But I feel as if you and I have shared something . . . something more than my name. I want to help. Don't speak if you don't wish to, but I must ask. Was it Jeremy?"

Peggy shook her head vehemently, her eyes fearful. "I d-didn't say . . ."

"No, you didn't. I just made a wild guess. You needn't be afraid to tell me, you know, even if he is my brother."

"No, please. I don't . . ." But all at once her face tightened to a knot of pain. "Oh, Georgy," she wept, collapsing on the other girl's shoulder, "I wish I were dead!"

Georgy put her arms about the weeping girl and rocked her gently. "Oh, my poor dear," she asked in dismay, "what did my brother *do* to you?"

Chapter 34

Peggy poured out the whole story, from her first glimpse of Jeremy, irresistibly resplendent in his gold-and-white uniform, to her last, when he'd cut her to the quick with his accusations and left her to her misery. Georgy listened to every word, flooded with sympathy for the poor girl who'd been forced into thievery but who didn't deserve the degrading assessment of her character that Jeremy had made. By the time the tale had been told, the afternoon had passed. Georgy washed the girl's swollen face, made her drink some tea and put her to bed. "Don't despair," she whispered as she tucked her in. "We'll think of what to do after we've both rested."

But Georgy could not rest. She went down to the sitting room and stood at the window watching the sunset. It was hard to accept the fact that her brother had been so cruel. During his boyhood he'd been her champion and her best friend. She'd always adored him. She hated to think he was changed, but time and circumstance were liable to change anyone. Had his years of war corrupted the sweetness of his character?

Memories of their happy childhood days together haunted her. She became so absorbed in them that she did not hear the front door open or the hurried footsteps in the hall. It was only when the sitting room door burst open that she was shaken from her thoughts and wheeled about.

Jeremy was standing in the doorway, not resplendent in his gold-and-whites but mud-spattered in drab riding togs, his face pale and his hair disheveled. "Peggy!" he exclaimed breathlessly. "Thank God you're still—" The words died on his tongue as he squinted into the fading sunlight that made almost a silhouette of her form. "Georgy?" he asked hesitantly.

She took a step toward him. "Jemmy—!"

"Georgy!" It was a shout of joy. He spanned the space between them in two quick steps, grasped her at her waist and swung her up in the air. "Georgy! You deuced, troublemaking runaway, you're a sight for sore eyes!"

She looked down at him, wishing to be angry at him, and could not. "Put me down, you . . . you blackguard!" she ordered, but when he did so, she could only beam as mistily at him as he was at her. "God forgive me," she muttered, throwing her arms around him, "but I *am* glad to see you."

"And why should God forgive you for being glad to see your brother?" he demanded when he released her from the embrace.

Her fond smile died, and she scanned his face intently for signs of the hardness and callousness she'd steeled herself to discover. But there were none. He was older, of course. There were deeper lines about his mouth and some incipient crinkles at the corners of his eyes. But she saw nothing of cruelty or coarseness. "How could you do it, Jemmy?" she asked bluntly. "It is so unlike you."

His eyebrows rose and he stiffened perceptibly. "Do what?" he asked.

"Hurt that poor, sweet innocent so cruelly."

His breath caught in his throat. "You've *seen* her!"

"Yes." She shook her head. "The likeness is amazing. I haven't yet got over the shock of it."

"She's here, then?" He expelled a long breath of relief.

"Yes, she is, although I don't know why you should care. You certainly didn't show any caring before."

Jeremy's already-pale face turned ashen. "Good God!" he gasped. "She told you?"

"The whole repellent story."

He winced in pain. "Damnation, Georgy, don't look at me so!" He sank down on the sofa and dropped his head in his hands. "I've made such a muddle of everything. What shall I do?"

"I don't know, Jemmy," she said with a sigh. "An accusation such as you made is not something a lady can forgive, ever." She scowled down on his bent head. "Why did you come? To tell her you're sorry?"

He looked up. "Yes. What's wrong with that?"

"I don't think being sorry is much of an atonement, do you?"

"No, I suppose it isn't. But I must do something! I'm beside myself with despair!"

"Are you, indeed?" she retorted. "How uncomfortable for you."

"Hang it all, Georgy, are you mocking me? Can't you see how wretched I am?"

"I see that you're very sorry for yourself. Since you have so much sympathy for your own wretchedness, I will save mine for Peggy's."

"Is that what you think? That I'm merely sorry for myself? Why do you think I've come all this way, riding without a stop on horseback through all last night and all today? Just to make a self-pitying whine?"

"Then why *did* you come, Jemmy?"

"To see her. To tell her I never really meant . . . never really believed . . . Dash it all, I want to explain to her why I said what I did. I didn't realize, you see, how insanely in love with her I was. How in love with her I *am*."

Georgy blinked at him in surprise. "Peggy didn't tell me that you said you loved her."

"I never really said it. I didn't realize it. I was so confused, what with Rosalind leading me a dance, and Peggy acting kittenish with Maitland, and strange, dark figures stealing out of her room in the dead of night. I felt as if I were going mad. I've read that love is a kind of madness, but I didn't know it would feel as terrible as this!"

"It does feel terrible," Georgy agreed, sitting down beside him. "I'm not surprised that you didn't recognize the feeling. One never expects how dreadful love can make one feel."

Jeremy eyed her curiously. "You, too?"

She shrugged. "None of us is immune to that particular madness."

Jeremy nodded glumly. "I thought what I felt for Rosalind was love. It was a shock to discover that what I thought was love was only a boyish fancy that I'd long since outgrown."

"It must have been more than boyish fancy. You've cared for Rosalind for years."

"Yes, I know. But what I thought was love was only an old habit. It never occurred to me to ask myself why she so often irked me with her childishness. I must be extraordinarily slow-witted."

"What finally did open your eyes?"

"Peggy, of course. She's in every way a woman, you see. Her feelings are all so deep and . . . full-bodied. Next to her, Rosalind seemed superficial and only half-grown."

"Then why, for heaven's sake, did you not tell Peggy all this?" Georgy asked impatiently.

"Because I didn't understand it myself. The awareness was coming upon me slowly, ever since I first laid eyes on her, but I didn't know how to interpret my feelings. Dash it all, why did I have to be so stupid?"

Georgy patted his hand comfortingly. "Well, at least you understand now. Just think of the pickle you'd have found yourself in if you had gone ahead and married Rosalind and *then* made this discovery."

"I shudder to think of it," he said with a rueful laugh.

"I'm glad you told me all this, Jemmy. I don't feel quite so angry with you now. And perhaps it *will* soothe Peggy somewhat to hear how you feel."

"It may soothe *her*," he said glumly, "but I don't think it will do much for me. She must feel nothing for me now but revulsion. I thought, when we first met, that she showed some signs of caring for me, but I've surely killed what little spark there might have been. She could never love me now."

"I don't know about that," came a small voice from the doorway. "Some sparks are very difficult to extinguish."

"Peggy!" He leaped to his feet, his heart pounding. "You don't mean it! You *can't*—"

"Yes, I can," she said softly.

He stumbled across the room to her and sank to his knees. "Oh, Peggy," he whispered hoarsely, tightening his arms about her waist and sinking his head against her, "I do love you so!"

She had to bend only slightly to put her arms about his neck and her lips against his hair. "I know," she murmured. "I know, now."

Georgy, choked with an emotion that was compounded of joyous relief and the slightest dash of envy, tiptoed silently out of the room and left them to their reconciliation.

Chapter 35

They sat at the breakfast table trying to pretend that this was just an ordinary morning. Peggy passed the coffee pot to Georgy with lowered eyes, hoping that her lips were not curling up in a too-radiant smile. Jeremy buttered his toast with serious concentration, attempting to control his embarrassing tendency to gaze adoringly at the girl across the table. And Georgy poured the cream into her coffee cup and hoped she would not burst into giggles. Finally she could contain herself no longer. "You two are behaving like a couple of mooncalves," she laughed. "If you think you're hiding your feelings with any success, you're fair and far off. Anybody even glancing at you would know at once that it's bellows to mend with you both."

"It is not bellows to mend with Miss Birkin there," Jeremy declared, pouting. "She keeps insisting she won't have me."

"What?" Georgy turned to Peggy in surprise. "Why not?"

"It is all so . . . so impossible," Peggy explained with a sigh. "You can't wish your brother to wed a nobody like me."

"I certainly can," Georgy insisted, "and I do."

"But he is Lord Verney! It would be highly improper for him to wed the sister of a common thief!"

"As to that, Peggy," Jeremy said with a sudden frown, "I have some unpleasant news to tell you about Ned."

Peggy bit her lip. "I know what you're going to say. You found out about the emerald. Did Ned plant it in your room after all?"

"Is *that* what he intended to do with it?" Jeremy's brows

lifted in surprise. "Why did he want to do that? He could have sold it for a fortune."

"He thought he could do better by squeezing Maitland."

"Squeezing Maitland?" Jeremy asked as both he and his sister leaned forward with interest. "How?"

"I'm very shamed to tell you." Peggy pushed her cup away and clenched her fists. "He wanted me to . . . to compromise Lord Maitland, so that then he could demand payment. To buy me off, I suppose. I told him Maitland had no interest in me, but he wouldn't believe it. He threatened to plant the emerald in your room and somehow make it known, and then *you* would be accused of thievery. So I . . ." She glanced up at Jeremy nervously. "So I agreed."

"You agreed?"

She looked across at him beseechingly. "I couldn't bear to let him embroil you in so distasteful a situation. I only agreed to it to gain some time. I hoped that I would think of some way out, or that something might happen to change the situation. Besides, I knew the plan was ridiculous. Lord Maitland is not the sort."

"Is *that* why you suddenly began to flirt with Maitland so outlandishly?"

She reddened. "Yes. Was I very dreadful? I was afraid Ned was lurking somewhere about, watching me. He can be very ugly if he thinks he's being crossed."

Jeremy reached across the table and took her hand. "Did you do all this just to keep me from embarrassment? When I think how I thanked you, I realize all over again how little I deserve you."

"Don't say that, Jemmy," she murmured. "I must have humiliated you horribly, flirting with Maitland that way. I can't imagine what all those people think of me. That's another reason why I can't marry you. I won't have the world whispering that Lord Verney has married a brazen flirt."

"As to that, my girl," Jeremy said with a wry smile, "Mama said you acted just as you ought. She said that any unmarried female has a duty to flirt with a catch like Maitland, and that you were not nearly as brazen as Lucy Traherne."

"Mama *would* say that," Georgy put in disgustedly.

"But my love," Jeremy went on, "I'm afraid there is more to my bad news than the discovery that your brother stole the emerald." He tightened his hold on her hand. "He's dead."

Peggy's eyes widened. "Dead? Ned is?"

"Yes. And that's not the worst of it. It was mostly my fault. I didn't know who he was, you see. I only knew that he was the man I'd seen leave your room. When I saw him again, we—Maitland and I—chased him up on the roof. I lunged for him and he . . . fell. I'm so sorry, Peggy, to have caused you this pain."

She pulled her hand from his grip and pressed it to her mouth. "Poor Ned," she whispered, shaken. After a while she rose from her chair. "Don't blame yourself, Jemmy," she said gently. "You did what had to be done. I always knew that Ned would come to a bad end. But please excuse me, now. I want to go upstairs."

Jeremy got up to follow her, but Georgy waved him back. "Peggy," she asked quietly, "do you wish me to go with you?"

"No, thank you, Georgy. I think I'd like to be alone for a little while."

Jeremy and Georgy waited silently at the table for more than an hour for Peggy to return. When she did, she was dressed in the shabby gown and bonnet she'd worn when she'd first come to this house. She paused in the morning room doorway, her eyes red and her chin lifted bravely. "I've just stopped in to say good-bye. I'm going now." She held up a hand to stop Jeremy who'd pushed back his chair and was about to rise. "Don't try to stop me, Jemmy, for I'm quite determined. I and my brother . . . we've brought enough trouble and embarrassment to this family. I won't bring anymore."

"Don't be a little fool," Jeremy said, jumping up and striding across to her so swiftly she had no time to move. He pulled her horrid bonnet from her head, tossed it away and took her in his arms. "You and I are going to be wed, Peggy Birkin, and we are going to live in blissful contentment in this house for the rest of our lives."

"Jemmy, *no!*" she cried, struggling unsuccessfully to keep him from kissing her.

When he at last released her, she made as if to run off again, but this time Georgy pulled her to the table and pushed her down. "I've heard just about all the nonsense from you that I can bear," she declared firmly. "Though I'm part of this family, I think I can be considered a disinterested party. And as far as I can see, there is not one good reason why you should not marry my brother."

"But I told you! A nobleman cannot marry into such a family as mine. It would be highly improper."

"If propriety were the best reason for marrying, then Jeremy should marry Rosalind. *That* would be a highly proper match, would it not? After all, they've been practically betrothed since they were tots. And her family is everything that's proper. Is that what you want . . . to see him 'properly' wed to that ninnyhammer? She would probably bankrupt him in a year, and we would all have to end our days in the workhouse. Is that what you wish for the Verneys?"

"He needn't wed Rosalind," Peggy persisted. "There are many other young ladies—"

"Not for me," Jeremy said flatly. "It's you or no one."

"But, Jemmy, you cannot wish for the world to whisper that you married the sister of the very thief who robbed Lady Denham's emerald! Since Ned died right on the grounds of Colinas Verde, everyone will know that—"

"No one knows who he is except Maitland, and you can be sure that Maitland will never tell a soul."

Peggy folded her arms on the table and dropped her head down on them. "You are both making this very difficult for me," she moaned.

"I hope we are," Georgy snapped. "You are being entirely too missish, Miss Birkin."

"But don't you see how impossible this is?" she insisted, lifting her head and looking at Georgy pleadingly. "Even if we managed to keep my background secret, there is still the business of the masquerade. I ran away from Colinas Verde, thus giving myself away. How will it look to the world if Jeremy Verney marries the girl who tried to pass herself off as his sister?"

"As to that," Georgy said slowly, dropping down on a chair beside Peggy and knitting her brows, "I've been giving the matter some thought. I think I have a perfectly sound plan. First, Jemmy, you must marry Peggy quietly right away and leave promptly on a lengthy trip."

"It sounds wonderful so far," he grinned.

"Then after a week or two I will place an announcement in the *Times* that says that Lord Verney has wed Miss Margaret Birkin of Whaley Bridge and has gone abroad on an extended honeymoon. By the time you get back, Peggy will have restored her hair to its natural color and to a more becoming style than that prissy coiffure of mine. She will dress in her own style and speak in her own voice. As a result of being uniquely herself, people will simply remark that Verney's bride looks remarkably like his sister and think no more about it. Then as time goes on, she will have babies and grow fat, while I will sink into lean and wizened spinsterhood, and the resemblance will grow so faint that no one will remark on it at all. How does that sound, eh, Miss Faint-of-heart?"

"I don't know what to say!" Peggy cried, burying her head in her arms again as if afraid to face the possibility of having her dreams come true. "You are making me tremble with wild hopes."

"That, my dear, is the most sensible thing I've heard you say today," Jeremy cheered.

"But I still can't believe your plan would work," she said, peeping up at them. "What about the problem of the party at Colinas Verde? My secret is probably out by now, and by the time the guests all return to town, it will be the favorite *on dit* of all society that a certain Peggy Birkin tried to pass herself off as Georgianna Verney."

"The secret is not out," Jeremy said. "When I left, Mama was shrewdly shrugging off all questions about your absence by saying that it is the curse of her existence to have so impetuous and unpredictable a daughter. And Maitland told me that, when he's asked, he will say that Georgy told him she had to rush off to town on urgent business. It all sounds a bit fishy, I admit, but when the party ends and the guests return to town, they will find Georgy alive and well, and quite recovered from her throat infection. And that, my dear, should effectively put an end to any smell of fraudulence that still lingers."

"Wait, Jemmy," Georgy said, putting up a hand to keep the others silent while she thought. A gleam of mischief lit her eyes and spread slowly across her face until it curled itself on her mouth in a wicked smile. "What if Georgy reappears at the house party herself, looking and sounding perfectly natural and at ease?" She gave a naughty, gleeful laugh. "*Then* there would be not the slightest *hint* of fraudulence."

Peggy and Jeremy stared at her in fascination. "Reappears?" Peggy ventured fearfully. "You want Georgy to return to Colinas Verde before the fortnight ends? Do you mean . . . *me?*"

"Of course I don't mean you. *You* will be much too busy getting married and going abroad."

"Georgy, you devil!" Jeremy chortled. "You're going to continue the game!" He pulled her from the chair and whirled her about in delight. "You're a regular out-and-outer, you are!" Then he turned to Peggy and lifted her up in the air. "And as for you, Miss Birkin, you are from this moment betrothed to me. Is it agreed?"

"Oh, Jemmy, yes!" she breathed, beaming down at him. "But I think all three of us have lost our wits."

Georgy watched for a moment while they kissed, but then she clapped her hands for their attention. "There will be enough time for that sort of thing later," she said briskly. "Right now we have something more important to do."

"Oh?" her brother asked, refusing to take his besotted gaze from the face of his bride-to-be. "And what important something is that?"

"We've got to get me ready. I'd better leave at once if I'm to have sufficient time to accomplish anything at Colinas Verde."

"But what is there to get ready?" he asked.

"A great deal. We must dress me up to look like Peggy."

"What do you mean?" her brother asked, bemused. "Don't you want to look like Georgy?"

"Not exactly. I don't think this change in the game will be as simple as you think. I shall not quite be Georgy on this excursion."

"No?"

"No. I shall be Georgy playing Peggy playing Georgy. And that, dear brother, is quite a different thing."

Chapter 36

To be Georgy playing Peggy playing Georgy was *not* simple. Georgy could not walk in on the assemblage and simply be herself. If she did, she would seem different and thus give the game away. She studied Peggy carefully to assimilate the small differences. She would have to be hoarse, of course, and speak in a whisper. She would have to chose the more daring and brightly colored of her gowns to wear. She would have to permit her hair to be a little more free of restraint. "And for goodness sake," Peggy warned, "don't be quite so opinionated and sure of yourself. I had to guard my tongue so carefully that I almost never expressed a strong opinion."

"Heavens!" Georgy exclaimed. "How could you have been a shy, retiring little mouse and still convince everyone that you were me?"

Jeremy laughed. "They all decided that illness had taken the starch out of Georgy Verney. Just remember that, my girl. You've been ill. Show a little less starch in your spirit."

Peggy gave Georgy the gown she'd worn when she'd left Colinas Verde and showed her exactly how she fixed her hair. While they were thus occupied, Jeremy went out to the stable where the carriage Maitland had provided for Peggy was housed and left word for the coachman that Miss Verney had decided to return to East Riding with him. By evening everything was ready. Arm in arm they went out to the carriage where many affectionate embraces and heartfelt expressions of good wishes were exchanged, and at last the happy couple assisted her into the carriage. Georgy waved good-bye from the rear window until her brother and his betrothed were lost from view. Then she settled back for the long ride north.

No sooner were the lights of London left behind when Georgy began to regret the impetuous impulse that had made her undertake this trip. · Her misgivings were so strong that she rapped on the trap door and shouted for the driver to stop. "Wait a moment," she instructed him. "I want to think."

This was a foolishly daring escapade, she argued with herself, and probably unnecessary. She had thought of it at first as a way to bridge the awkward gap that might occur between Peggy's assumption of her character and her own resumption of it. She would begin her stay at Colinas Verde as Peggy might have done and gradually become more herself. It would be a smooth, subtle transition from one personality to the other. In that way, no one would ever guess that a substitution had been made. It had seemed to her a very clever idea at the time.

But now she began to realize that she would again be placed in too-close proximity to Tony Maitland. Since she had determined that she could not accept him, she asked herself why she'd arranged to put herself in a situation that was bound to bring her pain. Seeing him in his own surroundings among his own friends would surely make him even more desirable in her eyes; and spending days and evenings in his company would certainly rekindle the spark that had ignited in Ruckworth Parish. Why had she done it?

She had done it, she told herself, to prevent the possibility of anyone's discovering her mother's idiotic trick. It was still a good reason. She would hate for her mother to become a laughingstock. It would be cowardly of her to back out now, after she'd promised Peggy that she would make things right. And besides, the whole game would be over in two or three days. She could manage to harden her heart toward Maitland for two or three days, couldn't she? She was certainly strong enough for that. There were no really good reasons for misgivings.

Thus having reassured herself, she rapped on the door again and told the driver to proceed. She spent the rest of the journey reviewing in her mind everything that Peggy and Jeremy had told her about the events that had taken place at the house party. She wanted to be sure to make no little slips. There seemed to be so many details to remember that she wondered with awed admiration how Peggy had managed to cram into her head the thousands of details about *her* past. She had to learn the details of nine or ten days of a house party; Peggy had had to learn the details of a lifetime.

Although she made only one brief stop during the journey, she did not arrive at the estate until late the following evening. Colinas Verde was not quite as brightly lit as it had been when the Verneys had arrived at first, but Georgy gasped at the sight of it nevertheless. The butler admitted her with only the merest raising of an eyebrow. "How nice to have you back, Miss Verney," he said, taking her wrap. "His lordship did not tell me you were returning this evening."

"I don't believe I informed him of it," Georgy said absently, looking about the grand entryway with interest.

"Ah, your throat is better, Miss! I am so pleased."

She bit her lip in self-disgust. "Thank you," she said, giving a belated little cough. "I think it *is* improving at last."

"Dinner is over, I'm afraid," he informed her as they crossed the hall, "but Cook would, I am sure, be pleased to warm up some soup and a portion of partridge filet. Shall I serve it to you in the morning room?"

"No, thank you," she muttered, wondering what the devil his name was. "I'm not a bit hungry. Where is everyone?"

"In the music room, Miss. His lordship has arranged a musicale for this evening. A string quartet."

"How lovely. I'll go up at once."

"Up, Miss?" The butler peered at her strangely. "You must have forgotten. The music room is just down the corridor there . . . in the east wing."

Georgy wanted to kick herself. Peggy had not made so many mistakes in her eight days here as she had made in five minutes! Her respect for Peggy was growing by leaps and bounds. "Of course I haven't forgotten," she said sternly. "I meant I'll go up to my room first."

"Yes, of course, Miss. Shall I wait for you to come down, to announce you?"

"No, thank you. I prefer to slip in quietly, without distracting from the music."

"Yes, Miss. As you wish, Miss."

She strode quickly toward the stairs. Peggy had described the location of her room, so she had no difficulty finding it. She gave herself a quick look in the mirror and sighed at the rumpled condition of her gown. She considered changing to something fresher but decided against it. Wearing the same gown that Peggy had worn when she left gave her a sense of connectedness with that part of the past that was—and was not—hers.

She slipped down the stairs again, looked uneasily at the two stony-faced footmen who stood like statues at the bottom of the stairway, and walked past them as if she knew exactly where she was going. She turned down the corridor the butler had indicated, and soon the strains of Haydn's *Lark Quartet* reached her ears. She followed the lilting sounds to her destination. The door of the music room was open, and Georgy paused in the doorway and looked inside.

The four musicians were seated in a circular niche in the wall between the two tall windows opposite the door where Georgy stood. Their faces and their music stands were illuminated by two large candlestands on which dozens of candles were burning. The rest of the room was dimly lit, but Georgy could see the assembled guests well enough to distinguish them all. Farthest to her left, Sir Basil sat puffing at his pipe and watching with admiration the fingers of the cellist lovingly stroking the neck of his instrument. In front of him, his head falling forward in sleep, sat Lord Traherne. While Georgy watched he gave a little snort, and his wife quickly but surreptitiously jabbed his ribs with her elbow. Georgy's mother sat in the first row, watching the players with her usual expression of attentive placidity, her hand on the shoulder of her youngest daughter, who sat on a footstool near her feet and was listening, enraptured, with her eyes closed.

Immediately to their right were Lord and Lady Denham, watching the musicians with what seemed to Georgy to be sincere pleasure. Their hands, resting on the arms of their respective chairs, were just close enough to touch, as if to assure each other of their devotion but without the least ostentation or intention of making that devotion noticeable to the world at large. If there was any couple among Georgy's acquaintance whose marriage she admired, it was the Denhams.

Lucy, Monte and Rosalind Peascott sat behind the Denhams. Monte was, as usual, making a show of his musical interests by nodding his head vigorously to the beat. Rosalind's hand was resting in his, but she was gazing up at the ceiling in unmistakable boredom. Lucy was, typically, fiddling with the satin band that tied back her curls. She was being minutely observed by a handsome, blond young fellow who Georgy immediately identified as the Austrian nephew of the Countess Lieven. The Countess, hands folded as if in ecstatic prayer, sat at the rear beside Tony Maitland himself. Tony was leaning back in casual comfort, his legs outstretched and his arms relaxed. But his eyes were lowered, his brow furrowed and his expression more solemn than Georgy had ever seen it. She did not know what dark thoughts were racing through his mind, but she could see that they had nothing to do with the soaring charm of the music.

As she stood watching, the bored Rosalind suddenly looked round. Her eyes widened, and she leaned over to Lucy, pointing over her shoulder. Lucy looked up, blinked and then smiled excitedly. "It's Georgy!" she whispered to no one in particular. "Georgy's back!"

Inexplicably, Georgy's heart began to pound. Her eyes flew to Maitland. He sat upright and turned at once to the door. Even in the dim light Georgy could read his expression clearly. His face took on a look of mild interest at the return of the girl he thought was Peggy. He even started to lift himself from his seat, his mouth turning up in a polite-host smile. But then Georgy saw his eyes become blank.

He seemed, for just long enough for the flicker of an eye, to suspend his breath. Her own breathing stopped, too, as she saw a wave of absolute gladness spread over his face. No one else could have seen it, for not a muscle moved. But to her, the feelings behind his eyes had been as legible as if they were words on a page. Something clenched in her chest so tightly it made her gasp. *Oh, my God*, she thought in joy and pain, *he knows me!*

Chapter 37

———◦❦◦———

Georgy put a finger to her lips and pointed to the musicians to indicate to Lucy, and Lord Maitland as well, that they should not get up to welcome her and distract from the music. Maitland sank back in his chair but did not take his eyes from her. She, however, forced herself to take her eyes from him.

Meanwhile, the word spread through the room: *Georgy's back.* Heads turned. A rustle of motion swept through the audience, alerting Lady Horatia that something had occurred. She, too, looked round. Surprised, she pressed her fingers into Alison's shoulder. "She's *back!*" she muttered.

Alison turned, peered at the figure in the doorway and then gave a sharp intake of breath. "Mama!" she hissed. "It's Georgy!"

"But of course it's Geo—*Georgy?*" Horatia's mouth dropped open and she gave a start. "Georgy!" If Alison had not laid a restraining hand on her knee, Horatia would have jumped up from her chair. At the back, Georgy met her mother's startled eye and wiggled her fingers at her in an utterly casual greeting. Poor Horatia choked, shut her eyes and fell back against her seat. Her breast heaved—not at all in time with Haydn's *Lark*—and, for once, she looked not at all complacent. She was overjoyed at her daughter's reappearance, of course, but it seemed as if her little plot had somehow gotten quite out of hand.

When the movement ended, Lord Maitland set a chair for Georgy and wordlessly led her to it. The next movement commenced at once, allowing no one time to greet her. She was grateful. As part of the audience, with everyone's eyes returned to the musicians, she would have time to pull herself together. Lord Maitland, however, edged his chair close to hers. "This is an unexpected pleasure, Miss Vail," he whispered. "Is this a school holiday of some sort? I am not aware of school holidays in November."

"No holiday, my lord," she whispered back, keeping her eyes on the musicians and barely moving her lips. "I was sacked."

"Were you indeed? How fortunate for me."

She could hear him settle back into his chair. A few minutes later, she stole a look at him. He had stretched out his legs and folded his arms over his chest, looking as relaxed as he had when she first saw him. But the solemn expression was gone from his face. In its place was a look of such obnoxious self-satisfaction that she would have liked to box his ears.

When the concert concluded, Georgy found herself surrounded. Everyone greeted her warmly but with no recognition of any particular change in her. Lucy, of course, wanted to know where she'd been, but before she could reply, the butler came in to announce that a late buffet supper was being served in the blue saloon. The group began to saunter out of the music room in the direction of the food.

It was then that Allie seized her arm and held her back. "You're the most complete hand," she giggled. "How on earth did you manage the switch?"

"You don't expect me to tell you *now,* do you, my love? It's too long a story. But I'm so glad to see you, Allie dearest. You can't imagine how much I've missed you. I feel as if I haven't seen you in years. You look so grown!"

"I've missed you, too, Georgy, but never mind that now. There's something much more urgent I have to tell you."

Georgy looked uneasily round the now-deserted music room. "Do you have to tell me now? We should be going to supper."

"I think I'd better, Georgy. You see, Lord Maitland *knows*."

"Knows what?"

"About Peggy. It might have been my fault, because I gave the game away only a day or two after we got here. But Tony said he knew anyway. It was really quite amazing. He's the only one who knew at once that Peggy wasn't you."

"It doesn't matter now, Allie. Don't worry about it."

"But it *does* matter. I've got to be clear about this or I shall get us in the suds again. Are you supposed to be *Peggy* to him now?"

Georgy let out a peal of laughter. "This is becoming a complete farce, isn't it? We should make a chart listing who I am to whom. I'm Georgy to Mama, Peggy to Maitland, etcetera, etcetera."

Allie giggled. "It does seem to be a dreadful tangle, doesn't it? But we shouldn't laugh, Georgy. We don't want to reveal Mama's sordid machinations to the world, you know."

"Yes," Georgy said, her laughter dying, "but it *is* sordid. When this is all over, I shall give Mama a proper talking-to. And you, too, for permitting her to do such a thing."

"Me permitting her?" Allie said indignantly. "Since when have I been able to 'permit' Mama to do anything? I haven't the slightest influence on her. She won't even let me wear long skirts!"

Georgy put an arm about her sister's shoulders. "I know. Mama can be dreadfully overbearing," she said as they strolled to the door. "But you'll be in long skirts soon enough. As for his lordship, Allie, you needn't worry about him. He knows perfectly well who I am."

"Does he?" She looked at her sister intently. "I hope that one of these days you'll explain to me how he does. Though I suspect it's because he looks at you with love. I think lovers' eyesight is especially keen."

"Good heavens, what a little romantic you've become!"

her sister laughed. "What makes you think Maitland loves me?"

"He loves you very much, I think. Are you going to marry him, Georgy? Because I warn you: if you don't, I will!"

When they arrived at the buffet, Georgy was surrounded again. "Where on earth did you run off to the other day, Georgy Verney?" Lucy demanded loudly. "And why didn't you say good-bye to anyone?"

"Yes, do tell us, Miss Verney," Lord Maitland said, smiling wickedly. "You had us all alarmed."

"Alarmed, my lord? But why?" Georgy asked in the hoarse whisper she'd rehearsed with Peggy. "You knew I'd gone to London. You lent me your carriage."

"Yes, so I did. But none of us could guess why you'd gone."

Monte, lifting a forkful of liver pâté from the plate in his hand, nodded in agreement. "It was very strange behavior, Georgy, I must say, to rush off to London while the party is still going on."

"I see no reason why the girl has to account to us for her movements," Roger Denham interceded.

"Quite right," his wife agreed. "I'm sure no one means to pry, Georgy, my dear. We're just happy to have you back with us."

"Thank you, Lady Denham, but I don't mind explaining," Georgy said. "It's no great mystery. You see, we received a message from Mr. Hitchins—he's Mama's man of business—telling us that he needed to go over some financial matters. Didn't Mama tell you? Since she dislikes dealing with business matters, and Jemmy didn't wish to go, *I* went. The next day, however, it occurred to Jemmy that now that his army service is over he ought to take some interest in the management of his estate, so he returned home and sent me back here." She turned to her mother with a bland smile. "Why didn't you explain it to everyone, Mama?"

Lady Horatia threw a quick glower at her daughter before turning to the others with a shrug of pure innocence.

"To tell the truth, I forgot all about the message from Mr. Hitchins. But I *told* you there was no need to worry about Georgy." She flicked her daughter another speaking look. "You know Georgy," she added, throwing up her arms in a gesture of motherly helplessness. "She always turns up in the end."

Chapter 38

"I know why you came back," Lucy remarked as she and Georgy sat together in a corner of the Blue Saloon munching happily on delicious little cheese buns and filets of pullet *à L'Indienne*.

"Of course you know," Georgy said calmly. "I already told you why."

"You mean that tale about Jemmy sending you back? That's not the reason."

"No?" Georgy took a bite of bun and chewed it with calm deliberation. "Then what is?"

"You've decided to try again to attach Maitland."

"I don't know what's wrong with you, Lucy," Georgy sighed. "I've told you and told you I shall never marry for wealth."

"If that's true, then why did you come back from wherever it was you've been hiding lately and replace the girl your mother was trying to pretend was you?"

Georgy gasped. "Lucy! You knew?"

"Not just at first, for your substitute was remarkably like you, you know. But after a while she gave herself away. Her voice, for one thing, wasn't enough like yours, even when she pretended to be hoarse. And there was much she didn't know. She didn't recognize the blue Norwich shawl you gave me for my birthday, for instance."

"But if you knew she was an imposter, why didn't you say something?"

"Why should I? If your mother and sister, who were obviously in on the game, wished to perpetrate a harmless fraud, I didn't see why I should interfere. Besides, I

wanted to see what sort of deep game you all were playing.
And now, of course, I'm beginning to sort it all out."

"Are you indeed?" Georgy asked drily. "If you are, you
are cleverer than I am."

"Well, perhaps I don't understand all of it, but I'm certain that it has something to do with capturing Maitland."

"Why won't you believe me, Lucy? I tell you I'm not
interested in making an advantageous match."

Lucy glowered at her. "You should know by this time,
Georgy Verney, that even if I'm not a bluestocking like
you, I'm not quite a fool. Your mother made that other
Georgy flirt outrageously with him all last week."

"I don't deny that captivating Lord Maitland was
Mama's purpose, but you can't believe it was *mine*. And
besides, I understand that Peggy's feeble efforts were nothing compared to yours."

Lucy nodded with refreshing honesty. "I know. I've
been behaving scandalously. So Peggy's her name, is it? I
hope, my love, that you intend to tell me the details of this
peculiar business."

"Yes, I will, one of these days," Georgy promised.

"But as to Peggy's and my efforts at flirtation," Lucy
went on, "we were both feeble, I think, as far as our effect
on his lordship was concerned. I don't think he showed a
spark of interest in either of us."

"Didn't he? I'm sorry, Lucy. Are you hurt by it? Are
you attracted to him?"

"I would be, if he'd give me the least encouragement.
But his mind always seems to be elsewhere when he speaks
to me. I shan't give up hope, however. There is still a little
time."

Georgy grinned at her friend. "You gudgeon! You never
say die when it comes to attempting to make a great match,
do you?"

"If you think that I intend to retire and leave the field
entirely to you, my girl," Lucy came back, tossing her
curls, "you'd better think again."

"Oh, have no fear, Lucy, my dear," Georgy told her,
rising, "I intend to leave the field entirely to you. But if I

were at all tempted to try my hand, I think I might do better than Peggy."

Lucy snorted scornfully. "Do you really think so? Why is that, may I ask? If Peggy, who looked enough like you to be your twin, didn't attach him, why do you think you'd do better?"

"Because it's really me, this time. Poor Peggy had to expend too much effort on the pretense. I, on the other hand, can simply be myself."

Lucy studied her carefully. "If this is a challenge, Georgy Verney, I'll take it. If you can get more of a response from his lordship than your double managed to get, I'll admit defeat and say yes to Algy Colclough."

Georgy chuckled. "So Algy has come up to snuff at last, has he? You always did have a secret yearning for that beanpole."

"Perhaps I did," Lucy admitted ruefully, "but no one could say *that* would make a great match."

"He may not be rich, Lucy, but he's a man of character. You could do a great deal worse."

"Nevertheless, I shan't give up on Lord Maitland until the bitter end," Lucy said, jumping up. "Shall we go back to the buffet and begin this competition?"

At the table they found themselves rubbing elbows with their host, but Lucy immediately discovered that she was to lose the first round, for Maitland turned to Georgy at once. "I've made some changes in the library since you left, Miss Verney, that I think you will find interesting," he remarked with studied casualness. "Would you like to see them?"

"Now?" she asked, meeting his eye challengingly.

"Yes, now, if you'd like."

She felt her heart begin to hammer. "Very well, my lord." She threw Lucy a so-there look and took his arm. They left the room and strolled down the hall with unhurried propriety, but as soon as they'd stepped over the library's threshold, he shut the door and leaned against it. It was an act of decided impropriety, and she raised a disapproving eyebrow in response. "Are you locking me in, my lord?"

"For as long as you'll let me." He gazed at her with a

kind of thirst, as if he'd been parched for the sight of her. "My God, girl, you're beautiful." He reached out and pulled her to him. "More beautiful even than I remembered," he murmured and kissed her hungrily.

She could not help responding for a little while. But then she pushed hard against his shoulders and turned her head away. "I only seem beautiful in contrast to the way you saw me last," she said with a breathless laugh, "in that dreadful cap."

He took her chin in his hands and forced her to face him. "Tell me why you're here, Georgy. Does it mean you've changed your mind about marrying me?"

She shook her head. "No, of course I haven't. Do you think my principles are so shallow that they can be overturned in only a few days?"

"Good God," he exclaimed in disappointment, "are we going to have to argue about those blasted principles *again?*"

"We won't argue at all. Since nothing has changed, there's no point in it."

He peered intently into her eyes, his own face sobering as he recognized the firmness of her intent. "Confound it, Georgy," he said, letting her go, "if you haven't changed your mind, then why the devil did you come?"

"To keep everyone here from discovering Mama's damnable trick, that's why. I must apologize to you for that, Tony. You do realize I knew nothing about it."

"Of course I realize it. That's why I said nothing to you about it while we were in Ruckworth. I thought it might upset you, and I knew my presence had upset you quite enough. But I don't understand, Georgy. What really happened at Ruckworth? Why are you not at school?"

Her eyes fell. "I told you. I was sacked."

"You *can't* have been sacked! You're an excellent teacher. Even that inflated, self-important pomposity, Lady Ruckworth, must have seen how those children adored you."

"They did, didn't they?" Georgy mumbled, feeling a sudden choking in her throat. "And I *w-was* a good teacher." She turned away so that he wouldn't see her unexpected and embarrassing tears. "But I was s-sacked nevertheless."

He came up behind her. "I'm truly sorry, Georgy," he said, putting a hand on her shoulder. "I know how much they meant to you."

"No, you can't really know," she said quietly, her head lowered. "I thought I could make some d-difference in their lives . . . that I could change things. Little Hester was *reading*. And Timmy was so enjoying the sketching. And Sarah's m-mother said she s-sang around the h-house!"

All at once she felt herself shaking with sobs. It was Tony's sympathy that had undone her. She had been so preoccupied with the life of Georgy Verney in the past few days that her life as Grace Vail had been shut away behind a closed door in her mind. But somehow Tony had pushed open that door, and the feelings she'd not permitted herself to face came rushing out.

Without quite knowing how, she found herself turned about, facing him and supported by his arms. He was looking down on her with such sincere sympathy that all she could do was throw herself against him and sob on his shoulder. "And B-Benjy!" she wept. "My sweet, b-bright Benjy! That hurts most of all. All that he'll ever do with his life now is make horseshoes!"

Tony put his lips against her hair and rocked her gently. "Don't cry, my love," he murmured. "I know it's painful to have to put that part of your life behind you, but your life isn't over. Marry me, and you can spend your days teaching our sweet, bright children. We can have lots of children, if you wish. As many as you like. Dozens and dozens."

She gave a gurgling laugh. "Dozens?"

"A whole classroom full, if it will make you happy."

She shook her head and pushed him away. "Damnation, Tony Maitland," she exclaimed, dashing the tears from her cheeks, "stop asking me to wed you. I won't do it!"

"But why not? You're not going to stand there and pretend you don't care for me, are you?"

She hid her face in her hands. "I knew I shouldn't have come. I knew I'd have to endure this sort of thing."

"I asked you a question, Georgy Verney," he said, pulling her hands from her face and making her look at him. "You do love me, don't you?"

"Yes, all right, I love you," she snapped angrily. "I *love* you. But that does not mean I'll marry you, because I swear to you I won't."

"Your blasted principles, eh? I'm too wealthy for you."

"You may laugh at those principles if you like, Tony Maitland, but if you think I'm going to allow myself to wed a man of wealth, and to permit him to humiliate me by supporting my impoverished mother and sister, and to be forced to accept from him an unending stream of jeweled necklaces and diamond brooches and all those other senseless luxuries I find so distasteful, and to be subjected to the sneers of the *ton* as they whisper that Georgianna Verney, who's family had not a feather to fly with, has managed— clever little puss that she is—to snare for herself the richest man in London and is now rolling in soft . . . if you think I could *ever* endure all *that,* my lord, you can jolly well think again!"

"Whoa! Hold on there!" Maitland laughed, stepping back from her and holding up his hands. "A simple 'no' will be enough. You needn't roll over me with a battery of caissons."

She blushed, abashed. "I suppose I sounded ridiculous," she muttered.

"Not ridiculous. *Idiotic.*"

"You are entitled to your opinion," she said, putting up her chin and sweeping past him to the door. "But idiotic or not, I shall not marry you."

"Very well, ma'am," he said, coming up to the door and placing his hand on the knob, "you need not repeat yourself. I've accepted your refusal."

She blinked at him. "You've accepted—?"

"For the moment. We still have a couple of days. I don't promise not to try again."

"It will only be another refusal, Tony," she warned.

"We'll see," he said, opening the door for her. "Good night, my lovely idiot."

"An idiot perhaps," she retorted as she sailed past him,

"but not *yours*. Remember that, my lord. And a very good night to you."

Idiot!, she repeated to herself furiously as she strode down the hall, *that's what he thinks of me!* And probably the entire population of the world would agree if they'd been privy to the conversation she'd just had. But she didn't care what the whole world thought of her. She would never marry money. That was something her blasted mother had better learn right now. If she was to continue to live at home, there would have to be no more game-playing, no more plotting, no more matchmaking.

She strode up the stairs to accost her mother in her room, but she realized before she reached the top that she didn't know *which* room was her mother's. And there was no one she could ask except Allie, but she didn't know the location of Allie's room either. In frustration, she turned to the door of the only room she could properly identify—her own.

She opened her door and stopped in surprise. Her mother sat on her bed, waiting for her! As soon as Georgy closed the door, Horatia leaped up and enveloped her daughter in an ecstatic embrace. "Georgy, you naughty puss, where have you been?" she cried. "I've been beside myself!"

"You have not been any such thing," her daughter said with asperity. "You've been too busy making mischief."

Lady Horatia drew herself up in indignation. "*I* making mischief? I? How dare you, Georgy? I will not be scolded by a disobedient, recalcitrant, obstinate daughter who thinks nothing of running away from home without a word and breaking her poor mother's heart."

"If your heart is broken, Mama, it does not show. You look in the best of health."

"Yes, that is my curse. I always look in the best of health." She sat down upon the bed and looked up at her daughter complacently. "Are you going to tell me where you've been?"

"I've been in a town called Ruckworth, teaching school."

"Teaching school?" Lady Horatia nodded knowingly, as

if that answer was not unexpected. "I might have known that's what you'd do. I must admit that it's something of a relief."

"Relief? Why?" Georgy asked, dropping down upon a chair.

"Allie thought you might be a barmaid or some such dreadful thing. What sort of school was it, my love? One of those new academies for girls?"

"No, Mama, it was a charity school. I think they called them Dame schools in your day."

"A *Dame* school?" Lady Horatia's brows rose in horror. "You must be joking! Do you mean one of those dreadful, filthy places where they gather together poor little dirty urchins and teach them to pray?"

"It was not as filthy as all that, Mama, but your description is more or less correct."

"Good heavens, Georgy," her mother sighed, "whatever did you do it for?"

"To earn a livelihood, for one thing. And to do some good in the world, for another."

Horatia frowned at her daughter in disapproval. "Georgianna Verney, are you still a blasted bluestocking? Or worse, an Evangelical? Because if you are, I almost wish you hadn't come back."

"In that case, ma'am, I can always go away again," her daughter teased.

"I said almost. You know I didn't mean it. I don't think I could endure another of your absences."

"Do you mean that, Mama? Really mean it?"

"What a perfectly ridiculous question! Of course I mean it. You are my first born, my most beloved offspring. I know I'm not given to showing my feelings, but I wept myself to sleep for weeks after you left!"

"I'm sorry, Mama," Georgy said contritely. "I didn't mean to make you unhappy."

"Then I trust you'll never do so dreadful a thing to me again," her mother said.

"I won't, Mama. I'll be happy to resume living at home . . ." she leaned toward her mother with an expression of unwavering determination on her face, ". . . under certain conditions."

Lady Horatia stiffened. "Conditions?"

"Yes, my dear. Conditions. The first one is that you accept Peggy Birkin as your daughter-in-law."

"*Peggy Birkin?*" Horatia rose majesterially to her feet. "What on earth are you babbling about. Jemmy would *never*—"

"Jemmy already has. Or he will have by this time to-morrow."

"My Jemmy is marrying that . . . that *thief?*" she uttered, choked. "You can't be serious."

"I'm perfectly serious. And Peggy is not a thief. She is a lovely, kind, warm-hearted girl who loves your son devotedly. And the fact that she was not raised in a noble house is, in this case, a blessing. She has not been spoilt, she will not spend your son's money recklessly (as some ladies I could name whom he might have wed may well have done) and thus will not drive him into bankruptcy. What's more, since she looks like me, and I am said to resemble you, you are quite likely to have grandchildren who are remarkably like their grandmama."

Horatia stared speculatively at her daughter for several seconds. Then she sank slowly down again. "I should have guessed that he was in love with her," she muttered. It took another moment for her to swallow what was a rather bitter pill, and then she drew a deep breath. "Very well. If Jemmy is happy, I will be, too. She is certainly more acceptable to me than Rosalind Peascott, despite the fact that the Peascotts have a noble line. What's your next condition?"

"That, Mama, will be harder. We must not be too great a burden on Jemmy. I will try to find another post, one that perhaps pays a bit better than my last, but if you and Allie and I are to live with him, we must not abuse the privilege. You must sharply curtail your expenses and give up most of your social activities. They are too costly."

"I knew we would come to this. You do keep harping away at the same string, don't you, Georgy? I shall do my best to curtail expenses, my love, but to ask me to give up all society is too cruel. If only you would listen to reason and try to make an advantageous match—"

"Aha!" Georgy exclaimed, leaping to her feet. *"That* was what I've been waiting for. That, my dear Mama, is the third and last condition."

"What is?" her mother asked, eyeing her daughter fearfully.

"That! Matchmaking! You must *promise*—on your honor, mind you—that you will never, *never* subject me to one of your matchmaking schemes again. If you promise at once, I will refrain from telling you what I think of the dishonest, conniving, despicable, deceitful, *loathsome* trick of yours that I've come to East Riding to untangle."

Lady Horatia merely lowered her eyes. "I knew you would fall into a rage if you learned of it," she sighed. "That's why I hoped it would never reach your ears. But you needn't fall into a taking now. It's almost over, and no one is the worse for it. And it was all for nothing. Lord Maitland is completely indifferent after all. I had thought, that night at the Denham's ball, that . . . but I mustn't let myself dwell on it. It was too impossibly splendid a match to actually come to pass."

"I don't wish to hear any more about splendid matches, do you understand me, Mama? And I particularly don't wish to hear about Maitland. What I wish to hear is your promise."

"Oh, very well, you have it," Lady Horatia said in surrender.

"Then *say* it," Georgy insisted. "I will never, never try to make a match for Georgy again."

"I will never, never try to make a match for Georgy again."

"Good. And we will never, never mention the words *splendid match* or *Lord Maitland* to each other as long as we live."

Lady Horatia glared at her daughter venomously. "We will never, never mention the words *splendid match* or *Lord Maitland* as long as we live."

"Thank you, Mama. That was not too difficult, was it?

Now we shall all be able to live together in loving contentment."

"If that is what you call contentment, you foolish child.
But I shall say no more. You've tied my hands. I shall let
you wither into sour spinsterhood without another word
from me." She rose in her usual magisterial manner and
went to the door. "In fact, Georgy," she said before stalking out, "though I'm your mother and as fond of you as a
mother could be, I'm not so blind that I can't see that
you're becoming quite sour and spinsterish already!"

Chapter 39

Georgy told herself firmly that she would not permit herself to feel even a soupçon of eager anticipation for the next day. She was here to accomplish a purpose, not to enjoy herself. But when morning came, she found herself unable to remain coldly purposeful. The mere awareness of where she was and that she would be spending the day in Tony Maitland's company made her hum aloud as she dressed. She even made a few dancing steps around the room. If one's *spirit* decided to be joyful and eager, she discovered, there was very little one's *mind* could do to depress it.

She chose a scandalously clinging gown of India pink to wear, released her hair from its old-maidish knot and ran down to breakfast. But Maitland was nowhere in sight. Nor did he make an appearance all day. Letty Denham resumed her duties as his substitute, explaining with a touch of embarrassment that he'd been called away again but had promised to return by evening. She herded the group out for a walking tour in the early afternoon and, later, for the long-postponed croquet match. The game was a merry one, the women beating the men handily, but Georgy, crushed with disappointment at Maitland's absence, did not enjoy a moment of it.

As promised, his lordship returned before dinner. Georgy's spirits, completely beyond her control, rose ecstatically. But Maitland took no special notice of her during the meal and made only the most distantly polite remarks to her afterward. While the card tables were being arranged, she saw Lucy prance up to him. "Last night you showed Georgy some changes you made in the library, did you not, my lord? Perhaps tonight you can show them to me."

"I don't know if the library changes would interest you, Miss Traherne," he responded (with what seemed to Georgy a lecherous gleam in his eye), "but there are some paintings in the second-floor gallery which you might enjoy seeing."

Lucy promptly took his arm. As they strolled past Georgy, Lucy threw her an even saucier so-there look than Georgy had given her. Georgy stared after them in irritation. This was the next-to-last day. Already servants could be seen carrying baggage down the hallways. Tony *knew* that these last few precious hours were all they would ever have! How could he have wasted half of them away?

But the card tables were ready, and Georgy had to put on a good face. She joined the Countess Lieven's table for a game of silver-loo (to the delight of the still-infatuated Rudi), but she could hardly keep her mind on the cards. She seethed with envy and disappointment. She knew perfectly well that Tony Maitland was doing what he was doing on purpose to distress her, but that knowledge did not keep her from being distressed.

When his lordship and Lucy returned to the card room, he refused the Countess's invitation to join their table but sat down with Lucy and the Peascotts. To add injury to insult, Georgy lost every cent she had on the card game.

It had been, she decided, one of the worst days of her life. As soon as the game was over, she excused herself. "No," she told his lordship when he reminded her of the late supper, "I don't care for anything tonight. I'm off to bed."

He bid her goodnight without any further attempt to persuade her to stay and turned to his other guests. But just before she left the room, he called to her. "Miss Verney, by the way, I have a suggestion for you. You haven't done any riding since you came here. I know you've not fully recovered from your illness, but you've seemed to be much better since your return from London. There's a lively little mare in my stables that I think would suit you very well.

Why don't you try her tomorrow morning? Ask the stable boy. He'll know the horse I mean."

"Thank you, my lord. Perhaps I will," she said coldly and went off to bed.

She slept only fitfully. Every time she woke she remembered how he'd avoided her all day. There was only one day left. Did he intend to behave in the same way again? It certainly looked as if he would, for he'd already suggested that she go riding *alone*. Well, she sighed in despair, she'd asked for it. She'd refused his offer in no uncertain terms, and he'd accepted her refusal. What more did she expect from him?

The next morning was cold and damp, but Georgy, in a sour, contrary mood, decided to try out his mare anyway. She put on her riding garb and strode out to the stables. The only person in view was a young boy in smock and cap, busily currying a roan stallion in one of the stalls. "You, boy," she called, "can you show me the mare his lordship said would be suitable for Miss Verney?"

The boy turned round. He was a strapping lad with a freckled nose and a large, fading bruise under his right eye. "Mornin', Miss Vail," he said cheerfully, dropping the curry-comb and emerging from the stall. "Lord Maitland *said* you'd be comin' in this mornin'."

"Benjy!" she gasped. *"Benjy!"*

He pulled off his cap and grinned at her. "I knew ye'd be right surprised."

She was almost speechless. "Wh-what are you *doing* here?"

"Lord Maitland brung . . . brought me."

"Lord Maitland? Brought you *here?* When? I don't understand."

"'E showed up at the smith's yesterday, see, an' made me bring 'im to my Pa. 'E an' my Pa 'ad a long talk—"

"Lord Maitland talked to your *father?*" she gasped, awestruck. "Was it very . . . dreadful?"

"Oh, no, ma'am, not at all. Pa was real polite to 'im. An' grateful to 'im, too. An' Pa said fer me to tell ye 'e's that grateful to *you*, too."

"To *me?* Mr. Kissack said that? This is all so . . .

astonishing! Although your father has nothing to thank *me* for. All I ever did for you was get you a black eye."

"You know that ain't so, Miss Vail. I learned a lot from you. An' ye sent 'is lordship to fetch me, too."

"*I* did? Did his lordship tell you that?"

"Yes, ma'am, 'e did. It was real good of ye, Miss Vail." He blinked at her in sudden unease. "Ye look very fine in that ridin' costume, Miss Vail. I s'pose I shouldn't've called ye that. 'Is lordship said yer Miss Verney now. A real lady, ain't ye?"

"No more than I ever was, Benjy. Oh, I'm so glad to see you that I can't catch my breath! But I still don't quite see . . . will you be working for Lord Maitland now?"

"Yes, ma'am. 'Ere in the stables. There's a nice ol' codger that 'as charge of me, an' I 'ave my own room. An' my pay is three times what the smith was payin' me. An' the best of all, Miss Vail, is that 'is lordship is sendin' me to school next year, after I get a bit of tutorin'. A fine academy fer boys, 'e said."

"Oh, Benjy," she murmured, clapping her hands on her trembling mouth, "I'm so glad for you!" She gazed at him tearfully for a moment and then threw her arms about him impulsively. "I'm so *very* glad!"

The boy reddened to his ears. "Thank ye, Miss Vail. I mean, Miss Verney. Shall I bring the mare out now, ma'am?"

"No, Benjy," she said, her face growing thoughtful. "Not right now. I have something I must do. I'll be back."

She turned abruptly and ran out of the stable. Lifting her skirt, she flew across the field and round the east wing to the entrance of the house. "Where is his lordship?" she demanded in panting urgency of the ever-present footman at the bottom of the stairs.

"In the morning room, I believe, ma'am," the footman answered, trying not to gape.

She ran down the hall to the morning room and flung open the door. Roger Denham, seated alone at the table sipping his morning tea, looked up in surprise. Maitland, however, was standing at the sideboard holding out a plate on which the butler was placing two coddled eggs, and he didn't see her enter. Georgy took no notice of anyone but Maitland. She flew across the room, crying out his name. He whirled around in time to catch her in his arms as she flung herself at him, dropping his plate on the floor as he did so. "Georgy? What on earth—?"

"You *darling!*" she cried breathlessly, throwing her arms about his neck. "You are the kindest, most thoughtful, most generous, most *lovable* man in the world!" She drew his head down and covered his face with kisses, while Roger and the butler watched in frozen fascination.

"Benjy?" Maitland asked her with a grin.

"Benjy," she nodded, smiling at him tremulously.

Roger cleared his throat. "I don't know what a Benjy is," he remarked, "but it seems to be something with magical powers. Perhaps I should go and try the word out on my wife. It might, if I'm lucky, bring out a similarly delightful reaction from her."

"Yes, why don't you?" Maitland urged, not taking either his eyes or his arms from the girl.

"Yes, I think I shall." With a pleased smile, he got up from the table and sauntered out, closing the door carefully behind him.

"I suppose, my lord," the butler said impassively, "that I, too, should depart."

"Yes, that would seem to be a good idea," the engrossed Maitland murmured.

"Without cleaning up the eggs, my lord?"

"Without cleaning up the eggs."

They waited, motionless, until they heard the door close again. "I knew you would be pleased," he said, smiling down at her, "but I didn't dream you would be as pleased as *this.*"

"That was the most wonderful thing anyone has *ever* done for me!" she said lovingly, letting her head fall on his shoulder. "To think that all day yesterday, when I hated you for ignoring me and wasting away our precious short time together, you were going all the way to Ruckworth to find Benjy."

"Idiot," he murmured fondly, "how could you believe I could ever ignore you?"

She ran a finger down the side of his cheek. "I suppose you think that what you did is so wonderful that it will overcome all my principles and convince me to wed you."

"No, I don't think so at all. You've told me many times, and quite vehemently, that your principles cannot be overcome. What I did think my act of benevolence would do was to tempt you to take a position in my employ. The boy needs a tutor, you see."

Her eyes widened. "You wish me to be his tutor?"

"Yes, why not? You would be the perfect tutor for him. Of course, if it became known that I'd hired a beautiful, desirable woman to take residence here and be tutor to a stable boy, there might be some who would interpret the situation as being . . . well, *peculiar*."

She giggled. "To say the least."

"If you *married* me, however, you could tutor the boy without causing the least gossip."

"I suppose I could at that," she said shyly.

"And if you married me, I could set up a school for you to run, right here at Colinas Verde. There must be many children in the district who would benefit from such a school."

"Dozens and dozens, I imagine."

"That, my love, is one of the benefits of being wealthy. One can set up schools."

"Yes," she said, lifting her hand and curling a lock of his grizzled hair with her fingers, "that is a consideration I hadn't thought of before."

He tightened his hold on her. "Will you consider it then?"

She buried her face in his neck. "But I *swore*," she said in a small voice, "that I would never marry for money."

"I won't give you any," he said promptly. "Will that do? And I won't buy you a single jeweled necklace or diamond brooch . . . except perhaps on very rare occasions like your birthday or our twentieth anniversary."

"Stop it, Tony!" she muttered into his shoulder. "You are making me feel very idiotic indeed."

"And so you are," he said, turning up her face and kissing her gently. "Of course," he went on, "it would be rather difficult to turn your mother and sister out in the snow, but if you insist—"

"All right, my lord, enough!" She broke from his arms and backed away, holding up her arms like a prisoner in the act of surrendering. "I admit that I spoke like an idiot. Will that do?"

"I don't know. Is that merely an admission that you made a poor argument, or is it an acceptance of my third and final offer of marriage?"

Her arms slowly lowered. "Your final offer?"

"The very last."

"Then my answer is yes. I'll marry you, dash it all, but in *spite* of, not *because* of, your being the catch of the season."

"Thank you, my dear," he said, gathering her in his arms again. "I'll ask the engraver to inscribe that disclaimer on our wedding announcements."

A little while later, the morning room door again flew open. Alison, standing in the doorway, could scarcely believe what she was seeing. Her sister and Maitland were locked in an absolutely scandalous embrace. "Well!" she exclaimed in shocked disapproval. "What have we *here?*"

"What we have here," Maitland replied, lifting his head and grinning at the girl, "is a fortune-hunter in the act of arranging for herself a very advantageous match."

Allie made a face. "I thought you were going to wait for *me*," she pouted.

"Sorry, my love," Georgy said, looking at her sister with eyes that glowed, "but by the time you're ready to come out, I'm sure there'll be another catch-of-the-season for *you* to hook."

Allie shrugged. "Anyway, if I can't have Tony for a husband, I suppose having him for a brother-in-law is the next best thing." She perched up on the sideboard beside them and burst into giggles. "Wait til Mama hears! She'll *explode*."

"Mama!" Georgy paled. "Good heavens, Tony, I forgot! Just last night I made her swear that we were not to mention your name to each other ever again."

Tony laughed. "That's priceless. She can go through life

calling me 'you there', or referring to me as 'that fellow, my son-in-law.'"

"Don't joke," Georgy moaned. "I don't feel like laughing. How can I face her?"

"You've no need to face her," Allie said. "I know just how to tell her."

"You do?" Georgy asked eagerly. "How?"

"Leave it to me. Just go on doing what you were doing when I came in."

"That," Tony said cheerfully, pulling Georgy back into his arms, "will be my pleasure."

Alison took a last, appraising look at the closely entwined pair and then scurried from the room, being sure to shut the door on them. She found her mother just coming down the stairs. "Ah, Mama," she greeted. "I was just going up to get you. Come with me." She took her mother by the hand and pulled her down the hall. In front of the morning room door she paused. "Are you feeling well today, Mama?" she asked.

"Well enough. What is the matter with you, Alison? You are acting very strangely."

"Nothing is the matter, Mama. I just want to be sure you are feeling just so. Able to face anything, so to speak."

"What are you babbling about, child? I assure you I'm quite well."

"And you are fit to withstand storm and strife and . . . and shocks of all sorts?"

Her mother sighed. "After last night, I can withstand anything," she declared.

"Very good, Mama. Because, you see, I have something rather shocking to show you." And she threw open the door.

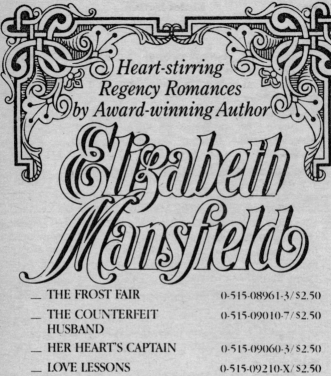